# LYNDA LA PLANTE

# SLEEPING
# CRUELTY

PAN BOOKS

First published 2000 by Macmillan

First published in paperback 2001 by Pan Books
This edition published 2007 by Pan Books
an imprint of Pan Macmillan Ltd
Pan Macmillan, 20 New Wharf Road, London N1 9RR
Basingstoke and Oxford
Associated companies throughout the world
www.panmacmillan.com

ISBN 978-0-330-45647-0

2 4 6 8 10 9 7 5 3 1

A CIP catalogue record for this book is available from
the British Library.

Typeset by SetSystems Ltd, Saffron Walden, Essex
Printed and bound in Great Britain by
Mackays of Chatham plc, Chatham, Kent

Visit **www.panmacmillan.com** to read more about all our books and to buy
them. You will also find features, author interviews and news of any author
events, and you can sign up for e-newsletters so that you're always first to hear
about our new releases.

*To my mother, sweet Flossie*

# Acknowledgements

MY SINCERE THANKS to Suzanne Baboneau at Macmillan for her constant support and enthusiasm for my work, a friendship I value greatly. Many thanks also go to Hazel Orme, Philippa McEwan, Esther Newberg and Peter Benedek. Thanks also to my agent Gill Coleridge, who steers my career and reins in some of my more erotic writing.

I'd also like to thank the team at La Plante Productions. The rough draft of *Sleeping Cruelty* bounced around the office until it fell into the capable hands of Alice Asquith, head of research, Kate Fletcher, Nikki Smith, Kerry Appleyard and George Weatherill. After testing some of the sequences out on random passers-by, the team found some of my more steamy scenes too hot to handle, so these scenes will be forever left to the imagination! A big thanks to Liz Thorburn, MD of La Plante Productions, 'mother' to us all.

Further thanks to my financial advisor Stephen Ross, who was disappointed not to have been allowed access to the censored sections!

Special thanks to the following for their generous contribution: Juliet Battersby, Bulgari, Hugo Waring for his wine expertise, Professor John Henry at the

Poisons Unit at St Mary's Paddington, the Ritz, the West Indies Tourist Office, British Virgin Islands Tourist Office, French Antilles Tourist Office, the Necker Island Office.

# PROLOGUE

## Summer 1977

THE VILLA was nestled in a hollow cut into the side of a cliff, overlooking the sea. A strange, low, sprawling building, it was shaded by the massive fir trees that surrounded it, almost encroaching on to the small paved patio at the front. The grounds of the house curved upwards steeply so that you could look in through the windows on the top floor. The nanny could tell that the villa must have had another storey at one time, a third floor, high enough to overlook the forest and give panoramic views of the sea and maybe even a glimpse of the beach below.

Though highly experienced, and with tip-top references, she was surprised when she received a call in answer to the advert she had placed in the *Lady* magazine, asking if she could start work immediately before she had met either parents or children. The wages were almost double what she had anticipated, and a first-class ticket and travel expenses were sent from a reputable firm of solicitors in Paris. She was told that her duties would be outlined to her on her arrival. It seemed a wonderful opportunity, and she felt fortunate.

The children's father, a handsome man in his late

forties, had shown her in. He was aloof and rather condescending, especially when she had questioned the weight of the household duties he was expecting her to take on. He spoke slowly, not looking into her face but staring over her head. 'I checked your references. Previously you have been paid a standard rate. I am offering substantially more. Surely it is not asking too much of you to run the household. There will be no interference. I will not be here. I have business commitments in Paris.' He went on to say that he would spend only the odd weekend at the villa but would always give her warning if there were to be any guests and then, if necessary, he would bring staff from his Paris home to cook and assist with the cleaning.

The interview was brief. She felt guilty about even mentioning the household tasks, especially when she saw her luxurious quarters: a huge bedroom with vast wardrobe space and *en-suite* bathroom. What a change from her London bedsit! She looked forward to spending days on the beach with the children and perhaps going for rambles and picnics.

No sooner had she unpacked, showered and changed ready to meet her charges than she heard a car departing. He had not even introduced her to his children. There was a sound at her door, a child's knock. It opened and there they were. The children stood together, sweet and shy. They shook her hand, welcomed her with downcast eyes and, as if rehearsed, said they hoped she would enjoy working at the villa. They looked so vulnerable that she was fired with enthusiasm to make the most of this job.

As she got to know them over the next few days, however, they began to make her feel uneasy, sometimes downright scared. Both children were astonishingly beautiful, but their faces were chillingly devoid of emotion and their wide, clear blue eyes oddly expressionless. Both had ash blond hair, bleached white by the sun. Their slender bodies had a golden tan, and for two such young children they were remarkably clean and poised. She soon realized they were both neurotically fastidious about their clothes. Though she was only eight, the girl changed numerous times during the day. The nanny also noticed that she washed her hands and face repeatedly. The boy, at ten, was just as meticulous about his appearance. But there was nothing feminine about him: he had an unusually mature masculinity, giving the nanny sidelong glances when he thought she wasn't looking. If she caught his eye, he would give a slow adult smile.

The nursery was always tidy, the toys lined up with military precision. They made their beds without having to be told, and asked for fresh sheets and pillow-slips every two days. The amount of washing and ironing ensured that the nanny's working day stretched well into the evening. When she questioned them, it soon became clear that they had not been forced into this disciplined lifestyle. It was how they liked it, they said in unison. They were always whispering and giggling together but fell silent when she approached. They ate sparingly, simple food with lots of salads and vegetables. She presumed the menus had been established by their previous nanny. But when she asked, they changed the subject. Once they spoke briefly of their mother, who had died two years before, they said, in the villa, in a fire. They didn't seem distressed, just stated the fact, then asked if she would like to come swimming. She

3

agreed to meet them in the garden as soon as she had put on her swimsuit.

They were waiting for her, but not in their swimsuits. They were still dressed. The boy strolled ahead, the girl took her hand and led her towards the pool. 'Dive in,' she piped.

The nanny was puzzled that the pool should be in such a shaded area, and from where she stood the water appeared murky. But the children told her again to dive in.

'Go on, close your eyes,' said the little girl. 'I'll guide you right to the edge.'

The nanny's toes were gripping the edge of the pool when she looked, *really* looked, at the water. It was infested with wasps and bugs, a seething, green, moving carpet. She was so shocked that she almost lost her balance as the children ran away, laughing.

Later she served them supper and watched them get into their beds before returning to her own room to read. The heat was oppressive and when she opened a shutter to let in some air, she was taken aback to see the children in a dark corner of the garden. The little girl, wearing a white nightdress, dragged a large doll with curly blonde hair, behind her. The boy pointed at the ground with a spade. In silence, she watched the children until they came back inside. Then she went out to see what they had been doing. Handmade crosses marked what appeared to be a row of graves. One cross, made from rough twigs and bound with string, had a piece of pink writing-paper pinned to it, with the word 'Papa'.

The following morning as she served them breakfast, she mentioned that she had seen them playing. The boy

4

pushed his plate to one side. 'You must have been dreaming. We were in bed.'

'Yes,' said the girl. 'We always do as we're told. We weren't outside.'

The nanny didn't want to make an issue of it, but after breakfast was cleared away, she went in search of the garden graves and discovered they had gone.

She was frightened. She knew she hadn't imagined it.

She tried to be cheery and inject some fun into their strict lives, but they weren't interested. They didn't want to go to the beach, or for walks. They preferred to sit together, reading or whispering. Their routine remained the same day after day, and she felt like an intruder in their world. She hoped their father would return one weekend.

No one ever came to the villa. There were no calls, there was no mail. The groceries were delivered on Friday, so she had no need to go to the nearest village. She was pleased when she saw the deliveryman roar up the drive. But he seemed in a great hurry to get the receipt signed and leave. He didn't even turn off the van's engine. 'Did you know the children's mother?' she asked, as he laid the carbon paper between the receipt and copy.

He shook his head. 'She burned alive, up there.' He used his chewed ballpoint pen to point to the flat roof of the villa. 'It used to have another storey – that's why the roof is flat.' His face glistened with sweat as he then leaned close. 'No one stays there now, not for more than a few days anyway. He stays away for months at a time, the father. He hates it here.'

'But what about the children?'

The deliveryman gave her a strange look. 'They're the reason no one stays. It was them that started the fire they reckon. They're . . . not normal.'

Later when she entered the nursery she found them lying side by side, their arms entwined around each other, whispering. They parted quickly and fell silent, as if annoyed by her intrusion.

'This afternoon we're going on a picnic,' she said. 'Which would you prefer, the beach or the heath? You choose.'

As if on cue there was a clap of thunder and heavy raindrops began to fall. The children giggled.

'Ah, well,' said the nanny, 'maybe tomorrow. These storms never last long. Let's see what's on the television.'

She turned on the set, but it was crackly and unwatchable, so she offered to play a game with them, but none of her suggestions drew so much as a flicker of interest. The two children sat, hand in hand, dead-eyed, until she became angry with her own inability to cajole them into animation.

'Why don't you want to play?' She couldn't stop her voice rising. 'Have you ever played like normal children? What on earth is the matter with you both? Stop looking at each other and look at me. *Look at me!* Now, tell me what's the matter. You behave as if you hate me.'

The boy kicked at a chair leg. 'We don't hate you,' he said. But he had a strange smile on his face.

'No, we don't hate you,' piped up his sister.

The nanny took a deep breath. 'Are you like this because of your mother? Because of what happened to her?'

6

The children held each other's gaze for a long time, as if having a silent conversation. Then the boy eased away from his chair and crossed to her. Reaching for her hand, he began to stroke it. His skin felt almost silky. He pressed his body closer and closer to her as if wanting to slip his arms around her waist. She found it moving, as if he was trying to comfort her.

Apparently encouraged by her brother, the girl crossed and hugged the nanny's knees, so tightly that she could feel the child's hot breath against her thighs. Suddenly her joy turned to panic as she realized that this was no show of juvenile affection.

The boy was easing up her skirt, his small hands rhythmically stroking her thigh, as his sister's hot breath centred at her crotch. Just as the boy's hand reached for her breast she pulled away. 'Stop this,' cried the nanny, standing and smoothing her skirt. '*Stop this right now.*'

They looked up at her, puzzled.

'But you said you wanted to play with us,' said the boy petulantly. Then he punched her in the stomach while his sister sank her teeth into her hand. The nanny let out a yelp of pain. The children responded with high-pitched shrieks of delight.

'Get away from me,' screamed the nanny. '*Stop this.*'

She ran to her room. She put a call through to Paris, to their father. He was curt, dismissive, and did not question her reason for wanting to leave. He asked if she would please remain at the villa for that evening until he had made alternative arrangements. The nanny stayed in her room, packing her suitcases, not wanting to face either child again. She was ashamed that she couldn't deal with them but she knew that someone far more experienced than her would have to unravel their psyches.

As dusk drew in she went into the kitchen and made up a tray of cold chicken and salad for herself, leaving the children's food laid out on the table. She could hear no sounds from the nursery, and was unsure if they were inside the villa or not. Then she returned to her room and locked the door. The rain lashed down: the storm had returned.

Later that night she awoke to a loud bang. The thunderclaps seemed to be centred on the villa itself. She moved around the house, checking doors and windows. A light was showing beneath the nursery door. She paused to listen, then bent down to peer through a crack in the door. An eye peered back at her and she straightened up fast as a high-pitched laugh echoed across the corridor.

She made her way to the master bedroom suite. The room was in darkness. The furniture was oak, as oppressive as the night itself, and a wardrobe door hung open. She looked inside. Rows of shirts, suits, trousers, racks of ties and handmade shoes, bottles of cologne with silver-backed hairbrushes were neatly lined up in open drawers.

She jumped in fright as a loud bang came from the bathroom. The shutters had come loose. Standing in a puddle on the blue and white tiled floor, she reached out to close them. At that moment the lights went out. She groped around for the switch. It must be a power cut. She found a hand towel and knelt to mop up the water – she didn't care that she was using a pristine white towel to dry the floor. Whoever had the misfortune to work here after her could deal with it. She was glad to be leaving. She wrung out the towel into the bath. Then she froze.

A sound came from above her, from the flat roof. It was as if something was being dragged across it, like a heavy, unwieldy sack. Frightened, she listened and, still carrying the sodden towel, she left the bedroom. On the landing outside she listened again, looking upwards. She wondered if perhaps an animal had jumped on to the roof. But as she could hear nothing, she hurried along the corridor to her own room, went in and closed the door behind her.

Then she heard the sound again, coming from directly above her room. She stepped out into the corridor again. Looking up, she inched towards the old staircase that once led up to the third floor, but now terminated at a bolted wooden trap-door.

A sudden flash of lightning momentarily flooded the corridor with a bluish light, but the staircase to nowhere remained dark and shadowy.

'What's happening?'

The voice came from behind her and she spun round. Both children stood there hand in hand.

'There's something on the roof,' she screamed. 'There's something *up there on the roof*.'

At that moment the lights flickered on. She felt foolish, standing barefoot in just her bra and slip. 'Didn't you hear it?' she asked lamely. 'It sounded as if someone, or something, was trapped up there.' She looked into their impassive faces. 'I'm sorry if I frightened you, but I was scared.'

The two children stared in silence.

'I'm sorry. You'd better go back to your room and try and get some sleep. Your father will be here tomorrow.'

They looked at each other. 'Why?'

The nanny wiped her face with the back of her hand. 'Because I asked him to come. I'm leaving.' She headed towards her room.

The children remained watching, their eyes wide.

'I'll be leaving in the morning, as soon as he gets here, so please just go back to bed.'

As she closed her door behind her, she was sure she heard the boy call her a stupid bitch. She looked at her watch. It was almost four in the morning. She shivered as she remembered their hands on her body. Was it possible she had been mistaken? But when she relived it, she knew she had not. Then the noise on the roof started again. She felt the draught as soon as she stepped into the corridor. The trapdoor was open. She climbed the stairs to peer out and scan the roof. What she saw froze her to the spot.

Their small frames doubled under the weight, the two children were dragging a body, using all their strength, and trying to roll it over the edge of the roof. The rain had left pools, which were now blood red, as were the awful marks where they had hauled their burden across the roof. The children seemed wounded; their blond hair was matted with blood, their night-clothes were drenched.

'Dear God, what's happened?' she whispered.

The boy spun round. 'It's all right,' he said, continuing to heave the body closer to the edge of the villa roof.

'No one will do anything,' added the girl, helping her brother. 'We're only children.'

The nanny knew without even seeing his face that the body was their father's. 'Just like they did nothing about Mama.' The little girl strained as she pushed at the dead weight. As the body rolled over the side on to the ground with a dull thud, both children smiled, as if congratulating each other, then turned to face their nanny.

'Nanny, will you help us bury him?' they asked in unison.

# CHAPTER 1

WILLIAM BENEDICT was fifty-three, and regarded himself 'well preserved'. He had never been a vain man, but recently his creeping paunch and loss of hair had started to play on his mind. It was the latter that he really hated. His blond hair had always made him look younger than he was and although you could never have described him as handsome, his boyishness had given him a certain attraction. Even the press nicknamed him 'Boy Wonder'. But his youthful looks had gone.

Standing just under six feet tall, William stared down at the scales: despite hiring a personal fitness trainer he had not lost a single ounce. Why waste time and money on press-ups and weights for nothing? And the pills, at least thirty different vitamin and mineral supplements, irritated him too – they seemed to stick in his chest for half the morning.

William muttered with annoyance as he inspected his face in the mirror. He struck a pose, sucking in his cheeks and raising an eyebrow. He was all right, really. His pale blue eyes were as bright as they ever were – his mother always said they were his best feature. They had a permanently alert quality that could be unnerving, particularly when they darkened in anger. He glared at himself: he was beginning to feel as if someone else had sneaked into his body and blown it up. He drew his lips back to inspect his teeth, which had come courtesy of one of the best dentists in Los Angeles. He had smoked cigars all his life but his second wife had been particular about teeth and had made sure that his never bore the tell-tale stains.

Clothes were a different matter: he dressed for comfort rather than style. He had always been told what was fashionable, and both his ex-wives had sent him to the tailor in an attempt to improve his sartorial sense. He had wardrobes full of tailored shirts, suits and handmade shoes – even his tracksuits were made by Armani. Everything looked fine on the hangers in the wardrobe, but once it was on William it gave the impression of sloppiness. The truth was, he had never really been interested in clothes. He felt he didn't need to be. William was a man to be envied. Few could match his fortune. He had recently floated his computer company and made a five-hundred-million-pound profit, and he had numerous other interests in property and industry.

His new project was politics. He had never been a political animal, but had voted Labour throughout both his marriages simply because it infuriated his in-laws. Now he had switched his allegiance, more or less on a whim, to the Conservative Party due to Andrew Maynard. He had heard the tall, pallid Maynard speak at some tedious charity function and the hairs on the back of his neck had stood up. It was almost as if something about the man reminded William of himself – not physically, more because, to all intents and purposes, he was an outsider. He made a note to watch the young man's progress. When he found himself in Brighton during the 1997 Tory Party conference and noticed that Maynard was to speak, he surprised himself by going to hear him.

As just another hopeful politician attempting to gain notice, Maynard might easily have been overlooked that week. But to everyone's surprise, though not to William's, he swept the entire conference hall to its feet for a standing ovation. The young man mesmerized his listeners.

The third time William saw Maynard was at a fund-raising dinner at the Grosvenor Hotel. Having decided to back the Conservative Party, William had made generous donations to Party funds, which had warranted an invitation. Once again the young man enthralled him, this time as a guest at the same table. Maynard, William noticed, drank little and hardly touched his food. It was not until coffee was served that William had the opportunity to talk to him. Maynard seemed shy, explaining that he held out little hope of gaining a seat at the election, but added that he fully intended to give the opposition a good run for its money.

Over the following weeks William continued, albeit half-heartedly, to monitor the young politician's career as the pre-election fever grew. However, Maynard lost, by a narrow margin, as the Labour Party swept to victory. His loyal supporters commiserated with him at a breakfast they had organized. They didn't stay long, and Maynard shook their hands as they departed, maintaining that he would fight on, and that next time he would win.

At the end only William remained with him in the

restaurant. He lit a cigar, feeling depression hanging in the air. Maynard loosened his tie and unbuttoned his collar. He picked up a lipstick-rimmed champagne glass and downed the remains. Until now they had hardly spoken more than a few words to each other, although Maynard had written William an appreciative letter thanking him for his financial backing.

Maynard turned to him now with a doleful expression. 'It was close. I'm sorry . . . you've donated so much. I'll never be able to thank you enough for your support.'

'Why don't you let me take you home?' William offered and ushered him to his car.

Maynard sat, head bowed, beside William in his Rolls Royce. They turned into Ladbroke Grove off Notting Hill Gate, and headed towards Maynard's small terraced house.

William cleared his throat. 'I donated to your campaign even though I didn't think you were ready. You were always an outside bet, but I don't regret it or worry about losing my money. It may still bring opportunities, so let's just put it down to experience.'

Maynard was clenching and unclenching his fists. He muttered that the new Prime Minister was young too, then turned to William. The weeks of day-and-night canvassing had taken their toll, and Maynard was thinner than ever. With his tie askew, and his unflattering black-rimmed spectacles he seemed like a fragile petulant boy. But when he spoke, his voice was cold with controlled anger. 'I appreciate your generosity, but I am sad that my political aspirations are not the reason you have supported me. It makes me wonder what strings you might have tried to pull for your own gain if this rank outsider you bet on *had* won!'

The chauffeur stopped outside Maynard's house, but before he could get out to open the door, it had been slammed shut.

Maynard opened his front door and just managed to close it behind him before the adrenaline that had been keeping him going for days evaporated. He leaned against the wall then slipped down it to the floor. He had not just failed to win his parliamentary seat but, without the continued donations from billionaire William Benedict, he had also lost future assurance of financial backing. With his rude remark, he knew he had made a foolish tactical error.

The following morning, Maynard's cleaner arrived as he was leaving. By eight fifteen he was at Claridge's – William's regular haunt for breakfast meetings. This morning when Maynard joined him he had every newspaper piled on the table and some stacked by his chair.

'I want to apologize for the way I spoke to you,' Maynard said, and flushed as he sat down.

They discussed the news coverage. The rival Labour candidate had expressed concern at beating Maynard by such a narrow margin. 'But he still won,' Maynard said, buttering his toast.

'Listen,' said William, 'I'm going to give you some advice. Take no favours, you'll have no debts. Show respect. A friend is useful, an enemy takes up your time. With that in mind, I have forgotten what you said to me last night.' Before Maynard could respond, he took out a pocket calculator, and a computer no larger than a wallet. Intent on the screen, he tapped away. Then he turned it to face Maynard. 'Is that up to date?'

On the tiny screen were Maynard's private bank statements, details of his mortgage, life assurance policies, the accounts for his office and staff during the campaign, lists of queries on personal expenses, claims, then details of tax and VAT payments, and sums owing to him.

'I pay my cleaner twenty quid a week,' Maynard said. It was the one item not listed. But he was angry, confused and dismayed by all the information William had amassed. He continued to scroll through the personal details: his school, his scholarships, university degrees, even the odd payments for speeches he had written for various MPs. He had been so engrossed he had not really listened to what William had been saying. But now it dawned on him. Had he heard correctly? He was not withdrawing any further donations? 'You will be in financial difficulties within months,' William said. 'You've taken out a second mortgage, you've no collateral left, and no fairy godmother in the wings to leave you a big inheritance. You need me, Andrew, more now than ever, and I'm offering you the deal of a lifetime. I'm going to back you to the hilt, all the way. Just you.'

William scraped back his chair and Maynard looked up. William needed a smoke, and it was not allowed in the dining-room.

Maynard joined William in the foyer where he sat with his cigar. He was unsure what William had meant by 'just you'. He felt as if he might be walking into a trap. What was the deal? What strings were attached?

William puffed until a halo of smoke formed round

his head. He suggested that Maynard should go for a good long holiday to recharge his batteries and think clearly about what he should do. William was certain that his election campaign had got him noticed; it would be up to him now to approach the Tory leader to discuss his future.

Maynard leaned forward. 'Why are you doing this?'

William stubbed out his cigar, only partially smoked, in the big silver ashtray on a stand by his chair. 'I have my reasons.'

'I need to know, sir. Please, you're offering me so much – why?'

William frowned. Then after a long pause he cocked his head to one side. 'Okay. It was just before lunch, a few years back, at the Party conference. Margaret Thatcher was sitting next to me. I watched her watching you. I saw her backbone stiffen. She never took her eyes off you until the end of your speech. You impressed me, and I saw that you had impressed her. That's it, really. Now, I have to go, old chap. You think about it. Call me tonight, or whenever.' He grinned at the confused young man, stood up and walked into the foyer.

William had to go only five paces across the pavement to reach his car. The passenger door was already open, his chauffeur standing by. He touched his cap when he saw Maynard.

Maynard stood rooted to the pavement, his heart thudding. William was getting into the car. 'Can I come with you? Could you drop me wherever you're going? Please?'

William shrugged, a little irritated: he wanted to get on with the day, but Maynard was fast off the mark, leaped in beside him and slammed the door.

'This is a Rolls Royce,' remarked William as the car glided away. 'The doors are perfectly balanced and hinged. They do not require a heavy-handed slam. You should learn that. One day, perhaps, you'll have one of your own, if we play our cards right.'

Maynard swallowed. His throat was bone dry.

William continued, leaning back against the soft leather seat. 'You need a makeover. It's all about image – get a professional. Lose those bloody glasses for a start. And you need a red hot PR person.'

Maynard felt as if he was hyperventilating. William leaned forward and opened a small compartment built into the back of the seat in front of him. Maynard saw that the compartment was stocked with all kinds of drinks, a cut-glass ice bucket, cigar boxes and cutters and cut-glass decanters with silver tops designed by Dunhill. William took out one of the decanters, poured a glass of water, and passed it to Maynard, who sipped it gratefully.

At last Maynard had pulled himself together. 'I have never done anything illegal in my life,' he said. 'As a politician I have to be scrupulously honest – and everything you're offering might be a potential trap – might ruin my career prospects. I'll get there the hard way, if I have to, no matter how long it takes. I have no interest in personal wealth – or a "makeover".' He took a deep breath. 'All those things are insignificant in comparison to the kind of changes I want to make to this country. Our current system is corrupt, we need to—'

'Stop the car, please.' William cut Maynard off before he could finish his sentence. He'd heard Maynard's speeches repeatedly during the campaign, and applauded the radical ideas he had urged on his supporters. But now he was trying William's patience. He leaned over and opened the young man's door. 'Get out, I've heard enough. Some people like to spend two million on a racehorse, but they never place a bet. It's not the money they want, it's not the winnings that excite them, it's the enjoyment of watching the horse race, and the thrill of when – *if* – it wins. That's all there is to it. That's all you are to me. Now go home.'

'Your *racehorse*? I jump when you say so?'

William shook his head in exasperation. All he wanted, he said, was to see Maynard win his seat in the next election and to be there to watch him do it. Then he took pity on him. 'No strings, no traps. *I believe in you*, you dumb bastard!'

William held out his hand for Maynard to shake. 'I mean it, I believe in you, son. You shine brightly, and you're right to be cautious. This is a career you've wanted since you were a kid. Well, I'll give it to you, with no ulterior motive. Now push off, I have work to do.'

Maynard walked away, his hands stuffed into his coat pockets. He must have looked such a wimp, but in fact he was highly ambitious and, at times, aggressive. Nevertheless, he would not allow himself to be treated like a commodity: he was not for sale. His career could not be compared with a racehorse. He had suffered too much already to get to where he was. Then he stopped and gave a humourless laugh. What career? In the cold light of morning, after all the hype, he knew he was still low on the political ladder. But maybe he had just stepped up a rung.

It took him three further days to contact William

Benedict. His excuse for not calling earlier was that he had been busy with post-campaign work. In reality he had taken legal advice. He told William that he had decided to accept his offer and made it clear there must be no possibility of any backlash against him. Then he relaxed. He had a benefactor whom most ambitious men would give their right arm for.

He was a little taken aback by William's non-committal response. He was quite cool; it appeared that his mind was elsewhere. All he said was: 'Good, but you realize it'll have little to do with me personally? Apart from the money, it'll all be down to you. I'll see you at my lawyer's tomorrow.'

Maynard's cosmetic makeover took more time to finalize than the legal accountancy and drawing up of acceptable bank accounts. It was imperative that the monetary transactions could not possibly be construed as a bribe from William, especially considering the fuss that had been made over the recent Aitken case. As Maynard had insisted it was all above suspicion: no ulterior motive could be detected behind his benefactor's generosity. The contract went back and forth and Maynard pored over it for anything that might be misconstrued if it ever became public knowledge.

Six months after their breakfast at Claridge's the change in Maynard's appearance was beginning to pay off. The fact that the tailoring and the dental work had taken so long was a blessing, because no one was able to pinpoint any dramatic change in Maynard and therefore didn't whisper about his growing show of confidence and polish, and William enjoyed watching his protégé emerge.

Neither did success come overnight – it took a great deal longer. Three years after that breakfast meeting, Maynard's star at last rose. He took his seat in a by-election, and became the young hope of the Conservative Party. Aged thirty-eight he was now courted by the Party elders, who showed interest in grooming him for a big political future.

For William, it was not a question of basking in the young man's glory, but of watching his protégé quietly from the sidelines with almost fatherly pride. Maynard became well known for his fearless stance, and was an almost constant media focus. Acting classes and elocution lessons improved his pose and diction, which meant that his television appearances gained him respect and attention. He ate up his fame with relish. Without doubt Andrew Maynard was earmarked to rise to the top.

Even though William had never hinted that he wished to be repaid for his generosity, it was at this time that he was knighted for his constant support to the Party. His charitable donations brought him to the attention of the peripheral socio-political scene and he was more socially active than ever before.

Sir William was inundated with invitations to fundraising events and charitable functions. He couldn't calculate on how many boards he now sat as an 'honorary member', and he enjoyed his new standing. He was a wealthy man but, until this stage in his life, had kept a low profile. It was not until Maynard had crossed his path that he had appreciated his fortune or used it for anything other than to expand his own companies. He continued to work on pet projects but only when he felt so inclined.

William knew that his seemingly bottomless wallet was his biggest social asset but he nevertheless found most of the company he attracted delightful. A number of ladies used him as their escort, and he took on this role with enthusiasm. Not that he found any of them sexually attractive – far from it. It was being at the hub of the social world that he liked, and he took to collecting all the newspaper photographs and articles in which he featured. And all of the changes in his life had come about through Andrew Maynard, who now occupied the place of the family he had lost. He had little contact with his own children due to his ex-wife's bitterness, and at times he looked on Maynard as a son. It was as if Maynard had opened a door inside William that allowed him, at this stage of his life, to enjoy living.

Even with all his millions, William had always felt second rate. His self-consciousness when moving in his ex-wives' aristocratic circles made him uncomfortable and aware of his social shortcomings. Now he blossomed, and for the first time discovered he was comfortable with himself. His background, which had been an embarrassment to his wives, was acceptable. As a self-made businessman he was applauded in the post-Thatcher line-up. And it was all due to Andrew.

Niggling doubts arose only on the odd occasion when he had dinner with Maynard. Sometimes William felt as if the young man only accepted his invitations out of politeness, but they were still pleasant evenings. The pair would discuss the present day's news, Party developments and so forth, but nothing personal. In fact William could not recall ever having any conversation with Maynard that embraced his private life, apart from on one evening. Maynard told him of how he had lost both parents and then, shortly after his mother's death, his elder sister had been killed in a car accident. William had commiserated, hoping for more details, but Maynard had been his usual reticent self: he said that his sister was much older and they had little knowledge of each other's lives – she worked abroad as a nanny and had never shown any interest in his political hopes. He invariably turned conversation back to William, fascinated by how he had accrued his wealth.

William had never known anyone to take such an interest in his career and enjoyed talking about his success. The first company he founded designed and developed computer chips, sold software programs, and designed and built computers. He had recently, partly out of boredom, begun manufacturing CD-ROMs, and had opened up a four-storey factory to develop computer games with experts brought in from Japan and the USA. He was selling on the Internet, and opening more factories to take over the European market. William had made his first million before he was twenty-eight.

Maynard, however, even in the relaxed atmosphere, would never talk about his own life and William did not like to press him. In some ways, though, their relationship was moving closer, albeit at a mutual-admiration level. It was, however, a deeper friendship than he had ever shared with another man. Yet after five years, all William knew about Maynard was what every newspaper reporter knew: his age, where he was brought up, and that he had been to grammar school outside Leatherhead before winning a scholarship to Cambridge.

At one dinner party hosted by a famous novelist and paid for by a glossy magazine, William defended Maynard when a gossip columnist, Meryl Delaware, spoke in a derogatory fashion about his lack of private life and his colourless background. 'My dears, that young man is like one of those awful Russian dolls. You keep on opening it up and out pops another and another, and they are all as *boring* as each other!'

At this point William leaned across the table and asked if perhaps she was confusing Maynard with herself: she appeared to have more in common with a rotund Russian doll than the intelligent young politician.

She sat back and glared hard at him, her mascara-caked eyelashes like tiny spikes. He should perhaps have taken this as a warning: the tentacles of Meryl Delaware's journalism crawled a considerable distance, and what might not do for her society magazine would perhaps find a place in a number of downmarket newspapers. Now Meryl Delaware leaned closer to William. 'Sweetie, you should be careful. Your protégé is *very* cagey about himself. Perhaps one of his layers will be peeled off to reveal a deep and nasty secret . . .' William laughed dismissively, but later that evening Meryl Delaware sidled up to him: 'I meant no offence, dahling. Perhaps the reason he's so hush-hush about his private life is because he's as flawed a human being as the rest of us.'

William gave a stiff smile. 'Speak for yourself, Miss Delaware.'

'Oh, sweetie, don't tell me you won't admit to having flaws?'

William shook his head. 'I doubt my faults would be of any interest to anyone, especially your readers.'

'You'd be surprised, Sir William . . .' And with that she swanned off into a small throng of people.

On his way out, William overheard someone say, 'God help this country if people like that vulgar fool and his protégé can buy their way into the cabinet!'

With clenched fists he walked out of Claridge's into Brook Street and signalled for his chauffeur.

# CHAPTER 2

WILLIAM WAS always up and dressed by six, his chauffeur standing by to take him to his first appointment of the morning. Recently he had been planning a takeover of a German electronics company. It was part of a large corporation owned by Baron von Garten, whose steel empire had been in his family for generations. However, it had been hinted that they were selling off their smaller electronics bases. Three previous meetings had been cancelled so William had sent his private plane and an invitation to breakfast at the Connaught. He was determined to get his hands on the prime site, sniffing out, with his fine business acumen, that von Garten was in financial difficulties. He knew that once he had his foot in the door he could make further inroads into the von Garten companies.

Sir William arrived at exactly nine for his breakfast meeting. He had been so busy making calls he had not noticed that one shoelace was undone and in danger of tripping him up as he marched through the Connaught Hotel reception into the dining room. William sat down at a table with a pristine pink cloth and a single rose in a tubular silver vase. He tossed aside the menu and ordered grapefruit, coffee, wholemeal toast and kippers.

He always had the kippers at the Connaught: they were perfect, not too smoked, and grilled with just a dab of butter. Just thinking about his breakfast, his mouth watered and he'd eaten two rounds of toast before his guest sauntered into the dining room.

Baron von Garten was accompanied by a shrewish little man wearing rimless glasses and carrying a soft leather briefcase. William waited, tetchily drumming his fingers on the table, but the Baron made no apology either for being half an hour late or for the previous cancelled meetings. His companion introduced himself as Herr Eric Kramer, the Baron's lawyer.

The elegant Baron said only a few words and left his lawyer to do most of the talking. Kramer explained that the Baron's family had to be a hundred per cent certain that, if they did agree to the sale, their name would not be connected to any of the factory's future products. He gave a blow-by-blow account of the Baron's ancestral history, emphasized how well connected the family still was, and declared that a transaction would be withdrawn at any whisper of scandal. He wanted a confidentiality agreement signed to ensure that any dealings would never be made public.

William was pretty sure that the Baron's Board of Directors had not been asked to approve the deal, so that when the business was sold to William it would be too late for anyone to do anything about it. He guessed that the Baron, for all his family connections, was hurting for cash.

'How much?' he asked softly, and both men leaned forward as if afraid to be overheard.

William shook his head. 'Gentlemen, that is a preposterous asking price,' he said, and withdrew from his own briefcase a detailed document about the property: its location, its present dilapidated condition. It emphasized that William was buying the shell of the old factory to tear down and rebuild; his major interest in the purchase was its location. He wished to turn it into a computer works, offering four hundred jobs, and bringing a team of experts to train the employees to his standards. He showed them a brochure about a similar factory up and running in Paris. As they glanced over it he signalled for the bill.

The deal was concluded quickly. William would arrange a banker's draft to pay a percentage of the fourteen million dollars he had agreed – exactly half the amount they had asked for. They would receive this as soon as all the documents were signed and the surveyors had completed their inspections.

Throughout the entire transaction the Baron had remained aloof, treating William with contempt. It was as if this business deal was beneath him. Perhaps it was no wonder that – if the rumours were well founded – he had got himself into dire financial difficulty.

William had to wait only a moment outside for his Rolls – Arthur was heading towards him immediately. The Baron walked out of the hotel accompanied by a rather well-preserved blonde woman. He introduced his wife frostily, and the Baroness smiled vacantly in William's direction as the doorman hailed a passing taxi. The taxi drew up at the same time as William's gleaming car, but he was already speaking into his mobile so they had no further interaction. Not that William desired any: his mind was already on his next appointment with his bankers.

After lunch Andrew Maynard joined him for coffee.

He seemed relaxed and confident, his face slightly flushed, although this was noticeable only to William, who knew him well enough to realize that Maynard was drinking more than usual. But the warning bells still did not ring and William was merely pleased to see his protégé looking almost handsome: he'd been away in France and the suntan suited him, and he had started taking more interest in his clothes. Maynard was wearing a slim gold watch and the lining of his expensive new suit was of a dark emerald green satin.

The conversation turned to the predilection of the British press for public hounding, and to the most powerful man in British journalism, the newspaper magnate Humphrey Matlock. Matlock's powerful control of virtually every newspaper in the UK made him a formidable opponent. Although William didn't know him, he admired Matlock's tenacious strength of mind. Maynard, however, believed that no single individual should be allowed such control of the national media. William pointed out that as long as Matlock was on their side they had no reason to try to stop him.

'We'll never know exactly which side he's on. And now that everyone is afraid to get on the wrong side of him, whichever party they belong to, he's unstoppable,' Maynard insisted.

'I don't understand why you suddenly feel the need to attack him. As I recall, he's never done anything but enhance your image,' William replied, then stood up to leave – he had a three-thirty appointment.

The next morning at five fifty-five William had had his morning shower and was throwing on his clothes. He caught sight of the documents he'd been reading in bed the night before, and his heart leaped with pleasure. He owned numerous sumptuous homes around the world, all run by a permanent staff and ready for occupancy at any time of the year. But his latest purchase was the jewel in his crown. He was looking forward to showing it off to Maynard. He wouldn't approve, of course: he maintained that one home was enough for anyone. William had bought a small island in the British Virgin Islands. In the sixties it had enjoyed brief fame as a jet-set getaway, and appeared in all the top magazines as one of the most exclusive playgrounds in the world. But in the intervening years the owner had grown infirm and his money had gone on health care rather than upkeep. Now the island was in a state of total disrepair.

William had spectacular plans to make his paradise rise from the ashes like a phoenix. He had bought it at a good price because the refurbishment costs would be astronomical. He invited a select group of designers to tender for the renovations, and took great delight in poring over their Toytown models. It was a huge job and, judging from the way the companies fell over themselves to produce their designs, a desirable one. Maynard would be appalled at the fact that no expense would be spared to make William's dream come true.

It was six thirty and William went downstairs for breakfast. As he sat at the table and shook open that day's *Times*, he smiled to himself. He was where he had always dreamed he would be, right at the top of the world, and he had, as he constantly reminded himself, got there solely by his own hard work. He read the social column: 'Not So Idle Rich' was the headline. William Benedict already had a knighthood they said, how long would it be, at this rate, before he moved into the Upper House? William raised an eyebrow. He'd like that. He'd like to sit in the House of Lords, perhaps become one of the government's advisers . . . and maybe, with the help and guidance of Andrew Maynard, it was within his grasp.

Andrew Maynard's cleaner, Mrs Skipper, always arrived promptly at six a.m. She would tidy the house, prepare breakfast and cook an evening meal he could heat when he wanted it. Andrew Maynard was meticulous about his domestic routines. He did not like her to be there all day, or to stay overnight. He hated to work in his study with the sound of vacuuming, or the smell of cooking lingering in the air. By nine he had jogged, showered and breakfasted and had given Mrs Skipper a list of shopping, laundry or dry-cleaning collections. By ten his secretary was installed, the coffee percolating and the newspapers neatly laid out, and Maynard was ready for work, as immaculate and fresh as his small terraced house. Maynard had chosen the house because of its location and politically correct lack of ostentation. William had offered to buy him a larger property, but he had refused point-blank.

Mrs Skipper had been working for Maynard for the past five years. She knew as little about his private life now as she had when she started, and what she did know she had gleaned from the newspapers: when he took her on, she had signed a confidentiality agreement. He had explained that in his profession it was imperative he could trust those closest to him. As far as she knew, Maynard was a man of unimpeachable character, a young man on the threshold of a glittering political career, which even she could see was about to soar.

That morning Mrs Skipper picked up the single bottle of skimmed milk left by the milkman and, frowning, noticed that the bedroom curtains were still drawn. She let herself into number twelve. Mr Maynard was always up by this time so that she could make his bed and collect the dirty laundry. She went into the kitchen, which was as she had left it the evening before. This, too, was unusual: he always put his dirty supper dishes into the sink ready for her to rinse and load into the dishwasher. As she put the milk into the fridge, she noticed that the evening meal she had prepared yesterday was still in its tin-foil-covered dish. Mrs Skipper began to unbutton her coat, looking around for the note that was left each day on the kitchen table.

There was no note. She hung up her coat and fetched her apron, then walked back down the narrow hallway towards the stairs. She looked up, listening, wondering if her employer was upstairs in the bathroom – perhaps something had made him late for his morning jog and he was still out. Maybe he was ill. 'Mr Maynard?' she called tentatively.

The house was eerily silent – she was used to hearing the radio or television news when she came in. She began to mount the stairs, pausing midway to call his name again, but there was no reply.

His bedroom was dark and the bed had not been slept in. The bathroom door was open, and a suit, shirt and underwear were laid neatly across the bed. She went back out into the hall and tapped on his study door. It swung open, revealing the tidy desk, a stack of memos and mail lined up by the bank of telephones. She pulled the cord to open the curtains and, in the light, looked at the desk for some kind of sign. A yellow Post-it had been stuck to his blotter with a phone number. His address book was open and another sticker on the open page bore the same number and, underlined, an odd message: 'Call this number. Do not go into the bathroom'.

More worried by the minute, Mrs Skipper returned to the kitchen. Now she noticed that the back door was ajar. She opened it wide and looked out into the garden, which was empty. Mrs Skipper closed the door and locked it. It was then that she felt the drip of water from the ceiling above. She looked up and listened. Maynard's bathroom was directly above the kitchen.

Mrs Skipper went upstairs again and listened at the closed bathroom door. Now she could hear water running softly and, looking down saw the creeping stain growing darker as it seeped into the carpet and edged into the bedroom. She turned the bathroom door handle. It was not locked, and she pushed it open and froze in shock at the sight of Maynard's body, partly submerged, and his hands, floating, with deep gashes at the wrists from which blood still trailed.

'Call this number. Do not go into the bathroom,' the yellow note had said, each word heavily underlined. Mrs Skipper moved back into the office, reached for the phone and dialled.

The telephone's shrill ring woke William from his reverie. He waited a beat, hoping his housekeeper would pick it up, but eventually got up and answered it himself. 'Yes,' he snapped.

35

It was an hysterical woman, babbling incomprehensibly.

'Who is this?' he said coldly. It was William's personal phone. Only a handful of people had the number; this woman must have misdialled. Then William heard Maynard's name. He tried to slow the woman down. 'I can't understand what you're saying,' he said, and told her to take a deep breath.

'He's dead, sir. Please come.'

'Has there been an accident?' William asked. The phone felt clammy in his hand. When he realized what she was telling him, his heart lurched. 'Listen to me! Do nothing until I get there, do you understand. Wait until I see you. Do not call anyone until I get there.'

His heart was still thudding as he drove from his four-storey house in The Boltons towards Ladbroke Grove.

When he saw Maynard, he became icy calm. Mrs Skipper was sitting at the kitchen table below. He could hear her sobbing. She had refused to accompany him up the stairs, so William was forced to confront the grotesque sight of Andrew Maynard's body alone. His first reaction was of stunned horror, as if the scene before him was some sick theatrical set-up. Nothing he knew about Maynard had prepared him for this. He didn't touch the body, but looked down into the open eyes, the dark hair floating around the head, and reached forward to turn off the taps. Maynard's blood had stained the water a soft shell pink. The cuts in his wrists were deep and blood had sprayed down the bathroom tiles. Beside the bath was an empty gin bottle, and an overturned crystal glass with a slice of lemon still resting at the bottom.

William went to Maynard's study, pocketed the note with his phone number on it, and looked around for Maynard's diary, address book and any personal papers. He placed them in his own briefcase, and searched for a suicide note before returning to the bedroom. He found it partly hidden beneath the bathtub. It was sodden from the overflowing water and the ink was blurred, which made the few hastily scribbled lines hard to decipher, but William could see it was addressed to him.

Dear William,
  I have no ambition left, just heartbreak and ter-
rible longing.
  I am sorry,
  Andrew

William read and re-read it. It made little sense to him. What heartbreak, what longing had made Andrew take his own life? He felt numb and confused, as if he still could not believe what had happened. Eventually he called the police and sat waiting for their arrival, study-ing the note as it dried in his hands. Maynard's death would create a media frenzy, and one part of his brain was already wondering who would be the best man to hire for damage control.

Five hours later William returned home. He had his own press office prepare a statement, but no matter what he said, Maynard's death would cause one hell of a scandal. William poured himself a brandy, retired to his drawing room and started checking through the papers he had removed from Maynard's study. He had made no mention of them to the police, but they had taken the suicide note. They had asked if it was

Maynard's handwriting, and William had nodded, but in reality it was so smudged it was hard to tell. The large bundle of personal letters he placed to one side as he flicked through the first leatherbound desk diary filled with appointments, then Maynard's private diary.

He couldn't believe he had been so blind, that he had failed to detect this other side of Maynard. It confused and angered him, yet he found the details of the man's bizarre, hidden life strangely compelling: the neat, meticulous handwriting, the lists of names, lovers, descriptions of sexual practices and a detailed account of monies paid out for years on sexual gratification. One name, Justin Chalmers, featured more often than most. This man had accompanied Maynard on trips to Paris, Vienna, Jamaica and Morocco. Maynard's bank statements recorded payments to Chalmers; large sums over several years. William wondered if he had been blackmailing Maynard. What else could account for the thousands of pounds Maynard had spent on him? What else could account for the lists of fictional companies, whose names he had used to redirect campaign funds to a bank account in France? The recipient was always J. Chalmers. Was Justin Chalmers the person Maynard 'longed for'? Had Chalmers broken his heart?

It was lunchtime before William moved through to his office and checked the answerphone. There were twenty-four messages, but he felt disinclined to play them. It was imperative that he found Justin Chalmers. Of all the names in Maynard's diary, this one had leaped out as the most dangerous. Slowly William punched in the number and waited. The phone rang three times, then an answerphone clicked on and a soft, drawling voice announced, 'Hi, I'm afraid I am unable to come to the phone right now. Please leave a message and the time and date you called and . . .' there was a pause, followed by a laugh '. . . if you're lucky I'll get back to you.'

At two fifteen, William let in his damage-control expert, Myers Summers. 'Well, this is a fucking mess all round, isn't it? You know the world and its mother are trying to contact you, old boy?' Summers shrugged off his coat.

'I guessed as much, but I'm not speaking to anyone until we've sorted something out. Come and have a drink.'

'Not for me, thanks, if we're to concentrate on making sure you escape the flak.' Summers sat down. 'Right, let's have it from the top, shall we?'

It was just after midnight when Summers left, by which time William was flushed with brandy – not drunk, but he had consumed more than usual.

Summers's parting shot was that it was imperative to get the boyfriend, or whoever he was, tucked away and out of public grasp no matter the cost. Especially as, according to the diary, he would have been the last person to have been seen with Maynard. He might even have had an argument with him that had resulted in Maynard slashing his wrists.

'I suppose he did slash them himself?' Summers asked, as if it was just an afterthought.

'How the hell would I know?' snapped William.

'Well, let's hope he did. It's murky enough as it is. If murder was mentioned, it would really whip up a frenzy. Is this Justin fella around at all?'

William shrugged. He obviously had been, and with Maynard on the night he died. But where was he now?

As the police did not have access to Maynard's private diaries, William was confident that he could deal with Justin Chalmers. Money, he had learned over years of having it, always had the desired effect on a certain type of person. He had no doubt that Chalmers could be bribed. He was about to turn off the lights in his study when he checked the time. It was two thirty. He hesitated, then picked up the phone and dialled, leaning back against the desk, staring at his brown brogues. There was no immediate reply, and he was about to hang up when a sleepy voice answered, 'Yes?'

'I called and left a message earlier today,' William said, then had to clear his throat as he was so nervous. 'Is that Justin Chalmers?'

'I believe so . . .' came the reply, followed by a yawn.

'I need to see you.'

'Really? You want to come over now?'

'No, in the morning, early. This is a most urgent matter, which concerns a mutual acquaintance. I cannot discuss it over the telephone.'

'Mmm, well, come whenever you want, and . . .' there was a pause, then what sounded like a giggle '. . . I can't wait.' The phone went dead. At no time had Chalmers even asked who was calling.

Exhausted, William went to bed and was asleep as soon as his head hit the pillow. He slept, untroubled by dreams, but his serenity was not to last long.

# CHAPTER 3

It was six a.m. when William drove into the mews. As yet the news of Maynard's death had not broken: it had not made the previous night's programmes, but there was no doubt that it would be this morning's main item. William arrived at Chalmers's address in Kensington. Flower-tubs and urns decorated the doorsteps of the row of pretty two-storey mews cottages. If he lived in that sort of house, in this part of town, William thought, Chalmers must be pretty well off. But as he reached the end of the street, the houses began to look seedier, obviously leased. Number thirty-two had the obligatory doorstep tub, but the plants were dead and the front-door paint was peeling. The bell was out of order, so William knocked. He did not have to wait more than a few moments before the door opened. A tall, tanned young man beckoned him in. He was wearing a pristine white T-shirt with pale washed-out denim jeans. His bare feet were encased in velvet monogrammed slippers and he wore a heavy gold bracelet on his right wrist. The interior was dark, all the curtains still drawn, but the furniture was antique and the carpets, though threadbare, were good-quality Turkish. Velvet cushions were scattered over the floor, and there was a sofa with stuffing protruding from its arms. 'Justin Chalmers? Sir William Benedict,' William said, and thrust out his hand.

The young man glanced down at it and, without a word, went through a bead curtain into what William supposed was the kitchen, from where the smell of coffee emerged. William stood uneasily in the middle of the room.

Minutes later the young man reappeared with a tray and put it down on an Indian brass coffee-table. 'Do sit down. I rarely entertain at this house, so excuse the mess. You obviously have something of . . .' He swallowed the word 'urgency', then smiled, and gestured to the coffee pot. 'Black or white?'

'Black, please.'

William sat gingerly on the edge of the sofa. 'Thank you for agreeing to see me.'

'I'm intrigued by how you got hold of my number and address.' Chalmers handed William a cup.

He was tall, at least six foot two, with a lean torso. He had exceptionally blond hair, not the same colour or texture as William's but naturally thick and streaked by the sun, well cut and worn quite long, touching his shoulders. He had penetrating wide-set eyes of so vivid a blue that the whites seemed brilliant. The deep lines at the side of his eyes and mouth did not detract from his overall youthfulness, but he was, William guessed, in his early thirties.

As he passed a chipped porcelain cup and saucer, William noticed that his fingers were long, slender and as tanned as his chiselled face. His nails were clean and manicured and he had a large embossed gold ring on the little finger of his left hand.

'You needed to see me urgently,' he said, 'so let's not waste time. What's the problem?' He curled up on a cushion opposite William, and looked at him over the rim of his cup. He took a sip, then tossed his hair back from his face.

William watched him carefully as he began. 'You know Andrew Maynard?'

'Yes, I do.'

'He was found dead yesterday morning.' Chalmers showed no flicker of emotion. 'With his wrists slit in his bathtub.'

'Really? Sorry, I forgot to ask, do you take sugar?'

'No, thank you.' William took a sip of coffee. 'I'm aware that you had an ongoing relationship with him.'

'So?' Chalmers sank back into his chair and blew on his coffee. 'There are biscuits too, if you'd like one.' William was alarmed by the young man's response. This was not how it was meant to go. Chalmers pulled a face. 'So you found him, did you? Must have been unpleasant. A lot of blood, I suppose? Cutting your wrists sends a massive spray.'

'You saw him last Thursday. What time did you leave?'

There was a pause as Chalmers gazed intently at William. 'You seem very well informed.' He leaned back and closed his eyes. 'I went round at about seven thirty in the evening. I was having dinner elsewhere, but Andrew wanted to see me, so I obliged. I left about an hour later. Around eight thirty, perhaps a quarter to nine.'

'Did you have an argument?'

'I don't think that's any of your business.'

William placed his cup down and leaned forward. 'You mind if I call you Justin?'

'I don't mind if you call me Jack the Ripper.'

William talked across Chalmer's laughter. 'You see, Justin, the press will hound you if they discover what was going on between you and Andrew Maynard. I am aware that he paid you large sums of money.'

Chalmers stared. William was unnerved by his assurance and turned away. He chose his words carefully. 'It would be preferable, Justin, if your relationship was not made public.'

'I have no desire to discuss my relationship with Andrew. We were good friends and I was very fond of him, although not as exclusively as he wanted.'

'Did he kill himself because of you?' William blurted out.

Chalmers shrugged. 'I have no idea. He seemed quite together when I saw him but, then, one can never tell another person's real feelings, especially when that person is a politician.' He laughed, softly, leaned back and stretched like a cat, his sexuality and sensuality filling the room.

William felt distinctly uneasy in his presence. Suddenly doubts started to filter through his mind. *Could* it have been murder?

As if reading William's mind, the other man leaned forward. 'I didn't kill him. I can tell you're thinking it's a possibility, but I didn't. He was too useful and, as you so rightly pointed out, I received a considerable amount of money from him and hoped to continue doing so.'

William stayed another fifteen minutes, in which time he agreed that a sum of money would be paid into Chalmers's bank account on the condition that he left London immediately and did not speak to the press or anyone else about his relationship with Andrew

Maynard. The young man did not quibble over the amount, but accepted a hundred thousand pounds immediately and said he would be on the next flight. William was relieved that the negotiations had gone so smoothly, but as he shook Chalmers's hand, he felt the man's fingers grip his own.

'You have his diaries?'

'Yes.'

'Do the police know you removed property from the scene?'

'No. They will be destroyed. No one will know of their contents.'

'Ah, yes.' Chalmers sighed and smiled simultaneously. 'But *I* know . . . and I also know I could make a lot more than a paltry hundred grand in one exclusive to any number of tabloids.' He let the veiled threat hang in the air briefly then continued, 'Because I *did* care for poor old Andrew, I'll accept your offer – but I'd appreciate it if you remember you're getting off very lightly.'

'I have nothing to worry about,' William said, removing his hand from Chalmers's grasp.

'Really? Then I've misjudged you, Sir William.' He crossed his arms and propped himself against the door-frame. 'Look at the facts. You have come here personally and you have taken possession of his diaries. It can only mean one thing: you are worried that Andrew Maynard's private life might contaminate your own.' Chalmers chuckled to himself. 'After all, you did finance his career and, knowing the gutter-press, they will dig deeply into your . . .' he snorted before continuing, making speech marks in the air '. . . "predilections". Perhaps they will assume that you too are a "friend of

Dorothy" as they say. They may force you to come out.'

He smiled at William's discomfort, but his eyes showed no signs of amusement. William grasped the subtext and reluctantly upped the kiss-off price to a quarter of a million. It was accepted.

William drove back to The Boltons in a fury. He didn't mind spending the money – that had not irked him – it was the arrogance of the man, the confidence with which he had played his hand so perfectly. Justin Chalmers had class and William knew it. No matter how rich he was, he would never be able to match that sort of man's aristocratic air, and he felt sure that that had not been the last time he would see him.

The crisp morning made William feel a bit better. The traffic in Park Lane was still moving freely, enabling the gleaming Rolls to move swiftly down and round Hyde Park Corner. On occasions, William enjoyed driving himself instead of being chauffeured and already he felt more confident, as if the power he was wielding over the car was somehow mirroring the control he had taken over his life. Two hundred and fifty thousand pounds was chicken feed to a man as wealthy as William, and he had been prepared to pay a lot more. He would clear up this unfortunate Maynard business quickly, and that would be that. A minor setback. He slotted a CD into the stereo and drummed his fingers on the steering-wheel as Beethoven exploded from the speakers.

As he drove towards The Boltons, his mood lifted even higher. He had a full day ahead: a luncheon with Lady Thorn to discuss a charity benefit, then back-to-back business meetings for the rest of the afternoon before dinner with a senior member of the Royal Family to discuss sponsorship for the Royal Horse Show. As he mulled over the day ahead he succeeded in putting Maynard's suicide to the back of his mind.

However, as he turned into The Boltons, it all came flooding back. The roadway outside his house was swarming with reporters and photographers, and a TV news team was setting up its cameras. William was forced to slow to a crawling pace as the hordes converged on his car. The flash of cameras made his eyes water, and there was a sudden burst of voices as they recognized him and attempted to stop the car to interview him there and then. 'Sir William, SIR WILLIAM . . . *Daily Mail* . . . *Daily Telegraph* . . . the *Sun*.' They surrounded the car, shoving microphones towards him, and he almost ran over a few as he attempted to get into his driveway. The electronic gates half opened, but the journalists took that as an invitation to move further on to his property.

He lowered the window, and barked, 'You are trespassing. Please move out of the way of the car. *Move away from the car*. No comment. *No comment*. Get out of my way, please.'

Not until the gardener, the valet and Michael, his secretary, came out did William try to step out of the car. As the gates closed behind him, he saw his employees trying to remove two men who were attempting to squeeze past them.

Michael opened the driver's door and gestured for him to hurry inside. 'We've been inundated, sir. The phones are ringing, the fax machines haven't stopped, and there are people trying to get over the back wall.'

Inside the elegant hallway, William headed straight for his study. 'Call the bloody police, Michael. They're trespassing, for God's sake. Legally they can't put a foot in the driveway.'

'I know, sir, but they've been out there since you left this morning. We have contacted the police and they—'

'Call the Chief Superintendent. No, get me Commander Jameson. I'll talk to him.' Michael bustled around the study, stacking documents on the desk. Every single phone was ringing. 'Turn the bloody phones off! This is ridiculous. Get Mrs Fuller to bring me some coffee and—' William snatched at one of the telephones and barked into the receiver. 'Yes?'

It was an irate Myers Summers. 'Where, in Christ's name, have you been? I've been calling since seven o'clock. Have you seen the papers?'

'Not yet. I've been trying to get rid of the press. They're like hornets outside.'

'Well, read them and call me straight back.'

William took half an hour to get through every newspaper. By the time he had finished, Myers Summers was sitting in his study.

'You're telling me you went to see this Chalmers in the flesh?'

'Yes.'

Summers rested his head in hands. 'Did anyone see you?'

'No. Why are you getting into such a state?'

Summers took a deep breath. 'This is serious, William. You walk off with diaries and documents. You spend – how long at Maynard's place before you call the police? You then pay some fucking fruit half a million—'

'Quarter of a million.'

'Why? What the fuck for? I mean, who is he?'

'The last person to see Maynard, that's who. And he's a screamer so I got rid of him.'

'Do you think he killed Maynard?'

'No, Maynard cut his own wrists, Myers, with—'

'Yeah, yeah, I know, with an open cut-throat razor, silver and bone handle, inscription from you! Now, it seems to be a bone of contention that the cuts were deep, and to both wrists. Apparently that's odd. If you slash one open it's pretty tough to slash the other. So we won't be certain it was suicide until after the post-mortem. He could have a six-inch blade shoved up his arse for all you know, and this poofter might have done it! And you go round personally and pay him off!' He sighed and flopped back in his chair. 'Why?'

'To minimize the risk of scandal I bought his silence.'

'Are you *joking*?' Summers sat forward again. 'Don't you *see* the implications of that?'

'Quite frankly, no, I do not. Right now the "poofter", as you call him, is probably on his way to Paris. Gone. Finished with.'

Myers Summers closed his eyes. 'Well, I'll have to find out more about him. You're sure no one else saw you visit him?'

'Certain. I told you, it was six o'clock in the morning, there wasn't a soul around. Just milkmen, newspaper boys . . .'

'All right. Now, yesterday, did Maynard's cleaner see you remove anything?'

'No, she wasn't in the room.'

'Well, that's something. And she called you as soon as she discovered the body?'

'Yes, there was a memo stuck on his desk telling her to call my number.'

'What? He left a memo? With some kind of instruction?'

Suddenly William found himself blushing: it hadn't occurred to him how strange it was that Maynard should leave a sticker on his desk for his housekeeper to find, with William's private number and instructions not to enter the bathroom. Of course it was suicide. Maynard must have known exactly what he was doing.

'Come on, man, was there anything else this woman might have seen you remove?'

William was irked by the way Summers was speaking to him. 'Listen to me, Myers, I took the personal items because there were details of how much he had been forking out to this guy and it was a lot of money. Whether it was blackmail or not is immaterial now. Chalmers is out of the loop. I was just trying to protect Maynard's reputation, and mine and the Party's. He'd have been misappropriating funds, for Chrissakes.'

Myers Summers got to his feet and walked round the room as he spoke. 'All right, then, let me put it to you another way. His bank will have particulars, won't they? His bookkeeper, accountant. Maybe friends of this Justin Chalmers character knew about the money. Maybe there are other Maynard pick-ups in other diaries – last year's for instance. The police will be looking into everything.' He laid a hand on the mantelpiece and turned to face the desk. 'Can't you see, Sir William? This is a huge story. I mean, the man was supposed to be some great political hope, and he's climbing the ladder like a trapeze artist when he tops himself because he's heartbroken about some bloody poof. How much sleaze do you need to make a juicy front page?'

Myers pulled at his pinstriped waistcoat, then his tie, then his jacket, as if to calm himself. 'Okay, Sir William, I'll tell you what'll happen. You give a statement – I'll get my people to write it for you – and in it you say nothing about the diaries or documents you took. Nothing. You happened to be there as you had a meeting scheduled. After finding the body you were deeply distressed and needed a few moments to collect yourself before calling the police. I'll talk to the house-keeper. I'll also run a trace on Chalmers. List the other names you found in the diaries and I'll give them the once-over as well.'

'Is all this necessary?' William asked.

Myers Summers picked up his bulging briefcase: he was already running late for his next appointment. 'If Andrew Maynard was murdered, then it's abso-fucking-lutely necessary and even if he committed suicide, drunk or drugged up, whatever, it's still gonna be headlines for weeks because the press will want to find out who his boyfriends were, what his relationship was with every male he knew, in fact. And you can bet they'll come after you. You found him dead, you financed him to the hilt, and it's public knowledge that he's your mentor when it comes to public-speaking. Everyone knows you scratch each other's backs. What they'll wonder is just what else you've mutually scratched.'

'It's OK, Myers. I get the picture. But no one's going to think *that* of me.'

Myers Summers raised an eyebrow. 'They'll believe

anything, if they're told it often enough. Isn't that why you have a publicity agent?' He rested his hand on the door-handle. 'I'm just warning you, as one of the mega-rich, you are just the type the tabloids will go for. The bigger they are, the harder they fall. And all those little people you may have forgotten treading on when you were climbing up will come crawling out of the woodwork.' He paused and faced William. 'Just for the record, were you having a scene with Maynard?'

William gasped. '*What?*'

'Are you queer?'

William sucked in his breath, shocked. '*No, I am not. And how dare you speak to me like that!*'

'Well, that's the best news so far. I'll deal with it,' Myers said, and with that he opened the door to the hall. 'I'll be in touch shortly – if I make it through that mob and live to tell the tale.'

William remained in his study. Up to now, he would have described himself as unshockable; a tough man who had made it to the top by his own hard graft but who now enjoyed rubbing shoulders with the British aristocracy. For the first time, he realized the depth in him of a naïvety he had never previously suspected. He checked his watch and buzzed for his secretary.

Michael scooted in. 'Yes, Sir William?'

'I'm due at lunch. Can you call the Ritz and—'

'Oh, I'm sorry, Sir William, Lady Thorn called, but I didn't want to interrupt your meeting with Mr Summers. She sends her apologies, but has come down with flu.'

William sat down behind his desk. 'Perhaps, under the circumstances, it's a good thing.'

'Yes, sir, I've got sheets of messages. There are also

numerous faxes, e-mails and an urgent call from Superintendent Hudson, Metropolitan Police. He's left his home number and direct line.'

Michael left the study and William unlocked the drawer that contained Maynard's business-appointment diary, and wondered why Myers hadn't asked to see it. It soon dawned on him that such a devious man wouldn't want to touch it. If the story did get out, Myers could say he knew nothing about any diaries being removed. William's eyes travelled to his wall-safe, which held Maynard's personal diary. It was as if he could see the red leatherbound cover through the steel door. It was dangerous to keep it, but he could not bring himself to destroy it.

Later, Myers Summers phoned William to give him details of the post-mortem: Andrew Maynard had died from loss of blood due to both arteries being severed on right and left wrist. Tests showed that his blood contained a vast quantity of alcohol and cocaine. There were no signs of physical violence. It was determined that he a practising homosexual but no traces of semen were found apart from his own. His naked body was devoid of pubic hair and smothered with Johnson's baby oil. Myers hesitated to draw breath. 'They also found numerous bottles of pills. You name any kind of speed and your friend had it, plus five grams of cocaine. Oh, and another tasty morsel that will, no doubt, be fucking leaked is that Maynard was suffering from genital herpes.'

William couldn't listen to any more. He was sweating. Only the announcement of a Third World War would knock this lot off the front page.

'The housekeeper's blabbed,' Myers went on. 'She's

told the cops about a diary and drawers full of letters and that you were the only person with access to them before they arrived.'

'I suppose the police will want to question me,' William observed.

''Course they will, but wait, just fasten your seat-belt. So far strong-arm tactics have kept it all under wraps in case it was murder, but it'll all hit the fan tonight. So far the press have only had the most meagre details. They only know he died at home. But tonight they'll have the titillating details. You know anything about his family?'

'No, I don't. His parents are dead. I believe he had a sister, but she died in some car accident. There's just an aunt in Bournemouth, as far as I know.'

'Ah, well. No doubt we'll know a lot more by tonight.'

William shrugged. 'You sound very sure. Why?'

'All right then,' Summers grunted. 'How about this? Someone has managed to get photographs of the body from the mortuary and some other bloody hack paper has been sent photographs of Maynard dancing in some gay night-club in Morocco, so Christ only knows what else they'll get from some bloody perverted bastard trying to make a few quid.'

'Well, what's all that got to do with me? I financed him. I didn't go down the Palais with him, dancing on a Saturday night.'

Summers hesitated. 'We only have your word for that.'

William was starting to get angry. 'I've told you, Myers, I knew nothing about his pervy life till yesterday, and I will make a statement to that effect and hand it

54

'over to the police. I've already spoken to them anyway – at his house before I left.'

'That won't satisfy the papers,' Summers was impatient. 'You were closely associated in life so you will be in death.'

'So what do you suggest I do?'

'Give a statement and, thinking about it, perhaps it'd be better in your own words.'

'You fucking said you'd write it!' William said angrily.

'Maybe I did, but standing back a bit, I think it should come from you. You knew him better than anyone else.'

'What's that supposed to mean?'

'One minute you were calling him the political saviour of the millennium, next he's pictured dancing with twelve-year-old boys in Morocco! You work it out. I can't be involved.'

'Can't or won't? Which is it, Myers?'

There was a pause. 'My wrists are tied.' Summers gave a humourless laugh. 'Sorry, under the circumstances, that was a rather crass thing to say.' He continued, 'I've been warned off you, William. I'm sorry, but a word of advice. For God's sake keep schtum about the diaries and stuff. Burn them, get rid of them, deny ever seeing them. And don't mention the note. Why did Maynard want *you* to find him, before the police? And don't mention this Chalmers bloke either.' There was a pause, this time at William's end. 'You still there? Hello? Hello?'

William had hung up. He'd never liked the squint-eyed son-of-a-bitch anyway. It was just that he was so well connected. Well, fuck him! William hadn't become one of the wealthiest men in England without being able to take care of some jumped-up journalist – or a pack of them come to that. And if they wanted to dig around in his past, let them. He didn't have anything to hide.

'Michael,' he bellowed. 'Call a press conference.'

'For when, sir?'

'First thing in the morning. Meanwhile I want you to cut out every newspaper article on Maynard and record every piece of television news coverage to date, even if it takes all night.'

'It's all over the Internet,' Michael said nervously.

'Then print out whatever anybody's saying. I want to read it all, no matter what it says. Is it bad?'

Michael nodded and his lips trembled slightly. 'Some of it's downright sick. Er . . . will you be arranging his funeral?'

'What?'

'Andrew Maynard's funeral, sir.'

William slumped into his chair. 'Yes, yes – well, you sort it out, I can't think about that right now. Go on, do what you have to, no expense spared, but keep it simple.'

Michael left the room, as William lowered his head into his hands. He had been too preoccupied, too shocked for it all to have sunk in. He had been blocking out the emotional impact of losing a man he had grown to admire and love like a son, and now the floodgates opened. The tears trickled down his cheeks, as he murmured his protégé's name in despair and bewilderment.

He tried to hide his tears when Michael tapped and re-entered. The police were waiting to see him.

William blew his nose, wiped his face and nodded for Michael to let them in. He stood up, hand outstretched to meet Superintendent Hudson and Detective Inspector Joan Fromton. He offered them tea or coffee but they refused, seating themselves in front of his desk on two hard-backed chairs that were usually placed against the wall.

The interview lasted two and a half hours. They questioned William in detail as to how he found the body, what the housekeeper had said, why she had called him before contacting a doctor or the police. William had no need to lie. He just did not mention that a note had suggested she call him: it was feasible that she would have anyway as he was so closely associated to Maynard.

Then came the obvious question; 'Just how closely?' With dignity William dismissed from their minds any notion that he was homosexual. All he was, and all he had been for the past few years, was a friend and business associate. There had been nothing more between them than friendship and admiration. He had had no inkling of Maynard's private life.

He was asked whether he had removed any items from Maynard's property and he said that he had not.

When questioned about Maynard's associates, he again extricated himself well by saying that, as he had already stated, he did not know of Maynard's private life so did not know any of his close male or female friends. The officers were polite, at times appearing genuine in their sympathy with his grief. Twice William came close to tears as he repeated that he had not really taken in the loss of someone he had greatly admired, and felt sad that, despite their friendship, Maynard had not spoken to him about his depression. This led the officers to ask William if he had been aware that Maynard used certain substances, and that a substantial amount of cocaine had been found in his house. William said he had not. The interview eventually ended with William admitting, 'It is hard, I suppose, for you to understand how someone like me could be foolish enough not to see what Andrew was, but I didn't. You see, I cared for him deeply, as a father would. He was special to me, but now I have to face the awful truth that I never really knew him at all.'

The Superintendent thanked William, and said that he would have Maynard's note sent to him as soon as it could be released. Hudson had a habit of appearing to dismiss a subject, then hopping back to it. 'You recognized the writing on the note as Maynard's, is that correct?'

William nodded.

'It was very blurred from the water, but you still believe it to be Maynard's own handwriting?'

William's nerves were ragged. 'Yes, I do. Is there any reason for me not to? He had very distinct, looped writing.'

'Yes, we are aware of that. But the letter was submerged in water so it's quite difficult to ascertain for sure . . . That said, the forensic experts believe it to be Maynard's.'

The policeman assured him that foul play was not suspected and offered William his condolences. When he was ushering them from the room, Joan Fromton asked if William would please contact them should any of Andrew Maynard's associates approach him; they would still like to make enquiries about the drugs discovered at Maynard's home. Then she threw William. 'Does the name Justin Chalmers mean anything to you, Sir William?'

William knew that he had flushed but he shook his head. 'I can't say that it does, may I ask why?'

'He is the main beneficiary in Andrew Maynard's will. He had no family, but no doubt Mr Maynard's lawyers will be able to assist us. Thank you very much for your time.'

William gave a long, weary sigh. Chalmers worried him greatly but, as the police had said, there were no criminal charges under review. But yet again, just as he went to shake the Superintendent's hand, he felt the carpet tugged from beneath him.

'Sir, if this case had proved to be other than suicide, and you had removed items from the deceased's premises, it would be a criminal offence. I am sure you are aware of that. I take your word for it that you did not remove any such items such as diaries, private letters . . .'

There was cold appraisal in the balding Hudson's hazel eyes. He knew William must have taken a diary, perhaps even letters, and he also understood why. These society types were all the same; their sole priority was saving their own backsides, and it infuriated him that he had been ordered to clear up the investigation as quickly and with as little scandal as possible. He knew that William was somehow caught up in this and given half a chance, Hudson would come down on him like the proverbial ton of bricks.

'Thank you for your time, sir,' the Superintendent said as he left, ushering his inspector ahead of him. He kept his head down as he walked out into the street beyond the high barred gates. The vultures hovering there with their cameras and microphones, screamed for him to stop and say a few words.

'No comment. No comment.'

A uniformed officer stood by the plain patrol car, the door open. Joan settled in the back seat, Hudson in the front with the uniformed driver.

'What did you think of him?' she asked, checking over her notes.

'Not a lot. Lying through his teeth about the "no items removed from victim's premises". He certainly had time enough to clean the place up. He's probably scared his own sexual peccadilloes will get out – every politician's hiding something or other.'

'He's not a politician, though. He was Maynard's benefactor. He's rich as Croesus.' She paused. 'Didn't you think he reacted strangely to Justin Chalmers's name? I wonder why.'

'Justin Chalmers . . .' the Superintendent mused. 'You ran a check on him, right?'

'Yes, sir, clean as a whistle. Neighbours say he keeps himself to himself – not at home much, apparently. He has a sister who visits regularly. She has some sort of psychiatric complaint. I think he looks after her pretty well. Oh, and he's openly gay, which explains Maynard's generous will. Probably partners.'

'Oh, well, there you have it. That probably explains Sir William's reaction then. Maybe he had a scene with him too and doesn't want it to come out. Half of the society set are in the closet, not that it concerns me.'

Joan smiled. She'd liked Sir William, and felt sorry

for him, but she said nothing more as they drove past the flashing photographers. She often wondered what they did with all the photographs they took, and laughed to herself.

'What's so funny?'

'Oh, I just wondered if they'd caught my best side.'

He grinned. 'Don't let it concern you. They're not interested in us – we're not rich or famous enough. Now, if it had been a murder, we might have made the front page departing from Sir William Benedict's mansion!'

# CHAPTER 4

O N THAT evening's news programmes William did not come across well. Blustering, he denied any knowledge of Maynard's sexual predilections, and refused to be drawn into any discussions on weird sexual practices. He said he was saddened by the death of a friend, and hoped people would remember Andrew Maynard as a young, highly intelligent, well-meaning man. When asked whether he had removed any items from Maynard's home, he remained silent.

The press had a field day. They printed exclusive interviews with Maynard's cleaner, Mrs Skipper, and his secretary, Sara Vickers. Both women spoke of Maynard's private life in a way that was easy to embroider. William's next few days were beyond his worst nightmare. The affair mushroomed and dragged in people from under every stone of his own past. A photograph of William with his arm around Maynard appeared on the front page, an innocent photograph, with four other people cut from it to make it appear over-affectionate, if not loving. Headlines screamed, 'GAY MP'S SUICIDE', and further details of Maynard's life appeared, more photographs of him taken in seedy nightclubs, and on beaches. Where they came from was a mystery, but they kept appearing, and William constantly featured in one doctored picture or another. The trouble the press took to make it appear that William was the lover over whom Maynard had slashed his wrists was beyond belief. His first wife, Lady Margaret Pettigrew, gave an exclusive interview for one of the Sunday colour supplements headlined 'My Husband – The Adulterer'. She had waited twenty years for her revenge and she took it with relish.

William's humiliation did not end with her revelations. His second wife, Katherine, the mother of his two children, jumped on the bandwagon with equal enthusiasm. It was as if the two women had got together to destroy him. In a double-page spread in one of the tabloids, Katherine painted him as a mean, vicious, brutal man who spent his days trawling the streets for nubile flesh, neglecting his two children in favour of prostitutes.

Every day brought another outrageous defamatory onslaught, another person creeping out of the woodwork to tell their story. Maynard's suicide was beginning to take second place to the hounding of William, as if his death had simply acted as a catalyst. William could do nothing but look on with stunned helplessness. None of the sexual slanders was true, but the fact that he had indeed used a few girls made it impossible to sue.

In any case his lawyer, Brian Sutherland, appeared frightened for his own reputation. William felt as if he was hitting his head against a brick wall. 'For God's sake, yes! *Yes*, I've hired a few call-girls over the years, but who hasn't? It doesn't make me some insatiable sex addict! If I'm not a homosexual, I'm a lusting pervert.

Something has to be done to stop them printing these lies about me.'

Sutherland was one of the most respected lawyers in England. He warned that if, as William had admitted, he had occasionally used call-girls, then to bring a massive and costly lawsuit against someone as powerful as Humphrey Matlock, the proprietor of the newspapers, would end in catastrophe: '. . . the reason being, William, that any one of the girls you've known in an intimate way could be tracked down and offered money to refute these denials of yours. And as you have admitted, albeit in the privacy of my office, that you have occasionally used the services of certain illegal agencies for, ah, intimate massages and so on, you could not swear otherwise on oath.'

William interrupted, 'But no more than any other man has, for fuck's sake. Name me anyone you know who hasn't,' he snapped.

'That, old fellow, is not the issue, because you are not "any other man" but Sir William Benedict. So I suggest, and this is my best advice, that you lie low and ignore the slanders. Look at Jeffrey Archer! For God's sake, don't antagonize them, just let it blow over.'

'But it's a bloody outrage,' William stormed.

'I admit that it is,' said the suave Sutherland, in mellifluous tones as he wandered around his elegant Mayfair office, 'but you must look at it in a logical way, old man. The fact is that you don't want any of these women with whom you have had sexual relationships, albeit infrequently, to testify against you. And as they will want their fifteen minutes of fame while Humphrey Matlock is known for cheque-book journalism, I really do think you should just let it blow over.'

The meeting was at an end, and William knew he should heed Sutherland's warning. He agreed angrily to do nothing, but he couldn't help wishing for a minute alone with Humphrey Matlock so that he could swing a punch at him.

The final straw came the following weekend, when yet another Matlock-owned newspaper gave centre-page coverage to interviews with William's children, who said they hated him for betraying their mother. He noted bitterly that neither made any reference to the substantial allowances he made to them, way over what he was obliged to pay, and that he maintained the entire family in a luxurious lifestyle.

Desperate to stem the flow, William tried to contact his ex-wives. Margaret refused to speak to him, and when he threatened Katherine with reducing his maintenance payments to the amount stipulated by the courts, he was met with screams of 'Do that, you bastard, and I'll make up the difference by selling the rest of our story to the highest bidder.'

For six weeks after Maynard's death – six horrific weeks of humiliation and degradation – the country was privy to the personal details of his two marriages, his household costs, his earnings and even his children's school fees. Now everyone thought he was an obsessive, sex-crazed man, hell bent on personal gain and even using his own children to achieve it. However, in every single article, there was still a kernel of truth, no matter how distorted, which made his lawyers balk at legal action. Had Matlock got to them, William wondered. Was there no one he could trust? Was he really so despicable?

The answer came from his sixteen-year-old son,

Charlie. William drove to the school to take his son to lunch. It was an awkward, strained occasion and Charlie was unable to look his father in the face. It was not until pudding was served that William asked, 'Why, Charlie? Why have you said these terrible things about me?' The boy shrugged, still refusing to meet his father's eyes. 'I've never stopped loving you, providing for you. You've wanted for nothing.'

Charlie looked up at last, and William noticed for the first time his son's resemblance to himself. 'You left us. You've never been a father. All you were ever interested in was making money. And now I think we should go back, Dad,' he said. 'My band's got the music room booked this afternoon.'

William drove his son back to school in silence. When he leaned forward to embrace him, Charlie recoiled. 'Bye,' he said stiffly and got out, slamming the car door. He walked straight through the gates, hands clenched at his sides. He was hoping and praying that none of his friends had seen him. Even the car was embarrassing: no one who was anyone had a two-tone Rolls Royce with a gold Spirit of Ecstasy.

The following day William had an equally excruciating luncheon with his daughter, Sabrina. She was more aggressive than her brother, refusing to eat, and sitting with pursed lips – so like her mother's. William had married Katherine because he wanted to be accepted in high society. She had bubbled with delight at the balls and at the races. She enjoyed posing for photos with William in the winner's enclosure, and showing them to her friends when they appeared in the society columns. But the effervescent, giggling young socialite of courtship had vanished immediately after the wedding. She began to reprimand him as if he were a child for the way he held his knife and fork, the way he dressed. She made little jibes that exploded into huge rows. Eventually she had hired Miss Drumgoole to teach him etiquette. The truth was, William had needed to learn from Katherine so that he could feel at ease in the social circles to which she introduced him, but her scornful carping made him uncomfortable and afraid to open his mouth.

And here was Sabrina, his offspring, as like the whingeing Katherine as if she had been spat out of her mouth. She was pale, with straight blonde hair, heavy-lidded eyes with fair lashes and braces on her teeth. She might have been attractive but her long, thin nose and full lips made her face lack animation and she seemed loath even to attempt a smile. William had no one to blame but himself: it had been his choice to divorce one vacuous titled blonde and marry another. Out of the frying pan and into the fire.

'I can't stay long,' lisped Sabrina. 'Besides, Mummy said I really shouldn't have agreed to see you at all. We've had these press people everywhere.'

'I am sorry,' he said flatly. 'Perhaps if your mother hadn't been so eager to spill her vitriolic lies about me, this would all have blown over.'

'I have been teased unmercifully because of you. The other girls do nothing but giggle about you, and mince around like willy woofters, pointing at me. It's embarrassing having someone like you for a father. They call me "Rough Trade", because of you and your boyfriend.'

'I'll take you back to school.' William folded his napkin. He was too tired and too hurt to argue.

Had he brought all this vituperation upon himself? Surely there had to be someone he could call a friend. He went through lists of names, people who had stayed on one or other of his estates, all those he entertained regularly. But then it dawned on him that no one except his employees had made contact in the past few weeks. He kicked at the sofa in a drunken fury, as his father had when the bailiffs arrived to remove the family's few possessions. Unlike his father, he had no woman on whom to take out his frustrations. At least his mother had always been there, even if it was only as a punch-bag.

His mother had scrimped and saved for him to stay at school for extra tuition, and it was she who had told him there was a way out. She always said, 'Get your maths, Billy. You got to have maths.' Why she had this fixation with maths he never discovered, but his high grade in that subject netted him a scholarship to Liverpool University. Sadly, she had not lived to see this and his father's advice was that he should go out and work, rather than 'loll around at university with a load of ponces'. Billy had rolled up his sleeves and punched his father – so hard that he sent him sprawling into the fireplace – and walked out. He never saw his father alive again.

Fortified now by anti-depressants and sleeping-tablets, William remained closeted in his bedroom where his past became his focus. There had been around forty mourners at his father's funeral from the bars and clubs at which he had virtually lived. They all told funny anecdotes about him, what a character he had been, what bad luck he'd always had in his business ventures, how near he had been to doing well, and how many times he had tried to earn a decent living. Hidden among various drawers at home, William had found the remnants of his father's so-called 'business ventures'. Most were unpaid bills, but astonishingly he found a life assurance policy worth four thousand pounds. William sold the family house and made a further three thousand. Throughout his university life he hardly touched the money; his grant was sufficient to live on, and he was too scared to mention his nest-egg in case it was taken away. Not until he graduated, with a double first in mathematics and electronic studies, and moved to London, did he begin to utilize it.

In 1968, seven thousand pounds was a lot of money. Today it would have been worth almost ten times as much. William began to study the *Financial Times* share index as meticulously as his father had studied the dogs and, still only twenty-three, he began to accumulate a small fortune. He invested it in a small factory to make a computer circuit board he'd worked on at university. In those days the most elementary computer filled a room, but William's circuit board was set to change that. By the time he was twenty-eight he was a millionaire – not in the same league as Bill Gates, but rich none the less. By thirty he was one of the most eligible bachelors in Britain.

But William wasn't very interested in women. He preferred a brief fling, usually with one of his employees. It was easier, because all he really thought about was work. It had been Angela Nicholls, one of his secretaries, who had first encouraged him to attend social events, go to the theatre or the opera. On her advice William bought an apartment in Knightsbridge and joined a golf club, a tennis club and a luncheon club, and soon had a wide circle of friends. Angela gave him a confidence in himself that he had previously lacked. She was an attractive girl from a good family, the sex was easy and comfortable, and William was fond of her. When Angela fell ill with glandular fever and was forced to take time off work, he was caring and considerate, sent flowers and paid for the best medical attention. He had imagined when she recovered that they would pick up where they had left off. But hadn't reckoned on Harriet Forbes, the willowy blonde sent by the agency to fill in.

William remembered Harriet clearly. Only twenty years old, she had an insatiable sex drive and represented all the girls he had lusted after when he was a teenager but was too shy to date. Harriet was the youth he had lost in making himself rich. He was quickly and foolishly besotted with her; Angela was forgotten. He was surprised to discover how well connected and wealthy Harriet's family was. One evening, as they strolled home arm in arm, they stumbled upon Angela. Harriet made some stinging remark about how plain she was, and Angela ran up the street in tears. William did not follow her. He was too intoxicated by Harriet. Too intoxicated to see his relationship with Harriet for what it really was.

One day Harriet arrived at William's apartment with an astonishing collection of ballgowns from some of the most exclusive boutiques in London. 'For the Berkeley Square Ball tonight,' she gasped, tugging at a zip.

'But you know I've got dinner with the Japanese.'

She looked up at him with amazement. 'Don't be ridiculous! I couldn't take you with me – it's a Society do.'

So he was good enough to fuck and pay for endless champagne, meals and clothes, but even with all his millions he was not good enough for her precious aristocrats! 'I don't want to go to some tin-pot ball with a load of overdressed slags cavorting round with a bunch of chinless twats anyway,' he snapped petulantly.

Harriet laughed, picked up her purchases and made for the door. 'You obviously do or you wouldn't be getting so uptight,' she said, over her shoulder. Then she flounced out, banging the door behind her.

He remembered how he had smarted with anger, and then how he had told himself that it was time he straightened out and got back to work. For the first time in months, he called Angela, but was told she had gone to Yorkshire to stay with her family. A month later he saw her at the opera, a few seats in front of him. He was alone, and during the interval asked if she would have a glass of champagne with him. She introduced him to her party of friends, one of whom was Margaret Pettigrew. That evening they all dined together: he was attentive to Angela, but intrigued by Margaret. As he helped Margaret into a taxi she slipped him her phone number.

Two months later William and Margaret were married. William paid for the wedding, an elaborate affair that made all the society columns, even 'Jennifer's Diary'. Margaret's family, it turned out, owned a stately home and acres of Hertfordshire, but didn't have two pennies to rub together, so it was an advantageous union on both sides. The Pettigrews needed the money; William desired the social status. Again Angela was dismissed from his thoughts. In a moment of madness, William invited Harriet to the wedding, thinking she would never come, but she did, in an overlarge hat and tiny dress in skin-pink. She strode up to him, kissed him on the lips, and whispered, 'She looks like a fucking horse!'

He smiled down at her. 'Do you think so? She reminded me of you.'

Harriet shrieked with laughter. She was later seen leaving hand in hand with one of the waiters.

Apart from William's business associates and staff, the rest of the guests had been from Margaret's side: dukes, earls, judges and Members of Parliament. Everyone knew William as a business tycoon, a multi-millionaire IT magnate, and he relished the attention. During the wedding luncheon he bought his first racehorse, and was invited to the Dunhill polo match. Later as they boarded his private jet, bound for St Lucia, William was convinced that marrying Margaret had been the best business and social move he had ever made. On the plane she made a toast: 'To Angela, for introducing us.' William raised his glass but felt a dreadful pang of guilt. Angela had been at the wedding, but he had not even spoken to her. He knew he had hurt her badly, but she gave no indication of this, just a shy smile when their eyes met over lunch. 'To Angela,' he had said, and quaffed the glass in one.

During the honeymoon, after their brief consummation, Margaret suffered a bout of cystitis. William slept in another bed for the entire two weeks. During the days, while Margaret stayed inside 'in the cool', William remained at the bar, wondering now if he had just made one of the biggest mistakes of his life.

Back in London, Margaret devoted herself to the marital home, lavishly decorating it to the tune of nearly a million pounds. She also found a country house in Berkshire with stables and twenty-two acres of land. The cystitis recurred virtually every time they had fumbling, dutiful sex. After a year they were sleeping in separate rooms.

Gradually William spent more time away from home, and this was when he began to pay high-class prostitutes for what he neither got nor wanted at home. At Royal Ascot he saw Harriet again. As usual he was alone: Margaret had a headache. Harriet was wearing a novelty hat and the usual short, tight skirt, her pregnancy visible to all. She was not in the Royal Enclosure, and was accompanied by a rather seedy-looking young man. William spent a considerable time with his binoculars trained on her. The sight of her made him wonder if theirs might have been a long-term relationship, but that was foolish.

'William, come and join us!' It was Cedric, Lord Hangerford, making drinking gestures with his hand. As he entered the private box William was struck by a beautiful woman sitting alone in a corner, studying form. 'What do I get for twenty to one?' she called, pen poised over her card.

'Put one pound on, you get twenty back,' William replied.

'God, I'm stupid sometimes,' said the beautiful blonde, without looking up.

William bought two more horses from Cedric Hangerford, and went home to find Margaret out, playing bridge with friends. 'She may stay with Mrs Castleton tonight,' said the maid, grimly.

William nodded as she shut the door behind her, then flicked at the blotting pad on his desk. Bored, he looked around the room at the décor, so carefully chosen by Margaret and that terrible old queen who claimed to be an interior designer. It was an elegant study, lined with hundreds of leatherbound books. White linen was draped as curtains and a large antique mahogany desk was placed beneath the window. Margaret loathed reproduction furniture: she said it was made for the middle classes. William had a sudden urge to swipe everything off the desk and hurl the Georgian ink-well at the curtains. He put his head in his hands: he was rich, successful, and bloody lonely. He dialled Madame Norton, who ran an up-market call-girl agency. He told her what he wanted, then informed the staff that they could retire for the night. Half an hour later the doorbell rang and William answered it personally.

Nina strutted in and followed William up the marble staircase towards the bedroom. She let her coat fall to the floor, stepped over it and threw a cheap black bag on to the damask-covered king-size bed. William poured two glasses of champagne and glanced at the girl, who was looking around the room. 'It's on the bedside table,' he said casually, and watched her pick up the roll of money then stuff it into her bag. She smiled sweetly as he passed her the champagne. His notion had been to try to re-enact the moments he had enjoyed with Harriet, but this girl was too cheap. He realized he had made a foolish mistake in asking her to come to his home.

'Cheers!' She took a sip and kicked off her shoes.

William was about to tell her that she could keep the money and leave when the bedroom door opened. He caught Margaret's reflection in the mirror and turned, holding out his glass of champagne. 'Why, Margaret,' he grinned, and went on with characteristic bravura, 'would you like to join us?'

Margaret was frozen to the spot, mouth hanging open in stunned amazement. Then she started to scream.

The divorce cost William the house and a substantial pay-off, negotiated by her weasel of a lawyer, who could hardly stop rubbing his hands in anticipation of his cut. However, William's own lawyers were clever enough to insinuate that if she did not accept his offer, they would issue a counter-action accusing her of frigidity and denying her husband his conjugal rights. He celebrated the decree nisi with Cedric Hangerford over dinner at Rules. Cedric brought along his cousin, Katherine, the leggy blonde William had met in his Ascot box. 'Twenty to one, you'll say yes to the coffee at my place,' she quipped, as they left the restaurant.

William married her within the year. It was a small register-office affair, with a private dinner afterwards. But that evening the couple threw a ball at the Ritz, ensuring the marriage made not only the social columns but the glossy magazines too. Two days later they were honeymooning on safari.

It was far from the disaster of his first marriage. During their ten days in Zimbabwe they enjoyed each other's company. Katherine's genuine interest in wildlife and her inability to handle a camera were endearing. However, the sex was unsatisfactory. Katherine was not exactly frigid, just unloving. She evidently felt that the sooner it was over the better. William's inexperience of dealing with someone like Katherine made it impossible for him to discuss his frustration with her.

When they returned home and moved into their new house, William discovered that Katherine was no house-wife either. She was useless at organizing, hopeless with money, loathed shopping, never read anything other than *Tatler* and was generally bone idle. After a few months she was pregnant, and demanded that they sleep in separate bedrooms and expected to be waited on hand and foot. William soon realized that he had traded in one nightmare for another. When Katherine gave birth to a boy, they moved to a larger house. Although they employed two nannies she complained incessantly that she was tired and depressed, and spent all day in her bedroom watching television. He noticed that she was always lively enough to attend the dinners, balls and society parties she was invited to, but when he asked her to accompany him to a business function she always had a migraine. According to her, his business associates were 'middle-class and boring', which made William acutely ashamed and aware once more of his background.

Two years into their marriage, to Katherine's horror and William's surprise, she was pregnant again. After the birth of their daughter, Sabrina, Katherine locked herself in her bedroom, complaining of post-natal depression, but was overjoyed to have a daughter. However, he had had enough of the marriage. Despite that he did not file for divorce for another two years, and then only because he had found out his wife was handing over thousands of pounds to her cousin Cedric, whose stud farm was in financial difficulties. It wasn't that William didn't have the money to 'donate', it was just that every relative of Katherine's seemed to treat him like a soft touch.

The divorce was drawn-out and costly. For all Katherine's perpetual inertia, when William decided to leave she found the energy of a maelstrom. She wept, screamed and threatened to take the children abroad so that he would never see them again. He fought for custody, but Katherine threatened to tell the court of his trips to Madame Norton's, determined to prove that he was not a fit father.

Since his last divorce William had been almost content. He had concluded that marriage was not for him and had vowed that he would never contemplate it again. He didn't acknowledge that he was lonely, but buried himself in his work. Then he had met Andrew Maynard and his life changed. He found he had not only a face and a purse, he had a voice too. In return for his sponsorship, Maynard had helped him realize that he should be proud of his achievements.

After Maynard's death William felt as though the light had gone out of his life. Now he sat alone in his study and thought. He poured himself a large Armagnac, lit a cigar, and decided to set fire to Maynard's diaries. Then, on impulse, he decided to read them. He needed answers. Deep down he could not believe he had so misjudged the man for whom he had cared so deeply. As he unlocked the safe and took out the first diary he felt strangely calm.

In the months before Maynard's death the diary

contained frequent references to 'JC'. William assumed this was Chalmers.

> *Lunched here in Grimaud. They used to live here with their parents. They are the most astonishingly beautiful couple. She is as blonde as he and just as charming. I never believed in love at first sight until this moment. It was as if every movement was held under a bright magnifying-glass. I could not take my eyes off them, it was all I could do to stop myself kneeling at their feet. It is so rare to find such perfection. I am an adoring slave, nothing in my life meant anything, all I wanted was to*

The rest has been blacked out, making it impossible to read.

William began to feel cheated as he turned the pages: there were more blacked-out passages. Then he read,

> *... took me to a place that I could not believe. I am ecstatic, I am flying, I am a slave. I have never known such total peace and tranquillity. I want nothing but to be embraced and tortured in such sweet pain. I am a dog to be chained and beaten into total submission.*

There then followed a long sequence of dreadful adolescent-style poetry, in which the word 'torture' featured over and over again. Maynard never referred to a 'he', or specifically named Chalmers, but wrote often that he was desperate to hear from JC. William found a note at the top of a page, decorated with a heart, that read, 'JC called. I am in heaven, must get more money'.

There followed a long list of items of clothing he had purchased, gifts for JC, and then

*I am beginning to realize that beneath the drugs and the debauchery, beneath his perfectly handsome, stunningly beautiful profile, his face sometimes takes on a coldness, just as hers does. Sharp like a knife-edge. I feel frightened . . . Justin was so sour to me today, he made me weep.*

Then more blacked-out lines, and then over the page, the ink was blotched, from tears perhaps.

*I think Justin hides in a bottomless well of cynicism, which at times is so deep there is no sun, there are no stars, only darkness, and I have such a need to reach out to him, as he has become the centre of my universe.*

William sighed at such twaddle, hardly able to believe this had been written by the man he knew. He flicked through the pages, then stopped at the sight of his own name.

*Mr Need-to-be-accepted, Sir William B, came round today. A tedious, wretched man with too much money. He believes I will be his political hero. If only he knew what I really felt about his persistent intrusion into my life, this inarticulate buffoon who got lucky with some computer chip and believes himself to be my equal.*

William felt sick. A buffoon! He had ploughed hundreds of thousands of pounds into this egotistical pervert. How could he have been so stupid? He hurled the diary across the room.

Alone in his vast bed, William tossed and turned, asking himself over and over why he had allowed himself to be subjected to such abuse. Did he have such an inferiority complex that no matter what success he achieved he felt unworthy of it? Why had he allowed himself to be humiliated by virtually everyone who had entered his life? He had been living in some fantasy world since meeting Maynard. He had deluded himself that at last he had found contentment. Eventually he fell into a restless sleep.

He woke feeling tired, wretched, unwilling to face the day, and stayed in bed with the curtains drawn. He told the servants not to disturb him, and refused to eat. For two days and nights he cried as he never had before, until at long last he felt he had no more tears to shed. Then a calm sense of relief washed over him.

When he got up for a pee, he saw his reflection in the full-length mirror. He was in appalling shape: his eyes were puffy and dark-ringed, his face was pasty. William had never been handsome, but he had believed he was attractive, particularly since his success. He laughed bitterly to himself. Who would want him now? The depression returned. He had never been in love, had never felt passion the way Maynard had. He had wanted sex and been willing to pay for it, but he had never experienced ecstasy. Now, he thirsted for love.

He walked back into his darkened bedroom and threw on some clothes. First he called his office to say that he would be away for some time. Then he instructed his valet to pack a suitcase with evening suits and casual wear. He asked Michael to arrange for his jet to be fuelled and made ready to depart from Heathrow's private airfield.

'What destination shall I tell the pilot, sir?' Michael asked.

'Nice.'

'Will you need your apartment prepared?'

'No, I'll be at the Hôtel Negresco. Book me a suite.'

'Would you like me to arrange meetings?'

'No, this is not business. I need . . .' he gave the ghost of a smile '. . . need some space, as they say. I'm taking a break.' He gave another wan smile. 'Taking a break from my life, Michael. No more questions.'

The flight to Nice was comfortable, and the drive to the hotel uneventful. On arrival he didn't unpack but telephoned the villa in Grimaud. Justin Chalmers' villa. Part of him denied what he was doing, but the other part knew perfectly well: he was going to find water in the desert. He believed that here he would find solace for his lost soul.

A woman answered. 'Countess Lubrinsky speaking.'

'Sir William Benedict,' he said. 'A friend of Justin Chalmers. I'm going to be in Grimaud at the weekend . . .'

'Really?' crooned the Countess. 'Then you must join us. We are having a small dinner party.'

'I'd be delighted, thank you. If your plans change, I'll be at the Negresco.'

'I look forward to meeting you.'

The phone went dead and he replaced the receiver on the cradle. He had no idea what he was doing. It was the beginning of an adventure. He liked the sound of Countess Lubrinsky's voice, but he really wanted to meet whoever had accompanied Chalmers to meetings with Maynard. Was this countess the beautiful woman to whom he had referred in the diary?'

He thought again of how Maynard had described him, and his lips tightened. A buffoon! His whole body flushed with indignation. Was that what they all felt, how they all saw him? God Almighty, he wanted to get back at Maynard – at them all – and he would start with Justin Chalmers. That was why he had come to France. It was because he needed space to think, to make plans for how he would take his revenge. He would pay back *every one* of the bastards. No one was ever going to call him a buffoon again.

# CHAPTER 5

THE COUNTESS Lubrinsky tied her silk sarong tighter round her slim waist, and stared at her reflection in the mirror above the telephone table. She ran her fingers through her thick auburn hair, the curls in ringlets around her neck. She had long tapering fingers with short, unvarnished nails, and wore no jewellery apart from a gold ankle bracelet. At forty years old, Sylvina was proud of her figure, and her sculpted face was without a wrinkle. Her slanting green cat-like eyes, fine straight nose and high wide cheekbones gave her the look of a mystic. She lit a cigarette and, turning to the right, caught Sharee's reflection behind her. 'Hello, darling, have you had your swim?'

'No, just about to. Who was that?'

'Some friend of Justin's. I invited him to dinner.'

'Oh, God, why do you always invite every stray he gives our phone number to?'

'Because I presumed he'd arranged it.'

'Well, don't presume. Ring the bastard up and ask.'

'Don't start. It's just for dinner, and I've left a message on his mobile.'

Sharee, blonde and fair-skinned, was twenty-four.

She had a fuller figure than Sylvina, slightly plump around her bottom and thighs, with full, perfectly shaped breasts. Sylvina stared at her, took a long drag on her cigarette and blew out a perfect smoke ring. It coiled around Sharee's right nipple.

'You smoke too much, Sylvina.'

'I know. Keep still. Let me see if I can circle the left one too.' She sucked at her Gitane, held her breath and pursed her lips. The smoke ring floated in the air and Sharee wafted it away, strolling out on to the patio.

She leaned against the balustrade and, one hand shading her eyes, watched the butterflies in the garden. Sylvina, not knowing their correct names, had called the various species after parisian couturiers: the blue was Dior, a deep black, brown and orange one Schiaparelli, a remarkable multicoloured one Versace, and a rather dull moth type she found amusing to nickname Chanel.

'Penny for them, sweetie,' Sylvina said now, pouring herself a Dubonnet.

'I was looking for a Gaultier,' Sharee said, and turned back to the garden.

'Did Justin use all those trees he cut down to build the bridges?'

'No idea, darling,' Sylvina said, flopping on to a teak sun-lounger. Its cushions were hot from the sun, and she yelped.

'You should open the parasols,' Sharee said, and started towards the curved narrow staircase that ran round the outside of the house like a spiral of small white marble pillars. 'I'm going for a swim,' she said, and Sylvina watched her climb upwards to the rooftop pool.

'I love you,' she called out.

'I should hope you do,' came back the reply.

Dinner was to take place in a vast room with floor-to-ceiling windows draped in white muslin, lit by hundreds of candles. The huge table had a gold swan as a base, its wings balancing a slab of green-tinted glass. A vase of wild flowers, ferns and lilies sat on a large side table giving off a sweet and heady perfume. Sylvina, wearing a white robe, moved around the table placing name-cards in gold butterflies. Satisfied that the table was perfect, she moved to the ornate stone hearth and lit the fire. She would have to turn up the air-conditioning because it was a very warm night, but the fire was such a focal point that it was a shame not to light it.

It was a stunningly beautiful room, every item chosen with great care. The heavy oak floor had been shipped in from England. It had once been in a castle but now looked as if it had always belonged here. The carved oak doors had been brought from a temple in Indonesia. Content, Sylvina walked upstairs to find Sharee.

She found her soaking in the bath, bubbles up to her chin, a towel wrapped around her hair and wearing an eye-mask. 'You should get out, sweetheart – you'll be wrinkled like a prune if you stay in any longer.' Sylvina sat on the edge of the bath. 'I called Justin again,' she said.

'And?'

'He wasn't there, and nobody seems to know where he is. But I have a feeling he might turn up, the way he does!'

'Will she be with him?' Sharee tossed the towel from her hair, and sat up in the bath.

'How should I know?' Sylvina snapped.

'Don't get ratty, I was only asking. She's so difficult. I mean, I can take him on his own but when they're together it's just awful. They're like . . .' She frowned, pursing her lips in an attempt to find the right description, but none came. And, anyway, Sylvina had walked out.

Alone in her room, Sylvina chose a cerise Valentino tunic, tight-fitting with a split to her thigh and a mandarin collar. Her high-heeled sandals, which made her almost six feet tall, had been dyed to match. She coiled her hair into a pleat and placed a fresh freesia on either side of her head. Lastly she clipped on a pair of sparkling diamond drop earrings that had belonged to her grandmother.

Sharee came in wearing an ice blue, figure-hugging dress with T-bone straps.

'You look cute,' said Sylvina. 'Are you going to put on some make-up?'

'No. If I look and feel terrible, maybe I won't eat.'

Sylvina laughed and wrapped her arms around Sharee. 'I love you the way you are. I wouldn't want you to lose an ounce.'

'I look like shit.'

'You don't, honestly.'

'Yes, I do. I wish you'd help me buy some decent things,' Sharee muttered, checking her appearance in a long carved wooden mirror.

'When I have the funds, darling, you'll have whatever you want.'

'Yes, I know. But in the meantime you look a million dollars and I look like some cheap hooker.'

Sylvina closed the wardrobe then bent to pick up the various shoes and sandals lying about on the floor. 'God, you're so untidy. Don't you ever put things away?'

In fury, Sharee bent down and started gathering up shoes. When she had an armful she went on to the balcony and threw them over the rail. 'Happy now?' She turned, but Sylvina had left the room and Sharee felt foolish. She followed Sylvina out to the patio.

Sylvina passed her a glass of champagne. Sharee's mood was beginning to irritate her. There wasn't anyone special arriving, thank goodness, because actually Sharee did look cheap. Sylvina checked her watch: the guests were due in under an hour. She always liked to be ready in good time, and went in search of the housekeeper, Marta, to check that all was as it should be. Marta, who lived at the villa full-time, had hired two local boys as waiters. The chef was tutting round the various tureens and dishes laid out on the large wooden kitchen table. When she was satisfied that everything was on schedule Sylvina had a quiet word with Marta about Sharee's shoes, then returned to the patio.

The grounds were floodlit, spotlights carefully placed round the fountain to make the spray look like shooting stars.

'Isn't it beautiful?' Sharee was happier now, reclining on the chaise, sipping champagne. She asked again who they were expecting, even though Sylvina had told her numerous times.

'Baron and Baroness von Garten, Meryl Delaware,

Count Frederick Capri and his guest Princess Constantina with her guest the actor Terence Hampton, and the unknown Sir William Benedict.' Sylvina was a regular in the cheap French and English gossip magazines. She no longer even bothered to read them. However, now that she was broke, she tried to maintain some exposure so that the invitations kept pouring in. It was only at social functions that she was offered these house-sitting jobs. Sylvina's relationship with Sharee was not public knowledge and she was keen to keep her sexual proclivities quiet. Luckily, so was Sharee, who entertained hopes of becoming an actress and knew how things like that could damage your chances – unless of course you were famous enough for it not to matter.

William sat back in the hired Mercedes. Mercifully the driver had not spoken a word since he had opened the door for him to get in. He looked down at his linen suit and wondered whether it was the right thing to have worn – linen creased so badly. He switched on the lights to examine his trousers, then worried that his shirt was too formal for the suit. By the time the car pulled up outside the gates he was sweating with nerves. He felt hot, badly dressed and wished he had not pushed himself on Countess Lubrinsky. And what if they didn't speak English? But of course she did – he had spoken to her on the telephone. Should he have brought champagne or flowers? It was too late to do anything about that now. He'd have Michael send an arrangement the following day.

'*Magnifique,*' said the driver.

William leaned forward and looked out at the gardens. What a beautiful place! From the road there had been no indication of what lay hidden behind the trees. A crescent of vehicles was parked in the wide horseshoe drive to the right of the villa's front door, two Rolls Royces, a Porsche and a Citroën. The driver parked the Mercedes beside the Citroën, stepped out and opened William's door. He stood to one side deferentially as William gave a nod of thanks, and made his way to the porch. Flowers in large white tubs were placed either side of the white steps, and the pillars were draped with pink blossom. William was about to ring the bell when the door opened and Marta, in a black dress and white apron, stood before him, smiling. 'Good evening,' she said. 'Please do come in.'

William walked past her into the hall as she closed the door quietly behind him.

'Who may I say it is, please?' Marta asked sweetly.

'Sir William Benedict,' he said gruffly.

She handed him a glass of champagne from a tray held by a young waiter, then ushered him into the drawing room where the smell of perfume mingled with lilies, Havana cigars and incense which made his head spin. Immediately he wished the ground would open and swallow him. The male guests were all wearing black or white tuxedos and the women, as far as he could see, long evening dresses.

'Sir William Benedict,' Marta announced.

The stunning woman in a cerise dress who approached him with a wide welcoming smile was the Countess. She introduced herself as Sylvina and said, 'How very kind of you to join us.' William saw immediately that she had recognized him from the magazines and glanced round the room. He spotted the horrified expressions on the faces of the Baron and Baroness von Garten.

'It's the ghastly parvenu who was going to buy one of the factories.' The Baroness's stage whisper to her husband echoed round the room. The Baron's lawyers had ceased all negotiations as soon as the scandal had become public. He had not wanted his family name tarnished by association with misdemeanour, particularly one with homosexual undertones.

William's smile froze on his lips. The Baron had cost him a lot of money by withdrawing from their deal. Worse still, he had sold instead to William's strongest competitor. It was not just a financial slap in the face, he had also lost out on a vast potential European market. He had not yet found another suitable site and, more infuriatingly still, the rival company that had bought the factory had made offers to the staff William had earmarked for positions and interviewed in Germany. The Baron and Baroness now turned their backs on him. If he compiled a list of people to take a swipe at, these two stuck-up sons-of-bitches would be close to the top.

Silvina had noticed William's embarrassment and now linked her arm through his and guided him towards the other guests. 'I am sure you know Meryl Delaware?' she purred.

William felt his belly turn over. It was bad enough to have the von Gartens cut him dead, but now he was faced with this fat, painted bitch with her gossip-tuned ears. Meryl, dressed in black lace with too many fake diamonds around her neck, turned to face him. Her red mouth dropped open in shock. Then she forced a brittle smile. Meryl Delaware had written one of the most unsavoury articles about him and Maynard for one of the glossy magazines. In it she had hinted that Sir William had appeared very close to his protégé, and had illustrated it with a photograph of William leaning forward to talk to Maynard. As with many other photographs, it had been doctored to exclude the other members of the party to make it look as if the two had been having an intimate, candlelit dinner. 'How do you do?' she said, before turning back to face the wall.

The atmosphere changed swiftly from sophisticated elegance to the deep silence of unease. Everyone but Sharee was fully aware of who William was and unsure how to react.

Sylvina gestured to Marta to refill her champagne glass, and told her to adjust the place settings. Sir William should sit next to her with Terence Hampton on his other side. Terence was a social 'actor': you could put him next to anyone and the conversation would never dry up, as long as it revolved principally around himself.

As the guests were ushered towards the dining-room, Sylvina fell into step beside William. Suddenly the von Gartens were standing in front of her. As though William was not there, the Baroness announced, 'I'm afraid it is inappropriate for us to dine here, after all.'

Nothing like this had ever happened to Sylvina. 'I'm sorry, Baroness. Are you feeling unwell?' she said. 'Please do stay, dinner is served.'

'Maybe if someone was asked to leave . . .' said the Baron, eyeing William.

'I'm sorry,' said Sylvina. 'Sir William is my own personal guest.'

William was appalled. He shifted from foot to foot and stammered, 'It's all right, I'll go.'

Sylvina gripped his arm. 'No way, baby.'

She was still smiling as the Baron and Baroness huffed and puffed their way out of the door. 'I hope you don't mind but I have seated you beside me, so we can get to know each other.'

William murmured that he could think of nothing he would like more. He felt even better when she patted the sleeve of his jacket. 'This is from the new Armani collection, isn't it?'

'Yes, it is,' he said, flushing deeply.

'I thought so, and so much more comfortable in this heat than a dinner-jacket.' She whispered, 'No smell of mothballs.'

He caught her warmth and her wonderful, genuine smile, and began to feel more confident.

'I'm sorry about that little unpleasantness earlier.' She leaned right into him and added, 'The Baron is no paragon of virtue and neither is his wife. How odd that they should show such bad manners.'

But as the chilled avocado and mint soup was served, the conversation became stilted. The other guests were talking under their breath about the von Gartens' exit or William's tabloid exploits. Aware of the awful silences around the table, Sylvina told Marta to bring in a very special wine she had been saving for such an occasion. Her energy and charm immediately lifted the atmosphere, and Marta bustled off down to the wine cellar. She wasn't sure what bottle of wine Sylvina was talking about but she scoured the shelves and selected a Château Margaux '78. Leaving the cobwebs and thick layer of dust behind, she hurried back to the dining room and passed Sylvina the dusty bottle. 'Marta! The cob-webs! You know I hate spiders.' She rose to her feet and raised her arms above her head. 'Never mind, at least we know it's authentic. Now, dear, please decant it and let it stand. We are all eager to taste it.'

Marta left the dining room and immediately replaced the bottle with a vastly inferior one. She decanted it, as instructed, into a Victorian cut-glass decanter, which was taken to the table by one of the waiters. Sylvina had often laid wagers with her as to who would detect a first growth from a simple Médoc. She looked around at her dinner guests as they peered and sipped at the wine and discussed its attributes. William picked up his glass and turned to face her. 'This really is so very kind of you,' he said, and obviously meant every word.

'It is my pleasure,' she said huskily. She had to wriggle in her chair because the thought of his money made her feel orgasmic.

'To our mutual friend, Justin Chalmers.'

They sipped their wine and smiled. When she asked him what he thought of it he held the stem of the glass loosely in his fingers. 'Not too heavy or fruity, quite light for a Pomero.'

William reached for his water. The wine was ghastly. If he had ordered it in a restaurant, he would have sent it back. He felt unable to bring up the subject of Justin himself, and hoped someone else would do so, but the conversation remained on the quality of the wine. It amused him to see them sipping and nodding.

Sylvina leaned closer to him. 'I've even started making my own cobwebs – you know, from that stuff they squirt over you at kiddies' parties. It's cheap plonk, but you knew that. I could tell from your face.'

He smiled, pleased, then leaned closer to her. 'No one else seems to.'

'Even if they did, dahling, they wouldn't say so just in case they were wrong.'

'Are you expecting Justin for the summer?' Terence Hampton enquired, after enthusing loudly about the wine.

Sylvina shrugged. 'Well, it is his villa, but you know Justin. I hear he's in Europe, so perhaps he will appear at some point, unless . . .' She turned pointedly to William. 'What do you know of our Scarlet Pimpernel, William?'

'They seek me here, they seek me there.' Between the arched oak dining-room doors stood Justin Chalmers, his shadow from the flickering candlelight falling across the table. He was as blond as William remembered, but his hair was short now, almost in a crew-cut. He was deeply tanned and wore a black T-shirt with one sleeve almost ripped from the seam, a pair of tight black leather trousers and black motorcycle boots. He had a row of fine gold bracelets around his wrist and a slender gold watch. He shook the bracelets in a theatrical gesture then yawned. 'Eat up, and excuse the interruption. I need to bath and shave before I join you.'

William felt apprehensive. He had only ever met the man once, and then it was to tell him to get out of England. Now, driven by loneliness and relentless curiosity, he had blustered his way into his villa, having lied to the Countess. To his astonishment, Justin gave him a dazzling smile. 'How nice to see you, Sir William. Quite a surprise.' Then he turned and walked back into the hall calling over his shoulder, 'Don't let me interrupt your dinner further.' He caught Marta as she was about to wheel in the trolley with the main course, cupped her chin and kissed her lips. 'Who's a good girl?' he said.

'I thought you'd want to know. I think he invited himself,' Marta said, then asked hesitantly, 'How is she?'

He twisted his gold bracelets and his eyes brimmed with tears. 'She's going to be fine, but it'll take a while longer.'

'She'll be coming home then?'

He nodded, and said caressingly, 'Yes, our beautiful lily will be home, but you know how these clinics like to take their time and my money. They said she simply needed rest. She's doing some new therapy with crystals, and she sounds much better. It wasn't such a bad one apparently, but I like to be careful.'

Marta touched his hand gently. 'You know I am always here for her.'

He started for the stairs. 'I'd better get showered. Oh, is the fat man staying or is he just here for dinner?'

'Just dinner,' Marta said, as she wheeled the trolley towards the dining room. Two waiters came out to take it from her, and both looked to the stairs. Justin always had an effect on young men: the aura of danger that hung about him acted like a magnet.


Justin stood beneath the shower jets, eyes tightly closed, and pondered. Why was Sir William Benedict sitting at dinner? What did he want? What did he know? Or maybe it was all going according to plan. Maybe he was ripe for the picking already. Justin sighed. He knew he would find out sooner or later. And Sir William could not have appeared at a better time: Justin was broke again but downstairs, sitting at his dining-room table, was the man who had financed the reconstruction of this villa and paid off his debts. Justin spent money like water, and the cash William had given him was gone. He reached for a soft white towel and wrapped himself in it from head to toe. He was not sure yet how he could use his golden goose. The plan only formed later when everyone except William had departed.

William had drunk too much, and the combination of alcohol and anti-depressant pills had made him red-faced, sweaty, and unable to stand unaided. Every time he rose, the room spun and he felt ill. Justin helped him to his feet, and they went out on to the balcony into the cool night air, which made his head spin even more. He almost fell, but Justin caught him, guided him to a chair and went to brew some coffee. Marta had gone to bed, as had everyone else at the villa, and they were alone.

William tried desperately to sober up. With his head in his hands, he took deep breaths and tried to concentrate on his own shoes. He felt wretched. When Justin returned, he placed the steaming mugs on a low table then went to stand behind William's chair and began to massage his shoulders.

'I'm sorry about this,' William said hoarsely. The strong hands were soothing.

'Don't worry about it. Just relax. You're very tense – your shoulders are rigid.'

Justin leaned over to the table, and passed William his coffee. 'This'll make you feel better, and maybe you should take a couple of these. They're just aspirin, but they'll stave off the hangover.'

'Thank you,' William said. 'I'm sorry to have just turned up on your doorstep like this. To be honest, I don't really know why I came.'

'I'm glad you did. And you're most welcome to stay over if you would like.'

'No, no, I must get back.' There was an awkward silence. William lifted his eyes to Justin's and flushed as the handsome man smiled. It was extraordinary, he thought. Even though Justin was in his early thirties he had the look of a well-scrubbed youth. 'I think I'm very tired,' he said lamely.

'You must have been through a lot,' Justin said, sitting opposite.

'That's putting it mildly!' William leaned back and gazed over the garden so that he would not have to look at Justin, whose handsomeness unnerved him. 'I just needed to get away to try to recharge my batteries. I've made a fool of myself.'

'It's understandable. Anyone would feel the same.' Justin lit a cigarette, watching him with lizard-like attention.

'Can't show my face anywhere in London without being ridiculed. Not that I'm asked anywhere any more. I'm like some kind of plague. The people I thought were my friends have turned their backs on me, scared to be tarred with the same brush, I suppose. Dear God, I'm normally so in control of my life.'

'Why don't you do something about it?'

William sighed and drained his coffee mug. 'That's why I feel so wretched. The Baron and his wife walked out before dinner rather than sit at a table with me. So, in answer to your question, what the hell can I do about it?'

'Well, instead of accepting it and weeping into your cup, so to speak, turn it round.'

William rose to his feet. He felt steadier now. 'Oh, I dare say it'll all blow over. At least my wealth is still intact. It'd be much worse if I'd lost that as well as my respectability.' He chuckled a little.

'It would be nice though, wouldn't it, to make all those two-faced society cunts eat their own shit.'

William stared at him, a little shocked by his language and his icy tone. 'Yeah, but well, my lawyers warned me the best thing to do was ignore it, and it'll blow over.'

'But it would be nice to lead them by the nose and rub it in the trash they've written about you. You see, Sir William, you made the biggest mistake of all. You got caught.'

'Caught? The only thing I did wrong was trust Andrew Maynard,' William snapped. 'He was probably scared that his private life was about to come out. But what a terrible waste to kill himself!'

'Yes, maybe, but you shouldn't have tried to cover up for him.'

'I think that's enough.' William had regained some of his decorum. 'I should be on my way.'

Justin stood up and moved closer to him. 'You could get back at them, you know. You just need the right connections.'

'And you have them, do you?' William said, with some sarcasm.

Justin moved closer still, and patted his shoulder. 'I have them, Sir William, and I'll tell you something else.

If you just swallow the situation, wealth intact or no, you'll hate yourself for the rest of your life.' Justin's voice was soft and persuasive, and he had the most hypnotic eyes William had ever seen. It was impossible to look away from him, even if what he went on to say was rather insulting. 'Regaining your social acceptance can be arranged. It's easily bought. But that should not be enough for a man of your standing. You want to regain the respect of others because, right now, you don't have any. I don't think you even have any for yourself. They've beaten you into running away, which is why you came here. Correct?'

'You're very intuitive.' William was more and more intrigued by the young man, but not yet prepared to discuss his situation in any greater depth, especially not with Andrew Maynard's ex-lover. But he sat down again.

It was then that Justin knew he had been right. He had an immensely rich fish on the end of his line, and the next few moments would be crucial in making him take the bait, and swallow it so that the hook lodged firmly in place. He must not wriggle free. Justin wondered how many more photographs of Andrew Maynard he could leak to keep it an ongoing front-pager.

'So, Mr Chalmers, if you were in my position – and pray God that you never will be – what would you do?'

Justin smiled. He'd got him. 'Pay every one of the bastards back twofold. Only then would I feel capable of getting on with my life. I wouldn't let anyone get away with treating me like a buffoon!'

By William's reaction, Justin knew that Maynard's nickname had hit him like a dart. William leaned forward. 'So what would you do?'

Justin looked deep into William's eyes. 'You own an island, don't you?'

'I do.'

'Then that is where you will lay the trap.' He laughed, throwing his head back and clapping his hands. Once more he became serious. A slender finger tapped William's knee. 'I have an idea. It'll take a long time, but you will need that time to get ready, and I can guarantee that it will work. But you must be prepared to arrange it, down to the smallest detail. Then you can step in for the kill.'

'I don't want to kill anyone, for Christ's sake,' William squeaked.

'Hypothetically you do, but if you won't admit it, then forget it.'

'Okay, carry on, I'm all ears.'

Justin lay back in his chair and closed his eyes. The flickering candles played across his beautiful face. Then his eyes opened and William recalled what he had read in Maynard's diary about a darkness, both frightening and exhilarating. Now he felt it. His stomach churned and the bile of his humiliation subsided as he felt excitement rise. 'Go on,' he said softly.

# CHAPTER 6

SYLVINA CARRIED her coffee and rolls out to the pool where Justin was swimming. He didn't acknowledge her until he had completed twenty lengths, then he stopped, resting his elbows on the edge of the pool. 'I have a brilliant idea,' he announced.

She slid on her sunglasses, and poured coffee as he heaved himself out, splashing water everywhere, then padded towards the sun-lounger next to hers.

'Go on, ask me what it is.' He picked up her roll, bit into it, then reached for her coffee.

You always do this.' She was irritated. 'Why don't you ever ask if you can eat my breakfast? Better still, get your own.'

'You, my darling, will have a retinue of servants to bring yours in the future.'

'Really? Won the lottery, have you?' She picked up the pool telephone and asked Marta for more coffee and rolls. Justin was towelling himself dry. He was obviously pleased with himself about something.

He flopped down on a sun-lounger. 'This is how it's going to work.' She sat next to him as he smothered himself in her suntan lotion. 'You're going to get engaged to William.' He gave her a wide grin.

'Really? And is he aware of this development?'

'No, but he'll be thinking about it. I'll get him to come by this evening so we can arrange it.'

'Really? Well, that is fascinating. What if I'm not interested in attaching myself to him and, more to the point, what if he's not inclined to attach himself to me? I'm not going to open my legs for him. I've refused a lot better and—'

'Not that much richer,' he interrupted, then lay back to sun himself. 'This is the way it will work. You will get engaged and start to iron out his social ineptitude. You will become the society hostess of the season: parties, balls, the works. You will begin to entertain on such a lavish scale that anyone refusing to be associated with William will be won around. With your contacts and mine we'll make them cream themselves to get close to him!'

She laughed, leaned over and rubbed his flat muscular stomach. 'You're such a dreamer, darling.'

He swiped her hand away. 'This is *not* a dream! We can make it a reality.'

She shrugged. 'Fine. I'm riveted. Is there a purpose to all these immensely costly social functions you intend to sweep the world with, or do you just fancy dressing up?'

'I swear to you, he'll pay you for the privilege of your company.'

'Sounds very Mills and Boon to me, sweetheart, but do go on.'

Justin began to pace, skipping between the cracks in the marble tiles. 'Payback time. You will be his reintroduction into the world he has always wanted to be part of. He could never get there on his own and needs you to get inside the inner sanctum. Once he's there . . .' he gave a shrill, almost hysterical laugh.

Sylvina couldn't follow what he was talking about and Justin was interrupted by Marta's arrival.

'I'll go and shower,' Justin said suddenly, sunbathing forgotten. 'We'll ask for a million in cash, all expenses on top of that, a new wardrobe, a car, anything you can think of to enhance your performance as the most beautiful, eligible and sophisticated society hostess.' He was still chattering to himself and, as he disappeared, she could hear him laughing at his own fantasy.

'He's crazy,' Sylvina said. Then, 'Do you know when she's arriving?'

'I think perhaps tomorrow,' Marta replied. 'He has asked for the white linen sheets to be aired, plus her lilies, and that bottled water she prefers.'

Sylvina sighed. 'I don't know why he wanted me to house-sit. It looks like he's going to be here for the summer. He really is annoying.'

Marta said nothing, but cleared away the dirty crockery and headed back into the house.

Sylvina picked at a roll. She was suddenly depressed. She hated being so broke she couldn't leave here. She'd let her Paris apartment for the summer and her family château was uninhabitable. Even the vineyard that had once flourished was now suffering from blight. She rummaged in her pocket for her cigarettes and lit one. It would be nice to have some of the fat man's millions. She knew she had borrowed too often and, in so doing had limited her circle of wealthy friends by exploiting their generosity. But she still had many high-powered contacts. She was still on the invitation list of society's upper echelon, but of late she had been unable to afford the price of the charity tickets. She stubbed out the cigarette.

'Is that coffee hot?' Sharee said, making Sylvina jump.

'Yes.' Sylvina closed her eyes.

Sharee, using Sylvina's cup, poured herself a splash, sipped, then filled the cup. 'You were miles away,' she said, sitting down on Justin's vacated sun-lounger and squinting up at the sun. 'It'll be a boiler of a day. We going to the beach? Are you listening?'

Sylvina looked over her dark glasses at Sharee. 'Justin's got this crazy idea.'

'Hasn't he always?' Sharee said, concentrating on a few leg hairs that had been missed during waxing.

'It's about William Benedict.'

Sharee took out a pair of tweezers and began to pluck out the stray hairs with relish. 'What would you think if I got engaged to him, for money? I mean, we wouldn't fuck, it'd be a business arrangement for me to introduce him into society.'

Sharee's head was bent low over her left leg. 'Well, he's not exactly a teenager, is he? I thought only debs and young guys got into that society thing. He's gotta be fifty if not more.'

'If it's what he wants.'

'Is it?'

'I don't know.'

Sharee laughed. 'You know, sometimes I think you're as bad as Justin. He's nuts!' She looked up. 'Maybe *I* should offer. I mean, I'm younger than you and if he's got that amount of money to throw around, I'd get engaged to him. I'd even fuck him if it made him happy.'

'You've missed the point,' Sylvina snapped.

'Oh, yeah, so what is it?'

'I am a countess. I know everyone one needs to know. I am socially accepted, sweetheart.'

'Who you kidding? You've not got two cents to scratch yourself with, and I wouldn't say the Euro-trash I've met with you are exactly the top social order. You're not exactly mixing with King Thingy of Spain!'

'I was invited to his son's wedding,' Sylvina said.

'Oh, were you?' Sharee laughed.

Sylvina became inceasingly angry. 'Yes, I was, and the *Euro-trash* you have met are about the only people I could introduce you to as, quite honestly, you and your appearance leave a lot to be desired. Looking like a shop assistant is not exactly—'

Sharee hit her so hard she fell off the sunbed. 'This shop assistant, you bull-dyke, hates your fucking guts, and unless you apologize I'm walking right out of this fucking Mickey Mouse villa.'

Sylvina lay stunned on the marble tiles as Sharee got up and stood over her. 'Apologize or I'll kick you.' She glared down at Sylvina.

'Go on. Kick me.'

'You're sick, you know that? Sick, perverted and *old*.' Sharee bent down and began to drag Sylvina by her leg towards the pool. Sylvina struggled and wriggled as the skin on her thigh was scraped raw.

'Is this a private party or can anyone join in?' Standing in the doorway, Justin laughed.

'Fuck off,' screamed Sharee.

Justin watched as both women fell into the pool and continued the fight in the water. Eventually they bobbed up, gasping, spluttering and exhausted.

'Are you going to . . .' Sharee puffed '. . . apologize for calling me a shop assistant?'

'No,' Sylvina spat. Sharee hauled herself out of the water, her bikini hanging off.

'You are not a shop assistant, you are the woman I love more than anyone else in the world.' Sylvina held out her hand and Sharee took it, helping her out of the pool. They embraced passionately as Justin watched. Sylvina's soaked robe was torn and he could see her body shape through the thin cotton. Suddenly Sharee ripped it away, dropped to her knees and eased Sylvina's thighs open and began to part her glistening pubic hair with her tongue. Sylvina gasped. The next moment, Justin had cupped her breasts in his hands and she moaned as he thrust into her from behind, guided by Sharee. They were both intent on Sylvina, thrusting into her and caressing her until she climaxed with such a howl of pleasure it disturbed a flock of white doves, which fluttered up over their heads.

Justin pulled back and zipped up his trousers. 'Well, that was most pleasant and so unexpected,' he said, as he wiped the sweat from his forehead. 'I'll not be in for lunch. Back around four.' He moved towards the door.

'Justin!' Sylvina called, wrapping a towel around herself.

'Talk later,' he said, without turning. 'William will be here for dinner.' He paused. 'I'd say he'll be hard to move out if you put on a display like that, girls, but please have a little more decorum. Make him wait . . . at least a couple of days.'

'You mean he's staying?' Sylvina asked.

'Yes – and he jumped at the invitation. We're to discuss our proposition with him,' he said, and disappeared from view. Moments later he called Sylvina's name. She stood up and followed him into the house, leaving Sharee now collapsed on a sun-lounger. 'One little thing my love. Get rid of the shop assistant. She really does let you down. Make some excuse. I would prefer it if she wasn't here when I got back.'

'But, Justin, she thinks she's here for the summer.'

He sighed with irritation. 'Tough.'

'What about your other guest? How do you think she's going to cope?'

He checked his appearance in the mirror, then his eyes strayed to hers, cold, expressionless. 'She will be part of it. As I said, sweetie, I have been planning this for months.'

'But you didn't even know he was coming here,' she said.

Justin gave one of his sly crooked smiles. 'Didn't I? Well, let's just say it's all worked out perfectly, or I'm just lucky.' Sylvina flinched as he twisted the skin on her forearm until it hurt. 'So get rid of the slag.'

Sylvina stepped back. 'I'll think of something,' was all she said, and he brushed past her before she could add anything else.

Sylvina showered and changed. She went into Justin's bedroom. It was tidy, apart from a stack of magazines strewn over the bed. She picked up an old issue of *Vogue*, and turned to where a yellow sticker protruded. It was in the property section, where she found, ringed in red felt-tip pen, an advertisement for an island in the Caribbean, for sale, price on request. She looked over numerous other articles, all referring to William Benedict's purchase for eight million of a paradise island. Sir William was quoted as saying he intended to refurbish the island, and there were lists of the designers he had approached. She laughed softly. Perhaps Justin was not as crazy as she had thought. It was obvious now what his intentions were. He wanted the job. And maybe, just maybe, he was going to use her to persuade William to give it to him, for a fee. Well, she'd do whatever she needed to – like Justin, she could smell money dripping from the glossy pages he'd underlined and flagged.

By the time she returned to the pool, Sharee was lying topless, smothered in oil, her big breasts flopping wide across her chest. Her tiny bikini briefs were still untied and she looked, as Justin had said, like a slag.

'You want to go down to the beach for some lunch?'

Sharee wafted her hand. 'Nah, I'm knackered. Let's stay here and flop around.'

'I'm going. Come on, take a shower. Make yourself look good.'

'I don't feel like it.'

'Terence Hampton just called, he's getting a party going. The producer of *Babylon Baby* will be there, with a whole bunch of actors. They're looking for locations.'

Sharee sat up and stretched. 'In that case . . .' She laughed '. . . will you gimme one of those tiger-motif sarongs to wear and those big mules with the white tie strap?'

'Sure. Have anything you want, but don't be too long. I've ordered a taxi.'

'Okay.' Sharee breezed past, catching her hand. 'You look real classy, Countess.'

Sharee had not the slightest idea that she was about

to be persuaded to leave. Her lover might care for her, but she loved money more.

The private beach area had a small but elegantly styled Moorish marquee, in which tables had been set. The champagne was on ice and plates of fresh shellfish laid out. A guitarist was playing bossanovas. In the evening, there would be a disco and the party would continue until dawn. Sylvina arrived neither too early nor too late: she timed it so that she was seen by the optimum number of guests, and could do the rounds of cheek-kissing and introductions. Today's guests were mixed, mainly actors and actresses, a few producers and studio executives. It was rent-a-crowd time. The guest list had been compiled by Meryl Delaware, who held court in a flowing white cotton kaftan with platform shoes, Armani dark glasses, a silk scarf tied round her hair and jangling gold bracelets. The outfit successfully disguised her squat body.

'Darling, that was a lovely dinner party,' she cooed to Sylvina. 'My dear, you do know about that awful Sir William, don't you? His appearance at any function will clear the room. Ghastly creature. I used to be at school with his ex-wife, Katherine Hangerford. Sweet, sweet woman and such adorable children. It's just too awful the way he's dragged them through the gutter press.'

Meryl's lipstick was already running into the rivulets that had formed around her collagen-boosted lips. Sylvina let her prattle on while she scanned the crowd for Sharee. She managed to catch her eye, and gestured for her to join them. 'You know Sharee, don't you,

Meryl? I've promised to get her an introduction to Bernard Goldberg.'

Meryl smiled bleakly. 'Such an adorable man.' She ushered Sharee ahead of her and glanced back to Sylvina, just a flicker to register that she was owed a favour in return for this intro.

Sylvina looked on, as her lover shook hands with the large balding man in a T-shirt, huge baggy shorts and a backwards red baseball cap. At least he had the manners to remove the cigar from his lips as he leaned forward to catch Sharee's name. He was in a huddle with Terence Hampton, a Brad Pitt lookalike – one of the many dotted around – and one of the Baldwin brothers, no one seemed to know which one.

Sylvina waited half an hour, moving around unobtrusively. She was asked to a couple of dinner parties that evening, but to everyone's surprise she politely said she was otherwise engaged. The joke about Sylvina was that even if she was stranded in the Sahara desert she'd know someone there who would give her a free meal. Eventually she made her way back to Sharee.

'This is Countess Lubrinsky,' Sharee said to Goldberg, who beamed and offered Sylvina a glass of champagne.

She declined politely, raising the half-filled glass from which she had taken no more than a few sips. 'I have a terrible headache. Do you mind if we leave?' she whispered to Sharee.

'What? Now?'

'Sorry.'

Sharee put on a sympathetic face. 'You go and lie down. I'll come later.' She leaned in close. 'They're all dining on his yacht later and he's asked me. What do you think?'

'Go for it.' Sylvina smiled and left her.


Just after six Sharee returned to the villa to change. She was quite drunk, and was with three of Goldberg's guests in their Rolls Royce Corniche. The volume of the CD player was so loud that Sylvina was forewarned of their arrival well before they appeared on the drive. Sharee was flushed with excitement at the prospect of the party on the yacht. The plan, she told Sylvina, was to potter around the bay then maybe sail along the coast to Monaco. She was hot, feverish and angry in case Sylvina threw one of her moods and insisted that she stay.

'It's entirely up to you,' sighed Sylvina. 'Go, if you want. They seem a great group of people.'

'They are. And Terence is coming along. Why don't you come too?'

'Oh, sweetheart, I don't want to move. Head, you know.' She sank dramatically into a chair. 'Pack your things, don't worry.'

Sharee blinked, swaying. 'Well, there's no need for me to pack everything. I mean, it's just a night or two.'

Sylvina smiled weakly. 'Make the most of it. This could be your movie break, darling, what you've dreamed about. He's very famous, isn't he? Go and have a lovely time. And you know I hate having Justin looming over my shoulders so I'll probably go back to Paris if you stay on board any longer. If you've got all your things there'll be no problem.'

'Sure you don't mind?'

Sylvina picked up her case and walked her out to the car, whose stereo was still playing Guns N' Roses's 'November Rain' at an ear-splitting volume. The Corniche vanished up the drive, leaving Sylvina waving wanly on the porch. It had been so easy.

By seven o'clock there was still no sign of Justin, and it didn't look as if the planned dinner with William would be going ahead. The headache Sylvina had faked earlier was now coming on for real so she decided to go up to the roof for a cool swim. She paused as she passed her suite: her clothes had been taken to Sharee's room earlier in the day. Vast clear glass bowls now held bunches of white liles, which complemented the white bedspread, white lace cushions and the white muslin curtains that billowed out over the polished wood floor. The room was looking bare to the point of bleakness, but Justin's impending house guest hated clutter. He always had to rearrange the furniture when she was around. He said she suffered from claustrophobia – or was it agoraphobia? Over the years she had had every phobia known to man. She was the most neurotic woman Sylvina had ever met.

Continuing up the stairs to the roof, Sylvina walked out into the clear night air, stripped off her clothes and eased her body into the pool. She loved to swim naked at this time of the evening. It was so perfect; the water cool and refreshing. She swam a few lengths then lay floating on her back, eyes closed.

'She's very beautiful, isn't she?' It was Justin, whispering to William.

112

Sylvina had not heard them walk out onto the roof, but hearing the whisper, she opened her eyes and smiled. 'I didn't hear you arrive,' she said softly.

'We got held up in some traffic,' Justin said nonchalantly. 'Then we did a tour of the villa, and here we are.'

'It's nice to see you again, William.'

William smiled shyly. 'I'm sorry if I'm intruding.'

Sylvina swam to the side. 'Don't be. I'll go and shower. Are we going to dine at home, Justin, or would you like to book a table?'

'Eat in,' he replied abruptly.

As Sylvina strolled past them she heard Justin speaking to Marta on the poolside phone and asking for chilled champagne. William looked even more uncomfortable this evening than he had on the previous night. He was wearing another crumpled suit, with a creamy shirt left open at the neck to reveal a patch of pale skin.

By the time they sat down to dinner, Sylvina observed that he looked marginally better having removed his frightful open-toed sandals in favour of canvas rope-soled shoes. She also noticed that he hardly touched his champagne but instead consumed copious amounts of water. She was quiet and thoughtful, allowing Justin to regale them both with one amusing story after another about his travels, then listened to him describing the numerous villas he has redesigned including his own. He told William that at one time fire had destroyed the entire top floor, and he had redesigned it. He 'happened' to have some of his designs on hand to show William, who seemed impressed, but not overly interested. Justin had already driven him around to show him various villas and gardens he had refurbished.

Eventually William leaned across to Justin and tapped his hand. 'No need for overkill, you've already got the job.'

Justin laughed with delight. 'I can't stop thinking about what I'll do.'

'Just give me some plans to look over, and an estimate of what it'll cost to do everything you've suggested.'

Justin turned to Sylvina. 'William has a wonderful paradise island . . . Well, it's not a paradise yet but I intend to make it into one.'

'For a price,' she said softly, and caught the ice in Justin's eyes. But then she made him smile. 'Justin's the best interior designer I've ever known. Exciting, inventive and, considering what he's made of this villa, a genius.'

'Thank you.' He grinned like a delighted schoolboy and then gave her a small wink. 'We've had long talks about you.'

'Really?' she said nonchalantly.

On numerous occasions throughout the meal, she felt William's eyes on her, but if she returned his gaze, he immediately looked away. Whenever possible, Sylvina took the opportunity to reappraise his looks. He had nice hands and wore an expensive slim gold Bulgari watch. On his left hand he wore a heavy signet ring on his little finger. His cufflinks, however, were multi-coloured enamel; not so good.

'Shall we go into the drawing room or on to the roof?' Justin asked.

'Drawing room. I seem to have been on the roof all day,' said Sylvina, smiling. William, very much the gentleman, eased back her chair to allow her to move from the table. He stepped aside and she walked ahead of him from the room. It was sweet that he was on his best behaviour, Sylvina mused.

As they headed for the drawing room, William disappeared to the bathroom, and Justin gripped her elbow. 'He's on the line, sweetheart.'

'I can see that,' she said coolly.

He whispered, 'Not just for me. I've worked him over for you too. You're gonna do the Pygmalion on him, and for one million.'

'What? Are you joking?'

'No. Ssh, he's coming back.'

Marta had set out coffee, brandy and port, plus chilled lemonade and more iced water beside the two large white canvas sofas. Justin and Sylvina sat on one, with William opposite. William lit a cigar, took a few deep puffs and then leaned back, crossing his legs as the smoke curled above his head. Sylvina was taken aback when he announced softly, 'One million.' His face was impassive as he went on, 'Would you like to tell me what you are prepared to do for that?'

Justin answered for her. 'I think it is right that you should know she's a lesbian.'

'My loss,' said William, and gave a wonderfully engaging chuckle. 'But I think I've had my days paying for sex. This will be purely a business deal.'

Justin gave her a sidelong glance.

Sylvina said, 'But you'll have to agree not to have any sex with another woman whilst I am with you, so there will be no hint of a scandal attached to your liaison.'

William nodded. 'How well known is your sexual orientation?'

'What?' she was puzzled.

'I'm prepared to buy your services to re-establish myself as a respectable member of high society, but you can guarantee that after we announce our engagement, the British press will start digging up your past. If it is public knowledge that you are a lesbian, I'm back to square one.'

'It isn't,' she snapped and, to her annoyance, felt herself blushing.

'Any recent affairs?' he asked, with a half-smile.

'One, but she's history,' she said, glaring at Justin. 'And it wouldn't be in her interest to let it out. She wants to get into the movies, you see.'

William was not entirely convinced. He had taken out a small black notebook and was flicking through the pages. Sylvina glanced at Justin, who raised an eyebrow.

'Justin said you will need a dress allowance, a car, servants. These will be listed as expenses, correct?'

'Yes,' Justin said.

'What figure are we talking here?'

Sylvina shrugged and looked again to Justin.

'Don't look at me, Sylvina darling, you know what designer clothes cost. Anyway, William, it'll be a good teaser sequence. You know, being see together at the Paris fashion shows.'

'My apartment's leased for a year,' Sylvina said, toying with her necklace, 'but my château is always good for name-dropping, even if it is only occupied by cats and fieldmice. The exterior is still magnificent. We could have some wonderful publicity shots taken together there and . . .' She was hardly able to take it in: he was paying her a million!

William jotted a note and turned to the next page, which was filled with neat lists. He had spent the afternoon working out whether Justin's proposition was viable. 'How much would it cost to refurbish?' he asked.

'I have no idea.' Sylvina sighed. 'It's in an appalling state. No one's lived there for ten, twelve years. Roof, plumbing, electrical wiring from the thirties. It was occupied by the Germans during the war . . .'

'I think I get the picture.' William made some more notes and pursed his lips. 'You know, I think it might be a possibility. My humiliation at being made such a public laughing-stock fired up an immediate need to get my own back, which I felt was rather childish. But I have now become genuinely excited by the prospect. I've decided to take a lengthy period away from my work. If I am going to be reintroduced to society life, I might as well enjoy it. How long do you think we'll need?'

Justin jumped in. 'Oh, quite some time. Don't forget, I'll have my hands full redesigning the villa. That could be at least six months.'

'Six months?' she gasped.

'Six months?' William said, astonished.

'Of course. I'll have to ship in most of the fabrics and furnishings, and I'll need time to prepare my plans.'

Sylvina was now in tune with Justin. The longer it took, the more money they could squeeze out of him. 'To ingratiate yourself into the top level of society takes time and patience. You'll need to get to know an awful lot of people. I can arrange dinners and parties to introduce you, but you also need a bit of refurbishment yourself, William. To get a perfect suit made up nowadays takes six to eight weeks.'

'So we're looking at even longer than six months,' William said, shutting his book and slipping it into his breast pocket. 'But in the cold light of day, let's face it, the proposition is a farce and mightly easily backfire. To play out such an expensive game would make me even more of a loser if it goes wrong.'

'It won't,' Justin interjected.

'I'll make sure of it,' Sylvina said firmly.

William was beginning to feel in control again. Clearly Justin and Sylvina needed him – or his money. The game might work, but William's business brain was still functioning at full speed. He would pay, but he would make sure he got his money's worth.

'Obviously the ball is firmly in your court, William, but last night when we talked you seemed so frustrated by all the crap you'd been subjected to,' Justin said casually. 'If you can live with it, that's your business. I couldn't – but, then, I'm not you.'

'No, you're not,' William said. He rose, and glanced at Sylvina for permission to help himself to a brandy. 'This would be a totally new venture for me. Even if I win the game, it will provide me with satisfaction but no financial remuneration.' He swirled the brandy in his glass. 'On the other hand it might be fun.' He smiled and leaned against the back of the sofa. 'Fun is not something I've had much of. What I had previously regarded as fun now seems rather wretchedly mundane. However, it sounds as if you wish to be the "ringmaster" – because you instigated the game you would automatically control the events. I can't let that happen. It is imperative that I am in control. I must be the manipulator, as I am in my business dealings.'

'So what are you saying?' Justin asked tentatively.

'That I'll play . . . but with ground rules that I set down. And if you do not come up to expectations, I walk away. Your pay-off will be dependent on success. In other words, I am perfectly willing to pay for the privilege of becoming . . .' he chuckled '. . . your Eliza Doolittle, with a very attractive Professor Higgins.' He beamed at Sylvina. His face was alert, his eyes bright. 'So, here's the proposition. If within eight and twelve months you can help me regain my standing in the upper echelons of UK society, you get your money.'

He had one final query. 'One thing I do need to know, though, and whether or not I agree to all we have just discussed will depend on your answer.' They waited with baited breath. 'Tell me about Andrew Maynard. You first, Sylvina.'

She glanced at Justin, then fingered her necklace. 'I know what happened to him, obviously. Very tragic, even more so because I had met him here, just the once, and he seemed to be a genuine and interesting young man. That's all, really, I didn't know him at all.'

William turned a cool gaze to Justin, and gasped. Tears were streaming down his cheeks.

'What happened, Justin? I need to know.'

Justin paused for some minutes before he spoke, his voice low. 'I met him about two years ago. It was his first time in France and he was trying to buy some batteries for his camera, down on the quayside. His French was appalling, so I introduced myself and—'

'And?' William interjected.

'We became friends. He moved in here to stay for the rest of his holiday. Then we became lovers.' Justin closed his eyes and sighed. 'He was obsessed with this place, with me, with France. It was like he had never enjoyed a moment of his life until then. But he was just a summer thing for me. I had no idea what I had ... encouraged. I mean, I'm a free spirit, but he wanted to own me, and because he couldn't, he got into some weird sex-trips with rent-boys. Andrew had been sexually naïve, but he made up for it and, from then on, whenever he could he came here. Sometimes I never even saw him.'

'But you were the last person to see him in England the night he died.'

'He was in a depressed state, and I will always feel guilty because I probably made him even more so. I suggested that perhaps I shouldn't see him any more. I told him I couldn't reciprocate, I didn't want him. That evening I told him not to be foolish, he was taking too many risks, especially in his career. So I left him. The rest you know.' William sighed and Justin added, in a soft, emotional voice, 'I will never forgive myself. The way he has been written about is unfair, so cruel. He did not deserve it. You want to get even, William, well, maybe I do too, not for me but for Andrew.'

Sylvina had not been paying much attention to Justin. He was putting on a show for William's benefit, obviously. All she knew was that Justin had got thousands out of poor foolish Maynard, the way he had with so many lovers; he used them and discarded them, enjoying their desperation almost as if that was what turned him on.

'Does this mean you won't hire me to refurbish your villa?' Justin said now, in a boyish voice.

'No, of course it doesn't. But, as I said before, I will need professional estimates. Truth is, with the problems

I've been through I've not had time lately even to consider the island, but if you have ideas and experience, and you evidently have, then yes, you can do it. Why not? As for you, Sylvina, here's a list of people who are high on the social agenda that I want to see eating out of my hands!'

The first two names on the list she knew. 'Well, this will be no problem at all, Baron and Baroness von Garten are friends of mine.' She recalled the way they had left dinner in front of William, and added hastily, 'Not close friends, of course. But . . . yes, I know most of these names. It'll be no problem at all.'

Justin rested his hand on Sylvina's knee and gave it a small triumphant pat. He knew now his fish wasn't even wriggling. The game was about to commence, and William, for all his business acumen, had no notion of where the ground rules began and ended.


It was quite some time before Sylvina was able to corner Justin alone, and ask him just what this deal to refurbish some villa was about.

Justin shrugged. 'Well, sweet face, you are getting paid for Sir William's entry into society, and I am doing the same for some island he's got in the Caribbean. Nothing wrong in feathering my own nest – I've certainly feathered your bankrupt one.'

'There's no need to rub my nose in it.' She moved closer. 'But what was all that about a game, taking revenge? He's not a crook, is he?'

'No, straight as an arrow, pussy.'

'So what were you talking about?'

'Mind your own business.'

'But if I'm going to be living in his pocket, so to speak, don't you think I should know?'

He turned to her, and his eyes were so cruel that she stepped away. 'You don't want to know because it doesn't concern you.'

'But it is something that concerns you, right?'

He glared, refusing to answer, but under his breath he whispered, 'It does, but he doesn't know it . . . yet.'

# CHAPTER 7

JUSTIN WAITED until he thought William was asleep, then crept into Sylvina's room. He eased the door closed and flew on to her bed. Lying on top of her, he gripped her face with his hands. 'We are rich, rich, rich, sweetheart! Didn't I tell you it would work?'

'Yes, you did, but it's going to take a long time. He's no pushover, and he'll be counting every penny in that bloody little notebook.'

He rolled away to lie beside her, a big smile on his face. 'Listen, he's up for it, and you'll not see that book out again. Just take your time and enjoy it. You'll never have had so much money to throw around in your life!'

She leaned up on her elbow and looked down into his face. 'Where will you be when I'm with him?'

Justin stretched and yawned. 'I am heading for the British Virgin Islands. Preparing the island for his future house-guests.' He giggled. 'Obviously my fees for refurbishing it in my own inimitable style will be exorbitant, but style never did come cheap.' He swung his legs from the bed and sat with his back to her.

Sylvina stroked his shoulder. 'I don't want any repercussions. I was serious about not wanting to get involved in anything illegal. I mean, he's not going to be hurling people off the cliffs, is he?'

'No, of course not. You heard him, he just wants to . . .'

'Mmm, go on. William wants to what?'

Justin walked across to the window and opened the white muslin curtains. He twisted one round him so that it hid his face. 'Everyone has a sexual fantasy. Everyone has wondered what it would be like to be taken to the ultimate erotic high. Unbridled lust and lechery is what is going to happen on the island.'

Sylvina laughed. 'My darling, I know you're an experienced screw, but you're not everyone's idea of the ultimate sexual partner.' She sat up. 'And don't think for one second that I'm interested in any of your erotica. I've agreed to spend as much time as it takes with William, but no sex. Then I'll be off, as soon as I've collected my fee. Do I really need a whole year with him?'

'Yes, it'll take that time to work over the island. I have to have enough time to prepare it.'

'This list of names he gave me – I mean, they're a bit ridiculous. I know the von Gartens, he met them here. What's so special to him about them?'

'No idea,' he said, shrugging.

'Cedric somebody, who's he?'

'Breeds racehorses, English aristo.'

She continued reading from the list: 'I mean, Meryl Delaware? Dear God, everyone knows that wretched scribbler.' One name had been underlined three times. 'This Humphrey Matlock, who's he?'

'Newspaper magnate. I'm surprised *you* haven't heard of him – you read his grubby papers.'

'Oh, well, he shouldn't be a problem, then. But no one on this list is remotely "high society". She put the list aside. 'Is she going with you? She's very fragile, you know.'

He let go of the curtain and sauntered to the door. 'She's never done anything she didn't want to,' he said quietly.

'Don't you mean she's never does anything without you pulling the strings? What is she going to be doing?'

'Mind your own damned business.'

'Fine, I will. But be careful because I know she had another fit and one day she might just snap. Be prepared for when she turns on the hand that operates her. I hope your devious little mind isn't setting me up to prepare William for her, marry her off for his money.'

He giggled. 'Don't worry. I'll keep her away from him until the time is right. She's my *pièce de résistance*, the perfect foil, my beloved sister.' He opened the door and blew Sylvina a kiss. 'Goodnight,' he said, and closed the door softly behind him. Then he swung it open again. 'Don't you even contemplate marrying him either. You can announce an engagement but then you have to ditch him publicly. Understand?'

'Oh, go to bed. One year with him will be sufficient, thank you.'

He closed the door again, and she lay back on her pillows. She'd done some crazy things in her life, but this one took first prize. Still, one million . . . *one million*!


Five days later, Sharee returned to Nice. She called the villa to be told by Marta that Sylvina had gone to Paris and had left no forwarding address. When she asked after Justin, she was told that Monsieur Chalmers was collecting his sister and would be departing for the British Virgin Islands, again with no forwarding address. She felt a little guilty about taking off for so long, but as no one was here, she couldn't apologize. Her sojourn had turned into a sordid group-sex session, which in itself had not worried her, except that she had been unable to get off the yacht. Still, she'd made friends with Terence Hampton, or thought she had – although when she'd called to ask if he could run her to the airport, he had been unable to come to the phone.

Sharee eventually flew back to London and her small studio apartment. She continued to phone Sylvina on her various numbers, but her calls were not returned. It baffled her at first, but then made her feel that somehow she had been moved aside, as if Sylvina had instigated the boat trip. Although she knew it had been her own decision to go, doubts began to surface, and Sylvina's rejection angered her. Not only had she been used like a whore on the movie producer's boat, Sylvina had treated her in the same way.

William's apartment in avenue Hoche was already lavishly decorated with the finest antiques and paintings. All it required were floral displays. Sylvina moved in and, for the moment, William stayed in a suite at the Ritz.

Sylvina checked every society-function guest-list, making copious notes of the hottest faces on the circuit and the most fashionable venues. She had not expected to enjoy herself quite so much, but having a man so dependent upon her was a new experience she relished. And with no sexual chemistry to complicate the relationship, she and William were surprised to discover a genuine mutual friendship growing.

That William knew from the outset that sex with Sylvina was out of the question made him much more relaxed when she questioned him about his affairs. He found himself admitting that perhaps the disasters of his loveless marriages had been his fault. He had been too eager to move up the social ladder.

'What on earth for?' Sylvina asked, never having had to climb so much as a single rung herself. Her own family had been titled and she had married Count Lubrinsky at an early age. She had not seen their union as social climbing, because it was his wealth more than his title that she'd married.

Sylvina's château had never really been a home, just a rambling, cold megalith, and one morning they drove down to the small hamlet where it was situated outside Tours. Even with its high turrets and splendid balcony, it seemed tired and grey.

'This is where I was brought up, apart from the years I spent at school in England, of course, which I hated but it was still preferable to spending time here.' It had been years since she had visited the place and she felt an unwelcome surge of emotion as she stopped the car. 'Do you want to see inside?' she asked, almost hoping he would say no.

But William got out and looked around, smiling. 'Yes! This is wonderful!' They wandered through room after room with empty walls and rotten floorboards.

Trees and shrubs sprouted in corners, as if nature had taken over like a secret army. It was a sad wreck of a once beautiful palace.

'My father gambled away his inheritance. I was never sure whether he married me off to a count so that he could still live here or so that he could still gamble. The Count was an elderly cousin. The marriage was not consummated, and he died a few months after my twenty-first birthday.' She fell silent. Then she said flatly, 'They should bring in the demolition people. It's dangerous.' Seeing it again, after so many years, had brought home to her her lonely childhood. The barriers placed across the stairs, cutting off rooms too dangerous to enter, were like the emotional barriers that divided her family.

'This is all I have left,' she went on. 'My father spent the money I was left by my husband. Papa was a wastrel,' she said, looking up to the massive barrel-vaulted ceiling where once chandeliers of the finest crystal had tinkled. The fact that William wanted immediately to restore the château while Sylvina wanted it torn down epitomized their differing attitudes to the past: he was awed; she was indifferent. 'Why live in the past? It's better to look to the future,' she said.

'But generations of your family lived here.'

'So they did, and they're all dead.' She was starting to feel depressed by it, and over everything loomed her hatred of her father.

On the drive back to Paris William said he could not believe that when she received her money she would not rebuild the place. Sylvina couldn't contemplate the idea. 'No one can live in such a monster of a house,' she said. She had no children to inherit it. Why would she want to resurrect something that was dead? It was a pointless exercise, as pointless, to her, as being overawed by wealth and a title.

'That's because you have it, and I haven't,' he said, as they returned to avenue Hoche.

'No, it's because you think it will give you something. I am telling you it won't. All you saw was a large white elephant.'

'No, I saw your past, your family's past. It's in every stone of that château.' She cupped his face in her hands and kissed his cheeks. 'They are dead and I am alive. The world has changed. I want to live in the present. If I were to spend all my money renovating the château, I would be living in the past. You should be angry that you wasted a second of your time worrying about what has happened to you. You are a rich man. You could have anything, be anything. Go and find yourself a young, beautiful wife. Have more children, and don't dwell on the past. It will swallow you up.' Suddenly she stopped. All this had made her forget why she was with him, which, as she had said, was all to do with the past.

'What are you thinking about?' he asked.

'Oh, nothing. Memories.'

Sylvina was still anxious when William left for the hotel, convinced she had made him think about what they were doing and worried he might pull out. Why had she been so bloody truthful? The million pounds looked as if it might disappear. But at the same time the images of her childhood would not lie quiet. Tomorrow she would have to work extra hard, just in case she had placed doubts in his mind.

\*

Sylvina need not have worried. William too was caught up in the past he had always tried to submerge. The voices would not lie quiet. He wasn't thinking about what Sylvina had said, just hearing the cries, seeing his mother press the ice-pack against her swollen cheek. He vividly remembered a particular night when, in tears, he had asked his mother if he should go to the police. She had slapped him and said, 'You'll do no such thing. This is private business. It's nothing, do you hear me? Nothing happened here.' He knew it had, but his drunken father was sleeping off the booze. 'Don't pay any attention to what you see, Billy love, just you get out. If you get to be somebody, this will all have been worthwhile. You can say it made you. Because if there isn't a reason for it, he might as well kill me now.'

What had his mother meant? He had never stopped asking himself that question. Now he thought of the abuse he had suffered at the hands of the bloodthirsty media. He didn't need to take their insults, as his mother, who'd had nowhere to run, had accepted his father's brutality. It frightened him now to think that perhaps he had inherited her wretched acceptance of fate. She had never fought back, and neither had he. Paying out a million pounds to save his face was a cowardly revenge, perhaps as bad as his mother telling him that his success was worth her pain. He was ashamed that he had not fought back, ignored the lawyers by suing, even if it had meant losing money. At least he would have had some respect for himself. And what had he done instead? Run to Justin at his villa.

He picked up the phone and called Sylvina. 'It's me,' he said hesitantly. 'I don't want to be on my own,

Sylvina, just tonight. It's not . . . Can I come round to see you?'

'Yes.'

There was a long pause before she surprised herself by saying, 'I was just about to call you.'

'Well, I beat you to it.'

When Sylvina opened the apartment door, they looked at each other then embraced. It was not a sexual gesture, just mutually comforting.

'After I left you,' he said, accepting the brandy she held out, 'I started remembering things that I didn't want to think about. And then I couldn't stop.'

'Me too.'

They clinked glasses.

As they lay next to each other in the big Louis Quinze bed, William felt an unfamiliar warmth. 'My mother . . .' he said shyly.

She snuggled against him. 'I was thinking of mine too.'

They slept that night in each other's arms. They had not found the answers, they were not even sure what they were looking for, but they had found a deeper friendship.

The following morning they had breakfast together. As Sylvina poured his coffee she gave him an affectionate smile. 'Had any more thoughts on what we talked about last night?'

He looked at her, surprised, a glob of marmalade at the side of his mouth. 'What? What do you mean?'

She sipped her chilled *citron pressé*. 'You're not having second thoughts . . . about going on?'

'Good heavens, no!' he said, slurping his coffee.

It almost made her wince. In a formal setting his eating habits were acceptable, as she had observed at the dinner party, but when he was relaxed, he reverted to childhood table manners; eating with his fingers and dropping crumbs everywhere.

'For one thing, the island isn't anywhere near ready, and for another, as good as you are at bolstering my confidence, I've still a long way to go. Besides, I'm enjoying myself. This is the longest period I've ever spent away from my work.'

She smiled. 'Well, you're not entirely away from it. You spend hours every day on the phone barking instructions, and I've seen the faxes at the hotel for you every night.'

'Ah, yes. Well, I've got to keep my beady eye on everyone. I've got damned good staff, but you can never trust anyone else to make your decisions.'

'You mean you can't delegate.' His sharp tone unnerved her.

'Oh, but I can, my dear. If I couldn't, I wouldn't be worth the fortune I have accumulated over thirty years. I have thirty-five board members, even more top-level executives. Some have been working for me for years. I believe in giving tremendous responsibility to my team – it's one of my talents. An even better talent is spotting new blood . . .'

Sylvina listened for a full ten minutes as William outlined his numerous business deals, down to the location of each of his endless factories. Then he described the new Internet site he had set up to sell his games on-line, even drawing with his sticky knife on the pristine tablecloth to demonstrate some new hi-tech computer link that kids could use to play for serious prizes across the world.

She gritted her teeth. The question on her lips was why William was playing around with her, albeit at a price, and why he was allowing Justin free access to his island at what she knew would be an astronomical cost. Darling Justin Chalmers could spend other people's money even better than she could steal it. He had no morals, unless . . . Was it some kind of blackmail?'

'Is Justin hitting you for cash?' she asked sweetly.

'Bloody fortune.' William stood up and tossed his napkin on to the table. Then he beamed. 'But he's building me a paradise.'

'Really? Well, far be it for me to give you any advice, if that's what you want . . .'

'Ah, that's only part of it.' He glanced at his wristwatch.

Sylvina couldn't resist asking, 'Part of what?'

He walked to the door as if he were not going to reply, but as he reached it he looked back at her. 'It's a private matter.'

'To do with Andrew Maynard?'

His face darkened. There were many layers to William, she thought, and from his expression, she knew that whatever Justin was up to had something to do with the death of Maynard.

'Indirectly,' William said quietly, and swung the door with the toe of his shoe. 'Most of all it's to do with me, and if Justin hasn't enlightened you then I feel I shouldn't. Now, it's getting late and we don't want to miss the entire morning. We're going to the galleries today, aren't we?'

'Yes, it's a private view,' she said, stubbing out her cigarette. Not that anyone would be examining the paintings, just who was there. The publicity wheels were already in motion and she and William would be photographed. 'I suggest you take your time over dressing. Wear the new Valentino dark grey suit, white shirt and silk tie. I'll meet you in two hours. I must have my hair done, my nails . . .'

'Okay, whatever you say, Ma'am.' He walked out, leaving her deeply frustrated and still no nearer the real reason behind her 'contract' with him and whatever the devious Justin was doing.

William had arranged a bank account for Justin to use during his work on the island. He did not place any limit on expenditure, but gave strict instructions that any new acquisitions must be agreed in advance. These were to be dealt with through his office at home, where Michael would monitor Justin's costs. Justin sent faxes several sheets long on the refurbishments, detailing everything from art purchases down to the price and size of each towel to be placed in the suites. Time and again Michael gasped with amazement as the costs soared, but whenever he mentioned it to William he was simply told to pay. So he did. The figure mounted daily.

That evening William and Sylvina were to dine with the British ambassador, after a first-night performance of *Dido and Aeneas* at the Bastille Opera. A photographer leaped forward when they alighted from their limousine, drawing the press-pack towards them, the battery of flashbulbs making them feel like royalty. Sylvina was pleased they could not be photographed inside the theatre, as William slept through the entire programme. Returning to the hotel he yawned until she wanted to slap him.

'I think I've had enough of Paris,' he said eventually.

She would have liked to tell him that she'd had just about enough of him, but instead she said she would need a couple of days to pack and make the arrangements to move on. He didn't argue. For two days he left her in peace as he took himself off to toy shops. Toy shops! At times he behaved so childishly.

William returned with his arms full of mechanical toys. Sylvina found him sitting on the floor winding them up and crawling around after them on all fours. A few hours later he had taken them all apart. He made fast sketches of each and beamed with delight. 'I can rip off every one of these. My factory can knock them out at a quarter the price. Obviously we'll have to make them slightly different, or I'll be sued, but—'

She interrupted, 'I have some shopping to do. Would you arrange with your pilot to take off later? I've had some alterations done and they won't be ready for collection till four.'

'No problem, dear heart.' He was squatting on the floor with an electronic device that made four toy mice scuttle across the carpet, followed by a larger creature representing a cat. Sylvina walked out as he yelped, 'Gotcha!' The furry cat scooped the little mice into its open mouth, and emitted a high-pitched screech.

'Bloody clever,' he muttered. Although William had never had toys in his childhood, he was not making up for it now, as Sylvina thought. This was money: this was what excited and cheered him. At long last he was looking forward to returning to work: his energy was back.

Sylvina was loath to leave Paris but now she saw that she had little choice: William was impatient to go home. She decided that Justin was getting a better deal than she was and feverishly upped her spending sprees. She ordered a new wardrobe from Valentino, Givenchy and Christian Dior, with matching shoes, hats and handbags. She had never liked London, but at least she was returning to it in style.


William got back to The Boltons with so much luggage that his chauffeur had to order another car to follow the Rolls. His servants looked on, speechless, as Sylvina was introduced, her suitcases filling the hallway. 'Michael, this is Countess Lubrinsky.' William's secretary gave a small bow, flushing as she acknowledged him with a glacial smile. She told the chauffeur to make sure that all the cases had been removed from the second car, and asked the housekeeper to see that they were taken up to her suite. Her perfume hung in the air, sweet and heavy. From her body language alone, everyone could see that she loathed the house.


A few days later William burst into Michael's office, demanding an update on his business. Michael wanted to discuss the exorbitant outgoings of Justin Chalmers. William dismissed his worries with a waft of his hand: he had little or no immediate interest in the island.

'Don't fret, for God's sake, Michael. I certainly won't be having financial worries for a fair few years yet. Just get me up to date on the business.'

'But, sir, this Justin Chalmers—'

'What about him?'

'Well, his bills are vast! Purchases being shipped in from India and heaven knows where else.'

'He's an interior designer, Michael.'

'So all the accounts I've sent you are acceptable? Fine. I'll confirm that with the accountants.' He hesitated before continuing. 'Er, what about the account you opened in the name of Countess Lubrinsky? It's already in the red.'

'Top it up,' said William, bored.

'But it's another twenty-five thousand.'

'Michael, she is to be my wife.'

'I'm sorry?' Michael's voice sounded strangled.

'You heard, Michael. Countess Lubrinsky and I are engaged to be married.'

'*Engaged*?' Michael stuttered.

'Yes, that is correct. Beautiful woman, isn't she?' Then William began to pass the sheets of drawings he had made of the toys in Paris. 'Get these over to the art department, then on to the factory. I like the cat and mouse one. But we'll have to come up with a different concept. Tell the artists to make it up as a fox and chickens.'

William tapped on Sylvina's door. He was told to enter and found her trying on a gown.

'Whoever did your décor should be shot,' she said. 'This is so ghastly, I feel ill.'

'I told my secretary,' he said, looking around irritably. He'd never noticed the blue and white flock wallpaper, depicting Chinese fishermen with little rods.

'Told him what?' she asked, as she looked at herself in the wardrobe mirror. Even that was hideous – and, worse, the mirror was so cheap it made her look fat.

'That we're engaged.'

She turned sideways for a different angle of herself in the spectacular black velvet sheath dress. 'Bit premature, isn't it? Weren't we supposed to discuss it first? I thought we'd only make an announcement if it was essential. They don't even know I'm in England yet. We need to be seen around a lot first.' She smoothed the velvet over her hips. 'Let's hope he doesn't run to the press, because we're not ready to make any announcement yet.'

'Christ, it's an engagement, not a wedding date. It's covered in your fee and you agreed.'

'I'm not saying I didn't but, I think you might have had the manners to *discuss* it with me first. It was a silly thing to do, especially after we've spent so long working on your profile.'

He flopped into an armchair and opened a magazine. 'Oh, Michael's not going to tell anyone. He's worked for me for years. Have you seen this month's *Paris-Match*? There's a photo of us at the races. Very good of you, but not so flattering of me.'

Sylvina peered at the series of photographs. 'Darling, it's me who has to be the catch of all time. And, besides, I think you look very sophisticated.'

'I think I look a bit of a prat.'

Sylvina told William she had hired a well-known PR agent who would ensure that wherever they went a paparazzo would be at hand, the flash of whose camera would draw attention to them. But William seemed to have forgotten that this had been paid for. Like a young movie-star, he had started to believe his own publicity. And he loved it.

'You never cease to amaze me,' she said, turning her back for him to unzip the dress.

'Why? Is it seeing the man emerge before you? Well, I've done everything you told me to do.' He chortled.

It was hard to believe that in such a short time he had changed so much. There was a confident air about him, and his voice was louder than it had been in Paris.

'You're very cheerful,' she said.

'I'm glad to be home.'

Sylvina let the gown slip to her ankles and stepped out of it, naked. William reached out, as if to touch her, and she stepped back. 'Don't get too confident, William.'

He snatched away his hand as if she had slapped it. 'It was just a bit of lint on your shoulder,' he snapped. 'I should be allowed to touch you, considering the money I'm paying you. But don't worry, I don't want to.' He walked out and slammed the bedroom door shut behind him.

Sylvina sighed. He'd done it to her again. It unnerved her, the way that at one moment he was under her control and at the next she would realize that he could get rid of her whenever he liked. She had to be more careful now they were on his turf.

The couple had dined with film stars and cabinet ministers in Paris, attended premières, had been seen at

Longchamps and Auteuil. Now that they were in England the wheels of publicity were turning here. Michael monitored the growing frenzy around the pair with trepidation. He couldn't grasp what was going on, but knew it was building towards something. Perhaps it was just the announcement of their nuptials, but he had detected that the Countess, far from caring for William, was at times almost disdainful of him. He was sure she was simply bleeding him of a lot of money. And Michael was aware of how much, because he oversaw her accounts. *Nothing* quite made sense – not just the Countess, but the vast fortune being paid out to Justin Chalmers. And when he took a call from William's financial adviser, who was fishing for information, Mr Flynn appeared as nonplussed as himself at the astronomical sums being moved to the British Virgin Islands. He asked if Michael had any notion of what was going on.

'I believe he's having the island refurbished.'

'The amount he's shelling out could refurbish bloody New Zealand. This is just a small place, isn't it?'

'I'm not aware of the detailed instructions, just that the island is being prepared for Sir William to stay there with some guests.'

'Well, please ask him to contact me. He's not returned any of my calls . . .' There was a long pause, then Michael heard a light cough. 'Just between you and me, Michael, I know he took quite a public thrashing over this Maynard business. He's not having some kind of breakdown, is he?'

'No, he seems in very good spirits.'

'Ah. Well, get him to call me because I don't want to continue throwing money at this chap Chalmers until I've spoken to him. I need more details.'

Michael hung up, and addressed himself to another of Sir William's scrawled messages. The Countess did not wish to remain in The Boltons so he had arranged to rent a house for her in Mayfair. Having now formally announced their engagement in *The Times*, they were at last holding centre-stage, and Sylvina felt it would look better if they did not appear to be cohabiting.

'We're not,' William had said petulantly.

'We're under the same roof, dearest, and that to Meryl Delaware means we're swinging naked from the light fittings. We must appear to be above reproach, exceedingly respectable.'

'Fine. Go ahead and do what you want.' William was growing bored with her constant requests for hand-outs.

Sylvina insisted on installing a maid, cook and butler in her new home and ordered that the floral displays be changed every three days. She adored her luxurious surroundings, but William was irritating her. She tried to contact Justin, but after leaving several messages she gave up. She knew that William and he kept in regular touch, but when she asked how the 'project' was coming along William said simply that it was costing enough to be more than just 'coming along' and he hoped it was almost completed. So did his financial adviser, who had demanded a meeting to discuss the island situation.

'I have the money, haven't I?'

'Well, yes, of course, Sir William, but I also have to do my job, and I am advising you—'

'Don't. I know what the costs are and I have agreed to them. That is all you need to know.'

'And the house in Mayfair?'

'That is also acceptable. My fiancée requires her own establishment so, if there is no other business, please excuse me.'

Yet again, the idea occurred to them that perhaps Sir William was having a breakdown.

As they left his office, Michael was waiting to usher them out. 'What do *you* know of this Justin Chalmers?' Mr Flynn asked. He and his company had worked with William for many years, but Mr Flynn had never been spoken to so brusquely or kept so much in the dark by William as he had today.

'I've never met him, Mr Flynn,' Michael said quietly, afraid to be overheard. I did check up with some interior designers I know of, and they have no idea who he is, but . . .' Michael hesitated '. . . I think he was an associate of Andrew Maynard.'

Mr Flynn nodded. 'I see,' he said, but he didn't really, and he was rather annoyed at the way he had been treated. But, as Sir William had said, he had the finance to do what he wanted, so if this island was what he wanted then so be it. Mr Flynn would keep the money flowing out.

The past months in London had been enjoyable to begin with, especially as William watched people's attitudes change towards him. But the 'intended marriage' was now constantly raised by the press. Reporters asked ceaselessly for an announcement of the wedding date. But there was to be no date, no marriage. William knew he must do something radical. Sylvina just repeated that he had jumped the gun in announcing it. She felt that to all intents and purposes she had done her job: it appeared he was already accepted socially again.

'You were invited to Baron and Baroness von Garten's summer festival, two people you had on your list. You wanted to be acknowledged by them. I just don't understand why, after the lengths we went to, you turned down their invitation.'

'That, my dear, was the whole point. I wanted to turn it down. I can't stand the bloody sight of him, or his stuck-up bitch of a wife.'

She sighed. 'Fine. Well, what about Lord Hangerford? He's underlined on the list, and I've made contact. You've been asked to dinner and the races. You've turned him down too. I thought you wanted to get to know these people.'

'I did know them,' he said angrily.

'So why have you had me pulling these strings?'

'*You're missing the point!*' he shouted.

She sighed. 'William, what *is* the point? You pay me to have you reintroduced and accepted socially, and now you tell me you don't want to be.'

'I don't want to socialize with them . . . not yet.'

'Oh. Well, why don't you tell me when you do? In the meantime I'll just stay at my house and wait for your call.' In a flash she regretted having said this. 'Are you backing out of the deal we had?' She was panicking.

'No. All I feel is that it's got out of hand. I'm grateful, you've done a good job, but I think maybe it's boring me now, as much as it is you.'

'Is that my fault?'

'No, I didn't mean that. It's just . . . I'm tired of it all.'

'*You're* tired! Well, let me tell you, I'm exhausted.

143

All right, you're paying me, but I'm not only exhausted. Most of the time I'm bored out of my mind by these people.'

'Don't get tetchy,' he said.

'I'm not tetchy, I just want this all over and done with, and it appears you do as well. So, pay me off, and let me get back to my own life.'

'That's all this has really been to you, isn't it? Money,' he said glumly.

She wanted to scream, but she took a deep breath, crossed over to him and slipped her arms around his neck. 'Sweetie, I am what I have always been, and I have never led you to believe otherwise. You've always known this was a game. You instigated it and I have played my part. I have not had an affair, I have remained, ready, willing and able, at your beck and call. But it's almost a year . . . so let's part as friends.'

He removed her arms from around his neck. Yet again she was taken aback. His voice was soft, hardly audible. 'If I'd offered more money, would you have fucked me?'

She laughed. 'Christ no. Well, maybe. If the price was right, who knows?'

'Someone of your age should be– ' He never got out the word 'grateful' as she slapped him across the face.

'Don't throw crass remarks, Willy. If I'd have opened my legs, you'd have dived in. I've earned every penny, so please don't try and back out.'

'Not just yet. There's one person you've not brought to the table. Humphrey Matlock. You've not even got close to him.'

Sylvina clenched her teeth. She had really tried, but

Matlock was a hard man to get to. He appeared to loathe social functions and, in any case, was often abroad. When he was in London, he went fishing at weekends or whenever he could get away.

'William, Humphrey Matlock's a very unsociable creature and, to be honest, I wouldn't include a newspaper magnate as high priority for social standing.'

'Bullshit! Newspaper magnates are high in the social pecking-order. I want to meet him,' he said pettishly, 'but on my terms. I want that son-of-a-bitch to want to meet with me.'

'Right. Come hell or high water, I will arrange for you to do that. But please pay me, William, and let me get out of here. Otherwise we'll end up hating each other and I honestly don't want that.'

He took out his cheque book, and dangled it in front of her. 'You get me to Humphrey Matlock. Forget everyone else.'

She pursed her lips. 'Have you tried picking up the phone and calling him? You're on the front page of every bloody glossy magazine, some of which he owns. Meryl Delaware's been working overtime for you.'

'What?'

'Pay her and she'd work for Jack the Ripper – she even works for Matlock but she can't get close to him either. She's never met him.'

'I want him to *want* to know me,' he said again, thrusting out his lower jaw.

Sylvina looked at the cheque book, and bit her lip. 'Okay, I'll arrange it. I'll see if Meryl Delaware can help, but it'll cost.'

Two days later an innocuous piece in one of the gossip columns said that all seemed to be going well for the new 'golden couple', Sir William Benedict and Countess Sylvina Lubrinsky. Shortly afterwards, William received a gold-embossed invitation to a midsummer fête at the Matlock's country home. He propped the invitation on the mantelpiece and stood looking at it, his hands stuffed into his pockets. When Michael walked in, William pointed to it. 'What a two-faced piece of shit, eh?' Michael took the invitation down to read it. 'That's the son-of-a-bitch who ran filth about me for months. Every one of his papers ran lies about me, and now, a year later, he invites me to his home.'

Michael shook his head in disgust, and replaced the invitation. 'So you won't be going, sir?'

'You accept, Michael, and send a bouquet of flowers to his wife. Then, nearer the date, you can telephone and say I have been unavoidably detained.'

Michael gave a quizzical look, but noted down his latest instructions. They were getting more bizarre every week – and he had detected a frosty atmosphere between Sir William and his countess.

Sylvina was looking ravishing, and William thanked her for the scrapbook of press-cuttings she had sent him.

'It was really just to make a point,' she said. 'All that coverage was hard work, and sometimes I thought you didn't know how much time it took.'

William smiled and passed her a white envelope. 'You'll find a cheque inside, certified, of course, plus a list of the extra expenses that I did not agree to pay. I have deducted them from the fee we agreed.'

Sylvia gasped. Three hundred thousand pounds had been deducted from the million-pound payment. Even the solitaire diamond engagement ring had been charged to her. He had a funny crooked smile on his face.

'You fat bastard!' she snarled.

'Maybe I'm fat but I'm not stupid. Not stupid enough for you to rip me off anyway.'

After Sylvina left, still cursing, she phoned Justin and at last managed to speak to him.

'Hi, gorgeous, how's things?' he drawled.

'My cheque was short. The mean bastard deducted three hundred thousand grand.'

'He's got *some* sense, then?' He laughed.

'Soon you might be laughing on the other side of your face too,' she said angrily.

'What's that supposed to mean?'

'Exactly what I said. He's back doing business again like a demented kid. Every time I got him invitations from those wretched names on his pitiful list, he did nothing about it.'

'Did you get to Matlock?' Justin asked sharply.

'Yes. He's going to some function at the man's home. That's why I'm out of here.'

'You're leaving London?'

'I'm on my way to the airport right now.'

'He's going to Matlock's?'

'I just told you so. He's got the invitation, squeezed out of Matlock's prune-faced wife. What a dull woman she is.'

'Shit,' Justin hissed. Sylvina laughed. 'Goodbye,' she said, as she switched off her phone. She leaned back smiling. She had just made herself a tidy sum and could look forward to enjoying herself. She certainly had the wardrobe for it, and all the press she had engineered for William had benefited her too. Life was good.

Meanwhile, far from feeling relief at Sylvina's departure, William felt seedy and foolish, and more so when he considered that *he* had instigated the madness of the past year. But for what? He thought of other men who had been publicly vilified by the press: Profumo, Lambton, Archer and, of course, Aitken, now released from his prison sentence. Admittedly, the scandals in which they had been involved were more sensitive than his. In fact, he hadn't even been involved in a scandal. He was innocent, but he wondered if those others felt as he did. Had they at some time wanted revenge for the way they had been treated, or had they simply accepted it and got on with their lives? The public hounding as journalists dug into their families' lives must have hurt each of them, just as it had hurt him.

William looked at the array of invitations to high-society functions that had come in daily while Sylvina was at his side. How ridiculous to have coveted such meaningless things. He knew that if he continued to lavish money on certain charities he would remain on their lengthy, highbrow guest-lists, but he no longer cared. Maybe that was what he had learned from Sylvina: all it took to penetrate the higher echelons was money and 'face'. He had been a self-made mega-rich tycoon with one fatal flaw: his need for social acceptability. Now at last he realized how hollow that had been. How could he find a real purpose in life?

William, too, placed a call to Justin. He asked,

uninterestedly, how the work was coming along. Justin assured him that everything was going according to plan, that the game would soon be ready to begin. William told him quietly that the game was off. It was pointless. Sylvina had gone, and as soon as Justin was finished with the refurbishments he was to go, too. Justin flew into a rage, but knew better than to show it. When William hung up Justin let out a furious scream.

'I'm off home now, sir,' Michael said, popping his head round William's study door.

'Goodbye.' His employer's voice sounded empty.

Michael stepped into the room. 'Everything all right, sir?' he asked, with some concern.

'Yes, everything's fine. Goodnight.'

'Will the Countess be coming back?'

'No, she won't. She's gone.'

William gave a small, sad smile. 'Not much luck with the ladies. See you in the morning.'

Michael closed the door quietly. He could think of nothing to say.

If he had seen William opening his locked desk drawer and taking out a Luger pistol, he would have been more than concerned. William placed it on his leatherbound blotter and stared at it. The awful loneliness had something to do with Sylvina's departure but more to do with him. He contemplated ending it all. All he had to do was pull the trigger. But that was easier said than done. The pistol had belonged to his father. It had not been used for thirty years, and the firing pin was bent out of shape. He held it to his head as he stared at his reflection in the mirror, and remembered the discovery of Andrew Maynard's body. Had he really died of heartbreak . . . or through fear of his private life being exposed? Suddenly William focused on Humphrey Matlock's invitation. He lowered his useless pistol and tossed it back into the drawer. A spark of anger ignited amid his spiralling depression. 'I want to get that bastard,' he muttered.

William decided then that, after all, he was going to fight back because he was an innocent man. He had not stolen, lied or destroyed anyone in his climb to success yet he had been vilified. He was still wary of Justin's plan, but the dream of revenge on Matlock had pulled him away from the edge.

In the middle of the night, an enraged Justin placed a call to Meryl Delaware. She was about to launch an angry tirade at him for waking her at such an hour but he didn't let her get a word in. Speaking in a low, urgent voice, he gave her a front-page scoop. It concerned a young actress called Sharee, and her relationship with Countess Sylvina Lubrinsky, Sir William Benedict's future wife.

Two days later, as William was sitting down to breakfast, he was surprised to hear Michael arrive and tap on the door. 'I'm sorry, sir but I couldn't have blanked it. It came right out of left field.'

William looked up expectantly. 'Blanked what?'

In an exclusive that seemed exclusive to every tabloid paper in Europe, Sharee had disclosed her sexual relationship with William's fiancée. The headlines were beyond belief – 'Britain's Bad Boy Falls Prey to Sex Goddess' – but the articles were explicit, and accompanied by photographs of Sharee either in a sexy pose, pouting, tits to the fore, or as an angelic baby 'used and abused by lesbian temptress'.

The nightmare began again. William's home was surrounded by pressmen. He couldn't move outside without cameras flashing and microphones being thrust under his nose. The press regurgitated all his past indiscretions with hookers, and his ex-wives' quotes were rehashed. The onslaught was relentless. This time Michael was impressed by the way William handled it all. He remained composed and quiet. His demeanour when he left the house was sad, resigned, and that belied his abject humiliation. Eventually he decided to give a press conference. The battery of cameras and television crews with reporters fighting for front-row positions was sickening, all for some ridiculous article that might titillate a few readers.

Fortified by a few glasses of wine, William walked out to face the baying mob. He read a short statement he had written himself, and felt his anguish rising. Eventually he broke down. The flashbulbs popped. On returning to his house, he felt that the press conference had been the straw to break his back. He was appalled that he had lacked such self-control, and refused to watch any newsreels or read another paper. Now he was seriously contemplating ending it all.

Then everything changed. The fickle world turns on a fivepenny piece. The press began to depict him as a wronged lover and the public loved it.

Michael hired a PR agent, who played heavily on William's shock and trauma at the revelations. William was amazed by an avalanche of sympathy letters and articles. He was now seen as a man seduced by a gold-digger who had betrayed him. The débâcle went on long enough for William to be sickened at first then amused that without making any effort himself he had come out smelling of roses.

Sylvina and Sharee had unwittingly given William a new public image, and to Justin, this turn of events was a gift from heaven. He had dropped the scoop to Meryl to spite William for dropping the plan. But the miraculous turnaround also meant that William's putative guests would be sure to accept an invitation from such a popular media star. He called William to talk him into leaving London to visit the almost completed paradise island.

'I can't right now, Justin,' said William, tired from all the interviews and phone calls.

'Right now is the perfect time. William, are you there?' There was a pause. 'I want you to think about our plan,' Justin began.

'At the moment I can't think about anything.'

'But you have to.'

'Justin, I can't talk now. Call me later.' He hung up.

At the other end of the line Justin's face twisted into a paroxysm of fury. Then, in a fit of rage, he smashed the receiver to pieces against the wall. He berated himself for acting too rashly.

He had been sure that the exposé would make William even more eager for revenge, but it seemed to have had the reverse effect. 'Will this idiot never come to his senses?' Justin muttered to himself. Gradually he calmed himself. It was just a setback. He'd leave it a day or so then call again. The fish was still on the line, he assured himself, just wriggling dangerously. Justin would land his quarry, even if it meant drawing him out to the island and slitting his throat himself.

# CHAPTER 8

A FEW DAYS later Justin called William again. William was surprised to feel genuinely pleased to hear from him, but with the Sharee story, he was desperate to get out of London. He couldn't face going to work. 'I'll get the next flight out,' he said.

'What?' Justin asked loudly.

'I said I'll be flying out as soon as I can.'

'Oh, fantastic. By the way, I've ordered four jet-skis, and I told you about the speedboat, didn't I? Expensive, but out here it'll be an eye-popper. Hopefully it's arriving today. Let me know what time your flight gets in, and I'll have a boat fixed up to collect you, if yours hasn't been delivered. Hello? Are you still there?'

'I'll have Michael call you, Justin.' William hung up and pressed the intercom. 'Michael, arrange a flight for me, would you? I want to leave as soon as possible.'

'Where to, sir?' came Michael's clipped tones.

'The island. So get Mrs Thingy to pack enough suitable clothes for a fortnight.'

'You have board meetings the day after tomorrow.'

'Cancel them.'

Michael accompanied William to the airport, ostensibly to take notes and instructions, but his boss seemed distracted.

'The new mechanical toys are ready for you to test, sir. Do you want me to send them out to you on the island?'

'What toys?' William asked.

'The fox and hens, remember?'

'Oh yes, yes, just go ahead.'

'What about the patent?' Michael asked, aware that they had been copied from some William had bought in Paris.

'Well, I reckon we can get away with it. I'm sure I remember seeing some designs for a similar toy done by one of my boffins years ago. If they do decide to take on the Benedict Corporation, which I'm sure they won't, we'll be able to pass it off as ours anyway. In fact, Michael, get my lawyers to look into the company that made that cat and mouse thing and root out our old files. Maybe we can sue *them*!' With that, they arrived at the airport.


The speedboat's engine was cut and it cruised into the small, immaculate dock. It was late afternoon and still blisteringly hot, but a sea breeze kept the air fresh. Justin, deeply tanned, was wearing cut-off blue jeans, a white T-shirt with torn seams and a faded pair of flip-flops. His gold Rolex wristwatch glistened in the sun, and a pair of black Armani shades hung from the neck of his T-shirt. A boy in white shorts and dirty sneakers was at the controls. He jumped deftly out of the boat on to the quay, and Justin hurled him a coiled rope, which he tied around a wooden post.

William was sitting in the small harbour café with a whisky and soda. He had landed in Miami, then booked the Cherokee two-seater to taxi him to Tortola, the adjacent island; his own had no airstrip. Another seaplane landed at the same time, and William was irritated to see Count Frederick Capri, whom he recognized from Justin's villa in France, greet the disembarking passengers.

His mood darkened as he watched the lithe, handsome Justin strolling towards him. He seemed to know everyone who passed, waving and laughing, speaking fluent French one moment, Spanish the next. William sipped his drink and squinted into the sun as Justin made his way towards the café veranda and leaned against the railing. 'You made it,' he said, smiling, his white teeth dazzling against his dark skin.

His hair had grown quite long since William last saw him and he wore it combed back from his high forehead. It was bleached almost white.

'The boy'll get your cases,' Justin added, slipping on his shades and checking his watch. 'We shouldn't leave it too long, there's a bit of wind and it might get choppy. Besides, I want you to see the island in the best possible light – when the sun is just slipping down.'

They walked to the quay, got into the boat and surged off. William pressed his back into the leather seat. Justin sat next to him, tilting his face to catch the last rays of sun. 'So the Countess buggered off,' he said.

William shrugged. He could smell Justin's sun-oil, and glanced at the small diamond ring he wore on his little finger.

Justin hooked his arm around William's shoulder.

156

'This is nerve-racking for me. It's been almost eighteen months, did you know that?'

'Time passes quickly,' William said, uneasy with the man's closeness.

'I have created a paradise,' Justin said, tightening his arm. 'Sometimes it was hard for me to remember that I was creating a place for you, not me. I've grown to love this island with a passion.'

William would never forget the next few moments. The boat cut through the water, passing between two jagged rocks. A mist began to sweep towards them, blurring the ocean and the sky, creating an illusion of nothingness. Then the island appeared, like a mirage. White turrets, boundary walls, white cliffs and sparkling latticed windows. As they drew closer, the mist parted, and William made out undergrowth, trees and shrubs in a blaze of different colours.

The quayside, jetty and pathways leading to the mansion were as white as the turrets. Large Chinese lanterns hung from ropes, swinging gently in the wind, and the tinkle of wind-chimes and bells echoed across the water. William half rose, his lips parted, as they cruised past man-made beaches and cascading waterfalls. The perfume from the lilies was so strong that the heady smell wafted over the water like incense. The boat passed hidden coves equipped with small jetties and lines of jet-skis, sailing dinghies and windsurfers. Sunbathing terraces, covered with brilliant white canopies, rows of polished sun-beds and picnic tables, jutted out from the rocks; diving boards reached out into the sea. As the boat curved inwards to the main landing, jettyboys in white blazers and shorts stood like sentries

157

waiting for their arrival. The boat-boy eased into the jetty alongside a sleek cruiser covered in white tarpaulins and a small, elegant launch. Five white golf carts were parked nearby.

Justin climbed up on to the jetty, speaking in French to the boys, who then assisted William from the boat, collected his luggage and stacked it on a golf cart. William stood still, taking it all in. 'Stunning,' he said, in awe.

Justin was delighted at the impact of his creation. But this was just the beginning and he was determined to milk every second. 'I'll show you the grounds first.' He veered off the pathway into a shaded, narrow, rough lane where the ferns and the palms made it darker and more mysterious. They turned a corner on to a clearing with an Olympic-sized marble swimming pool. The water, lit from beneath, was a vivid turquoise. Sun-loungers were covered in the same brilliant colour; parasols and tables were placed on different levels. A straw-covered gazebo accommodated a bar, where a man stood waiting to serve drinks. Crystal glasses glittered, and mountains of fruit in ceramic pots were dotted on the tables around the pool. Justin escorted William to a jacuzzi built on a higher level, and a large swirl pool with an elaborate mosaic floor.

The tour continued round the entire island, taking in secret pathways, or 'lovers' walks', as Justin described them, until at last they headed around the rear of the mansion, past the servants' quarters to a shady cobble-walled yard. 'The servants live in the area away from the master rooms, but they're connected by phone and intercom,' Justin said, pointing out the hidden wires. Following his gaze, William looked upwards. 'The cameras are for the security monitor in your master office. You can see what's going on over the whole island with one flick of a switch.'

They returned to the cart and headed back towards the main mansion entrance. Justin had restructured the building, turning a warren of small rooms and corridors into vast open spaces. The doors leading into the main hall were thirty feet high and had come from an Indonesian monastery. They were carved with spectacular fretwork, and in the centre of each was a wooden lion's head, its jaws wide open, holding a gleaming brass knocker. Justin had a flair for mixing the old with the new and the combination was perfect. The hallway was tiled in black and white marble. Above, a huge domed ceiling was vaulted with thick wooden beams, a minstrel's gallery snaking its way around the hall. Overhead, fans whirred quietly, and carefully positioned lights cast beams on paintings the size of living-room walls. Tapestries, oil paintings and a full suit of armour gave the feeling of a medieval castle, yet the room was light and airy. The wide double staircase was made of polished Japanese pine and had a frail appearance that belied its strength and weight. The windows opened on to balconies and verandas. All the rooms seemed to be interconnected: one wall slid back to reveal a modern, open-plan drawing room with white cushioned sofas, low tables, paintings, china displays on plinths of polished wood, Japanese bowls, rough local pottery, and, dominating each room, a wide open fireplace. 'I've installed the finest air-conditioning system. The engineers were here for months.' Justin pointed around the room, to the floor and ceiling, but William could see no grids or outlets – they were all hidden from sight.

Besides a row of six small bungalow-type residences for staff and guests, there were eight suites, each with their own bathroom. There was also a drawing room and a dining room with a long monastery table and big carved chairs, plus a smaller table for more intimate dining. The breakfast room had no walls, and was designed so that guests could drink their morning coffee with spectacular views on every side. However, when it was windy or wet, the touch of a button would electronically activate glass panels to shield them.

Nothing in his wildest dreams had prepared William for this extravagance. Justin insisted on tours to the servants' living-quarters, going into long descriptions about the kitchens and wine cellar, which he wanted William to see. Then he led William into a gargantuan study. It was a modern room, with a futuristic-looking desk, a hi-tech computer and printer, a huge television and a bank of security monitors. Although William was now aching with tiredness, Justin gestured for him to sit. He crossed to the desk, spread out the architect's drawings of the mansion, and with a red pen indicated the areas they missed on the tour and the positions of the hidden cameras. He began to fiddle with an array of switches in the large panel at the side of the desk. The monitors fizzled into life, revealing every possible area of the island.

'You can keep an eye on everything, William,' Justin said, unable to hide his pride in his work.

'Very impressive,' William said, so exhausted he could hardly keep his eyes open.

'We need to discuss the finances,' Justin said, rolling up the drawings.

'Not now. I need some sleep. Perhaps in the morning.'

Justin checked his watch. 'Will you want to dine? Only you should really meet all your staff.'

William removed his jacket. His shirt was stained with sweat. 'A light supper in my suite. Offer them my apologies. I'll meet them tomorrow.' He looked around, unsure where to go.

'I'll send the chef to your room,' Justin said, opening a door in the corner of the study. 'Tomorrow we'll discuss the grand plan.'

William took a deep breath. 'No, we won't, I'm here for a holiday, nothing more. All that revenge stuff was nonsense, as stupid as my arrangement with Sylvina.'

Justin's heart sank, but he kept a smile on his face. 'You get a good night's sleep. Maybe you'll think differently in the morning.'

William glared. 'No, I won't. As I said, I'm here for a break, and God knows I certainly need one. All that silly stuff is best forgotten. I don't even want to discuss it again. Goodnight.'

As William made to leave, Justin gave a small bow. 'Welcome home,' he said softly.

'Thank you. You've done one hell of a job.'

Justin directed him to his suite, then closed the door and leaned against it. 'You've done one hell of a job,' he repeated sarcastically. 'Fucking prick,' he muttered, under his breath. The dumb bastard didn't want to play! Well, so be it, *he* would play. He hadn't spent eighteen months setting it up and half of his life waiting for this opportunity just to let it slip away. It might take a little longer, but he was sure he could persuade the buffoon to do exactly as he wanted. No one was going to stop him now.

William showered and changed into a pair of cotton pyjamas that had been laid out on his bed. His suite seemed bigger than the first floor of his London house. He padded to the balcony, opened the doors and walked out. Like a golden globe sinking into the sea, the sun's last rays reached out like tentacles into the darkening sky before it disappeared. William gasped. It was the most extraordinary sight he'd ever seen. Soft lights came on automatically, and he rested his hands on the veranda rail. He breathed deeply. The air was cool and sweetly perfumed, the night caressing, almost like a naked woman reaching out to hold him. As emotion welled up inside him he felt close to tears and gasped to regain his composure. He felt as though he were caught in a dream. But it was reality. This was his paradise. It belonged to him and no one else.

There was a light tap on the door and William let in a small Frenchman who introduced himself as Monsieur Dupré, the chef. He handed William the menu, a thick sheet of manila paper with looped writing. William barely glanced at it. 'I'd like some melon, a little scrambled egg and maybe some salmon.'

'Of course, Monsieur, and . . .' He passed William the wine list. One glance told him it was on a par with that of the Ritz. He asked for a bottle of chilled Pouilly Fumé and some iced lemon tea. Dupré bowed and backed out, closing the door silently behind him.

The tray arrived on a steel trolley with silver domes placed over delicate pale blue porcelain. The cutlery, of silver and eighteen-carat gold inlaid with ivory, was laid out on the damask cloth. The fluted goblet was chilled and frosted, and the wine stood in an ornate silver bucket.

'I'll serve myself,' William said briskly, anxious to be left alone to savour yet another of Justin's touches of elegance. The eggs were cooked to perfection, the salmon melted in his mouth like butter. The warm crusty rolls were fresh, just as he liked. The melon, cut into fine slivers, was garnished with segments of lemon, strawberries, pineapple and apricots. William ate sparingly, and after a glass of wine, his eyes drooped. He didn't finish his meal but went into the bedroom, fell onto the damask-covered bed and into a deep, dreamless sleep.

At some point during the night, the tray was removed and the hand-made mosquito nets released above the bed. William turned and his eyes opened and, for a moment, he was unsure where he was. The netting above him felt like hands touching his face and he cringed. He must make it clear to all the servants that his rooms were not to be entered unless at his express permission. Returning to a half-sleep, he saw winding dark corridors, secret rooms – eerie, frightening places. He felt so cold he woke up. Pushing the netting aside William reached for the bedside lamp, patting its base to find the switch. The lamp filled the room with a soft yellow glow. Looking around, he suddenly noticed a painting.

For a moment it looked like a mirage, suspended in the air, but then he realized that it had been framed to stand away from the wall and was intended to appear to float. It was of a woman, her blonde hair cascading from a central parting almost to her waist. A pale blue chiffon scarf covered her shoulders, revealing her perfect breasts. One hand, with long fine fingers and short oval nails, held a white lily. The other rested against the side of her pale neck, as if she was touching her pulse. The painting was in washed, muted colours. Only the face had clarity, as if the artist wanted it to be the focus. It was a childlike, innocent face. Pale blue eyes stared out above a small, delicate nose and the full lips were slightly parted. William turned off the light, but kept staring towards the painting, unsure whether he wished it to remain in the room. Eventually he fell asleep, her face the last thing he saw that night and the first when he woke next morning.

Standing on the veranda, William saw Justin in a white robe heading back towards the house.

'Morning,' Justin called up.

'Morning,' he replied.

'I've been for a swim,' Justin said, shading his eyes. 'Have you had breakfast?'

'Not yet, will you join me for coffee?'

'Absolutely,' said Justin, disappearing.

'Justin!' William called after him. 'The woman,' he said, as Justin reappeared. 'The painting of the woman in my bedroom.'

'Ah, yes,' Justin called up. 'Beautiful, isn't she?'

'Who is she?'

'My sister,' Justin said. Almost as an afterthought he added, 'Her name is Laura.'


At breakfast, William was wearing a pair of Bermuda shorts and a loose floral shirt. On his feet were Gucci sandals, leather uppers with rope soles, but his legs above his socks were unhealthy pinkish blobs. His pale freckled skin never tanned, but turned red and blistered if he sat in the sun too long. His fine blond hair, thinning at the back in a neat round crown, was perhaps the only thing the tropical sun enhanced, turning it from mousy blond to white-silver. Justin, in comparison, was so deeply tanned from months of working outdoors that it was hard to tell what race he was. He was wearing a cheesecloth kaftan and the flip-flops he had worn the previous day. He hitched up the kaftan around his thighs as he stretched out his long legs beside the table.

A large trolley loaded with fresh fruit cascading from iced bowls had been wheeled to within easy reach of the table, with fresh rolls, pastries and home-made breads under a covered silver warming-dish. Various jams and sweet and sour marmalades in silver basket-weave jars, matching silver coffee- and tea-pots with hot-water jugs in the same but larger-woven pattern sparkled in the morning sun. The table wore a starched pale blue linen cloth, with matching napkins and heavy cutlery. Added to the array of knives and forks were diamond-shaped grapefruit spoons. Iced flutes held freshly squeezed orange juice. Jugs offered lemon water, or grapefruit juice with sprigs of mint. A small, heated tray held covered tureens with bacon, sausage, scrambled eggs, liver, kidneys and onions.

'No cornflakes?' William said, looking over the trolley.

'I'll send down for some,' Justin said.

'No, don't bother. It was a joke.' William poured more coffee and proffered the pot to Justin, who shook his head, holding up a glass of iced water.

'Not until midday. Gets me too speedy.' He sat munching at an alarming rate.

'Is she dead?' William asked, out of the blue.

'Who?' Justin enquired.

'The woman in the painting.' William dabbed the corners of his mouth with his napkin.

'Laura? No, she's very much alive.'

'You've never mentioned her.'

'I'm sure I have.' Justin took out his cigarettes, noting the way the debris from William's breakfast now dominated the table. He had read somewhere that the space a person took up on a table was representative of their perceived status in relation to their fellow diners. William clearly felt he was the dominant personality here.

'Laura?' William said, his head cocked to one side. 'The name suits her. She's very beautiful.'

Justin nodded, picked up a book of matches and lit his Gitane. He drew the ashtray close and laid the match in the bowl then slid it, with a half-amused smile, directly in front of William. He had now reclaimed his space. 'We should go over the accounts,' he said quietly.

'Fine. Whenever.'

Justin stood up and stretched his long arms above his head. 'Half an hour? Your study would probably be best. Then I can lay out all the plans.'

'What does she do?' William asked, looking up at Justin.

'My sister?' Justin drew deeply on the cigarette, then let the smoke drift from his nose. 'She fucks.' With that he strolled away, the smell of his cigarette hanging in the air.

\*

Justin was waiting in William's study. He had changed into a pair of white shorts, frayed at the edges and a washed-out blue vest. William pointed to a stack of receipts and invoices. 'Has Michael been privy to all of this?'

'Most,' Justin said, concentrating on the account books.

'He'll need copies of everything,' William said, wandering around the room, noting the contents of the bookshelves and cabinets.

'Absolutely.'

William stared out of the window. 'Christ, it's a wonderful view from here,' he said.

'From every room,' Justin corrected, concentrating on his papers. 'Shall we get started?' He stepped away from the desk, gesturing to the carved chair behind it. William sat as he placed an open, leatherbound account book in front of him. He pointed to the control panel on the desk. 'You have a high-tech calculator there if you need it. It'll give you the costs in any currency, plus exchange rates. This is the master copy.'

William nodded and flicked briskly through the pages of neatly handwritten accounts until he got to the last page and glanced down. Justin was becoming irritated. He knew that William was looking for the final total. 'If you have to look for it, you can't afford it,' he said. 'The truth is, it's peanuts compared to what some interior designers would have charged.'

'Jesus Christ!' William uttered under his breath. The total was one hundred and twenty-six million dollars. 'Peanuts?' He looked up as Justin averted his eyes.

'I'll start at the beginning. Go to page one, structural repairs,' he snapped.

'Yes,' William said flatly, adding a curt, 'I think you had better do just that!'

At last there was some energized response from William, even if it was not necessarily a good one. His depression hung around him, pervaded the island and infuriated Justin. He simply could not understand his lack of energy and enthusiasm. He was like a dead man set in cement. Only the money angle seemed to have given him a spark of life.

Later, a business lunch of crisp salad and chicken breast wrapped in spinach leaves on a bed of saffron rice was brought in to them. William did not want a break, and Justin, under a barrage of questions, didn't eat a morsel. William demanded to know the cost of every item. By mid-afternoon Justin had to get out. He needed to clear his head. He'd not even left the room for a piss. Neither had William.

No wonder the man was rich, he thought. Nothing went unnoticed – he even inquired about bars of soap.

'Look, Sir William, we must discuss more than nit-picking costs. There is more at stake here.' William peered at him quizzically. 'I suggest we both take a break. I'll arrange for a drink to be brought up to you at the jacuzzi.'

Reluctantly William acquiesced. He didn't like jacuzzis and he could have easily continued all day and into the night.

'I'll take some of these folders,' he muttered.

'Fine. Just don't get them wet.' Justin was trying hard to control his temper.

Justin walked to the edge of the pool, kicked off his shorts and dived naked into the cool blue water. William was sitting in the jacuzzi on the higher level, wearing

168

Justin's baseball cap with a cigar clamped in his teeth. He was checking through the lists of paintings and tapestries that had been shipped in from Sotheby's and Christie's showrooms in New York and London. The hot water was pumping and shaking over his rather flaccid thighs and buttocks. He had put on at least two and a half stone since Maynard's death, partly due to Sylvina's constant round of dinners. His pot belly hung over his maroon bathing shorts. He watched Justin swim length after length.

After about half an hour William showered and changed, gathered up the folders and returned to the study. He was surprised to see Justin already at work, bent over the computer, with a glass of chilled wine.

'You mind?' Justin asked, holding up the bottle, which was already three-quarters empty.

'Not at all.' William gestured to the chair beside him. 'I need you to run these by me. Mexican artefacts? Were they necessary?'

'No, not at all, but rather nice, don't you think?' Justin slumped down into the chair.

'At this price they should be.'

And so it continued.

At last, by nine that evening, William was satisfied that he had covered the entire expenditure on his island paradise. He closed the last book and reached for a cigar from the specially designed humidor, embossed with his initials in gold. 'You took some liberties,' he said quietly.

Justin leaned forward. 'I'm sorry?'

William pushed back his chair. He puffed at his cigar then spat out a fragment of tobacco. 'I said, you took liberties. Some of the costs are ridiculously high.'

'You'll find it worth it.' Justin handed William a pen and blank piece of paper. 'Now, can we discuss the original reason for my rebuilding this place?'

William wrinkled his brow. 'We did. I thought I'd cleared that up on my arrival.'

Justin smiled. 'Fine. You're the one who's been made to look the arsehole, so it's your decision. I mean, I've seen you publicly humiliated. If I were you I'd want revenge. But I'm not you, obviously, and it's always been your decision about everything.'

'Revenge?' William shifted uneasily, recalling that late-night conversation all those months ago in the South of France. 'It's been too long now.'

'William, everyone has called you a wanker. The press, your family, everyone. Doesn't that bother you? Even with all your money, you'll never be free of that. The only thing you can do is pay the bastards back, but you're too much of a pussy to do it. I've set it all up for you, worked my butt off.'

'You'll be paid.'

Justin lifted his hands in exasperation. 'Fine, pay me off like Sylvina and I'll walk out of your life. I don't care any more, I just don't want to waste any more of my time on you.'

William sat down, head in his hands, and fell into the trap. 'This grand plan you've conceived . . .'

'I didn't, you did. It was your idea.'

'Refresh my memory.'

Justin's eyes narrowed as he wondered how much to elaborate. He must choose his words carefully.

'Okay, the original plan was for you to become socially accepted again, which partly worked via Sylvina.

You listed the specific names of people who had, to your mind, done the dirty on you. People like—'

'Baron von Garten,' William muttered.

'Exactly. Then everyone on the hit-list would subsequently be invited to join you here on your island, where they would be at your mercy.'

Justin looked for a reaction, but there was none.

'Once here, they would be lulled into a false sense of security, entertained on such a lavish scale that they would relax . . . unaware that you had another motive. Pay-back. You would systematically get every single one of them.'

'Caught in a sexual scandal,' William added quietly.

'Exactly,' Justin said softly, then got up and touched William's shoulder. 'That was what we hatched up. Don't tell me you've forgotten.'

'Of course I hadn't,' William said hoarsely. 'I hadn't forgotten, Justin, but so much has happened, and the Sylvina débâcle turned round to my benefit. Sometimes the press that I despise so much—'

'Makes you look even more of a buffoon,' snapped Justin.

There was that word again. William clenched his hands in anger.

'Go to bed. You think about it tonight. Then if you decide to go with it, we can start things rolling. If not, then I'll be finished here and I'll leave, with no hard feelings.'

Justin strolled out. He might have been discussing something as mundane as cushion fabric, not a complex revenge plot.

William felt as if he had been holding his breath too

long, and let it out. 'Oh, my God,' he whispered. He wondered whether Justin was unbalanced. But it was himself who had sown the seeds of the plan. That night in France he had wanted to make someone pay for what had been done to him. His injuries had still smarted then. But did he still want that? William patted his pockets and removed his wallet. Neatly folded into a small square was the original list he had made out of people whom he believed should pay for what he had been put through. But now that he had just such an opportunity, he found it didn't make him feel good. Instead it disturbed him. He needed to think hard before he made any decisions.

The sound of speedboat engines drew William to the balcony of his room. The night-lights and lanterns illuminated the path all the way to the water's edge creating a carnival feeling. He could see a group of people on the jetty watching the Sunseeker Hawk 34 being tested. Justin was shouting instructions to Sammy at the wheel, and the engine came to life with a sound almost as loud as Concorde. The boat lifted out of the water leaving a foaming wash behind as it disappeared out of sight.

After a moment, the Sunseeker returned with Justin at the wheel. He circled the boat, putting it through various fast turns and surges, laughing and waving to the boys on the jetty. Then he cut the engines, drifted back to the shore and tied it up. He jumped out, then walked away from the jetty, each arm hooked around a boy's shoulder. As they disappeared into the darkness, their disembodied voices and laughter hung in the air.

William wondered where Justin slept. Perhaps he was living in the servants' quarters or in one of the thatched bungalows. He decided to take an evening stroll. Walking through the hallway, he paused and looked up to the ribbed ceiling, then at the paintings and tapestries. The elegant flowers, plants and ferns that hung and draped the stairs and balconies were so thick and voluptuous they might have been growing there for years. He had to admire Justin's artistry, the way he had made the hallway a powerful, but not daunting, centrepiece of the mansion.

'I like this,' he said. He thought again of the Grand Plan as he surveyed the hall. It might just work. He had laid the groundwork during his year with Sylvina and the press had unwittingly made him a social star. He was sure the people on his list would accept his invitation to stay. It was just a matter of deciding when.

William stepped through the massive oak and iron doors, which appeared to be left open at all times, and walked down the white stone steps. He turned back and looked upwards: the night-lights threw gentle beams across the roof of the mansion, illuminating its magical structures. Plants cascaded in tumbling waterfalls of colour, and thousands of lilies, in hanging baskets and ornate pots, gave off a powerful aromatic scent. William had never given a moment's thought to plants or flowers before, but now he touched, smelt and admired them. His pleasure grew as he walked along the main pathway to a smaller, darker lane that Justin had called Secrets Avenue.

William walked for about a quarter of a mile, and calculated that he was heading to the east side of the island towards one of the small coves. As the pathway sloped downwards, he could hear the thunder of the sea.

It will work. They'll be bewitched by the place. He took such a deep breath of fresh air that he felt light-headed. It's even got to me.

The path curved to the right and a white wooden railing with a thick rope marked out the steep slope to the side. The pebbled path was also slotted with thick wooden slabs, each one lower than the next, to create a set of steps down to the beach. The cove was carved out of the white cliffs, discreet lamps and platforms built into the rocks. The sun-loungers and cushions were lined up like soldiers, and tables with white parasols had been positioned to accommodate diners who wished to eat in the shade. Then, to his surprise, William thought he heard Justin's laughter, carried on the wind, then the clink of glasses and a guitar playing softly in the dusk. He stayed in the shadows, scanning the darkness for him.

He spotted Justin lying stark naked on a small wooden jetty that extended into the sea. Sammy was with him, wearing an orange sarong tied loosely around his waist and a crown of flowers around his head. He was smoking a long joint, leaning back with his eyes closed. A beautiful girl with long braided hair entwined with flowers was massaging Justin, while another with red and white beads in her hair was dancing nearby, dressed only in a white chiffon scarf. A small girl was sitting between Justin's legs placing strawberries along his thighs and eating them off him, one after the next. A fourth exotic creature, wearing Justin's white kaftan, was playing the guitar. William watched in awed silence. The scene was like a painting by Gauguin.

He was just about to make his presence known, when the girl eating the strawberries began to eat Justin. For a moment William felt deeply embarrassed, then so shocked he couldn't move. All of Justin's beauties had begun to massage, suck and lick him. But when the girls stripped off their gauzy garments, William was aghast. The figures unintentionally revealed to him were male. William turned and ran away like a schoolboy.

The next morning William had already had breakfast and was sitting by the pool when Justin sauntered towards him. 'Morning,' he said, and flopped down on the sun-lounger next to William. 'I've ordered corn-flakes and every make of cereal you insist on crunching at breakfast. There's also a selection of muesli. Did they leave them out for you this morning?'

'Yes,' William said. He hated muesli: all those nuts and bits got stuck in his bridge.

'So, did you sleep well?' Justin enquired, yawning.

'Yes,' came the crisp reply.

'That's good.' Justin scrutinized William's pink flesh. 'You need some protection cream – there's plenty in your room, plus some self-tanning lotion.' He touched William's thigh. 'Look. You're already burning.' William pulled his legs away. Justin stood up. 'Finish your breakfast while I have a swim,' he said, heading back inside. 'Then we can talk business.'

William tried to stop himself watching Justin stroll away through the double doors.

*

Twenty minutes later, William appeared at the pool, dressed in a dreadful pair of khaki shorts, a white shirt, loafers and a Panama hat. Justin clung to the rail at the side of the pool. 'Going on safari, are we?' he remarked.

William flushed and hitched up his pants in a defensive gesture. 'I need to do some exercise,' he said lamely.

Justin hauled himself out of the pool and placed a dripping arm around William's shoulders. 'There's a well-equipped gym, and one of the boys is a fitness trainer. He'll have you in shape in no time at all.'

'I used to work out regularly,' William muttered, ashamed of his body next to Justin's.

'I can see there's still some muscle tone, so it won't be too much of a strain,' Justin lied. He felt sorry for William, surrounded by beauty but so deeply uncomfortable with himself. He led him through to where a large woman sat flicking through a magazine. 'This is Ruby, Sir William. She's the skin expert.' He turned to her. 'Check his sun lotions. And use some of that self-tan on him.'

'Yes, sir, will do, sir.' Ruby bobbed up. 'Any time you wish, sir.'

Justin smiled at William. 'Before you go outside again, Ruby will see to you. That's an order.' He threw his head back and laughed. 'Now, let's have that talk.'

Settled in the study, William tried to resume his authority. 'I've given this thing a lot of thought, and no matter which way I look at it, it's farcical. I mean, do I really want to invite these people here?'

Justin sighed. 'You'll never get it, will you?' He leaned forward and looked William in the eye. 'It's a scam, William. We're going to pull a scam that exploits the greed and selfishness of all these ghastly people.' He gestured expansively towards the open window. 'Look at the place. It's the nearest you'll find to paradise on the planet. We publish pictures, get a few articles in the press. It'll be easy. "The Most Exclusive Villa in the World. The Most Expensive Villa in the World". They'll all fall for it. They'll be over here and ready for the plucking.'

William slapped his hand down hard on the desk. 'Read my lips. I *do not* want them here. And even if I did agree, and we got everyone here who has made my life hell—'

Justin put his face in his hands, screeching, 'No! No! You've got it wrong. You still don't understand. Let me give you an example.' He sat back again, talking deliberately as though addressing a simpleton. 'Your ex-wife is at the hairdresser's. She picks up a copy of *Hello!* magazine. The page falls open at the headline that has grabbed everyone's attention: "Tycoon's Island Paradise Affordable Only By Mega-Rich". She sees the pictures of the beaches, the rooms, the pool. Then she sees the words: "Exclusive – only multi-millionaires, pop mega-stars, the top fifty wealthiest people on the planet will ever be given the opportunity to see this playground for the world's élite."' William couldn't help but smile as Justin pressed on. 'The pictures and the words will stay in her mind, haunting her, tempting her. What wouldn't she give to be a fly on the wall, just to see the place, *see you*? Until one day, opening her post . . .' Justin mimed a bored woman opening an envelope, then feigned surprise and delight '. . . what should she find but an invitation. A *free* invitation to taste for herself the delights of this paradise on earth.'

'Sorry. Don't buy it.' William shrugged. 'If she knows it's my place, she'd never accept, even if it was free. Besides, I have no desire to have either of my ex-wives set foot on the island.'

'Fine, cross them off your list.'

'I already have. I've crossed them all off. We're not doing it.' With that, William stormed out of the room.

William ate alone at lunch, Justin having taken the boat to pick up some stuff from Tortola. He tucked into a lobster salad followed by a sorbet, and sipped a light sparkling rosé from a small vineyard in California. Afterwards he could hardly keep his eyes open, and decided to take a rest.

Ruby was waiting in his suite. A massage-table covered with white towels was positioned in the centre of the room, an array of oils and lotions laid out on the table. William just wanted to crash out, but Ruby assured him he would sleep even better after a massage. After a quick shower he lay face down on the table. The oils were cool against his hot skin, and Ruby's touch gentle and soothing. First she massaged him, then applied an astringent lotion to remove the residue of oil from his back. She removed the small towel from his waist, and continued to massage him, gently easing the tension from his muscles. Then she rolled him over, and started to masturbate him. When he came she wiped away his semen and continued the massage. William drifted into a deep sleep, unaware of the slices of iced cucumber laid on his eyelids, while Ruby performed a delicate cleansing facial.

At eight Dahlia, the housekeeper, delivered a message that Justin was held up and would not be returning till the following morning. William felt cross. He wanted company that evening, conversation, perhaps even a game of backgammon. He didn't feel like eating alone again. He looked at the housekeeper. 'Dahlia, will you join me?' he asked bluntly.

'I would be delighted,' she said courteously, and took his order for dinner.

William looked at Dahlia and wished he'd changed into a suit. Justin referred to her as Mrs Danvers whenever they discussed her. She was about thirty and exceptionally tall with a taut, muscular figure and waist-length hair combed back from her face and tied in a tight braid. 'There's nothing in the mansion that Mrs Danvers doesn't monitor,' Justin had told him. 'She rules with a rod of iron.'

William couldn't see it. She stood before him in an elegant dark turquoise dress, slit to her thigh, which reminded him of the one Sylvina had worn the night he had met her in France.

They ate together by candlelight. It was a sumptuous dinner, and they conversed easily, discussing wines, restaurants and favourite dishes. William told her about his planned weight-loss and she promised to arrange a low-calorie eating-plan so delicious he would never know it was a diet. William said he liked the idea of her controlling his food intake, and that was when the *doubles-entendres* started. He enjoyed Dahlia's titillating questions about how he liked to be controlled, and when she asked if he was too strong-minded ever to release himself into another's hands, he chuckled and said that he'd never had the opportunity to find out. Dahlia leaned across the table, drew his face towards hers and kissed his lips. She released him and sat back. 'You have the opportunity now, sir.'

Justin was eating a large slice of watermelon, his feet on the desk in William's study, watching the security monitors. He couldn't help but shake his head in admiration. Dahlia was brilliant. He flicked on a second monitor, which showed William being led up the stairs like a puppy by her. He flicked on a third monitor, which showed William's empty suite, then Dahlia and William entering.

Justin reached for the phone and dialled an internal number. 'Ruby,' he said quietly. 'Wake up, Ruby, and get ready. She's cracked it.' He giggled down the line. 'And even before coffee was served.'

'Okay,' came the soft reply, and the phone went dead.

In her small but immaculate room in the north servants' wing, Ruby selected oils, masks, handcuffs, a leather-thonged whip and various other items she knew Dahlia sometimes used. She took her time, humming tunelessly as she placed them in a wide basket. She was still dressed in her white masseuse's overall and white sneakers, naked underneath.

Meanwhile Justin slotted a tape into the video-recorder and clicked it on. He waited until he was sure the machine was recording then returned to the security monitor where Dahlia sat astride William's naked body, his face blindfolded with iced cloths.

Now Ruby entered the room, unheard and unseen by William. Justin checked the headphones to ensure that the microphone was picking up the sound. William might have forgotten the initial reason for the island's redevelopment, but Justin hadn't. He had worked towards it with relish and the length of time taken just made this moment even sweeter. Surely William wouldn't say no to the plan after he'd seen the video of this! When the show was over, Justin would have earned enough money never to have to work again. He and Laura would live the life they had dreamed of. He had always believed that everything he did was for his beloved Laura. Just thinking of her, saying her name, made his body prickle. He was missing her, and couldn't wait to see her again and tell her that the game was moving into action. All they needed were the players. They would arrive and be treated like royalty, unaware that cameras were filming every second of their intimate moments. Justin had arranged for these intimacies to go well beyond the boundaries of flirtation: the guests would be seduced by the luxurious surroundings, and drawn into a false sense of security, just like William.

The staff were not ordinary domestics, far from it. They were giving William a taste of their real calling in life and they had no limits. The victims would happily pay a fortune to keep out of the press. It would, Justin mused to himself, be a lucrative blackmail weapon. William *has* to agree. There were endless possibilities, and soon Laura would become a major player.

Justin closed his eyes and remembered Laura standing up on the high rocks near their villa in the South of France. She had been holding what appeared to be a perfectly almond-shaped piece of green glass. She had laughed softly, that husky, whispering laugh. He had never heard such a sound on anyone else's lips, and as always it touched him. He could see her in his mind as clearly as if she was standing next to him. He remembered the way she held up the glass to the light, transparent, delicate and frighteningly fragile.

'I have a frozen piece of the sea, Justin,' she cooed. 'Look, doesn't it remind you of me?' Then she turned away from him and that sweet, delicate laugh he loved so dearly was swept away with the wind and swallowed up by the sea below. She held the glass in the palm of her hand. The light glittering off it made it appear like a green eye. 'You look at it and it seems smooth,' she whispered, stroking it. Then she turned it over, drew one slender finger across it and blood came to the surface. It formed a single droplet, which she pressed against Justin's lips, then licked off the residue herself.

'Don't break your promise, Justin, we have a right to draw blood. We have waited so long. We need to make it happen, and make it happen soon.' Justin was sure that, after this evening, at long last he had in his grasp the one person they wanted to bleed to death.

# CHAPTER 9

IT WAS after eleven when William finished his breakfast. He had been apprehensive about seeing Dahlia, but when he went into the kitchens she hardly acknowledged his presence. She had been reprimanding a delivery service about certain supplies that were due to be collected from the mainland. She behaved as if the previous evening's events had not occurred. 'Excuse me, Sir William,' she said, cupping the receiver in her hand, 'I won't be a moment. The fruit I ordered hasn't arrived.'

He gave her a rueful smile, and asked if Justin was back. At that moment the man himself breezed in. 'You want a spin in the Sunseeker?' he asked.

William followed him. Dahlia was still immersed in her phone call.

Sammy was waiting with the boat already uncovered and the engines ticking. William and Justin climbed aboard as Dahlia ran towards them, out of breath. 'Can you pick up the groceries, Justin? They'll be ready for collection.'

'Fine,' Justin yelled as he gave the signal for Sammy to move off.

William staggered backwards as the boat surged forward. Justin took off his sunglasses, and slipped them into his pocket. 'I'd remove your hat and shades. The wind'll whip them off. We're going to open her up today. She can do sixty-eight knots, you know.'

William lowered himself deeper into one of the leather seats and did as Justin advised. The boat's engines were so loud it made conversation impossible, but Justin tried nevertheless, shouting for William to look at the small navigational computer by the wheel, and then at all the various dials and speedometers. The wind billowed his shirt and ruffled his hair. Justin laughed with the sheer exhilaration of speed, then turned to William. 'You want to take the wheel?' he shouted.

'Better not,' William bellowed, then changed his mind. 'Okay, show me what to do.'

He made his way to Sammy's side, where the force of the wind was eased by the shelter of the windscreen. Justin stood right behind him, and at first he helped him steer, shouting instructions into William's ear.

William felt like a schoolboy, bellowing at the top of his voice, 'This is marvellous. *I love it.*'

Justin took over the wheel as they came in to dock at Wickam's Cay on Tortola. The marina was crammed with yachts and cruisers of all shapes and sizes. Navigating a path between the buoys and moored boats, he pulled in as close to the delivery warehouses as he could get. As he manoeuvred into the marked collection zone, Sammy jumped out to catch the mooring ropes.

He and Justin tied up the boat and started off towards the warehouses. Turning back to check that William was following, Justin saw him staring into space. 'William!' he called. 'Do you want to meet us up at the Harbour Bar? We'll be about an hour.'

'Oh, right, fine, see you there.'

William watched them for a moment, then patted his head. The sun was burning his scalp so he climbed back into the boat and retrieved his crushed Panama.

The Harbour Bar was a crude place with a straw roof and one long wooden counter with rows of bottles stacked on shelves behind it. An old-fashioned Coke dispenser stood on one side next to an ice-maker. On the other was a row of pinball machines. Formica-topped tables spilled out on to a small, shaded veranda. The bar regularly caught fire, so the walls were brown and discoloured; paint peeled from the doors, which were never closed. At night fairy-lights decorated the railings, curling round the posts that held up the roof. There was no air-conditioning, but two large fans spun in a slow, hypnotic cycle, more effectively whipping up dust than circulating cool air. The PA blasted out home-made tape recordings of local bands, mixed with a variety of pop, rock and disco. The mindlessness of the continual music was all part of the scene at the Harbour Bar, which was one of the main meeting places for anyone using the harbour.

Other more sophisticated bars and hotels, with elegant palm-filled air-conditioned saloons and waiters stood further along the marina. But none did the thriving business of the Harbour Bar, which was constantly packed. At night, the smell of ganja was strong and local bands played live. A small platform had been built just outside so that people could dance. Now it was peak season and the bar was heaving. White girls on holiday flirted with young black guys who hit on them for money. The local hookers led a carefree existence, their eyes roaming for rich pickings as they sat drinking Coke at the bar. William attracted no more than a perfunctory gaze before they returned to their conversations while he ordered a lager and lime. He felt hot and uncomfortable, his shorts chafing his thighs, and he could feel mosquito bites erupting. By the time Justin strolled up the steps of the bar's veranda, he had consumed two more lagers.

'Get you another?' Justin called, but he shook his head and watched as Justin sauntered to the bar. The hookers slapped his hand and the barman was already fixing him a mixture of fresh orange and lemon juice with crushed ice. Justin stopped at two other tables, chatting and laughing, before he joined William. 'We're all stocked up. We can leave any time.'

William's shirt was dripping with sweat and he took himself off to the shack at the back of the bar, which served as a lavatory. He splashed tepid water from a chipped basin over his face, but it didn't cool him. He was looking forward to getting back into the boat for the air. His chest felt constricted and he could hardly breathe.

He and Justin walked the short distance to where the boat was moored at the harbour, passing charter yachts and gin palaces. One yacht, in the most prominent position with a wide wooden gangplank, had numerous white-T-shirted crew setting out a dining area under a canopy.

More crew were carrying on crates of fruit and drinks

past the four people at the foot of the gangplank. The women wore skimpy, buttock-revealing shorts and bikini tops, their bronzed bodies gleaming. A blonde had a white baseball cap pulled low over her eyes, the other wore a wide-brimmed straw hat with a scarf knotted around the rim, flowing down her tanned back, over her sarong and matching bikini top. William identified them as English. One of the men, in a moth-eaten straw hat, was lighting a cigar. William recognized him instantly. Henry, Lord Bellingham was probably the same age as William, but looked at least fifteen years younger. The woven embroidered bracelet on his wrist gave him a hint of the hippie.

Bellingham oozed social confidence. He was the type of man who immediately made William feel inferior, the type that William had once wanted to emulate. Instead of succeeding, though, he had become the butt of their jibes. The Bellinghams of this world were involved in far worse scandals than poor William ever had been, but they never came to light: friends in the right places made sure of that.

'Do you know Sir William, Lord Bellingham?' Justin asked casually, as William joined them.

Bellingham gave him no more than a cursory glance. 'I believe so.' He turned away. 'Annabella, darling, we should make moves,' he said. He gave William another glance as he strode up the gangplank.

Justin turned to the women. 'Lady Annabella Bellingham and Countess Maria de Coveney, Sir William Benedict.'

They gave aloof smiles and Lady Annabella shook William's hand, which was hot and wet. She withdrew hers quickly. 'Do be on time,' she barked to Justin. 'We've got so much security to deal with – it's a real headache.'

Justin bowed over her hand and kissed it. She laughed and tapped his cheek. 'Oh, you sexy boy.'

She started up the gangplank. The Countess, at least, acknowledged William, before following. Now the second man shook Justin's hand before turning to William. 'I'm Gabriel, Frederick Capri's brother. I believe you know him?'

William nodded. He couldn't think of anything to say as he'd only met him fleetingly at the villa in France. 'Justin, I'll see you on the boat,' he said flatly, and walked away.

As he left the group, there was a burst of laughter behind him. William blushed angrily.

It was another ten minutes before Justin joined him.

'Let's go!' he said, hurling the ropes to Sammy and jumping aboard. He patted William's knee. 'You seem a bit out of sorts,' he said kindly.

'I'm bloody hot and just want to get the hell out of here.'

Justin gestured to Sammy, who opened up the engines and they started to move out, weaving their way between the moorings and passing the Bellingham yacht. There were now eight people sitting on it under the canopy, laughing and drinking. One young boy with blond hair was sitting with his legs over the side. He waved to Justin.

'So pretty, isn't he?' Justin mused. 'That's Oliver Bellingham. He's not allowed off the boat – just been kicked out of school for dealing drugs. The other guests on board—'

'I'm not interested,' said William curtly, refusing to look towards the group, who were now all watching the powerboat draw away.

Justin settled into the seat next to Sammy. 'Open her up! Jog a martini out of Annabella's hand!' The engines throbbed, all six kicked in, the bow lifted out of the water and the boat sped out of the harbour.

By the time they reached the island William was frozen stiff. It took an hour and a half, and the pounding of the engines had given him a throbbing headache. By the time they got there, William was shivering. An hour later he had a temperature of a hundred and two.

Dahlia took great care of him. She arranged for trays of tasty food, tea, lemon drinks and iced fruit to be brought up to his room. Some time later Justin caught her as she carried down a tray. 'What the fuck is wrong with him?' he asked.

'Heatstroke, but he thinks it's malaria. His temperature is quite high.'

'How long is he going to be up there?'

'Maybe a day or so. He's not eating too well, and he's sleeping a lot. He'll be fine.'

'I bloody hope so.'

William remained in bed for three days. His linen was changed and he was washed and shaved like an invalid. He was rather tickled when he discovered he had lost fifteen pounds.

On the fourth day, at William's request, Justin arranged for Kurt to give him a gentle workout in the gym. After three gym sessions, the loss of fifteen pounds, daily massage and three more self-tanning treatments, William began to feel rejuvenated. He discussed his diet with Dahlia, and eventually sent a message to Justin that he would like to have lunch with him. It consisted of salad, chicken breast, an array of apple, carrot and vegetable juices and a row of vitamin pills.

'My! We're on a health regime, I see,' said Justin, as he sat down.

'You can order anything you want,' William said, picking at his chicken. 'I just want to lose at least another ten pounds. Kurt's getting me into shape.'

'Well, that's wonderful.' Justin could just about manage some enthusiasm.

'How do you want to be paid?' William was pouring more apple juice.

'I'm sorry?' Justin leaned forward.

'Well, you can have a cheque, but it's quite a sum, and for tax reasons I wondered if you had some offshore bank account. If you like, I can set one up for you.'

'Cheque,' Justin said quickly, then frowned. Maybe he should have a think about his tax situation. He rarely, if ever, paid any. The truth was that what came in went directly out again.

'Cheque it is, but it might be useful to have a word with my accountant. It's up to you.'

Justin could hardly believe it: he was paying him off, getting rid of him. He had to get William to agree to the plan, and fast.

'You're very quiet,' William said, smiling.

'Just thinking about what you said. I've never been all that good with money, you know. If I have it I spend it. But this is quite a tidy sum.'

'Well deserved, though.' William was smiling again. Justin found this new, cheerful William a little unnerving. 'Have to say, I had some doubts . . . I mean, more than doubts. After all, you overspent the original budget by four million, and to be honest I was none too pleased. But the more I've taken in your work, the more I see it was necessary. I have never, until now, had any interest in any of my homes, but this one I like.'

'We aim to please.' Justin helped himself to salad.

'I wanted you to help me out on another little area,' William said, 'if you have the time, that is.' He gestured down at himself. 'I see how dreadful I look. How deadly my taste has been.' He looked up at Justin. 'I know it's silly, but I want to wear clothes that make me feel good. When I shopped with Sylvina, she made me buy what other people thought was good – you know what I mean? Like my ex-wives – they togged me out too and, to be honest, I want a . . .' he gave a boyish shrug '. . . younger look.'

'We can get you some local summer gear. You don't want anything too . . .'

'Safari?' William said, and sniggered.

By mid-afternoon, the gardeners and the boat-boys had been handed plastic bags filled with discarded clothes to burn. Needless to say, they were thrilled, knowing they could resell them on Tortola, or even across the strait on Puerto Rico.

While William went for a workout in the gym with Kurt, Justin started sorting out a costume for the Bellinghams' summer dance. The British loved dressing up – the more outlandishly the better. It was as if they were trying to revert to childhood. He'd been working away for an hour when there was a knock at the door.

It was William. 'I was wondering whether you wanted to watch some videos with me tonight?'

'Any other time,' Justin said, wrapping some pale blue silk around his fist and pulling it into a shape. 'I'm going over to the Bellinghams' and I've got to fathom out some kind of costume.' He plonked the turban on his head.

'You were invited?' William said, jealous.

'Yes. The son invited me, Oliver. They invite a select mob and dress up. Prizes and games. Awful, really. But quite good for me, you know, drumming up business.'

He was lying. He never used social events to ply his trade.

'They didn't ask me,' William said, disgruntled.

Justin spun round and winked. 'Come with me?' he said, holding up a bolt of pink shot silk and silver-threaded organza.

'But they know who I am. It would be hell.' William stood watching Justin wafting blue and pink dyed ostrich plumes, ready to pin them to the turban.

'Far too unacceptable for their sort,' Justin lisped, as he pranced in front of a long mirror. 'We could have some fun together.' He wafted the plume at William. 'Come as my secret partner. Everyone wears masks. Nobody need know who you are.'

William leaped back. 'No bloody way! You're not getting me done up like one of those boys.'

Justin gave a lascivious grin. 'I doubt, William dearest, that anyone could mistake you for one of my little friends.' He swished a swathe of gold lamé into the air, and draped it over William. 'How about if I dress you up as King Tut, and I'll be your servant?'

'No way!' William had never been to a fancy-dress do, even as a child. He wasn't about to make a fool of himself now.

Two hours later, he was dressed in a flowing gold lamé kaftan, with a matching turban and four huge white plumes pinned to it with a gold brooch. Justin was tinting William's face with burnt cork, mixed with some boot polish. It took ages to dry, but gradually his face became bronzed, his lips were pinked, and his eyelashes darkened with mascara.

'Take a look,' Justin said, stepping back to admire his work.

'I don't know about this,' William said, secretly enjoying himself. Justin pushed bracelets and rings onto his stained brown hands, and hung big gold hoops from his ears. William reviewed himself in the mirror, while Justin finished his own costume. When they stood side by side they looked fabulous, and when Justin sprayed a heavy perfume over them, William started to get quite excited.

'I've never gatecrashed anything, you know,' he said, preening.

'Tonight's the night, then! Come along, Your Majesty, let's knock 'em dead.'


It was after ten when Justin and William descended to the jetty where the cruiser stood ready to transport them to the Bellinghams' estate. Four boat-boys, in turbans and sarongs, carried large fans to welcome the pair aboard. Fairy-lights were strung from stern to bow. Music blasted out of the stereo as the cruiser pulled out to sea. In the cabin, buckets of champagne and plates of caviar were laid out, where William, now in the spirit of the evening, sat relaxing on silk cushions.

The Bellinghams' jetty was ablaze with lights, flickering torches and flowers. William and Justin could hear the band as they approached. The sea was calm. Rows of bobbing yachts and cruisers were moored by servants. There were loud cheers as the King and his servant disembarked. William surveyed the array of costumes from behind his disguise. There were women dressed as cats, trapeze artists, semi-naked servant girls, Tarzans and Janes in skimpy strips of leopardskin, pirates and princes in multi-coloured lamé.

The heavy smell of incense and marijuana filled the billowing marquee, and tables were laden with fruit, lobsters and exotic dishes. Butlers in masks and loincloths carried around trays of elaborate cocktails laced with vodka, gin or rum. The centrepiece was a champagne fountain surrounded by ice sculptures.

As William surveyed the room, he recognized Meryl Delaware, draped over a dark-skinned boy who appeared to be no more than twenty. There were pop stars, models and actors whose faces he vaguely knew. Sections of the marquee were cordoned off by flowing drapes. William peeped behind them. Couples were copulating on low couches, others snorting from bowls of cocaine. In another section of the marquee sat a fortune-teller – average party material, thought William, except that she was stark naked apart from a glittering G-string and a long blonde wig that tumbled over her breasts. Nearby, leather-masked men with leather-studded cocks strapped to their legs, strutted between women dressed in PVC corsets, wielding whips. Other men were crawling on all fours licking the women's black patent stilettos.

'And those bastards whipped up all that shit about me!' said William to Justin.

'Over a couple of bloody visits from call-girls.'

No one asked who William was, and after about half an hour he started to relax, enjoying his anonymity. He moved from one group to another until he stumbled across Lord Bellingham. Sitting cross-legged on a large cushion, with a backgammon board in front of him and four other people around him, he was wearing a kaftan and turban and smoking a large cigar. It was obvious to William that he was stoned. William watched him for a moment, then moved back, passing two women in a passionate, semi-naked embrace on the grass. He felt himself flush under his cork.

'I want to slide under your robes, Your Majesty.' A woman wearing nothing but a PVC loincloth stood at his side and tried to slither under his gold kaftan. William sprang back, clutching the cloth around him. 'No, thank you,' he stuttered, and scurried away.

William went in search of Justin. The last time he had seen him he was heading out of the tent with Bellingham's son, Oliver, who was so drunk he could hardly stand. William wandered about, stopping to watch the cabaret of exotic dancers, then the local rock star, who jumped up on stage to sing with the band. Those with enough energy were still dancing, but most were scattered around in groups, talking and giggling as the drugs kicked in. Cocaine bowls were constantly topped up and there was an endless supply of thick joints.

Eventually, drunk and exhausted, William hitched up

his kaftan and sat on a low couch beneath a clutch of palm trees away from the main action. His head was throbbing so violently he couldn't raise it more than a fraction and when he did, he felt nauseous.

'Pull your frock down, old boy.' It was Justin. 'Look I've got something to do, then I'll be back.'

'Have they spiked the drinks?' William asked, squinting up at Justin.

'Probably.'

'Dear God, I feel terrible. You'll have to help me back to the boat.'

'Just stay here, I won't be long.'

The party was winding down. William lay immobile, hoping to ease his aching head. Two women had sat down on a lounger on the other side of the palm trees, unaware of his presence.

'Ghastly man,' one said to the other. William could hear the clink of glass.

'The Bellinghams saw him on the quay the other day with that boy Justin.'

They were talking about him! William lay still, listening. Bellingham and his cronies joined them.

'The stupid bugger got hammered because he was so desperate to be accepted. It always happens with his kind – they get caught with their pants around their ankles.'

One disembodied voice recalled William's engagement to the Countess Lubrinsky. This created hoots of laughter and a few lurid anecdotes about Sylvina's past. Then William heard a voice he recognized. It was the hideous Meryl Delaware, desperate to ingratiate herself with Bellingham. She claimed she had it on good authority that William had paid Countess Lubrinsky to broadcast their engagement in the hope that he would be accepted by the Royal Family. But the closest he had got to them was walking past the Royal Enclosure at Ascot. 'He's more than pitiful,' said Meryl. 'He's a laughing stock.'

'Paying a trashy countess to say she loved him and was prepared to marry him! He's pathetic.'

Suddenly, a voice William didn't recognize entered the conversation. 'You're not still discussing that awful man. Just keep the money-to-burn lowlife at arm's length. I suspect he's a poofter like his crony, that sicko Maynard.'

Suddenly there were shouts that the fireworks were due to start and the group heaved their tired bodies towards the quay side without glancing back at the prone figure a few feet away from them. Bellingham, however, had recognized William. Before he left he turned and said, 'That'll teach you to gatecrash, you jumped-up parvenu.'

A few seconds later Justin was back. He helped William along the harbour to the boat. William felt the screeching rockets and fizzing fireworks reverberating in his head, smashing through his thoughts: Pathetic! Pitiful! A buffoon!


At noon the next day, William woke up with the worst hangover he had ever experienced. He had breakfast alone. Just after two, when paracetamol had eased the throbbing between his ears and ice packs had soothed his swollen eyes, he went to Justin's bungalow on the lower path beneath the main house. There was no sign of him and, worse, William was shocked to see a line of packed suitcases on the bed and wardrobes and drawers emptied. With a sinking feeling in the pit of his stomach, he went to find him. He discovered Justin down by the jetty.

'Afternoon,' Justin said brightly. 'I'd given up on seeing you today, but I'm glad I have as I didn't want to leave without saying goodbye.'

'You're going?' William said.

'Yes. I need to get back to France. I'm on my way to Paris.'

William pursed his lips. He wasn't sure how to say it, or even what he wanted to say. He just knew that he didn't want Justin to go.

'You feeling all right?' Justin asked.

'No, I'm not. Come up to the house, have a drink with me.'

Justin glanced at his wristwatch. 'I really wanted to get the late tide.'

'I would like to talk to you,' William said.

Justin had expected this to happen.


William was sitting at his desk when Justin came in. 'What about my makeover?' he said petulantly.

'Well, I've left you a list of designers; suggested who you should contact. You can hire people to do this kind of thing, you know.'

'I want you,' William said.

Justin sighed. 'Well, that's all very well, but I have a living to make and I have things to do. Especially high on the agenda is seeing my sister.'

'If it's money you want you can have it.'

'Look, if someone fucks me over I fuck them back. You can't let people get away with humiliating you. I've prepared everything here for you to pay the bastards back. But I'm tired of your indecision. Either you want revenge or you don't.'

Justin left the room and went to the control room. The time was perfect now, he was sure of it.

William walked in as he was putting a tape into the VCR.

'William, take a look at this. You never even knew it was happening, but think what I could do with it.' William stood, aghast, watching the video of himself with Dahlia and Ruby, tied to the bed, being oiled and massaged, moaning with pleasure.

'Shocked?' Justin asked, smiling. 'You ever been taken that far before?' He was enjoying himself.

'No,' William said hoarsely. 'Did you drug me?'

'You did that all under your own steam! Impressive, wouldn't you say?'

'It's disgusting.'

Justin laughed gleefully. 'Rubbish, it was done in the privacy of your own bedroom.' He stopped the tape. 'Stop whipping yourself with guilt, Willy-boy. Like I said, get even. You've got all the trappings right here on Island Exotics. All you need is your guest-list – then we can line 'em up and shoot 'em down. One by one.'

Justin waited. Had he overplayed his hand?

'No more prevarication, Justin, I'll do it. But I need you to tell me what to do.'

Which, of course, was exactly what Justin had planned. 'Fine, and since you seem so concerned that your "guests" won't show if they know *you're* their host, I think there's no need to make your ownership of the island public. You could be some mysterious tycoon.'

'"Some mysterious tycoon." You love to play games, don't you, Justin?'

William remained silent for a long time.

'Tell me, what makes *you* so eager to play out this charade?' William asked eventually, his eyes sharp as flints. 'What's in this for you?'

Justin licked his lips, averting his eyes. His mind raced. He played his hand to perfection.

'Andrew Maynard. I lost a friend and it hurt to see him vilified and abused. That's why I care about you. I knew what you meant to him.'

'I think I meant to him the same thing I mean to you. A meal ticket,' William said.

'Wrong on two counts. I've already earned enough from you, and you'll no doubt reward me for assisting you in getting some satisfaction. Also, Andrew only spoke of you with admiration and respect.'

'Mmm,' William said.

'Make them eat shit like you were forced to. Don't back down or you'll regret it till the day you die. And then, when it's over, you can settle down to enjoy your life on the most exclusive private island known to man, once again renowned as the charming, debonair tycoon, Sir William Benedict.'

William contemplated the idea for a moment, then stretched out his hand. 'Very well, we'll have a go at it. I must be mad, but yes, why not? You're on. Let's get the bastards. Just so long as you know I'm the ring-master.'

'Absolutely. It's your trap, William, not mine. I'll

just do whatever you say . . . I have a few conditions, though,' he said softly.

William gestured for him to continue.

'I think we should get Laura here.'

'Why?'

'Well, you may need her. She's very beautiful. I guarantee no man could refuse Laura.'

'Would she agree?' William asked.

'She might. It's up to you. I think you need a hostess – you know, to welcome everyone . . .'

William nodded.

'No point in her coming here directly – the season's almost over and we don't want to rush into anything. We must have a perfect time of year: Christmas is the best time in the Caribbean.'

'God, that's a while away,' William said, sighing.

'Well, we're not quite ready yet. We've a few finishing touches to make – decoration, press releases . . . and Laura will need to be primed.'

'I'll come to Paris with you.' William said.

'That's a good idea. While we're there I'll start the press frenzy,' said Justin, 'while you think hard about who you want on that list. That should be fun.' He paused. 'Talking of press, I've been looking at your little problem. I think I have identified your main *agent provocateur*. One group of publications seems to have led the way in attacking you: News Syndicate International. It so happens that those papers and magazines are all owned by Humphrey Matlock. He's still on the list, isn't he?'

William nodded, his lips tight. 'Yes, well, he was. I got invited to his place for some charity fête, but I never bothered to go.' He sighed. 'Truth was, the Sylvina thing blew it all up in my face again and I couldn't face anyone.'

'So he should be a priority.' Justin stared at William, who was now deep in thought. He could be so irritating. 'Hear what I said?'

William nodded. He was listening, but his thoughts were miles away as he calculated how much money Matlock must have made out of his misery. 'Yes, he's top of my list,' he said softly.

# CHAPTER 10

WILLIAM AND Justin installed themselves in adjoining suites at the Ritz in Paris. From there, the two made sojourns to boutiques and back-street stores, William following his style instructor like a lamb.

His diet and fitness regime began next day with an early-morning swim, then running up and down the shallow end until his legs felt like jelly. Next they went into the gym. They did weights one day, stretching and abdominal exercises the next. For the first six days William ate a soup concocted by the hotel chef to Justin's specific instructions. It had been originally conceived for heart patients awaiting surgery, to enable them to lose weight quickly but safely.

William lost weight rapidly. He felt fitter and more energetic than he had in years. Daily massages and sun-bed treatments were interspersed with shopping expeditions, and William enjoyed watching his size drop. His excitement was contagious – even Justin had to admire his protégé's determination.

Ten days after they had left the island, Justin and William were having their usual early-morning juice and fruit while reading the English newspapers. Justin noticed an article in *The Times* and muttered something to himself. Then he said nonchalantly, 'Bellingham's son died. His funeral is today.'

William reached over and peered at the article.

'OD'd on the night of the party,' Justin went on, spooning strawberries into his mouth.

William was shocked. 'I'm sorry. How do you know that? It doesn't say so here.'

'He was found dead in the grounds after the party,' Justin said. 'He was a drug-addict, and a raving queen.'

He tried to change the subject to the day's itinerary, but William said, 'Curious that not a breath of scandal has touched Bellingham over this. Can you imagine if it had been my son? It would have been all over the—'

'Come on,' said Justin, glancing at his watch. 'No point in dwelling on the past. We've got to make a move.'

'Where are we going?' William said truculently.

'To get your hair cut.'

'My hair?' Instinctively he stroked it. 'It's looking good. I've never worn it this long before. What's the matter with it?'

'Pass,' said Justin, as he got up and left the room.

William caught up with him. 'It's just, well, I don't know if you'd noticed, but I've got a bald patch at the back.'

'No, really?'

'Yes, I have. Don't you think this sort of covers it a bit?'

Justin grinned. 'When you're swimming, the water drags your hair forwards and all you can see is that bald spot. So don't hide it. It makes you seem vulnerable when you don't need to be.'

'You're not going to make me wear a rug, are you?' William stuttered.

Justin laughed at the thought. 'We'll see what Louis has to say. Trust me.'

Arriving at the salon, William was not convinced that he should trust his precious locks to Louis, who was wearing one of the worst wigs he had ever seen.

Louis began to cut his hair at an alarming pace. When he reached for the clippers William froze. Finally, with mock-bravado, Louis swept off William's cape, stepped back and said, '*Voilà!*'

William inspected his cropped head. He liked his drastic new look. Stubble short and bleached blond from the sun, the haircut said: 'I don't give a shit!' and to a man who always had, it was just what he needed.

That evening William was going to join Justin in the dining-room. It was the seventh day of his diet, and he could eat as much meat as he wanted. He planned to order three fillet steaks with spinach and green salad. He was wearing a pale blue suit, a white silk shirt with a high collar and no tie. He was looking good, but at the door to the restaurant he was stopped by the *maître d'*.

'You must wear a tie in here,' Monsieur,' he snapped.

'Are you telling me I can't eat here? I'm paying for two bloody suites. You should let me in in my underwear!'

The *maître d'* shrugged in his Gallic way. William was just about to demand a table when his elbow was gripped from behind. 'Stop being such a crass, English yob,' Justin said. 'Rules are rules. Forget it, life's too short.'

They ate in a small bistro, not far from the hotel. William remained in a bad mood but then, to Justin's surprise, he suddenly said, 'That bastard Matlock. The more I think about him, the more angry I feel. I've thought about it a lot. It was really as if he had some personal grudge against me, as if the man was hell-bent on destroying me. The other papers just followed his lead. But then he invited me to that garden fête, albeit courtesy of his wife.'

'So what? You were invited, weren't you?'

'Via his *wife*. I asked Michael to check it out for me. I think Matlock's got it in for me because of his wife, Angela.'

'Do you know her?'

'She used to be my secretary.'

'Your secretary?' Justin asked, his jaw open.

'Well, the name is the same. I've not seen her for years. I had a bit of a scene with her.'

He signalled for the bill. This was a different William. He was obviously angry, but there was a steely quality to him that Justin had not witnessed before.

'I intend to find out, and if it is Angela, I want her on the island too. We leave tomorrow.'


They took the Eurostar to London to make preparations and for William to check his business affairs. When Michael saw the new-look William, his jaw dropped. 'Good heavens, you look—' he stuttered.

'Yes?' William said gleefully.

'Like a different person, sir.'

'Thank you Michael. Did you check out Matlock's wife for me?'

'She's the same Angela Nicholls who used to work for you. They have a son, James. He's at Eton and—'

William wafted his hand – he didn't want to hear any more. Could Angela *really* have been behind the onslaught to which her husband's papers had subjected him? If so, she would pay for it. Returning to his study, he couldn't help smiling to himself.

The two men stayed in London just three days while William attended numerous quickly arranged board meetings. His games company had been accused of plagiarism by a German toy manufacturer: William's company had ripped off their cat-and-mouse mechanical toy, they said.

'It's a fox and hens, nothing *like* a cat and mouse! Refuse to back down. We'll counter-sue if necessary. Did you check out the manufacturers as I asked? Who are they, anyway?'

His team passed him a detailed dossier. To William's fury, he saw that the action had been taken against him by the factory he had attempted to acquire from Baron von Garten, which was now owned by William's biggest competitor. The team had determined that the original cat-and-mouse product had been designed by one of William's former employees, who had been headhunted by the rival firm, who in their turn had illegally registered the toy's patent in their name: it had already existed when the designer worked for William, which could be proved because William owned the original designs. He'd sue and he knew he would win. And he would get another stab at the Baron, who was a shareholder in the company and had paid a fortune to market the toy. William was buzzing with energy at the thought of the battle ahead.

\*

Over a breakfast meeting, William showed his lawyers the drawings and proposals the Germans had used for their own gain; they had used the scandal that had erupted around William to escape their agreement to sell on a contractual nicety. Baron von Garten had reneged on the deal, retained William's goodwill down-payment, then gone on to sell to his closest competitors. Since Geffin's Toys had opened they had made vast profits and all their toys would be under review: William was sure it wasn't just one item they had ripped off. His lawyers gained the right to assess all the present Geffin's Toys on the market and to compare them with any from William's design departments.

William's researchers then discovered that Baron von Garten owned rather more than a 'small' portion of the business; he had fifty per cent. This discovery pleased William even more because, by retaining a fifty per cent shareholding in Geffin's, the Baron had opened himself up to being liable for all the legal costs and fines involved in actions brought against them for plagiarism. William was going to come down hard and heavy on 'Geffin's Toys'.

William could not keep the smile off his face as he gave orders for his legal team to sue the backside off Geffin's. They were to keep him informed of every move, even though he would not be staying in London. The new Sir William was like a hurricane, so it was with some relief that his London staff saw him depart.

William and Justin boarded his private jet for Nice. Justin had finished preparing a press-pack for the 'Billionaire's Paradise Island Home' and delivering copies to the most prestigious and influential magazines: *Country Life*, *Tatler*, *Vogue* and *Hello!*. Like conspiratorial teenagers, they sat side by side on the plane, reviewing William's invitation hit-list.

'My ex-wife Katherine, and her cousin Cedric. I hate that bastard, he's always ripped me off. Humphrey Matlock and his dear wife, Angela.'

'Who are all these people?' Justin queried.

'The journalists,' William said.

'For God's sake, you have the organ-grinder, Matlock. You don't need his monkeys. Cross them off.'

'You're sure he and his family will be easy to get over there?'

'Leave that to me,' Justin said softly. Then he went to the lavatory. He needed to be alone: he could hardly contain his excitement.

His hand stroked the worn old wallet in the breast pocket of his jacket. It had belonged to his father, the monogram faded now with years of use. It rarely contained folded notes – Justin preferred to stash those in the back pocket of his jeans. It held something more precious than money: a newspaper article, folded over and over, the creases brown with age. He eased it out and opened it. He knew every line, every word by heart, but this was the first time he had read it with a smile on his face.

'Gotcha!' he hissed. 'Humphrey fucking Matlock! Gotcha!'

# CHAPTER 11

THE VILLA was hidden in darkness, but the car headlights lit the main veranda. Justin jumped out and ran inside, leaving William and the driver to remove the suitcases from the boot. The lights came on in the gardens, throwing the villa into focus, and the driver stood open-mouthed as the magical garden came to life with fountains and shaded lights over the rock pools and flowers. Justin returned to help with the cases.

Suddenly Marta was running towards them. She flung herself at Justin and kissed him frantically, held him at arm's length then kissed him again.

'Is she here?' Justin whispered, and Marta nodded.

After unpacking, William found his way to the dining room. The table was beautifully laid, with candles, bowls of salad, and every conceivable cold cut. He heaped a plate, poured some chilled Chablis and sat down. After a few moments, Justin joined him and helped himself to food and wine.

'She asleep?' William asked, his mouth full.

'Yes.'

'So I won't get to meet her tonight then?'

'Maybe, maybe not.'

Laura did not make an appearance. It was after two in the morning when they both decided to go to bed. 'You want to see her?' Justin whispered. 'Come with me . . .'

Laura was lying on her side, naked, one arm stretched out, the hand cupped as if begging to be touched. One slender leg crossed over, the other leaving her hip rising like a wing. Her breasts were partly hidden by her other hand, which rested against them almost in an attitude of piety. Her silken blonde hair splayed across the pillow and fell over her shoulder like gossamer. Even in the flickering candlelight, the beauty of her sleeping face was heart-stopping. She had high sweeping cheekbones, fine arched brows and the lashes resting on her cheeks were dark. Her nose was straight, in perfect symmetry with her cheeks, and her wide pink lips were parted. She was almost too beautiful to be real.

'What do you think?' whispered Justin.

'She's perfect,' was all William could say.

'She is the bait, William.'

William went to his suite, changed and slid between the cool cotton sheets. He was aware of a strange sensation of fear in the pit of his stomach. He had no notion of why he felt afraid. He had spent enough time with Justin to think that he knew him . . . but did he? At some point he fell asleep, so he did not hear the soft moan or the conversation that went on for hours. He didn't hear a sound from above as brother and sister lay entwined like lovers, their perfect bodies catching the light of the candles: he so bronzed, eyes deep and tortured, she with the paleness of lilies that belied a terrible darkness.

*

'Morning,' William said to Marta, who was setting the breakfast table. She was hardly able to give him a pleasant look, never mind a 'good morning' in return. 'Lovely day,' he said. He had just received a call from his lawyers that two more toys were being inspected, and the chink-chink of the money it would cost the Baron was music to his ears.

Marta moved closer to him. 'Get away from this place,' she said tersely. Her expression said more, but she stopped abruptly when Justin appeared and swept her into his arms.

'Who is the love of your life?' Justin asked, kissing her cheeks.

'You both are,' she said.

William thought she seemed near to tears as she hurried out of the room, but he put it to the back of his mind. He beamed at Justin. 'Just spoken to my legal boffins, I'm going to squeeze Baron von Garten's balls so tightly. It's gonna cost him millions.'

'You ever think of anything else but accruing dosh, old man?'

'I do now. The dosh, as you call it, has nothing to do with my good humour. It's getting that stuck-up son-of-a-bitch.'

'That's good,' Justin said, and now he smiled. 'Like I've always said, pay-back is the best feeling you can have. You'll more than pay him back. You'll hit his reputation as well as his pocket, right?'

'Right,' said William, grinning.


Laura did not come down to breakfast that morning, but William saw Marta carrying a tray up to her room.

He was going up to the roof for a swim. Perhaps Justin would be up there. He was. Peering over his dark glasses as William approached, Justin held out the copy of *Vogue* that he had been reading. 'Have a look at page forty,' he suggested.

William sat down next to him and picked up the magazine. Flicking through the pages, he stopped at the spread of his bedroom on the island. 'Good God!' he said. He read aloud, ' "This extraordinary bedroom suite, with its canopied bed festooned with exquisite fabrics, its tasselled curtains and gorgeous rugs, like an Empire period fantasy in French opulence, announces the secret owner to be a man of taste and immense wealth. No doubt the fortunate guests will be universally famous, beautiful and strictly millionaires." ' William dropped the magazine. 'My name isn't here, is it?'

' 'Course not,' laughed Justin. 'Don't want to put them off.'

William read on, ' "Everything in this room, from the wallpaper to the doorknobs, is handmade, its grandeur counterpointed by its elegance and restraint. It is a room to inspire, and indulge a man's dreams. Only a high-flyer could come to rest in a bed that would have suited the Sun King himself." Did you write it, Justin?'

'Don't be ridiculous, it's that slag Meryl Delaware. I gave her the photos and the specifications. Now she's wild to see the place for herself. She believes it's owned by a mystery consortium of reclusive millionaires or royalty.'

'Maybe it wouldn't be such a bad thing to tell them whose island it is soon. I mean, we've got them all wondering now, and that thing with Sylvina has put me back on the social map.'

Justin had to admit that William was right, but he had grown bored with this exchange and was moving inside.

'Justin!' called William. 'Look!'

He was pointing towards the wooded area below them in the gardens. He stepped back in shock as Justin sprang on to the balcony rail and proceeded to climb down the front of the house, clinging to the ivy. 'Laura! *Laura!*' he shouted, as he ran towards the woods.

William shaded his eyes to watch Justin tear across the gardens. In a long white dress and a wide-brimmed picture hat, Laura waited among the trees. Justin caught her in his arms and swung her round, her feet off the ground, her arms around his neck.

William made his way down the stairs and out through the big french windows, then strolled through the paved Japanese gardens, past the fountains, ferns and palm trees. 'Justin?' he called, but there was silence. He headed into the forest of tall pines. 'Hello, where are you?' he called.

'Hello.' It was a woman's voice.

William turned to face her. She was standing in deep shadows between two massive fir trees, her hands resting on their bark. She was barefoot, and her dress was transparent so the light shone through.

'Laura?' said William shyly.

'You must be William.' Her voice was light with a hoarse quality.

'I saw you from the balcony,' he said, rather lamely.

As he moved closer, William noticed that she had threaded daisies between her toes. He felt like a schoolboy. 'Justin has told me a lot about you,' he said hesitantly, wishing he could think of something more interesting to say.

'Did he?' she said. He still could not see her face clearly: her long hair fell like a curtain, obscuring her profile.

'It's cold out of the sun,' he said, looking upwards.

'It's nice and cool. Don't you find it refreshing?' She lifted one hand and brushed her hair off her face.

William was mesmerized by her incredible blue eyes. They were deep like her brother's, but so pale and weirdly expressionless, that it seemed as if her thoughts were trapped miles away.

He felt awkward, and his body was covered in goose pimples. 'I find it chilly,' he said.

She cocked her head to one side. 'Chilly? *C'est quoi*, chilly?' Her accent was quite strong, unlike Justin's.

Suddenly she moved towards him and slipped her arm through his. William's heart lurched. Her perfume smelt familiar, of lilies. He realized she was very tall.

'I'm hungry,' she said, and her voice had no trace of an accent at all.

'How odd,' William said. 'One moment you sound French and the next you speak perfect English.'

She laughed. 'I was brought up in England, so if I wish I am English. But I can also be French.' She wrinkled her nose. 'I think, for you, I should always be English.'

'Yes . . . but you are a very good actress,' he mused, then asked, 'Have you ever been on the stage?'

'Oh, no, I would hate to be constantly portraying other people. I'd lose myself. I have a hard time holding on to who I am anyway. Does that happen to you?'

'I've never thought about it, but I suppose so. When I am in a good mood, I feel like I have more energy to deal with people, but when I'm in a bad mood, I feel inadequate and then I wish I could be my other self. Does that make sense?'

'Of course, because sometimes it is hard to be confident. Do you envy people who are always confident?'

'You mean like Justin?'

She looked up into his eyes. 'Justin is not always confident. He may appear to be so, but I know sometimes he goes to a place of deep despair.'

William was interested, he had never considered that Justin might be prone to depression. 'Sometimes he feels very lonely, so he hides. We are very alike.'

'You feel lonely?'

She hesitated a moment, then shook her head. Her voice was soft and hardly audible. 'I am alone if I am not with Justin.'

Her eyes brimmed with tears and he wanted to hold her, protect her, wrap his arms around her frail beauty. Instead he coughed and changed the subject. 'Er, I'm hungry too. Shall we make our way back to the villa?'

As they broke from the darkness into the splendour of the gardens, he said, 'It's wonderful, isn't it? Everything so alive, growing . . .'

'Mmm,' she said lightly, then, almost as an afterthought, added, 'Everything but me.'

It was a disquieting remark, which played on William's mind.

They walked in silence for a while. Then, wanting to make conversation, he said, 'I've grown very fond of your brother.'

She smiled, 'I adore him, I could not live without him.'

'He speaks well of you.'

'He loves me too much – but then I love *him* too much. Sometimes it leaves no room for anyone else. It has always been that way.'

'Do you work?' William changed the subject.

She frowned. 'Has he not told you about me?'

'How do you mean?'

She gave a soft laugh. 'He obviously hasn't, or you wouldn't ask. It's just that I have a frail constitution. I get very nervous of people. It's silly, but I get agitated very easily and then ... I get sick, just a nervous condition, but Justin looks after me, and Marta too. She's like a mother, we love her.'

Her voice was soft, musical, and there was a childlike innocence about her that took his breath away. William recalled Andrew Maynard's description of her, and could understand why the young man had been so drawn to these two creatures. The more time William spent with them, the more he, too, fell under their spell.

'Lunch is served,' bellowed Justin, from the first-floor balcony, and the moment was broken.

Laura picked at the food with her fingers. Often brother and sister ate from each other's plates, sometimes popping morsels into each other's mouths. The conversation revolved around the island: Justin described it all to her in minute detail, and told her how hard he had worked since she last saw it. Then he showed her the

217

magazine articles. Laura watched him intently, and at one point she reached over and used her napkin to wipe the side of his mouth. Marta served coffee, and hot water and lemon to Laura who had refused wine, leaving William and Justin to consume a bottle each. Afterwards Justin jumped up and said he would be waiting for William in fifteen minutes to go water-skiing, and Laura disappeared. Marta materialized and proceeded to stack a large tray with all the plates and glasses.

William pushed back his chair and stood up. 'This morning, Marta, at breakfast, you were about to say something but stopped when Justin came in.'

'You must have been mistaken.'

'I distinctly heard you say something about—'

'I didn't say anything.'

As she went out with the tray, William held open the door for her. 'Laura is very beautiful,' he said softly, and he saw the look of sadness in Marta's face. 'A rare thing. A very delicate, fragile woman.'

William went to his room to change for the beach, then set off to find Justin. He was waiting in the garden. 'What did you think of her, then?' he whispered, his face close to William's.

'She's gorgeous.'

'Perfection. Lovely firm natural tits, big pink nipples, and her pussy is like a silk purse.'

William pulled away from him. 'For Christ's sake, Justin, she's your sister!'

'Oh, God,' Justin sneered, 'don't be such a prude. She's an experienced woman. She knows what's going to be needed of her. Like I said, she's going to be the bait. You telling me any man would turn her down?

She may not be every man's trip, but let me tell you, if they fuck her, they always go back for more. Laura is an adulteress with more tricks than—'

'Stop it!'

'What's the matter?'

'I don't think you should talk about her in that way.'

'You see? She's got you hooked.' He laughed. 'Imagine fucking her, William. See the swan turn into a demon. She'll have every man on that island, every woman and child eating out of the palm of her tiny innocent hand. And she can bite, you know, and draw blood like no other woman.'

William refused to listen. He hated Justin when he talked like a pimp. But he was angry with himself too – because he couldn't stop thinking of her asleep, naked, her perfect thighs, her breasts, and it made him feel ashamed.

'Maybe you should try out the goods, huh?' Justin said, hopping into a jeep parked outside.

'Why don't you shut your foul mouth before I put my fist in it?'

Justin started up the engine as William got in. 'Anything you say. You're holding the purse strings. I don't suppose she's told you how much she wants yet, has she?' William refused to answer. 'Well, you can discuss it tonight, but her services don't come cheap.'

'Services?' William was appalled.

'She'll charge a lot more than those Mayfair whores you got hammered for screwing. Laura isn't a cheap hooker, she's a courtesan. If you get Matlock, he'll bring his wife and his son. If you leave them alone with Laura she'll have each one of them.'

'Really?' William said flatly. He was sure now that

Justin was joking, but refused to join in with his sick humour.

Justin smiled to himself. He'd never met a man who hadn't wanted to protect Laura on first meeting. Tonight William would witness the other side of Laura – the temptress or maybe the seductress. She had numerous different personalities and Justin loved every one of them. He admonished himself, though, for his reckless conversation: sometimes he forgot that his straitlaced friend did not think as he did. He must not do anything that might make William scuttle away from the trap, which was now in place.

When they got back from the afternoon's waterskiing, William rested until almost nine. He was so tired he hardly felt like dressing for dinner. As he sat morosely by his dressing-table, Justin came in, wearing a white suit and a black T-shirt.

'Every bone aches. I'm not hungry, I am totally exhausted,' William said.

'Just get dressed. I've a little something to give you a boost.'

William went to his wardrobe, selected a cream linen suit, then saw that Justin had chopped out four lines of cocaine on a small hand mirror. 'I don't do drugs,' he barked.

'Just this once,' cooed Justin. 'It'll give you some energy. We don't want you falling asleep half-way through dinner. Go on, everyone should try it once.'

William hummed and hawed, then accepted the rolled banknote and snorted. His eyes watered and he coughed, but Justin pointed to the next line. 'That's enough,' William said.

'Do the other line and stop stalling.'

'Justin, I have never used drugs. I abhor them,' he said, but he bent his head to do the other line as he spoke. 'I really don't approve of this,' he justified himself, blinking back tears. 'And I don't feel anything but a runny nose,' he said, sniffing.

'Believe me, you'll be needing this tonight. Let's go down,' Justin said.

William sniffed again. He wondered why Justin thought he'd be needing the cocaine. As he started down the staircase, it hit him like a thunderbolt. His head cleared and his body felt weightless. He felt incredibly fit and alert, almost jumping down the last few stairs. 'You know, I bet any money if I went back on the skis tomorrow I'd be able to stay up. We can do it first thing before breakfast.' William crouched on the stairs with his hands held out in front of him, as if he was waterskiing.

Justin turned and looked at him, then gave that wonderful, slow smile. 'You should trust your friend. He's always going to take care of you. Now we'll have a little caviar, some iced champagne, and party.'

'Fine by me,' William said, with an inane grin.

What William had not been expecting downstairs, though, was dinner guests. 'What the hell are they doing here?' he muttered.

'Don't fret, old boy, this is all part of the plan. I've arranged a small *soirée* so that you can drop the news that it's *your* island everyone's been getting excited about.'

221

'We never discussed this.' William was anxious.

'Trust me. Now is the right time. That Sylvina thing has made you look all squeaky clean. Go ahead, give it a go. You'll enjoy it.'

Before he could argue, one of the guests, in the shape of the blowsy Meryl Delaware, almost threw him sideways. She was aiming for Justin, but he sidestepped her and she stumbled into William.

'Miss Delaware,' he said, thankful for the wall behind him.

'Oh, good evening. Sir William Benedict, isn't it?'

'Generally speaking,' he said, and she looked almost puzzled.

'You look very different. Is it your hair?'

'Maybe the lack of it,' he said, with a charming smile, as she backed away and bumped into Terence Hampton.

William looked around. Rent-a-crowd, he thought. He helped himself to a glass of champagne, and drank it down as if it was water. He had such a thirst! He wasn't in the least bit self-conscious or worried that no one was approaching him. Instead, he was enjoying surveying the room, and quickly realized that Laura was absent. Marta was moving quietly around, collecting used glasses and half-empty dishes of caviar, the remnants swimming in melting ice. As she passed William he asked if Laura was joining them.

'I believe so, Sir William,' she answered, and reached out to catch a glass that Princess Constantina had inadvertently knocked off a bookcase.

'I was so sorry to hear about your break-up with Countess Lubrinsky.' Meryl had had to resort to talking to William.

'I'm still broken-hearted,' he said, smiling. 'As you can see. Inconsolable.' He dipped into some caviar. He was enjoying himself and decided that this was the right moment. 'Actually, I've been recovering on my island in the Caribbean.'

'The Caribbean?' Meryl's mind was whirring.

'Yes, I think you wrote an article about it. "Billionaire's Paradise Island Home",' he quoted.

He laughed inwardly when her jaw dropped.

'Tragic about Lord Bellingham's son, wasn't it?'

Meryl blinked her mascara-caked eyelashes and nodded. Rivulets of lipstick gathered in the crevices around her mouth, giving it the appearance of a tight pink arsehole. 'I was in the Caribbean when it happened,' she said, adopting a sorrowful expression.

'So was I,' said William. 'My island is next door to theirs.'

'*Really?*'

'I noticed you at the party, too.'

'Party?' she said guardedly.

'I'd say it was one of the most decadent evenings of my entire life.'

Her hands were trembling. 'My dear,' she whispered, 'a little word of advice. Don't discuss that evening. It's best forgotten. I left early. I had a dreadful migraine.'

'I remember you being there well,' he persisted. 'Life and soul of the party as I recall.'

Meryl pursed her lips. 'I suggest you forget it.' She glared over his shoulder and caught Terence Hampton's eye. 'Ah, Terence, dahling! Are you my chauffeur for this evening?' She rolled her eyes towards William. He did not miss it. 'We should really be thinking about leaving.'

'I only just got here,' he moaned, but Meryl grabbed him and bundled him away.

William strolled out onto the balcony. Princess Constantina stood with her back to the open doors, having a heated discussion with Count Capri. 'Well, it was drugs as well,' she was saying, 'but he'd been abused and tied up. That's what I was told. You know Lord B, he'd never let that out. It was bad enough that the boy was always in a drugged stupor.'

William was eavesdropping and didn't care if he was caught. Tonight he didn't hover or hide his new slim-line figure, but leaned confidently against the balcony viewing the Eurotrash. He would have happily remained so, if Laura hadn't appeared. She was wearing a long gold satin gown that draped her breasts, while the skirt was cut on the bias and swung around her body as she walked. Her pale skin shimmered and her hair had been drawn back tightly against her head, one long plait hanging down the centre of her back. She wore no jewellery at her ears or throat, but a gold bracelet hung low on her slender wrist. 'Ladies and gentlemen,' she announced, 'I do apologize but we are expected at dinner, so if you will excuse us . . .' She stood poised in the doorway. Frederick Capri gaped. 'Who's *that*?' he squawked.

In the drive below the cars started revving up to take the guests to dinner. A Rolls and a large open SL Mercedes were preparing to leave. The room emptied fast, leaving William and Marta alone.

'Well, that was all very . . .' He tailed off and shrugged as the cars disappeared up the drive.

'Typical Justin,' Marta said. 'He bumps into someone and the next minute he has that wretched group here. Laura hates it. She won't have any part of it. He's such a bad boy. Dinner has been ready for over an hour.'

William made his way to the south veranda, where dinner was being served. As he approached, he heard a loud crash.

'That was a stupid thing to do,' Justin shouted.

'No. *You* are stupid. Why did you let those wretched people in here? They are freeloaders, gossips. I hate the *filthy bastards*!'

There was another crash and the ominous sound of tinkling glass. 'That's seven years' bad luck, you soft cow.'

'I don't care. You have those people in here and you'll have more than bad luck. They are trash, Justin, and that fat bitch Delaware is the worst of them all. You could see her scrawling her filthy little articles in her head as she talked to you.'

'Well, you'll be all right – you hardly showed your face,' Justin snapped.

'You know why? If we go through with this, the fewer people see me the better.'

William coughed and stepped into view. Broken glass and china littered the long table, which had been so elegantly laid.

Justin waved at William. 'She's throwing a tantrum. Are you hungry? If you can find a space between the broken crockery we'll get Marta to dish up. I'm starving.'

Suddenly Laura seemed to calm down, and took a seat opposite William. 'Careful you don't cut yourself. Justin'll clear up.' She picked up a napkin. 'So, William, did you enjoy these ghastly clingers-on?' She pronounced the word 'ghastly' with a wonderfully accented lilt.

'No,' he said. 'I loathe them. Especially Meryl Delaware.'

'William, we all loathe them,' said Justin. 'They would turn up at a public lavatory if they thought there was a free drink in it.' He gathered the broken crockery into a napkin. 'But Meryl is very useful. How do you think we've had such a terrific press about the island? You could feed her dog-shit and, with the right price tag, she'd make it smell like roses.' He walked into the house.

William had almost reverted to his usual self-conscious self. The cocaine had worn off, his nose was running and his head ached. Laura poured him some wine. 'Justin has told me what those horrible people did to you. I am so sorry. But we'll get back at them. It'll be fun . . . Well, it will be for you. *They* won't think so,' she said, and crumbled a bread roll. 'If you would like me to help, I am available. But I don't want to be paid in cash.'

William said nothing, watching her. She was one of the most perfect creatures he had ever met and in the glow of the flickering candles she seemed like an exotic bird. A long finger traced the rim of a glass, and William watched as she dipped her forefinger into the wine, lifted it, and caught the drop on her tongue. 'According to Justin, you are going to hire me. But I need to hear it from you. If you do want me to help you, then I must make arrangements.' He leaned forward and she moved her hand across the table to touch his lips. 'Don't interrupt.'

'I'm sorry.' She was like a different woman: colder, more sophisticated, as if the childlike quality he had found so appealing had been a figment of his imagination. There was no trace of any French accent. She was speaking like a well-educated upper-class débutante.

'Justin suggested that I should be your woman, but not in the ridiculous way you were engaged to Sylvina. It's public knowledge in Europe that she prefers women. Ours should be a more loving match. It's usual, is it not, for British men to like younger girls? Perhaps it is that they fall in love with what they could not acquire before they had amassed a fortune.'

William smiled. It was so true. As a young man he could never have hoped to date a woman as beautiful as Laura. Not even with his fortune had he ever attracted a woman like her.

'What about this? We met in Paris, and you fell in love with me. You are desperate to propose. Would you find that acceptable?'

Had Justin arranged the candles so they formed that Madonna halo?

'Falling in love with you would be any man's reaction. You look so beautiful, Laura, you take my breath away. I doubt if anyone would ever believe that I could be fortunate enough.'

She giggled seductively. 'But you do have a fortune, William, and I mean to please you. But tell me, what do you think about what I've just said? Do you think it's a good idea? Or do you have another plan?'

'I'm not sure how much Justin has told you. To be perfectly honest, I don't know all the details myself,' he said, pouring more wine. Truth was, he didn't want to get into the sordid 'hidden' cameras, the plan to catch his enemies engaged in compromising sexual activities. And Laura frightened the life out of him.

Laura continued, staring into space, 'Justin has explained the details.' It was as if she was reading his mind and he flushed. 'Justin suggested that I compromise each of your guests. I am to have a sexual relationship with all of them . . . or use whatever or whoever is necessary.'

William was sweating. It sounded so unlikely that he wanted to say it had been some kind of fantasy.

Laura moved closer to him. She lifted his arms away from the chair and sat on his lap. Taking his right hand, she wrapped it around her waist. Resting against him, her face close to his, she was silent. She lowered her hand and began to rub him lightly. Her body heat warmed him and he felt his loins stirring. He could hardly breathe. She held his face between her hands and kissed his lips, so softly. 'I don't want money,' she said, and now her lips brushed his ear.

She stopped stroking him and eased away to perch on the edge of the table.

'I will play your game.' She laughed. 'I think the men will be easy. The women will be more difficult to seduce, especially if they have never had a lesbian relationship.'

'Women?' he said, flushing deep red.

'Yes, of course. The wives and sons will be there, and I think one of your guests has a daughter, does he not – Lord Cedric?'

'Yes, but—'

She cupped his face in her hands and kissed him, her

gown sliding aside to reveal that she was naked beneath it. 'I don't want any money,' she repeated, and slid away, returning to her seat, with the grace of a dancer. Languidly she picked up a champagne glass and sipped, then ran her tongue round her lips. 'Payment will be . . .' she paused, teasing '. . . a diamond for each conquest.'

'Depends on the carat,' he heard himself reply, trying to be nonchalant and failing.

'You want to try the goods?' She smiled, showing her small, white, even teeth. Then she yawned, stretched her arms above her head, and was gone.

William wasn't clear about what went on around him after that. At some stage Marta brought him some coffee and a cigar. Justin had disappeared. After a while he decided to go to bed. He showered and lay down, but he was not ready to sleep. He considered reading, but in the end he turned out the lights and remained wide awake, staring at the ceiling. The Egyptian cotton sheets felt good against his skin – he had only taken to sleeping naked since meeting Justin. He did not hear her enter, but knew she was in the room by the strong smell of lilies. He also knew she was moving slowly round the bed, but he was too afraid to move. Then he felt the mattress dip to his right.

'Give me your arm,' she whispered, and he lifted it a fraction. She bound his wrist with a silk band, then fastened it to the bedpost. 'Now the other.' Her voice was barely audible. Next she drew the sheet away from him, tossed it aside, and forced his legs apart, tying his ankles to the foot of the bed. William lay spreadeagled, unable to move. He kept his eyes tightly shut, afraid to open them. She sat astride his chest and he winced at his impotency. His mind was aroused but his body was not answering.

'I'm sorry, I can't do this with you. Please,' he mumbled.

First she licked each nipple till he felt goose pimples break out across his body, then his neck and ears. He wanted to feel her mouth on his, but she suddenly bit into his ear-lobe, which hurt. He nearly cried out, but she covered his mouth first with her hand, then she stuffed something into it. It felt hard, a roll of leather or plastic. He bit into it, as she drew blood from his ear and began to bite down on the vein in his neck. He felt as if he was being suffocated. Her hands felt strong, masculine, and they massaged and rubbed, twisted and pinched until he was on fire, heaving for breath. Then she inched down towards his now swollen cock. Easing him into her, she leaned forward across his chest, pressing her hands against his throat, so that what little breath he had was cut short. His gasps were painful, his head thundering as she rode him, strangling him, slapping and kicking at him, until he exploded with such intensity, such agonizing pleasure that he blacked out.

Later that night, William woke with a start and looked at the clock; it was three a.m. He thought he must have dreamed the sex, and Laura, but the bands still hung loosely around his wrists and ankles, although Laura had cut him free. He dragged himself from the bed and stumbled into the shower, rubbing his body hard, to bring the blood to the surface of his skin to stop bruises forming. He returned to bed, so tired he could hardly be bothered to wrap the sheet around himself.

Just as he felt sleep descending, she slipped into bed beside him. She snuggled up to him like a child and her kisses were soft and sweet. She whispered to him that he was special, that he was a king, a prince. He was the love she had dreamed of finding, he made her happy. He had never felt such a powerful emotion: a consuming need to protect and provide for the child-woman he held in his arms.

'That must never happen again, Laura.'

'What mustn't?'

'What we did earlier. I don't ever want that to happen again.'

'Why not? Don't you like me?'

'It's because I like you too much, I respect you too much. I'm not a stupid man, I know it was to prove something to me and you succeeded. But I can't use you, even if I desire you. It's wrong.'

He was holding Laura in the crook of his arm when the naked Justin slipped in beside him and hooked his arm around them both.

'She's good, isn't she?' Justin said into the darkness.

Laura reached across William to kiss Justin. Then she flopped back. 'That was just a free sample,' she said to William. 'What carat would you rate me?' Her voice was singsong, a little girlish. 'I want a big whopper each time. You promised me, William, that's right, isn't it?'

'Yep,' said William, out of his depth.

He was unable to think straight, aghast at the proximity of Justin's nakedness.

Justin, who had hooked a long leg over William's, said, 'Listen, old boy, tomorrow we're waterskiing again, so I suggest you get some kip.' He brushed William's face with his hand then kissed him sweetly on the cheek like a young boy. 'Come on, Diamond Lil, bedtime. Get your beauty sleep.'

She jumped up and Justin, with his sister's ease and grace, got up too. Naked, they walked out, arms around each other, leaving William alone.

William patted his pillow afraid of all the demons inside him. He needed to step aside and look from a distance at what had taken place. He found he couldn't do it. What was he thinking of? It had got out of hand, this talk of Matlock and vendettas, and his ex-girlfriend Angela. He would put a stop to it first thing in the morning because he was afraid. Suddenly he thought that the paradise trap might be intended for him.

As sleep enveloped him, his fears turned into nightmares. When he'd read Andrew Maynard's secret diaries, he had envied his exploration of his sexuality. He remembered the blanked-out sections. Had Justin taken Maynard that step further, the step that William had half contemplated?

He knew without doubt that Justin had drawn the naïve Andrew Maynard into an erotic world that had eventually obsessed him, ultimately killed him. Yet that night he had experienced such powerful emotion, not just for Laura but for Justin as well and, no matter how he had protested, she had made love to him and it was as if she had opened a closed door in his mind or in his soul. Whatever had happened had not been merely an erotic excursion but some kind of baptism.

William forced himself to remember the night, on the island, with Dahlia and Ruby. He could see Justin laughing as he watched the video. He sat up quickly, his breath caught in his chest. Had they filmed him this evening? The aim of the game was to capture his guests in pornographic situations, but what if the intention all along had been to entrap William himself? Might this be an elaborate blackmail scam, into which he had unwittingly played? Fear consumed him, and then it subsided. He realized *he* was the one controlling the game; he had instigated it. From now on he would take control, not just of Laura and Justin but of his life. He knew he was the stronger; he knew he had *become* stronger. And he also knew that he had been taken on a journey. Far from destroying him, it had made him become a man. Tomorrow he would make it clear there was to be no further sexual intercourse between himself and Laura. That was the only way of knowing he was in control. He felt easier, and his eyes were heavy. He slept with the perfume of lilies, unable not to recall what it had felt like to have both their bodies entwined with his own.

# CHAPTER 12

A T NINE William was served breakfast by Marta. He felt refreshed and alert, and ready to take control. He asked if Justin and Laura were still sleeping.

Marta looked surprised. 'Goodness, no, they were up and out to the market at seven,' she said. 'They always like to buy their vegetables fresh from the vendors rather than the big supermarkets. They'll have gone down to St Tropez to the fishmonger first.'

'How long will they be?'

'Maybe a couple more hours.' She walked out, then paused in the doorway. 'She is a child you know, sir. I blame Justin. He's been so domineering all her life, she looks to him for everything.'

'What about their parents?' William asked.

'They died when the children were small.'

'Marta,' he said sharply, 'tell me more. I need to know.'

'They are orphans. They were educated in England, and then they returned to France. This was their childhood home. Justin bought it a few years back.'

'How long have you worked for them?'

'Since they were in their teens.'

'Have they always lived together?'

'After England, I believe so. Money used to be very short at times, but Justin always found some way to provide. I think they've had difficult times, especially with Laura being the way she is . . .'

'And what way is that?' he asked not looking at her face.

'I think you know, sir.' He detected a tone of disapproval. 'She was the reason I stayed, even when money was short. I love both of them as if they were my own.'

'Educated in England?' William mused. 'Any idea where?'

Marta hesitated. 'Their mother was French, their father English. Their father's sister took care of them.' The telephone rang, and Marta seemed relieved to escape. He was perplexed and wanted to ask her more about Laura but Marta returned to the room in a hurry. 'It's your secretary. He said it's urgent.'

'Charlie has been expelled from school,' Michael stuttered. He had been accused of dealing in drugs. William called Katherine, his son's mother. She took ten minutes to come to the phone. 'William?' It was his ex-wife's nasal voice. 'Where are you?' When he told her she groaned. 'I think you should make an effort to get here as soon as possible.'

'Is he addicted?' William asked.

'He's not spoken to me. His housemaster called and I went down. He got in with a bad crowd.'

'Others have been expelled?'

'No, they were local boys . . . I don't really know. They found stuff in his room and his locker. He was caught in a seedy club and arrested.'

'Jesus!'

'I sent Daddy's lawyer to get him bailed, and now I can't find Charlie. I've called everyone I can think of. You're his father, for God's sake! Come and sort him out, and Sabrina too.'

'Sabrina?'

'Your daughter, in case you've forgotten. You have to go to her school parents' day. I sent all the information to Michael. I can't go and, as you've never been to one, I thought perhaps you should. I've not had time to think of anyone but Charlie. Cedric went into a frenzy.'

'What the hell has your cousin got to do with it?'

'He's more of a father to Charlie than you ever were. I'd just like you to try and talk to Charlie. Our worry is the press'll get hold of it. Anything linked to you seems to get us all on the front page.'

That was rich, coming from her, William thought. Katherine sold the story of her 'terrible life' with him to the press for a tidy sum. 'I'll get the next plane out,' he said. 'I'll contact you as soon as I'm home. Leave Charlie's address with Michael, if you trace him, and I'll see Sabrina at the parents' day thing. But—' Before William could add that his ex-wife had never wanted him to be at any school social even in the past, she had hung up.

Justin charged down the stairs with William's note. 'The bloody idiot's gone back to London,' he shouted. 'Marta!'

She appeared, drying her hands on a towel. 'He got a call from his secretary and arranged to leave immediately. But he left most of his clothes here. I think he intends to come back.'

Justin read the note again, pacing up and down the hall.

'It'll be all right, Justin,' Laura said, trying to soothe him.

'What would you know about anything.'

'Don't speak to me like I'm stupid!'

Justin wheeled round and grabbed her arm. 'Can't you get this through your thick skull? We've lost the big fish. He's off the hook. He's backing out, Laura, everything we've planned has been a waste of time. My God! When I think of the time I've wasted on that buffoon.'

Laura ran upstairs and locked herself in her bedroom, trying to ignore the thuds, shouts and crashes from below. She tried to calm herself with the thought of the diamonds William had promised her. Her fascination for them had been sparked off when she was given her mother's engagement ring. Now she took out the little Moroccan box in which she kept her collection. Each diamond was stored individually in a black velvet bag. In a notebook she had stuck cuttings from old De Beers diamond mine catalogues, which listed the carat, cut and cutter, and the estimated value of each stone. She liked to line up the diamonds on a piece of black velvet and knew every stone by touch alone. She liked their coldness and to watch them sparkle in the light. If she ever had to leave in a hurry all she would take with her were her darlings, the diamonds. Laura knew she was secure while she had them. No one knew about them, not even Justin. It was the only secret she had ever kept from him.

As Laura came out of her reverie, she realized that the house was quiet. She tiptoed to the door to listen, and could hear Justin crying. He was sitting hunched at the bottom of the stairs. Laura went to sit beside him and slipped an arm around his shoulder. 'Well, that was short and sweet,' she said softly.

He sniffed and wiped his face with the palm of his hand. 'It's just that I was so looking forward to it all, you know. I've been planning it for eighteen months, longer.' Laura stroked her brother's hair. 'I wish I'd killed that bastard Matlock when I was a kid. They couldn't have done much about it then,' he said quietly.

'You should sleep,' she said, easing away from him.

Justin drew her back and held her tightly. 'I can't move right now. Don't leave me.'

'I'll stay with you, always. Come on, now, let me take you to bed. You must sleep.' She helped him stand, then took him into his own room. A single bed stood beneath the window and tucked into it was a ragged doll. He allowed her to turn back the covers, tuck him in and stay as he curled into a tight ball clutching the doll. She sang to him until he slept, then sat with him stroking his hair.

No one saw Justin like this but Laura and, once or twice, Marta had witnessed his regression into child-like fear. When Justin was like this, he lost his bravado, his energy, and his confidence in who he was. Sometimes he lay curled up for days before he found himself again. This time, though, he joined her in the garden that afternoon. 'I'm being a ridiculous queen.' He laughed. 'I'll phone him. Maybe it's nothing to do with us. And even if it is we'll get him back.'

'Of course we will, my darling. You just needed to rest.'

He knelt down beside her. 'Thank you for taking care of me,' he whispered.

'Thank *you* for taking care of *me*,' she said, and they kissed and walked arm in arm back to the villa as they discussed their next plan of action.


William answered the phone personally, anxious for news of his son's whereabouts. It was a while before he could piece together what Justin was saying.

'I'm going to start sending out the invitations, William. They need to go out while the mags are showing the place off, and now that Meryl knows it's your place, it'll be all over the—'

William closed his eyes. 'Justin, right now I can't think about anything but my son. He's in trouble.'

'What's the matter with him?' Justin said impatiently.

William sighed. 'Justin, Charlie is my son and right now I can't think about entertaining a group of people in the Caribbean. Sometimes I really don't understand your obsession.'

'My obsession?' Justin's voice was strained. 'Fuck you!'

'Now don't get like that—'

'I am beginning to loathe the sound of your voice. I've been your friend, William, probably the best friend you ever had.'

The phone went dead, and almost immediately rang again. It was Katherine. 'Panic over. He's home,' she said.

'Thank God for that. Do you want me to come over and talk to him?'

'Could you check out clinics and things? We should think about sending him somewhere where they know how to handle these things.'

'Right, I'll get on to it and be with you tomorrow.'

The long gravel drive crunched beneath the tyres as William's car approached the large old manor house in Buckinghamshire. It had five acres of garden, a large paddock and a swimming-pool. As he drew up outside the front porch, two Labradors with muddy paws growled and padded off. William had never liked dogs.

His ex-wife was even paler than he remembered and age had not been kind to her. Her hair was tied back in a bun at the nape of her neck, and wisps of hair hung around her face. She was wearing a pink twinset, a tweed skirt and Gucci loafers. His emerald and diamond engagement ring was still on the third finger of her left hand.

'He's in the bath. He was filthy,' Katherine said, pouring herself a large sherry and offering the bottle to William. He shook his head, and wondered why she was drinking so early in the day. 'I can't get any sense out of him.' She paused. 'You look odd. What on earth have you been doing to yourself? It's your hair, you look awful. The Bellinghams have been on the phone,' she went on. 'They understand what I'm going through. Oliver was on some drug or other when he committed suicide. Lord B was saying that Ollie went to a rehab place in Cornwall. I asked him to talk to

Charlie, give him all the grisly details, try to scare him into straightening out.'

'I'll pay,' he said, with a resigned sigh.

'Of course you will.' She got up to refill her glass. 'It's already in the headlines. Have you seen it? "Terrible Tycoon's son in drugs raid." The press have been phoning here. Have they contacted you?'

'No,' he said warily.

'He's got to go before a magistrate. He was selling the stuff. No doubt the press will be in court.'

'Probably,' he said quietly. Then he asked, 'Why did you talk to the papers, give them that load of bullshit about me?'

'You deserved everything they threw at you!' She turned on him, her thin lips set in a tight line. 'I had them hanging round the house for days and it was the only way I could get rid of them. If you think I liked having my name, my children's name, dragged through the gutter press then you're very much mistaken.' She was on a roll. 'And if you think that this problem with Charlie isn't anything to do with your shenanigans, then you're wrong. It all stems from you and that wretched Maynard. Is it any wonder he's gone off the rails?' William didn't rise to the bait. 'I have never been so humiliated. I couldn't even walk into the village. And it looks like you haven't learned your lesson. You look like mutton dressed as lamb. That haircut!'

He felt his temper rising, but kept his mouth shut. 'You were a laughing stock and we all had to pay for your antics. Then flaunting yourself with that lesbian! You have no idea what harm you caused my family.'

'Katherine, you were paid handsomely for your

contribution to my downfall. Lucky for you, I didn't go right down. The business stayed firm so I was still around to pay your bills.'

'Oh, yes!' she screamed. 'Money! That's all you ever thought about. Money and sex.'

At that moment Charlie appeared, a half-smile on his lips. 'Ah, happy families. I'd forgotten how it used to be!'

William watched the thin, pale-faced boy saunter into the room and sit on the arm of the settee, his skinny legs protruding from a towelling bathrobe. 'Katherine, I'd like to talk to Charlie alone.'

She flounced out, slamming the door behind her.

Charlie dug into his pocket, took out a pack of cigarettes and lit one, his hands shaking.

'So you've cocked up,' William said quietly. 'You were caught selling drugs, you are to go before a magistrate and you could end up in prison.'

'Doubt it. It was only a few tabs and I'm a first offender, under age and all that. They'll let me off with a fine and a few months' probation.'

His upper-class drawl grated on William. 'What are you on?'

'What am I on?' Cigarette smoke drifted from his lips. 'What are you offering?'

'I'm your father. Show some respect, Charlie.'

'That's terrific coming from you Pa. Any woofters slashed their wrists over you recently?'

William took a deep breath and held on to his temper. 'I'll pay for you to go to a rehab centre. If you don't agree, then you get no money and neither will your mother nor your sister. I'll force them to take me to court and I'll drag the lot of you through the press.'

'I don't give a shit about your money.'

'You're throwing your life away if you give in to drugs. It's stupid, and you are not stupid.'

Charlie patted his pocket for another cigarette.

'So will you go to a clinic?'

'Yep.'

For a brief moment William wanted to hug his son, but he couldn't make the move. Charlie lit the cigarette with nicotine-stained fingers. He was close to tears but trying hard not to show it. As William moved to the door he said, 'You were never around when we needed you, or when I needed you. But in some ways I understood it was Mother's doing. She loathes you. Even at Christmas she hated it when you sent us presents. Sometimes she wouldn't let us open them.'

William hadn't expected this and he wasn't sure how to handle it.

'Oliver died. Did you know him?' Charlie said suddenly. And started to cry. 'He was my best friend.' He wiped his cheeks with the back of his hand.

'He was older than you, though, wasn't he?' William asked.

'Yeah, but we sort of hit it off. In fact I got a letter from him after I was told he'd killed himself. It didn't make any sense to me. I mean, he was arranging for us to go sailing together when he got back from the Caribbean and he had this girlfriend he was really keen on. I asked the Bellinghams about him at the memorial service, but they said it wasn't the right place. Then when I went round to their place they didn't want to talk about him. It's like he never existed.' He was looking down at his lap. 'Do you know someone called Justin?'

'Justin?'

'Yes, Ollie said he'd met this fantastic guy out there, Justin Chalmers. In his letter he mentioned him, said I'd get on with him too.'

'Yes, I know Justin very well.'

William sat down on the arm of the settee still wanting to put his arm around his forlorn son, but it hung limply at his side.

'Ollie was really good about getting the other bastards off me when all that filth came out in the press. I had a really bad time. It just went on and on, especially with that chap Maynard being a pervert.'

'Charlie, most of it was lies, you know.'

'Then why didn't you do something about it? Why didn't you sue them?'

'Whatever I did seemed to make it worse, so I buried my head in the sand. Reckoned if I kept quiet it would all go away, people would forget.'

'They nicknamed you Willy Wanker at school. They used to pin up pictures of you and write things on them. I hated it – and I hated you more than you could believe. I used to pray you'd die, pray you weren't my father.'

William stood up. 'Charlie, I'll make a deal with you. You really focus on getting straight, then come out to the Caribbean. Come and see the island. Get to know me. I have never stopped loving you – and you're right, I should have kicked ass about those press articles. But at the time, I just didn't have the . . .' He tailed off. He was silent for a while, then said, 'Sometimes, Charlie, we don't always do the right thing. But I want your respect more than anything else in the world. I want you to be proud to say, "That's my father."'

Charlie stood up and went to the fireplace. He kicked

at the grate, his shoulders hunched. 'Okay, it's a deal. Thanks.'

William went over to him, pulled him close and hugged him. 'Got a lot of catching up to do, lot of straightening out, but we'll do it.'

He could smell Pears soap on his son's hair and neck and remembered that Katherine had always liked it. It took him back to when he had bathed his son as a baby. It was a clear, sweet memory, the feel of his son's head beneath his hand. He cradled Charlie to his chest, and then did something he never had before. He cupped his son's face between his hands and kissed him. 'Everything will work out. We'll do it together, all right? Let me back into your life, Charlie. Let me show you I love you.'

Charlie suddenly put his arms round William's waist and held him tightly. Then he said, 'I'd like to meet this Justin.'

William felt uneasy, he didn't know why, but he smiled. 'Yes, why not? He's made a good job of rebuilding my villa on the island.'

'Yes, I know, I've seen the pictures. It was in the papers this morning. Everyone's talking about it. I'd like to come over.'

William was impressed at how quickly Meryl's gossip machine had swung into action, but he only said, 'Good, then that's something to set your sights on.'


On the drive back to London, William felt elated. He'd got through to his son for the first time ever. As he left he'd kissed Katherine on both cheeks and told her she was still an attractive woman.

Katherine had flushed, becoming almost girlish, which amazed William. Just by using some of Justin's phrases and a little of his manner, he was making more of an impact than ever before. He began to realize how much he had changed and how he owed it all to Justin. He saw it as a good omen that Charlie had mentioned Justin, although whether or not Justin represented a good example for his son was another thing; he doubted it. The first thing he did when he returned home was call Justin. There was no reply, so he went to bed, but he woke three times and made three further calls. He still received no reply.

William was preoccupied with business for a further three days as a costly legal case was looming: the German company had refused to accept they did not own the patent on the fox-and-hens toy. William's lawyers pointed out to him that it would not be a good idea to bring up the reason von Garten had withdrawn from his original deal, as the story would no doubt resurface in the press.

'I no longer care what is printed about me, and I'm going to kick a few arses!' William thundered.

'But it won't be cost-effective, William,' came the reply.

'Sometimes the cost of proving you can't be shat on is worth it,' he snapped, and hung up. Therefore he was not party to the conversation that ensued between his lawyers and business advisers.

As he put the phone down, the man to whom William had been speaking said, exasperatedly, 'We sue, no discussions. He wants us to hit hard and heavy no matter the cost. He also appears to be on another planet. Either that or he's losing his marbles . . .'

One of the young assistants spoke up nervously: 'Perhaps Sir William has a point. Rumours are rife that Geffin's may go public. A contact in Germany sent us some information about a Max von Garten, the Baron's son. Apparently, Max von Garten has recently bought shares in Geffin's Toys. You can bet that the purchase has been made on behalf of his father. The Baron must know the company is going to float; I'd say he's got hold of information that has not yet gone public. He already has a fifty per cent share in the company, and now he has used his son to buy up even more, based on this inside information. Well, that's illegal share trading! All we have to do is prove that he knew the company was going on the market *before* he bought the shares, and we can nail him for rogue trading as well as copyright. Double whammy!'

The senior men looked at each other, then began to sift through the mounds of paperwork already accrued on the case. They read and reread it. The trouble-shooters William had hired had dug deep and dirty. They even had transcripts of private phone calls, not to mention private bank accounts.

'Sir William's right,' said one of the seniors. 'This'll take more time but it will be worth it. We'll have proof of insider share trading and that von Garten's company have stolen – four patents, is it now?'

'Five,' said the eager young man. 'And their share price has gone through the roof. Sir William's been monitoring them for months. It just goes to show that his designs were worth stealing.'

The team were a little uneasy at the methods used to

247

acquire some of the damning material, but it became obvious that Sir William and his business acumen had run rings round them as always. An elderly man, Douglas Alexander, who had worked with William for many years, tapped the table with his pen. 'It seems to me that Sir William has some personal grievance against Baron von Garten. Do we know whether anything might crawl out of the woodwork, so to speak?'

He was reminded that von Garten had sold his factory to William's strongest competitor and had poached his employees. Maybe that was reason enough for him to be hell-bent on hitting the von Garten company hard.

'But Sir William has never been vindictive. I hope there is no ulterior motive as this case will make headlines.' Douglas closed his files. 'I have also been asked by Sir William to look into the financial situation with regard to Cedric Hangerford, particularly in regard to substantial loans Sir William wishes to be repaid. If that is not possible, we are to file bankruptcy orders. Again, this is rather a delicate matter as Lord Cedric is his ex-wife's cousin, so I suggest we are polite in our dealings with him. In the past we have corresponded with him on this matter but got little response. This time, Sir William appears to want him pressured.'

William was looking forward to seeing his daughter. He wanted to get closer to her, as he had with Charlie. He was driving down the motorway on the way to Parents' Day when Douglas Alexander called him on his mobile. What he had to say made William feel even better: Douglas felt now that they could nail von Garten to the proverbial mast.

'I don't suppose there's anything personal in this, is there, William?' he asked.

'It's just business, Douglas. You've known me long enough by now, surely?'

'Indeed I have. But it'll create a fuss and, after what you've been subjected to already by the media, I wondered whether you wanted to open yourself up to any further trouble.'

William's lips tightened. 'If you are referring to the scandal surrounding Andrew Maynard surfacing again . . .'

'Of course not.'

'Good.'

William hung up. He had not thought of Andrew Maynard for some time. Now he did, and he felt more than saddened. His suicide had made him weep, but had not really grieved him. In many ways his sadness now was that he had not, for inexplicable reasons, ever formed a closer friendship with Maynard. The truth was, he had wanted Maynard to like him. He had wanted to be his friend the way he had so wanted to be Peter Jenkins' friend! Peter Jenkins, William muttered, shaking his head at himself. Dear God, why was he suddenly recalling Peter Jenkins, the freckled-face kid that sat next to him at grammar school? He remembered his overlong, curling eye lashes that made his tawny eyes look like a cat's. Poor little Jenkins who had such a bad stammer he was bullied and constantly the butt of daily jokes. Jenkins had kissed him once. Suddenly, unexpectedly, he had kissed William's neck and the shock of his small, wet lips had sent waves through William's young, pubescent body. Only now did William ask himself why Jenkins had kissed him. Perhaps he just wanted to be his friend and this was the only way he knew of expressing it. Jenkins knew that William was often bullied too. Perhaps he thought that if they became best friends, they would at least have each other. But for some reason, the kiss had only annoyed William and he had ignored Jenkins after that. He had so wanted to be close to Peter, so why had he rejected him? Shortly afterwards, Peter Jenkins was killed on a level crossing on his way home from school. William couldn't recall what had happened next, even now, but he could remember how he had felt, seated next to Peter Jenkins' empty desk, because he had felt the same way after Andrew Maynard's suicide.

William had to pull the car over and park on the hard shoulder of the motorway. He had never gone into Andrew's death this way, never asked himself so many questions. He was now even questioning why he had believed that Maynard was worth the vast sums of money he had paid out. But deep down he knew he was. He recalled how he felt on the last afternoon he had seen him. He remembered his suit with the emerald-green satin lining, and he remembered his attractive smile. His eyelashes were as long as little Jenkins', but dark like his eyes. That afternoon he had known Maynard was in some kind of emotional turmoil. That was why he had asked him for dinner. If he had accepted, if that dinner had taken place, would he still be alive? Or would William have avoided probing into his private life or taking their relationship one step further?

He turned on the radio and felt a strange feeling of

relief, as if opening the memories and facing them was yet another step in his progress towards understanding himself. Then he continued driving to his daughter's school, looking forward to seeing her and hoping to have the same success with her as he felt he had started with Charlie.

'Sir William Benedict,' said Sabrina's school secretary, rather loudly, 'would you like to come through?'

'Thank you,' he said, and followed her to the head-mistress's study.

'Sir William Benedict to see you, Mrs Harper-Nathan.'

They shook hands and he sat.

'I am so pleased you were able to join us today. We have great hopes for Sabrina. She's certainly Oxbridge material.'

He leaned forward. 'I'm very aware of how difficult it must have been for her, for all my family, during my recent troubles. But everything has settled down now and I am grateful for the way you and your staff have protected my daughter. In gratitude I would like you to accept a small donation towards the building fund.' He withdrew an envelope from his pocket and passed it to Miss Harper-Nathan. She glanced at the cheque for a second, then did a double-take. 'This is really most generous, Sir William,' she spluttered. 'A quarter of a million pounds. Thank you so very much.'

William rose. 'It's been a pleasure,' he said, and shook hands with her. The secretary told him that his daughter was waiting for him in room Four Omega. She would take him there.

He found Sabrina sitting half-way down the room facing the blackboard with a book open in front of her. She didn't look up when William came in.

'Sabrina?' he said quietly, and closed the door. She didn't speak, so he walked further in and sat on the edge of the teacher's desk. 'Is this your classroom?'

'We move around,' she said.

He sighed, and stuffed his hands into his pockets. 'Well, I didn't think this was going to be easy, but you might make some effort to be pleasant. I've driven a long way.'

'What do you want me to do? Clap?'

He laughed. 'I got a call from Charlie. He's at a rehab place in Wales. Has he written to you?'

'No.'

'I'll leave his address, then you can write to him. He needs all the support he can get.' He shifted his weight. 'I'm sorry your mother couldn't come with me. She had a doctor's appointment, but she sends her love.'

'Playing happy families, are you?' She looked up and glared at him.

'It's about time, isn't it? Sabrina?'

'You think you can just pick up being Daddy? What a farce! You make me sick. I didn't want to see you. They forced me. They all make me sick, two-faced bitches! You should have seen the way they whispered about you.'

'They seem to think you're very clever. You've had impressive exam results.' She chewed her nails and kicked the side of her desk. He continued, 'Especially your computer studies. I'm pleased about that. Maybe one day you'll take over the firm. There's plenty of opportunities for you to think about. According to Mrs

252

Harper-Nathan you're top of the league, Oxford or Cambridge. I'd have given my eye-teeth to go to either.' Sabrina said nothing. 'Why don't we try to be friends?'

'You may be able to buy Charlie, because he's as thick as two short planks. You might even be able to buy off Mother. She's in need of cash right now – that'll be the only reason she's even talking to you. She hates you, and Charlie's only being nice for what he can get out of you. And I've got a life of my own . . . a secret life. There'll be no Oxford or Cambridge.'

'All right,' said William. 'That's fine. But I want you to know that if you ever need me, I'll be there for you. I always have been, you know, not just financially. It was impossible for me to be a good father when your mother refused to let me see you.'

'Bullshit.' Sabrina picked up her book, snapped it shut and walked to the door. 'You're in for a big surprise soon, Daddy-oh.' And with that she strode out.

As William drove back to London fog was drawing in. The drive was murderous and he was angry with himself. He realized he'd allowed Katherine to turn his children against him. She had forbidden him to keep in touch with them and had poisoned them against him.

It was just after midnight when he arrived home. He was about to head straight upstairs to bed, but heard the soft murmur of voices. He wondered if it might be Michael, or perhaps his valet. But then he heard music, some dreadful rap beat. He switched on the hall light, and saw a leather valise in the hall, a sports bag and a tennis racket. Puzzled, he headed towards the drawing room. When he opened the door, he was surprised to come face to face with Charlie, who was dancing around the room, a cigarette hanging from his lips. 'Oh, hi, Dad!' he said nonchalantly. 'We wondered when you'd get back.'

William turned to see Justin sitting on the sofa with a glass of champagne in his hand. 'Hope you don't mind, but Charlie let me in.' Justin stood and wrapped his arms around William's shoulders. 'I missed you,' he said, and kissed him on both cheeks.

William was at a loss for words. Charlie poured him a glass of champagne and handed it to him. William rounded on him. 'I only spoke to you this afternoon, for God's sake. What are you doing here? Why aren't you at the clinic?'

Charlie looked evasive. 'Oh, we get weekend leave, Dad, didn't I tell you? It's a fantastic coincidence that Justin's here.'

William accepted the chilled champagne. Justin gave William a covert look and almost mimicked Charlie's voice. 'Thanks, Dad.' William raised his glass but felt a deep undercurrent. What was going on? Having Justin turn up out of the blue with Charlie felt ominous.

'When do we leave for the island, Dad?' said Charlie.

William downed his drink in one. 'I'll think about it in the morning after a good night's sleep. Go to bed, Charlie. It's late, and I want to talk to Justin.'

Charlie groaned, but his father hadn't made a fuss about his departure from the clinic and he was grateful for that so he trudged off. That is, he hadn't made a fuss yet – but he would when he discovered that Charlie had lied about the weekend leave.

William stood at the bottom of the stairs watching

Charlie disappear. He called goodnight, then turned his attention to Justin and indicated the study. 'What's going on?' he asked.

Justin raised his eyebrows. 'What on earth do you think is going on? I missed you so I came over. You called enough times, I thought you'd be pleased to see me.' He laid his hand on William's arm.

William shook it off. 'Cut the crap. What do you want?'

'Oh!' squealed Justin. 'Mr Tough Guy.'

'Is it money you're after?'

Justin sat down beside him, and pulled out a large file from his case. 'Look, the trap is set.' He tossed a wad of newspaper cuttings about the island on to William's lap. 'It's finished, all set up. It's up to you now. If you need my help you can have it. If not I'll be off.'

William started to look over the cuttings. Suddenly the phone rang. 'Who the hell . . .?' William lifted the receiver. 'Yup?'

It was Mrs Harper-Nathan. 'Thank goodness you're there, Sir William. I've been trying to get hold of Lady Benedict but there's no reply.' William wished she'd get to the point. 'Sir William, I'm afraid your daughter has gone missing.'

'But I only saw her this afternoon.'

'Well, she did leave a note, but she's packed her case and left. We were rather hoping she might have come to you.'

'What does the note say?' There was an embarrassed pause. 'Well?' asked William.

'Well,' said Mrs Harper-Nathan, 'it seems she has eloped with the school caretaker's son. She says in the note that she's pregnant by him. I've spoken to the caretaker. He thinks his son is staying in a squat in Notting Hill Gate, above a pub. The Six Bells, I think he said.' There was a short silence. 'I'm so sorry, Sir William.'

'The boy's name?'

'Jacob Mkomazi.'

'Fax me that note. And, Mrs Harper-Nathan, no police, no press.' He hung up.

'Bad news?' Justin asked.

William gave a gesture of despair and went into Michael's office. Justin trailed after him, and by the time the fax had come through, William had told him about Sabrina. 'It's one bloody thing after another,' he muttered, passing the fax for Justin to read. 'First my son, now my daughter. Dear God, if the press get hold of either story they'll have a field day.'

Justin was pulling on his jacket. 'Look, William, you may be knackered, you certainly look it, and I know there's trouble, but the best way of dealing with trouble is action. OK?' He was holding the door open. 'I'll drive you wherever you want to go.'

Justin and William sped off in William's sports car to Notting Hill Gate. They cruised the streets until William spotted the Ten Bells. 'That must be it,' he shouted.

Justin swerved into the kerb. It was pouring with rain. William got out; crossed the pavement and pushed open the graffiti-covered side-door. The dank, carpetless hall smelt of urine and stale food, overridden by the powerful smell of ganja, which made William's head reel. There were several doors, and the sound of a jazz trumpet mingled with televisions and muted voices, then, eerily, a loud, cackling laugh.

He knocked at one door and received no reply. Looking down the dingy hall he saw that there was a basement, and another apartment further along. He decided to listen at each flat, rather than knocking. On the third floor, he heard Sabrina laugh, a joyful sound, so unlike the bitter, hard little girl he had encountered that afternoon.

He rapped lightly and waited. The door inched open and a tall, handsome boy with shoulder-length dreadlocks looked down at him. 'Yeah?'

'I'm Sabrina's father,' William said. The boy gave a half-smile before he turned back to the room.

'Tell him to go fuck himself!' came Sabrina's high-pitched voice.

The boy turned back to William and his beautiful, dark, slanting eyes twinkled. 'Guess she don't want to see you, sir.'

'Don't call him "sir", Jacob. You don't ever have to call anyone sir, and especially not him. Shut the door.'

Jacob turned to William. 'She don't want to see you.'

He was about to shut the door when William stuck out his hand. 'Listen, Jacob. I want to see my daughter, and I want to talk to her. It'll take a few minutes then I'll walk away. She need never see me again if that's what she wants.'

Jacob hesitated, then swung the door open.

Sabrina was lying on a moth-eaten couch, with a portable TV set balanced at one end amongst cans of Coke, packets of crisps and a bowl of apples. The room was untidy and dirty. Even the bed in one corner had not been made. Jacob gestured to a dilapidated wing-back armchair, the stuffing and springs bulging out, barely concealed by a big wool rug that had been thrown over it. Two guitars and a set of conga drums were stashed beside it.

'Sit down,' Jacob said, hitching up his jeans. He wore an old miner's shirt with a knitted sweater over it, dirty sneakers and no socks. 'You want some coffee?' he asked.

'Yes, please,' William said, easing himself into the chair, afraid it would collapse under him.

'You want a milkshake, Sabby?'

'Okay.' She had not even looked at her father.

'Be two minutes.' Jacob opened her purse and took out some money.

'I'm sorry, I didn't think you'd have to go out for it,' William said, but the door closed. Then he turned to his daughter. 'You're pregnant?' he said.

'I'm not going back to school. Never, never, never. OK?'

William looked at the guitars and asked if Jacob played in a band. She shrugged her shoulders. 'Right now he's cleaning tables in a bar,' she said defiantly.

'You need money?' he asked.

'Oh, for Christ's sake, it didn't take you long to get around to that, did it? Listen, I don't need a cent from you, I've got my trust fund.'

'And the fairies made that up for you, did they? Well, you can't get your hands on that till you're twenty-one. That's quite a few years to wait. If you're having a baby, you're gonna need more space than one room.'

She was unsure how to take what he had said. He hadn't been angry – in fact he seemed to have accepted her situation.

'Are you going to get married?' he asked.

She laughed humourlessly. 'Yeah, all in white with four bridesmaids.'

'Do you love him, or are you just doing this to get back at me?' He moved closer.

She nodded as tears spilled down her cheeks. 'Please go away,' she whispered.

'I will, but we need to talk about maternity bills, hospitals . . .'

'For fuck's sake don't tell me to get a nanny! I had my fill of those. This baby is all mine. At last, something of my own that no one can take away from me. We're going to bring it up, me and Jacob.'

William reached for her hand, but she pulled it away. Again she asked him to leave, but this time without anger. He stood up and laid his hand on her head. 'I love you. If you ever need me, I'll be there. Take care of yourself, Sabrina, and I hope you'll be a lot happier with Jacob than I ever was with your mother. I'll call her and tell her you're looking well and happy.'


William sat on the stairs waiting for Jacob to return. He came in carrying a cardboard tray with their coffees and the milkshake.

'Hi,' William said, trying to appear relaxed.

'Hi. She's into these milkshakes and crisps.'

'You're lucky. With her mother it was *pâté de foie gras* and champagne. Sit down, Jacob.'

Jacob squashed down beside him, his long legs stretched out as he passed over the coffee.

'You are going to marry my daughter?' William asked, removing the lid and dripping coffee over his raincoat.

'Yep, when we got some cash. Right now we're having to be real careful. She's half-way. We've got to take care of the baby.'

'You love her?' asked William, sipping the strong coffee.

Jacob's dark eyes bored into William's. 'No, I'm after her trust fund, man!'

'No need for sarcasm. Anyway, you're going to have a long wait. She's only sixteen, and she can't touch it until she's—'

'Twenty-one. Yeah, I know.'

'You work in a bar?' William asked, and sipped the coffee.

'Yeah. Sorry I'm not no accountant.'

'Jacob, I don't give a fuck what you are just so long as you're going to take care of my daughter. Listen to what I have to say.'

'I'm all ears.' Jacob drained his coffee and crushed the cup in one hand.

'You needn't tell Sabrina, if you don't want to, but I'm going to open a bank account in your name. All I ask is for you to take care of her and contact me when she's in labour. I'd like to see the baby. After all, it'll be my grandchild.'

'No thanks, no bank account. I'll take care of her 'cos I'm crazy about her and we'll get along fine.'

William stood up and looked down into Jacob's face. 'Don't turn it down. Everyone needs a break. It won't be millions, just enough to get you started in some kind of job, whatever you want. Get a decent place to bring up your kids. I may not have been a decent father, but . . .'

'Money's no object, huh?'

William leaned over him. 'I earned every cent I've ever made. If you love her you'll take what I'm offering, because if you don't you'll not stand a chance of making it work between you. It's a game for her right now, but she's scared shitless.'

Jacob bowed his head as William took out a visiting card. 'Ask to speak to Michael. He'll have all the details.'

Jacob held the card loosely in his hand before he stood up to face his soon-to-be father-in-law. 'Thank you.' William reached out and hugged him.

When William reached the car he saw that Justin was asleep, his head resting against the car window and his mouth slightly open. He looked like a small boy. William tapped on the window and Justin's eyes sprang open. There was a moment, it came and went so fast, but for that second, as Justin stirred, he seemed terror-struck: his hands flailed and he covered his face as if protecting himself from a beating.

'Sorry,' William found himself apologizing, 'do you want me to drive?'

'No, get in. Did it all go okay?'

'Yep, but I don't want to talk about it. All I can think of is getting some shut-eye.'

Justin grinned as he started the engine. 'Right, home it is.'

When they got home William directed Justin to a spare bedroom and was thankful that Justin said that they'd talk in the morning. But when he leaned close and kissed his cheek, it was perhaps the best moment of William's wretched day.

# CHAPTER 13

WILLIAM STARED out of the window. The heavy rain and dark grey skies made visibility so poor that he couldn't even see the end of his walled garden. It had been lashing down all night and, with the trauma of yesterday, sleep had been impossible. When Michael arrived at nine William gave him strict instructions that if any press phoned he was to say he knew nothing and that William was out of the country. He was explaining that Charlie and Justin were both still asleep upstairs, when Charlie strolled in. 'Hi there, Dad.'

'I need to speak to you for a few minutes, Charlie.' They went into the drawing-room. 'I *will* take you to the island and I'm very glad that you've met Justin but—'

Charlie groaned. 'I knew there'd be a but.'

'But you've really got to get straightened out first. Now, you'll have to go back to this clinic and don't give me this bullshit about weekend leave. It's mid-week. Do you think I'm stupid?'

'The place is full of wankers.'

'You liked them last week.'

'Yeah, but I've never been into all that therapy stuff

and the group-leaders are full of shit. They were addicts themselves and all they ever talk about is their old scene.'

Justin was standing in the doorway. 'There's a great place you'd really like in Minnesota,' he said. 'It's where all the superstars go. I'm sure your dad can pull a few strings.'

William spun round. Justin was grinning at Charlie.

'Minnesota, America? Wow! Yeah, I'd give that a go. Yeah, that's cool, I've heard of that place,' Charlie said enthusiastically.

'So that's that settled,' Justin concluded. 'Now, for God's sake, can we have some breakfast?'

William gripped Justin's elbow and drew him aside. 'Stay clear of my son, Justin. Do you understand me? You stay away from him.'

'Yes, sir. Now can we have breakfast?'

By three thirty Michael had arranged a five-month stay for Charlie in the high-powered American clinic, the finest rehabilitation clinic in the world. As Justin had said, a queue of movie stars and ex-presidents' wives were waiting to be dried out and the cure rate was amazing. Charlie was frightened. It had all happened so quickly, but he agreed to leave England immediately.

The three arrived at Heathrow in good time for Charlie's flight. Justin and William waved him through the gate, then walked back to the car-park.

'Justin, if you'd like me to drop you off somewhere . . . I've been trying to contact my ex-wife all day to give her the news about the kids, but I can't rouse her. As we're on the motorway here, it wouldn't take me long to whizz up to her place. But I don't want to bore you.'

Justin put his arm round William's shoulder. 'What else would I do? Sit in front of the TV?' He clicked the remote control to open the car. 'Think of me as your chauffeur today. We can chat, listen to music. It's a good system you've got here.' Justin sat in the driver's seat and buckled up. 'So, William, fire away with the directions and off we go.'

It was dark when the car rolled up the drive of Katherine's Buckinghamshire home, splashed through the pot-holes, and drew up outside the porch.

'You wait here, I won't be long,' said William, and climbed out of the car. In the semi-darkness the house looked run-down. William noticed broken panes of glass in the stained-glass door. 'Katherine?' he called, as he opened it. 'Katherine.'

He made his way first to the kitchen, which was a shambolic mess of dirty cutlery and blackened, greasy pans. 'Katherine!' he called again, as he walked towards the drawing room.

The door was ajar, the room a mess, the fire burned out in the grate. He was worried.

He made his way slowly up the creaking staircase. Even though he presumed she would be in the old master bedroom, he glanced into his children's rooms. Charlie's was still full of cricket bats and skateboards. Sabrina's was papered with Spice Girls posters and there was an array of Barbie dolls. The spare room was dusty, unused and cold. He realized that the whole house was damp, and when he felt one of the radiators on the landing, it was cold. He sighed. The stupid woman hadn't turned on the heating – in this weather. The master bedroom door was ajar and he could hear the soft sounds of a radio turned down low. Again he called his wife's name.

She lay on her side, with a cashmere shawl draped around her shoulders. An empty sherry bottle lay on the floor beside the bed and a half-full one sat on the bedside cabinet amongst numerous sticky glasses. As he drew nearer William knew, from her grey complexion, that she was dead. The lamp gave a soft pink light through the frilly lampshade over her peaceful face. The remains of the sleeping tablets she had taken were spilled over the rose-pink satin-covered duvet. William checked her pulse, but her wrist was cold. Her eyes, half open, were glazed in an expressionless stare. A white envelope was propped against a silver racing trophy on the mantelpiece. William ran his finger beneath the flap, which opened easily. 'To whoever reads this: I am very tired, and not very well. So I have decided to go without bothering anyone, in particular my husband. I have made a mess of a lot of things, so forgive me. That's all really. Katherine.'

The next morning Michael arrived. He, too, was shocked at the state of the house, but said nothing. He offered his condolences and began to sift through the papers and outstanding bills littering Katherine's bureau.

'I'll have to get Charlie back, and he'll have only just arrived,' said William. 'Damn her timing. And Sabrina. I'll go round this afternoon, when I'm through here.'

'You'd better have a look at this, sir,' Michael said, passing over a thick file of accounts. 'They were in the locked drawer at the bottom of the bureau.'

William looked down at the files. 'Jesus! I don't believe it!' he said, under his breath, turning over page after page. Then he tossed the papers aside. 'We're leaving now.'

He went outside and leaped into the car.

'What's going down?' asked Justin, as William switched on the engine and drove away.

'Katherine has robbed the kids' trust funds, and most of the money I ploughed into them went into her fucking cousin Cedric's stables. I mean, it's one thing that she got herself into debt to the tune of two million, but she's been keeping that bastard going with my children's money!' He was shouting.

'William,' Justin said calmly, 'you have the island. Everything is in place. We'll get the son-of-a-bitch,' he said firmly. 'Remember, you have only to say the word and we start the Paradise Trap.'

'For Chrissake, shut up about it!'

Justin knew he had to keep his mouth shut. Often old Willy surprised him: he had quite a temper on him.

The funeral arrangements were taken over by Katherine's depleted family. The service was conducted in the private chapel of what had once been the Hangerford ancestral home, long since sold to the National Trust to cover debts. The coffin was bedecked with floral tributes and the chapel almost full. Even Lord Bellingham and his wife were there. Just before Katherine was carried up the aisle, Sabrina made her entrance. She was wearing a floppy straw hat with a large poppy attached, clogs and a long print dress with a big black overcoat on top. She clutched Jacob's hand, who, William was sure, was wearing exactly the same clothes as when he had seen him. The pair walked down the aisle with their heads held high.

The luncheon afterwards was tedious and rather embarrassing. The old hall, opened for the occasion, was freezing. The food was appalling and the wine no more than plonk.

'Great nosh,' said Cedric, piling his plate high. At one time he had been handsome; now he looked seedy, over-weight and nervous. William watched as he smothered butter over his roll, crunched into it and spat bread-crumbs as he spoke. 'Shame about Katherine, what?'

'Poor woman was driven into a corner, wouldn't you say, Cedric?'

Cedric looked up, a smear of mayonnaise on his chin. 'So you admit it?' he said. William was taken aback. 'Oh, yes, you and your shady life,' spluttered Cedric. 'It was always clear to us she'd made a mistake marrying you. Marrying money's all very well, but . . .' He dived down to the table and spooned more potato salad on to his paper plate. 'Mind you, funny that with all your millions you couldn't keep her in the manner to which she was accustomed. Pity you couldn't have been more like me. I'm very protective of my wife and young Clarissa.'

William looked him in the eye. 'It's just other peo-ple's families you steal from? Is that it, Cedric?' The other man returned his stare, wide-eyed. 'Maybe you haven't actually calculated just how much you sponged off Katherine, but in case you are not aware of it, I have it all in black and white.'

'You feeling all right?' Cedric enquired. 'Maybe all those high jinks addled your brain.'

'I could take it to the police, of course. To fund your bloody stables and to support her gambling, Katherine embezzled her own kids' trust funds.'

'Not a police matter, you'll find. She was family.'

'Family? You piece of shit. I've seen the letters she wrote, begging you to repay her because she was scared she'd get into trouble. She was stealing money I'd provided for my children's future.'

Cedric shrugged. 'Well, you've plenty more.' He pointed his white plastic fork at William. 'Matter of fact, I was going to ask you whether you'd like to invest in a little filly I've got my eye on.'

William threw back his head and laughed. The man's gall was beyond belief. 'You ever heard the expression "pay-back time"? I instructed my lawyers to contact you about returning loans dating back to—'

'Pay-back? I don't know what you're getting at, old boy.' Cedric was concentrating on recharging his fork with a dollop of Coronation Chicken.

'You are in financial shit, Cedric. By pay-back I mean cough up what you owe. And another meaning of that expression is to do with getting you back for being a thieving two-faced bastard!' William strode across the hall and, nodding at his children and Jacob, indicated that he was leaving. He waited at the door while they all made their excuses.

Cedric's daughter, Clarissa, sidled up to William. 'Uncle William,' she simpered, 'I'm coming up to my last term at school, and I was wondering whether you could find me a place in your office or whatever it is . . .' She gave him a winsome smile.

'What are your qualifications?' he said.

'Oh, I haven't any. I just need something to tide me over for a while.'

'Or somewhere to sit and file your nails while you get paid for it?' said William.

Clarissa giggled. 'Well . . . Daddy said you wouldn't mind.'

'Did he indeed? Well, dear, get some qualifications. If a job comes up and you're better than the other applicants, I'll think about it.'

Clarissa stared and reddened. 'Daddy and Mummy were right. You *are* a pig.'

William strode out to the car and climbed in, breathing deeply to regain calm.

He was exhausted that night but, yet again, couldn't sleep. It had been one hell of a day. Cedric and his wretched daughter's remarks at the funeral had put the tin lid on it. What had he got to lose? Justin had gone back to Paris, but the more William tossed and turned, the more he thought about him and about all the vicious backstabbing. His mind drifted back to the day he had discovered Maynard's body, and all that had happened since then. He would like to put them all through the same torment they had inflicted on him. Then it dawned on him that that was exactly what Justin had described. My God! He'd like to see that bastard Cedric caught on camera with more than his pants down. Only now did William see the funny side of it. He reached for the phone, but then realized the time. He lay back on his pillows and laughed.

\*

As though by divine intuition, Justin phoned the following morning. His timing was perfect, as always. 'I'm on the four o'clock train,' he yelled down the Gare du Nord pay-phone. 'I'll be with you in a few hours.'

'I'll pick you up at Waterloo.'

'Let's get the invitations out today,' William said as they drove away from the station.

Justin laughed. 'Sure, why not?'

William leaned forward and opened the glove compartment. 'I've made out a new list, short and sweet.'

Justin unfolded it. He glanced down it, then closed his eyes in relief. Humphrey Matlock's name was at the top of the list, followed by the Hangerford family. Then came Baron and Baroness von Garten, Meryl Delaware and a few others he hadn't heard of.

Justin looked at William and shook his head. 'Too many. Do you really need to bother with that wretched Delaware woman? She's a raddled old cow, not worth the effort.'

'She was one of the gossipmongers sniffing around poor Maynard. I'd like to see her squirm.'

'Fair enough, but just get her sacked. She's not worth any more trouble than that.'

'Scratch her off, then.'

'The von Gartens have a son.' Justin giggled. 'Maybe invite him along. He'll be company for Matlock's boy.' Justin stared out of the window. 'No drug clinic for him, not like your poor Charlie. This kid's a real golden boy. Athletics, tennis, does the lot.'

'Invite him, then,' said William, recalling the boy's shares in his father's company.

'Good, it'll look better. The kids can have a holiday of a lifetime . . . whilst your Charlie's in a rehab clinic and your daughter . . .' Justin had to think this one out carefully, get the balance right. He wanted to rub it in, but he didn't want to go too far. 'I'd say your public humiliation made Sabrina throw away her career. Son-in-law's perhaps acceptable, but—'

'I don't mind that she's with Jacob,' William snapped, flushing.

'But you have to care that she's only seventeen, for Christ's sake. She's a clever kid, isn't she?'

'Yes,' William said. His lips tightened and his anger against his dead wife resurfaced. It wasn't just the divorce, the refusal to allow him access to his children, it was so much more, culminating in the loss of their respect and love, not to mention their trust funds. 'Yes, we include their kids,' he said coldly.

Justin smiled. He and Laura would quite enjoy the boys for starters, especially Matlock's son.

'So, it's Matlock, his wife Angela and son, Baron von Garten, his wife and son, and the Hangerfords. Nine is a nice easy number to control. You don't want to get too ambitious.'

They drove in silence for a moment before William laughed. 'I'm looking forward to seeing them all arrive on the island. Let's just hope they accept.'

'They will,' Justin said, and even placed a fifty-pound bet on who would reply first.

But William shook his head. 'No, I won't play around, not any more, Justin. This is too important. If we don't hear within a week or so, we'll get Michael to make a personal call on my behalf. Fuck it, I'll make the calls myself, better that way.'

'If you have to,' Justin said, and suggested that, if need be, William could renew his friendship with Angela Matlock, just to ensure an acceptance. 'After all, it's a very special Paradise—'

'Trap,' William said.


First to reply was the 'horse thief', as Justin had nick-named Cedric. He was soon followed by Baron and Baroness von Garten's acceptance, but the Matlocks did not reply, and William, to Justin's frustration, flatly refused to make personal contact with Angela. 'You just remember who's running the bloody show,' he said. 'I do not want to contact Angela fucking Matlock. You get him there, or get that bloody Sylvina to help. Just get Matlock on to the island.'

'If you want Matlock, you shall have him.'

The truth was, Justin was at a loss as to how to handle Matlock's lack of interest. He never replied to an invitation and he was impossible to get to. He was an obsessively private man whose only interest apart from making money was fishing.

Strangely enough it was an article published in one of his own newspapers that gave them Humphrey Matlock. Meryl Delaware lunched with Justin at the Ivy and Justin leaked to her there, in confidential tones, the names of the guests who were to stay at the spectacular island. On pain of death, she must not mention Sir William Benedict's name, he said. Neither should she mention that the Prime Minister and his wife had been invited. So was . . . Justin leaned close to her ear, and whispered.

'No, that can't be true. Are you kidding? But he's Matlock's biggest rival. Are you sure?'

Justin grinned and rubbed together finger and thumb. 'Money, my darling. He's switching parties, so rumour has it, and with wealth like that . . .'

Meryl Delaware had a scoop she had to handle carefully. But that blond boy couldn't be trusted and printing even the smallest hint about the 'Big White Chief' might have dire repercussions for her waning career. At five she decided to call his PR woman, who she detested but lunched with. Perhaps now all those lunch bills she had met would start to pay off . . .

Elaine Dunn's crisp voice was eventually on the line. 'Sorry to keep you waiting, Meryl, but the Chief's in today. What can I do for you?'

Meryl dragged on her cigarette. 'Actually Elaine darling, it's about your *numero uno*. I've heard a rumour and I just wanted you to verify it.'

'Well, you know, Meryl, if there's anything—'

'It's just an enquiry, Elaine. I don't want to know who he's shafting! It's just – can you tell me if it's true that he's a guest with the Prime Minister on Sir William Benedict's island this Christmas?'

There was a pause then Elaine's voice lowered. 'I don't think so. I know he received an invitation but I'm sure he turned it down. For God's sake don't print that.'

'Oh, I won't, of course I won't. I just wanted to check out the truth of the story. Both Matlock and his *bête noire* have been invited, you see. Do you know anything at all?'

'No more than I've just told you and now I really have to go – we must have lunch.'

'Yes, we must,' Meryl said, as the phone went dead. She drained her glass and lit another cigarette. 'Lying little shit.' She thought of Justin. Still, she'd had a free lunch.

Elaine, however, wrote a memo and passed it to Matlock's private secretary: the note said she had it on reliable information that the Prime Minister was to join a party on the most exclusive Caribbean island for Christmas. The other guest rumoured also to have been invited was Matlock's biggest competitor.

Meryl Delaware had played right into Justin's hands: there was no way Matlock would walk away from an invitation of this calibre. But she had slightly overplayed her relationship with Elaine. After Elaine discovered that Matlock had accepted the invitation, she was warned that he wanted his privacy guarded and required the source of the rumour about his vacation. Elaine was asked to speak to him personally. 'The woman really is a bit of a lush nowadays, sir. I have no idea how she came to know about the guest lists, but I'll make sure it's never printed.'

'That has already been taken care of, but thank you for your diligence. It is greatly appreciated.'

Elaine sighed with relief. Matlock never appeared to acknowledge Meryl Delaware, or Elaine's indiscretion in speaking with her, but the cryptic message that went round to all editors and magazines was that Matlock's organization no longer required the services of gossip-columnist Meryl Delaware.

\*

274

Later that evening, as Justin made arrangements for their departure to the island, William was in his study, sifting through documents that required his signature. He was pleased to note that the case against the Baron was now moving forward swiftly. Perhaps that was why the stuck-up bastard had accepted the invitation.

Then his mood swung to a darker place. He had found an envelope from the Metropolitan Police. It contained a short note of sympathy and enclosed Andrew Maynard's suicide note in a plastic cover. William sat staring at the waterstained note with the blurred writing. Then he opened a drawer and searched through it until he found an old memo from Maynard. He compared the two pieces of writing. Obviously the police must have checked that it was authentic but to William something was wrong. He took into consideration that Maynard must have been drunk and drugged, so perhaps his scrawling, looped hand would appear different.

Dear William
    I have no ambition left, just heartbreak and terrible longing.
    I am sorry,
        Andrew

William delved around in his desk and withdrew more letters. In one, written to him on thin airmail paper, Andrew had signed off 'Longing to return to work'. It was the word 'longing' that did not match the suicide note. The letter 'L' was looped on the note but Maynard's Ls were straighter. He chewed his lip.

The office door banged open and Justin appeared.

'Right, we're all set. We leave early in the morning, first flight out.'

William looked up, covering his papers.

'Did you hear what I just said?'

'Yes, yes, just clearing my desk, join you in a moment.'

Justin closed the door and William sat for a few moments longer. He knew that Justin had been the main beneficiary in Andrew's will, but that had been a mere few thousand. *What was he thinking of?* He gathered up his papers, replaced them in the drawer and joined Justin in the drawing room.

# CHAPTER 14

WILLIAM WAS holding his 'script', making final notes as Justin joined him after his morning swim.

'Morning,' Justin said cheerily.

'Morning. I've been rethinking a few moves.'

Justin held out his hand for the thick pile of carefully typed notes.

'Can't afford any mistakes,' William said. 'We've only got two more days. So let's start from the top. I don't think I should be on the jetty to greet everyone.'

Justin raised an eyebrow. 'Why not?'

'Angela might just freak; who knows how she's going to feel at seeing me again. She might persuade Matlock to do a U-turn off the island.' Justin nodded. 'So, you make up some excuse, say I've been delayed. It'll be more dramatic and I'll make a good entrance *after* they get nice and relaxed . . . What do you think?'

Justin nodded. It irritated him that William was making this last-minute adjustment but he had to admit it made sense. 'Anything else?'

'Yes.' There was a heavy pause. 'Partly to protect myself . . .' William began and paused. 'When things get under way, perhaps I should find some excuse to leave the island. This will obviously protect me from any repercussions, should there be any.'

Justin couldn't have asked for an easier way to make sure William was out of the way when the game commenced. Nevertheless, he sighed and studied William with a concerned look. 'I don't know about that. It sounds as if you're backing out.'

'Think about it, Justin. I get called away – we'll make up some emergency. I travel to London for a few days and what goes on here has nothing to do with me because I wasn't here. And it'll leave Laura alone. It's a far better idea than me staying.'

'You're right,' Justin said. 'You're a wily old codger, aren't you?'

William shrugged. His plan meant that whatever Justin and Laura got up to his hands would be clean. He hadn't liked the ruse about the Prime Minister being a guest and was worried it might cause problems.

'But you'll be here for their arrival. You don't want to miss that, do you?' Justin asked.

''Course not. I'll hide in one of the beach houses and make a grand entrance. In fact, you could say I got called away again to check on security for the rest of the guests.'

'My, my, you've thought of everything, haven't you?' Justin said, with a grin.

William was thoroughly enjoying himself. He loved the script sessions, which invariably involved discussions with the staff, who had been briefed one by one: Dahlia would co-ordinate the 'girls' who, on the surface, were attentive servants, their other attributes to be offered quietly at the right moment. The handsome Kurt had been primed to prepare workouts and 'special extras'.

The massage rooms, sauna, steam room and the gym were all filmed continuously, as was every other area of the island. Every sexual predilection could be catered for and recorded.

Opening night was near, the cast waiting in the wings, but the man still nominally deemed the ringmaster remained supremely unaware that Justin was pulling the strings. It was obvious to all except himself that William Benedict was dancing to Justin's tune. Nevertheless, all the staff were instructed to maintain the pretence that William ran the island, and due to his rearranging sections of the plans, there was no reason for him to believe otherwise.

Justin lowered the binoculars. He was standing precariously close to the cliff edge he had nicknamed Suicide Point because of the sheer drop down to the rocks below. He could hear the plane but it was hidden by clouds. He looked down, without trepidation, at the swirling, foaming water below, battering against the lethal, jagged rocks.

'Here we go,' he said. 'William, time for you to hide.'

William's stomach churned. So many months and all this preparation. He crossed his fingers. 'Good luck,' he said.

'You know the agenda, William. Wait till the coast is clear, then into the seaplane. A launch is waiting for you just beyond the two rocks.'

'Roger and out,' said William, saluting.

Through the clouds, the seaplane suddenly emerged, much lower. 'I'll wireless you when we need the love scene!' Justin yelled after William, who laughed as he headed for his prepared hiding place.

Justin trained his binoculars on the seaplane. It dropped lower and lower, and then, like an osprey, hovered before swooping down to the waves. It made a smooth landing on the water, then motored slowly towards the jetty. Justin made his way down there, training the binoculars on the disembarking passengers. Baron and Baroness von Garten were already on the quayside, looking around with astonishment. Even with their nonchalant disregard for the trappings of vast wealth, they were unable to hide their surprise. 'You ain't seen nothin' yet,' murmured Justin.

He looked down at his list and ticked them off in the column headed 'Arrivals'.

Klaus von Garten was six feet tall, wearing white shorts and leather thonged sandals, his Gucci shades pushed back on his forehead. His statuesque wife Christina stood beside him. At forty-four, she was still the envy of many women: the surgery to her face and neck had ensured she was unblemished by age, and enhanced her Germanic high cheekbones and full lips. She was beautiful, intelligent, bilingual and had great social graces. She oozed class.

Next to alight from the plane was a rather handsome boy of about eighteen, whom Justin recognized as the Baron's son, Max. He had a lovely, rangy adolescent body with long, slender arms and legs and strawberry-blond silky hair. Behind him came another boy. Justin double-checked with the profile in his folder: James Matlock. Smaller in stature than Max and already tanned a deep golden brown, Justin could tell that, although James was around the same age as Max, he was far more worldly. He was athletic, with strong muscular legs, a tight torso, and even his worn shorts and T-shirt had a groovy 'I'm cool' look, unlike the beige chinos and white shirt worn by Max. Justin knew he would enjoy breaking them in.

Next came Cedric, Lord Hangerford, fat, puce and sweating, just as William had described him. He was followed by his fatter wife, Daphne, and their daughter Clarissa. Then came another woman, mousy, plump and nondescript. Her face was pleasant enough and she obviously took care of herself: her pale skin was barely wrinkled, even though she was in her late forties if not early fifties. Her blonde hair, probably natural, was cut into a simple style, neither elegant nor flattering. So this was William's ex-girlfriend, the 'pretty, sweet' Angela, Matlock's wife.

Justin's heart beat fast as a man emerged from the hatch behind her. It could only be Humphrey Matlock. He double-checked with the folder. The man looked bigger and heavier in the flesh. He was at least six foot two and his black hair, greying at the temples, was thick and glistened with hair oil. He wore dark glasses, had a cigar clamped between his teeth and wore a light alpaca suit and open-necked shirt. Bingo! They were all here.

Dahlia stood in front of a line of boys ready to take the luggage. Justin giggled with pride. She was a stunner, Dahlia, tanned to a dark gold, wearing a demure YSL black dress, neat black ballet slippers, her dark hair coiled severely at the nape of her neck. Justin observed the way the Baroness ran her eyes over Dahlia, struggling to ascertain who she was. Since when had a housekeeper looked like this and worn such elegant clothes?

'Welcome,' Dahlia said, 'to the Paradise. I am Sir William's housekeeper.'

Buggies were waiting to drive them up to the house, leaving the luggage to follow with the boys. The sun beat down and they fanned themselves as they drove the long way round to take in the wondrous gardens, eventually pulling up at the main entrance. There Justin stood in the doorway.

'Hi there, folks,' he said, grinning at the Baron and Baroness.

'He seems at home,' said the Baron to his wife, as they passed into the hall.

'According to the magazine clippings we were sent, he designed the place. Remember how much we liked his villa in France? Met him at one of Sylvina Lubrinsky's dinner parties.'

The Baron raised his eyebrows. He had not wanted to accept the invitation, especially after insulting William and even more so after his withdrawal from their business transactions, but his wife had insisted. They were in financial trouble and perhaps a new deal could be negotiated with William.

The next buggy held the Hangerfords and close behind them came Matlock and Angela. They were discussing the gardens. The Matlocks were avid gardeners – or, at least, avidly capable of instructing their gardening staff. Neither of them had ever seen such opulence, though, quite so many rare blooms in such profusion.

Dahlia arrived in the foyer in time to introduce them to their personal maids. Ruby for the Baron and Baroness, Kiki for their son Max, Nina for James Matlock, Ella for the Hangerfords, and Dahlia herself for the

Matlocks. The curvaceous Ruby, with her wide brown eyes and long hair, wore a simple white linen tunic, white shoes. Kiki was darker, almost six feet tall with beaded hair that sparkled around her head. Her sister Nina was stockier, with the muscular build of an athlete. Ella was the shortest, with a square, masculine body, wide shoulders and strong hands, whose strength she demonstrated by picking up a large carry-on bag belonging to Daphne Hangerford. 'This way, please,' she announced, her voice deep.

Last but not least was Kurt, in white shorts and tight T-shirt. He was the type to make any teenage girl swoon. Any adult woman with any sense would bypass him fast.

The Baron and Baroness passed covert looks to each other as they were led to guest suite three. Ruby opened the massive oak doors to reveal inside a male servant awaiting their orders, a tray of iced drinks already laid out on their private veranda. The Baron accepted a glass of chilled vintage Krug champagne, while his wife poked around, noting the fridge stocked with caviar and chilled wines, and fresh fruit piled on iced platters. She grabbed one of the magazines left for her perusal then saw the folder titled 'The Paradise'. It gave details of the facilities: the gymnasium, masseurs, the beauty treatments, the cinema, beautifully drawn maps of the island, which highlighted the sporting facilities and the beaches and coves. She carried it to her husband on the veranda and sat next to him.

Sipping his Krug, the Baron could hardly take it in. No hotel or private residence he knew could match the island's outrageous luxury.

'Well!' she said softly. 'Sir William certainly knows how to put on a good show. The place feels more like a hotel than a private residence.'

'You complaining?' said the Baron, irritated by her need always to find fault. But for once she wasn't and by now they had both been silenced by the stunning view.

Their son Max had been allocated one of the bungalows and he loved it. Initially he had not wanted to join them on holiday, hardly relishing the thought of being hemmed in on an island with them both. He had spent little time with his parents during his childhood: he had been sent away to school at an early age and his holidays had been spent in the care of nannies as his parents jetted around the world. But when he had come into adolescence, they had suddenly wanted to have him constantly at their side. His mother found him especially useful, using him as her walker when she was invited to a function that his father would not attend. At these events she monitored what he wore, to whom he spoke, what he ate and drank, and never gave him an opportunity to move from her side, a protective diamond-studded wrist resting firmly on his shoulder at all times. She would laugh and tease him about being the man in her life, and God help him if he so much as glanced in the direction of any young female his own age: his mother would immediately run through the girl's social background and her unsuitability. As a result, Max was naïve and shy at eighteen, having only a fleeting knowledge of the opposite sex.

Suddenly James Matlock jumped over from his veranda next door and strolled into Max's bungalow suite. 'It's fucking mind-blowing,' he said, looking around. Max flushed as James opened the fridge. 'We can get really pissed,' he exclaimed, and laughed.

The boys had met on one or two occasions before, and had sat next to each other on the plane; Max had been reduced to tongue-tied shyness, as James talked about the girls he hoped to get his hands on. Unlike Max he was well experienced, and enjoyed broadcasting the fact in a loud whisper.

'I've got my own maid,' Max said, nodding to the bedroom to indicate to James to mind his language.

'So have I,' James said, winking. 'You want to do a tour?' he asked, going back out on to the veranda.

Max followed. 'Okay. But perhaps I should see my parents first.'

James shrugged, he had no intention of getting a lecture from his old man. He climbed back to his own quarters.

Max found himself alone with Kiki, who passed him a menu. 'All you have to do, sir, is request the time and state where you'd like to eat – the beach, sun deck, here in your room, wherever – and your order will be brought to you. Dinner is served in the dining room from seven thirty until ten.' Max smiled shyly, wondering if he should tip her. 'May I suggest, sir, I put some sun block on you, especially on your shoulders? It's very dangerous to go without at this time of the day.'

Max hesitated, but Kiki gestured for him to go into the bedroom where she had already set up a padded massage-table covered in soft white towels with a tray of oils.

*

In the adjoining suite James was already lying on his veranda while Nina rubbed sun-oil over his back and shoulders. He had a hard-on, feeling her strong hands smoothing on the sweet, perfumed oil, her big breasts sweeping over his back. He reckoned this was going to be the best holiday of his life. Nina leaned in close, letting her breasts slide up his arm. 'If you need any extras, sir, you only have to ask,' she said.

'Extras?' he repeated dumbly.

'Intimate massages. I am here to see that you are totally satisfied.'

This was a cocky little sonofabitch, Nina thought, and she could see his crotch swelling as she moved her hands expertly over his beautiful young body. She was rather glad she'd been allocated a boy rather than one of the older men. She liked breaking in young guys, but she reckoned this one was no virgin.

'Oh, yeah, that's great,' James said closing his eyes. Nina bent low and whispered into his ear, 'I can also provide any substances you require.'

His eyes sprang open just as the top button of her stretched white tunic released itself. His already swollen cock was upright now, like a gun primed to shoot.


Matlock was lying on the vast bed, wearing just a short cotton dressing-gown. Unlike his wife, he paid little attention to the elegant suite. She crossed the room now to open the floor-to-ceiling Gothic windows. With the touch of a button, the electric blinds glided back into virtually hidden alcoves to reveal the large patio. It was partly shaded with tropical plants and a striped awning around a private dining area, leaving the other side bathed in bright sunlight. Two sun-loungers were laid out and a chilled bottle of champagne with two glasses stood in the shade on a small marble table.

'Nothing has been overlooked,' Angela said softly.

'What?' her husband enquired, tossing aside the brochure. It made him feel as if he was supposed to put in a bid for the place. 'What was that?' he barked to his wife.

'One's every need is catered for,' she said, shading her eyes to look down to the glistening water then upwards to the cliffs. Matlock came to stand beside her and saw James way below walking with Max. 'He's really going to enjoy himself,' she said.

'We all are, darling. That invitation was heaven-sent. It's so rare for us all to be together. I'm glad I changed my mind about coming – it would have been a shame to miss all this, and I'm sure there's some great fishing to be had, deep sea. I'd love to try my hand at that.'

'Yes, I'm sure.' Angela's calm exterior belied the fact that she had had to take extra Valium to prepare herself to face William.

Matlock changed the subject. He didn't want to give her the real reason for changing his mind: two weeks with the Prime Minister and his biggest competitor had been too good an opportunity to miss. 'Apparently there's a damned good library and gymnasium. Must say that is one hell of a pool,' he said.

There was a knock on the door. Angela went to open it. It was Dahlia. 'Just checking you have everything you want,' she said.

'A cup of tea,' yelled Matlock. 'Good old English tea.'

'Everything's lovely. I was just going to take a

287

shower.' Angela nodded to Dahlia. 'Thank you so much for unpacking. It's something I always loathe doing.'

'Would you care for a massage?' Dahlia asked. 'I am a fully trained masseuse, ma'am, reflexology and therapeutic herbal massage.'

'Another time, perhaps.' Angela was unable to meet Dahlia's direct gaze: for some reason she couldn't identify the maid unnerved her.

'Very well. I'll order tea. Would fifteen minutes leave enough time for your shower?'

'Oh, good heavens, yes. Thank you.'

Dahlia closed the door and left. Angela looked out onto the veranda, but her husband was already snoring. She had wanted to ask him when they were to meet William, but decided against it. They would confront each other at dinner.

The Baroness, wearing a white bikini, her hair tied up in a flowered scarf, lay with her eyes closed in the jacuzzi. She loved the feel of the herb-scented water as it massaged her body. She had a second glass of champagne at her elbow and one of the white-coated servants had unobtrusively placed a small platter of canapés beside her. She sighed. This really was perfection.

'You should see the gymnasium,' her husband said, perching on the side of the jacuzzi. 'It's better equipped than any place I have ever been to, and the instructor seems pleasant. He's from Berlin.'

'Really?' she said, eyes closed.

'I'm going to work out while I'm here,' said the Baron, accepting a glass of champagne from the same hovering servant. 'According to Kurt, I could still lose some weight. When you get to my age, it gets harder to lose those few extra pounds.'

He accepted a fresh platter of canapés and, despite his talk on weight-loss, began to eat them.

'Where's Max?' his wife asked, yawning.

'I have no idea. He went off with the Matlocks' son, James. He's a good-looking boy, isn't he?'

His wife's eyes opened and she squinted up at him quizzically. 'A word of warning: be careful.'

'For God's sake, I only said James was good-looking.'

'I know you and your good-looking boys.'

'But he's Max's friend.'

'Hasn't stopped you before, has it? But this time just remember whose son he is. Those two are so prudish, and if you cross him he'll crucify you on the front page of so many newspapers.' She sighed with impatience. 'He did it to William Benedict and look what happened to him!'

'Judging from this place, that scandal didn't hurt him.'

'Perhaps not, but tread carefully. He must have a hidden agenda. Why else would he ask us here? Maybe he wants to do business again. Let's hope so.'

They had shelled out thousands to pay the press to keep his homosexual dalliances private and his wife had protected him for years. The Baron's face tightened as she continued languidly, 'I'm surprised he wasn't waiting to greet us with a sledgehammer, considering the way you backed out of that deal.'

'All's fair in love and business deals,' he snapped.

'I'm sure it is. I just wish you had a little of his success. I presume that was why you accepted the invitation, in the hope of getting into bed with him, so to speak.'

'For God's sake don't start. Don't you think that maybe, just maybe, he wants to get into bed with me? In a business capacity, obviously.' He made no mention to her of the legal case he was fighting with Benedict. His lawyers had suggested that this trip might be a good opportunity to discuss it, perhaps in an informal way.

'I say! This is all rather lovely, isn't it?' Angela Matlock was wearing a large-brimmed sun-hat, a pale lemon dress and flat white sandals. She carried a straw basket with her cross stitch sticking out of it. 'It's a little too hot for me in the sun. I'll sit in the shade. I can't go too far, Humphrey's sleeping. He hates it if I'm not close when he wakes.'


In the control room, his feet up on the console, Justin spoke into the mike.

'William?'

'Yup,' came the crackly reply.

'You in position?'

'Yup, I'm in the charter-boat. We're just inside the two rocks.'

'Then this is your call for onstage,' he said.

'Roger!' said William.

'Roger yourself!' replied Justin, then hesitated. 'Hang on, what are you wearing?'

'What you and Dahlia put out for me.'

He was about to describe his clothes when Justin cut him off with 'Break a leg.'

*

290

The Baroness stepped out of the jacuzzi, selected a robe from the pool-side table and put it on. She looked around and then decided to sit at the far end of the pool, beneath a yellow striped awning near Angela Matlock.

'Who else is expected?' she asked Angela. 'Have you any idea?'

'I'm not sure, but the place is big enough to accommodate goodness knows how many. Have you see William Benedict yet?'

'No, I presume he'll be at dinner, though,' mused the Baroness. 'Does Justin Chalmers count as a guest? Or is he staff?'

Angela pointed towards the sea. 'It looks as though someone is arriving,' she said, reaching for her glasses.

The Baron strolled over to join them. 'Boat coming in,' he said.

William stepped out of the cabin and looked up at the island. Dahlia was on the quay waiting, her hand held out to guide him down the ramp. They saw him kiss her cheeks.

'Oh, my God! Is that his latest? His housekeeper!' the Baroness said sarcastically, then leaned forward.

Angela shrivelled into her cross stitch. With every fibre of her body she wanted to see him, but she refused to look.


Matlock woke with a start when he heard the powerful engines of the boat at the dock. He was sweating like a pig and had spent too much time in the sun. He swore, wrapped a towel around himself and stood up in time to see William step into the waiting buggy and head for the house. He sat like a king, tanned and relaxed, smiling: a happy man.

In the control-room, Justin was applauding. 'Bloody Oscar-winning stuff,' he said, into the mike. 'I'll see you after dinner. Just do as instructed, then meet up at the westerly cove. Now I've got to set some tapes recording . . .'

'My God, he looks like something out of a movie. How many servants has the man got, for heaven's sake?' asked the Baron, downing the rest of his champagne. 'Certainly splashing his money around, as if he was printing it himself.'

They all laughed. Within moments, they were joined by Cedric Hangerford, who'd been monitoring William's arrival from his own veranda. 'Typical of that jumped-up parvenu,' said Cedric.

At that moment, Humphrey Matlock appeared. 'I see our host has arrived. Rather like Anthony Steele in one of those sixties movies.' He laughed.

Angela couldn't help thinking that William looked rather good. Then she remembered how much he had hurt her, ignored her, treated her like a nobody. Seeing him again had unsettled her. She reached out and patted her husband's arm. 'You look very hot, darling,' she said.

'A few lengths will cool me down,' he replied, turned and dived into the pool with a tremendous splash.

Angela watched her husband swimming up and down and recalled her first meeting with him. At first she'd found him loud-mouthed and frightening, but she'd soon discovered his deep-seated insecurities. It was a touching evening when he told her that he longed to better himself. He knew he was going to be successful and he wanted, or needed, someone like her to smooth off his rough edges. 'Excuse me,' he had said, 'if I'm a bit unrefined. I don't have your high-society connections.'

She'd laughed and told him the truth: her family was middle class with social aspirations. They'd saved every penny they had to send her to Roedean, so that she would meet all the right 'gels'. But despite that, Angela was still a greengrocer's daughter. Her elongated vowels and Sloane style were cultivated. She'd told him how frightened she was of love. She said she had been in love before, but she'd been hurt. Twice. Later that evening Humphrey told her all about his childhood, told her things he had never mentioned to another living soul. It was as if they had found sanctuary with each other. Six months later they married.

In many ways, Matlock was like William. He had the same insecurities and the same need to be educated in the social graces. But, unlike William, Matlock had married Angela. Perhaps deep down, though, Angela always knew that for her Humphrey Matlock was second best. As the years progressed, she learned to put up with his moods, his aggression and his terrifying temper. He grew more and more successful and Angela felt the need to hide herself in his shadow. She knew about his mistresses, nothing ever escaped her, but she felt this was a cross she had to bear. She doted on her son, but at times she couldn't help seeing he was a mirror image of his father.

Sinking deep into depression, Angela's hatred of William resurfaced. She was a woman who appeared to have everything, but in truth had nothing. She had a wretched, loveless marriage, for which she blamed William. He had taken her youth and love, and had humiliated her twice. She had waited many years to repay him. She had badly wanted to hurt him and she had used her husband to do so. It was reading about Andrew Maynard's death that had set it off. She urged her husband to dig deep, to ruin William, even hurt him through his own family. When he questioned her obsession, she murmured only that he owed her: she had turned a blind eye to his own philandering. Matlock had laughed and then, of course, had obliged.

# CHAPTER 15

T HE NEXT DAY dawned with a cloudless azure sky and just enough breeze to blow away the humidity. The guests explored the island, swam, rode the jet-skis, played tennis, worked out in the gym. Now they gathered on the veranda overlooking the jetty for tea. Plates of sandwiches, pastries, muffins and fruit were placed in the shaded buffet area, with every conceivable variety of tea: Assam, Formosa Oolong, Orange Pekoe, Earl Grey, and herbal. They chattered excitedly, sharing their day's discoveries, all relaxed and enjoying the food. They turned as a powerful speedboat appeared on the horizon, heading for the island's jetty, the boys running hot-foot to welcome the new arrival.

The guests shaded their eyes against the sun to stare.

'Here comes someone else,' Cedric Hangerford stated unnecessarily, as the boat's engines were cut. To Matlock's disappointment, only one figure could be seen, and it was that of a woman.

Laura remained in the stern of the boat, her eyes shaded by dark glasses, an ice blue chiffon scarf draped around her head, matching her Chanel shift. The staff hurried to remove her Louis Vuitton suitcases, but she remained a serene figure. Extending one slender hand to a waiting boy, she stepped from the boat in a fluid movement, like a dancer. As if in slow motion, she unravelled her trailing scarf and her white-blonde hair swirled around her shoulders as perfectly as if she had been in a shampoo advertisement. Laura was not tanned: her skin was translucent, pale, like that of some exotic ice maiden.

Max let out a long sigh of admiration. 'My God, she's so beautiful . . . like a mirage.'

The Baroness gasped and turned to her husband. 'Isn't that . . . it is, isn't it?'

'What?' said the Baron, buttering a scone.

'Laura. It's Laura Chalmers.'

The Baron looked up, butter trickling down his chin.

'Justin's sister, remember? We met her once at Grimaud.'

'Ghastly temper,' the Baron said, holding his empty teacup for Kiki to refill. 'You remember Christa, that evening when she appeared like a Hollywood Oscar in that gold lamé dress?'

'There's Benedict again,' shouted Hangerford, grabbing the binoculars.

William was walking casually down the jetty, and they saw the beautiful woman turn, and then, to their astonishment, fall into his embrace. To even further amazement, they watched the couple kiss.

'Bloody hell, she's young enough to be his daughter,' spluttered Hangerford. 'The dirty old sod. After all that scandal, I think I'd have shot myself if I was him. But look at him!'

They all expected Laura and William to join them for tea, but by five thirty, they had not made an appearance, so they drifted off to their various suites to digest the day and rest before dinner.

Dinner was well attended that night. The Baron and Baroness were seated at a table for four with Cedric and Daphne Hangerford. The Matlocks were at an adjoining table with their son James. Max and Clarissa sat at a table by the open balcony doors. The main dining table, which could seat twenty, remained empty, save for two Mexican silver candlesticks that stood in the centre. A mellow light threw shadows around the wall, enhancing the oil paintings and tapestries and making the suit of armour shimmer. The room could just as easily have been in England, Austria or Russia; the ambience was theatrical.

The guests, including the younger ones, had all dressed up, the women in long gowns and the men in dark suits, except the Baron, who wore a white dinner-jacket with a white bow tie. A boy sat in a corner, quietly strumming bossa novas on his guitar. The waiters moved around quietly and efficiently. The wine flowed and the level of conversation lifted as each group relaxed and enjoyed their dinner. Nobody could fault the food, except the Baroness, who only took one spoonful of her avocado and lime soup.

The diners had all but forgotten their host when the door opened and he walked in. Momentarily the room fell silent. Then an animated conversation began again. William led Laura to her table like a lover. She did not acknowledge anyone and sat with her back to the room.

William fussed over her, making sure her chair was in the right position. She wore a delicate gown of silver chiffon, which fell loosely from a halter neck and swirled like gossamer. Her blonde hair was braided down her back and tied with a fine silver ribbon. Her shoes were silver, with a spiked heel and a band of silver leather around the ankle.

The adults were impressed, but disguised it by continuing to talk. The younger guests stared openly. William was wearing a white dinner-jacket, with a black, tight-collared shirt and well-cut black trousers. Now, at last, he turned to his guests. Moving around with an elegant confidence, he shook hands with them all, apologizing for not having been there to greet them but explaining he had had pressing business meetings. He came last to Angela and Matlock.

'Angela, what a long time it has been. I can't tell you how delighted I am that you accepted my invitation.'

Angela's cheeks flushed as his hand reached for hers. When he kissed her fingertips, she had trouble breathing and had to gulp before she was able to speak. 'You look better than ever,' she said nervously.

'Thank you. And this must be your husband. I don't believe we've actually met. I am delighted that you and your family are here. I do hope you enjoy my island.'

Matlock's voice boomed, 'It's a paradise, wonderful place. This is my son James. James! Say good evening to your host. William Benedict, James Matlock.'

But James could not stop looking across the room at the wonderful naked back opposite him. He drank in the woman's every move as she picked up a glass – filled, James presumed, with the champagne his parents were guzzling – and sipped it.

'James, dear, do stop staring,' Angela said softly.

'Nice to meet you, sir,' James said eventually, and William smiled warmly as his eyes, like James's, turned back to Laura.

Then William rejoined Laura and took her hand to help her rise. 'One of the main reasons I invited you all here, and we are hoping more guests will join us shortly, is because I wanted to introduce to you the love of my life. She is soon to be my wife: Laura.'

Laura gave a dazzling but demure smile, as William paraded her from table to table. She rested an arm around William's back as she walked. On her hand glistened a diamond ring that made the Baroness gasp. William raised his glass. 'A toast to my darling. She has made me the happiest man alive. To Laura.'

They all lifted their glasses, and Laura cupped his face between her hands and kissed him, before turning back to implore them gently, 'Please, continue eating, we've interrupted your dinner long enough. Come and sit down, darling.'

Clarissa Hangerford also kept her eyes on Laura, but with a look of envy. She had been getting on well with both James and Max and had been secretly hoping for a fling with one, if not both of them, though Justin of course would be preferable to both. But seeing this gorgeous creature had shattered all her confidence. She had blonde hair too, but of quite a different type: it didn't shine like Laura's, and swimming had made it frizzy and dry. Clarissa had also caught the sun, and was blotchy, red and sore. The gown Laura was wearing was any young girl's dream, and Clarissa wondered how on earth it stayed up with just a tiny strap around her neck. It made her own white cotton dress seem dowdy.

She looked down at herself and noticed that it was already crumpled, with a nasty crease running around the waist. She immediately hated her thick-soled, trendy platform shoes, which she was sure made her feet look enormous.

Clarissa's dinner companion, Max, had already decided he was in love with Laura, but believed her to be beyond his reach. He had returned to his hamburger and French fries. His parents rarely, if ever, allowed him to eat such fatty foods and his mother would not have a bottle of ketchup in the house. He ate with rare relish. Clarissa munched fried chicken and salad, but delved constantly into Max's chips.

Max appeared not to notice, his eyes glued to Laura's exquisite back. 'Is she a movie star?' he whispered to Clarissa.

'I dunno. If she is, I've never seen her in anything and didn't your oh-so-elegant mother tell you it's rude to stare with your mouth open?' Then, unable to contain herself, 'How old do you think she is?' she whispered.

'No idea,' said Max, as he moved his wine glass to the left, to enable the waiter to refill it. He glanced at his parents to see if they were monitoring him, but they were deep in conversation. As he turned back to the table, he saw James cast him a rueful look and tap his glass of mineral water. Unlike the Baron, his father watched over him like a hawk, and as he'd been caught drunk recently, he had to be on his best behaviour . . .

Laura was served a green salad, followed by a Dover sole. Max watched the way she held her cutlery and wished he could feed her morsel by morsel. James was still staring too and his mother had to kick him beneath the table as his father asked him about his exam results for a second time.

He was stoned. Knowing he would not be allowed to drink, he had rolled a spliff before coming down to dinner. At first he had not felt the effects, but now, confronted by his father's burning red face, he did.

'I'm sorry, Dad, what did you say?'

'We must discuss your last exam results, James, because if you need extra tuition we should arrange it before you return next term.'

'Oh, well, yes, but you know part of my problem was being on the rowing team. It meant I had to do so much practice in the mornings and evenings it didn't leave all that much time for cramming for the exams.'

'I thought it was tennis,' Matlock said, wiping his mouth with his napkin.

'Yeah, well, I'm in the first team for that as well,' James lied. He hadn't played for months and the rowing team had dumped him.

Matlock sighed and looked at his wife as she toyed with her food.

'Don't you like it?'

'It's delicious. I'm just not very hungry.'

Matlock looked across at the intimate couple, and leaned closer to his wife. 'Making a damned fool of himself with the girl. What did he say her name was?' he whispered, too loudly.

'Keep your voice down,' she hissed.

'Do you always have to tell me what I should or shouldn't do, for Christ's sake? They can't hear me.'

'I'm sorry, I've got a headache.'

'Yes, a permanent one,' he snarled, and she cringed into her seat.

The desert trolley was wheeled in, laden with sweets so tempting that even the Baroness could not resist. As the boy with the guitar began to sing softly, Laura kissed William lovingly and slipped out of the room.

'Will you all excuse us?' asked William, as he drew back his chair and followed her.

As soon as they left, the dining-room broke into loud conversation, like the tidal wave after a dam has broken.

'Well, where on earth did he find that little filly?' Hangerford wondered aloud.

Matlock was more concerned with when the PM was expected, not to mention the other guests he had been told would be joining them. But no one appeared to know and the abundance of such exquisite food became the focus of all their attention.

'How's my princess?' whispered Justin, as his sister hugged him tightly, giggling.

'You should have seen their faces. We were so good, weren't we, Willy?'

William kissed her cheek. He felt like a conspiratorial child. 'I am having a good time. What a pompous, fat-arsed man that Matlock is . . . and I did such an elegant eye-to-eye with his wife. To think I almost married her. Dear God!'

Justin looked at Laura then back at William. 'It's phase two now. Time to make yourself scarce.'

'Oh, no! Can't you give me another day?'

'No. Don't start messing around with the schedule, it was all agreed. You can't back out of it now. And, anyway, you decided it, William.'

'But I don't want to miss the fun.'

'You won't, and as it's all recorded you'll have it for posterity. If you're here it'll hold things up.' William sighed. 'Make yourself scarce, you old bugger. It was your idea, so get your arse out of here and let the fun and games begin. Besides, it'll keep them waiting for the extra guests who aren't going to appear,' said Justin, pushing William through a door.

Before disappearing, William turned and blew a camp kiss. 'Knock 'em for six,' he said, and was gone. But just to make sure he didn't change his mind, Justin kept the monitor running, watching as he made his way out through the back corridors.

'I'll not start on the younger ones,' said Laura quietly. 'They'll be too easy. I think I'll go for his lordship first. Then I'll work my way to Angela. Is that OK?'

'Save the pig Matlock until last. Make him beg,' said Justin quietly, his eyes on the screen. William was in one of the golf carts being driven down to the jetty where the boys were waiting to take him off the island.

'Of course he has to be last. I'm not stupid.'

Justin switched the monitor screen to the main hallway. 'Here they come. Go into the lounge and be waiting.' He left her side to welcome the guests as they drifted up the stairs into the drawing room for coffee and liqueurs. As they entered the light, airy room, their bellies full, tired from the day in the sun and the sumptuous dinner, they were surprised to see Laura, who looked ravishingly fresh. Justin made a show of serving coffee alongside the servants, but was watching Laura as the men moved closer, like bees to honey.

Max looked into her eyes then immediately dropped his gaze, even though she said no more than how pleased she was that he had come to the island. She eased away from Max and moved on to James, then to Clarissa. When she shook Cedric Hangerford's hand, he held hers far too long. He only let go when his wife interrupted them to admire Laura's gown. The Baron and Baroness mentioned that they had met before. Laura smiled sweetly but made no attempt to recall when or where. The Baroness examined the woman who made her pale into insignificance. She was adept at fast appraisals, and wondered which designer had created such a delicate dress. She reached out and took Laura's left hand. 'What a beautiful engagement ring. So simple. I always think diamonds look best with platinum. Who designed it for you?'

'William. It's sweet, isn't it?'

Sweet it was not. It had to be worth a few hundred thousand pounds.

'Lady Matlock, this is my sister, Laura,' Justin announced, ushering her away from the Baroness. Angela smiled but did not take Laura's hand. She turned to her husband. 'Darling,' she said, in turmoil. The girl's eyes were magnetic with the colour of the sea, her lily perfume like clean air.

Humphrey Matlock, cutting a slice of cheese, turned round. He wiped his hand on a napkin. 'You have stunned us into silence yet again, like an angel passing over.' He kissed her hand.

She allowed it to remain against his lips just a fraction longer than necessary. 'Thank you,' she said softly, and watched as he returned to his cheese.

Then Justin slipped his arms around her shoulders. 'But this poor darling is going to be all alone for a few days,' he announced.

304

Everyone turned their attention to the brother and sister.

'My fiancé has been called away. He's expecting other guests so he's gone to the mainland. Something to do with security,' Laura said lightly, before Justin assured them their host would not be away for more than a few days. Then he led her out of the room. Again, as soon as they disappeared, a hubbub of conversation broke out as they wondered who the guests might be – the island already seemed entirely secure.

'I heard it was the Prime Minister,' Matlock said flippantly, and they looked from one to the other.

Angela's lips tightened. She knew now why he had insisted they accept the invitation, even though he had been aware of what torment it would cause her. 'You never said anything before about the Prime Minister,' she said softly.

'Only just found out,' he lied, and made no mention that he had been told his main competitor was also expected. Still, it meant that he had a couple of days to enjoy himself and not think about business. He began eagerly enquiring about fishing.

Justin unhooked Laura's dress and she stepped out of it, kicking off her sandals. He fetched a robe and put it around her shoulders. Then she sat at the dressing-table while he unplaited her hair and began to brush it.

'So?' he asked.

She half turned and lifted her hand. 'Kiss it,' she said. He did so and she laughed. 'Now give me your hand. You be me and I'll be Matlock.'

Justin held it out to her. She lifted it to her lips,

brushing them against his fingers, then darted her tongue between two.

'He did that?'

She nodded, and turned back to the mirror. 'It's going to be easier than we dreamed. I will have him crawling, begging for it. And you know what'll make him crazy? I think he'll find out that his son has been there before him.'

Justin flopped on the bed and laughed. He loved to hear her talk dirty. 'Shall I fuck him too?' he asked.

'James? Why not?' she said, creaming her face.

'What about William's ex? The strait-laced Angela,' Justin asked. He didn't relish the idea of screwing her. 'God, that man had lousy taste.'

'You take her first. I think she's got to be given something, maybe half a tab.' Laura plucked a tissue to wipe over her face.

Justin rolled on to his stomach and told her what the maids had said to him, that despite her frumpy look, her lingerie was lacy, flimsy and sexy.

Laura got up and lay on top of him, nuzzling his neck. 'The Baron and Baroness seem tedious. Do we need to bother with them?'

'He'd roll over for a monkey,' smirked Justin, 'as long as it had its mouth taped up so it couldn't give away his secret.' He turned on to his back.

Laura remained on top of him, feeling him erect beneath her.

'What about Clarissa?' he said.

'She's wet just looking at you. The skinny boy Max isn't a push-over, though. And he's got the hots for the Hangerford girl. He looked as if he'd never had an erection before, never mind fucked anyone.'

306

Laura sat up and moved away from the bed. Justin yawned; he was really tired. He stretched, and his jeans slipped down to reveal his tight, flat belly. No man had ever made Laura feel so aroused. She sighed and reached over to unzip his pants. 'This'll make you sleep.' She knelt down between his legs, taking him in her mouth.

'We have to be careful,' he said, eyes closed, loving the feel of her mouth around him. She sucked harder, clawing his thighs and twisting his testicles. The pain made him gasp and with a moan he climaxed into her mouth.

'That was a quickie,' she said, wiping her lips with a tissue. Usually it took much longer.

'It's been a while.' He zipped up his trousers. 'And I've had a hard-on all evening thinking about you.'

She went into the bathroom and started to clean her teeth. Justin lolled at the door. 'Willy must be on the flight by now,' he said. 'You know, I've become fond of him.'

'Oh, no.' Laura sighed. 'Don't tell me you've fucked him. I told you not to.'

'I haven't, and I like him. He's good company. Sure he can lash out a bit, but considering all the tedious family situations he's had to go through, he's impressed me.'

'I like him too,' she said softly, then laughed. 'He kisses like a teenager. He was so nervous of taking me in his arms, even if it was just for show.'

'He means us no harm, Laura, I know that. Sometimes I think he's the only man I've ever trusted.'

'Are you in love with him?' she asked, her voice soft and afraid.

'Hell, no, I mean . . . it's more that I love him like . . .' He thought about it for a moment. '. . . I don't know.'

'Love him like a brother, perhaps?' She stared at Justin in the mirror.

His brow was furrowed in a deep frown and he shook his head slowly. 'No, not like that. Maybe it's because I've never known anyone for such a length of time. I dunno. It's a new one on me, but the old codger grows on you.'

He stood behind her and slipped his arms around her, hugging her close. He had a vulnerable side, and it was the side she cared for most of all. 'I miss you so much when you're away from me. I love you, Laura,' he whispered.

'I know, I know. Now go on. Go to bed.' She cupped his face between her hands and kissed his lips. 'We only have two weeks, then it'll all be over and we'll be free.'

'You won't leave me?' he said anxiously.

'No, of course I won't. Will you leave me?'

'Not even with all the diamonds Willy's going to give you?' Justin insisted.

'We'll be together, Justin, I promise. We'll live in our villa, just you and me, and no more nightmares. We'll have paid Matlock back and we'll be free. It'll all be over.'

'Yes,' he said, then kissed her lightly before he left the room.

This was the side of Justin that William had rarely seen. Hardly anyone had ever seen it, apart from Marta and Laura. This was not the vicious, twisted Justin, or the over-confident, witty, talented Justin. This was the child who hid in the darkest recess of his adult mind, when Laura became the stronger of the two.

Next morning, Justin and Laura went to the control room to survey the guests at play. Justin's mood had lifted, and he was chuckling at the film footage.

'Well, I'd better start work,' she said. 'If I have to begin with Cedric Hangerford, you'd better stand by. I doubt if it'll take long. His kind never do. Where is he?'

Justin flicked on a monitor and pointed at the screen. 'As arranged. He's midway through a workout with Kurt in the gym. He's got a massage booked immediately after with Kiki.'

'Tell Kurt,' Laura said softly, 'to suggest to his lordship that he has a sauna. Justin? Did you hear me?'

'That's not on the list.'

'No, I know. I've just had a good idea. I'll work him over in the sauna. So arrange it.' Then she leaned towards him, and whispered further instructions.

'Sauna it is, my darling. And just remember, Big Brother is watching you.' He picked up the intercom phone. He adored Laura: sometimes her mind was even more warped than his. She was right, though: they needed to move fast on William's tedious guests, get rid of them as soon as possible, leaving Matlock for the plucking.

Kurt replaced the receiver.

'I've arranged a sauna for you,' Kurt said to Hangerford, now flat on his back, arms splayed at his sides.

'Christ, I don't think I can get up,' he said.

Kurt put out his hand and hauled him to his feet. 'I'll take you through, sir. I'd keep to the lower bunks,' he added, 'it's hotter and better for your skin.'

They went in and Kurt laid out a towel for Hangerford, who flopped down with an exhausted sigh of relief. Then he passed him a bottle of chilled water. 'Drink as much as possible,' he said encouragingly, and waited a moment as he watched Cedric gulping it down.


Laura lay on the top shelf of the sauna, naked apart from a small white towel across her thighs, her body glistening. When the door opened she didn't move a muscle, but remained still with her eyes closed. Hangerford sighed again, as soft relaxing sounds drifted into the sauna, the noise of waves and whales over the sighing ocean.

Hangerford did not notice that the sauna was already occupied, until one perfect white hand swung down from the bunk above. Then Laura sighed, and yawned as if just waking. She dropped her towel, which brushed his shoulder, and he half sat up, wondering who was above him. As the sighs grew louder, he realized it was a woman, and that she was masturbating. His body flushed with anticipation. Laura began to mew like a kitten and then she moaned. Hangerford could feel the tremor of the bench above him and he was now fondling himself. As she became more and more vocal in her arousal, so did he. His body felt as if it was on fire.

Laura swung her hips and legs down over the side of the upper bunk, and gripped the slats with her hands to keep from dropping to the ground. Cedric raised himself on one elbow. She thrust herself into his face.

He put his head between her legs and began licking and sucking, grunting. She pushed her hips forward and wrapped her legs around his shoulders. He was virtually buried inside her when the sauna's incredible heat enveloped him. His brain felt as if it was about to explode. He tried to draw his head away from her legs. He was gasping and unable to get his breath, but the more he panted, the dizzier he felt. He couldn't breathe and his heart felt as if it was about to explode. Darkness descended and he passed out.

Laura shoved him away from her, picked up her towel, and opened the sauna door. As it closed behind her she turned up the temperature and walked into the shower. By the time she felt cleansed, her skin tingling from her body scrub, she reckoned Hangerford might need assistance. As she passed the sauna, she lowered the temperature and headed for the changing cubicles. Justin joined her. 'Get him out quickly,' she said.

Justin and Kurt carried Hangerford out of the sauna and into the shower. They remained with him as he spluttered and shrieked from the ice-water jets. From her changing cubicle, Laura saw Dahlia walking towards the sauna with Clarissa. With a white towel clutched to her naked body, she told Dahlia that she could never take more than a few minutes in a sauna. Dahlia laid the towel along the top bunk and assisted Clarissa up the ladder; then she lowered the heat, threw some pine essence on to the coals and closed the door. Laura left the changing rooms with Dahlia.

Hangerford was resting, another glass of water in his hand. He wished Kurt would stop hovering around him. He insisted he was perfectly recovered and, in fact, felt remarkably fit. Just thinking about getting back into

311

the sauna gave him an erection. It had been the most exciting sexual encounter he had ever experienced.

The moment Kurt left him, he went straight back inside. His heart was thudding in his chest, yet he felt focused, full of energy and sexual drive. He closed the door and dropped his towel, proudly revealing his bloated penis. He walked to the bunk he had used before, lay down and stretched his hands up to fondle beautiful firm breasts. His hands roamed over the young body and he grew more excited as he masturbated the woman, pressing his fingers between her legs. Feeling her opening he could no longer contain himself. 'Come down, I want to finish where I left off. I want to fuck you.'

Clarissa raised herself on her elbow. She could hardly catch her breath. *'Daddy!'* she gasped, leaning down to behold not Justin, as she had hoped, but her father.

Hangerford charged out like a crazed bull.


In the control room, Justin sat smoking a cigar, the camera still focused on the terrified face of Clarissa. Beautiful! The film would splice together perfectly. He also knew that his lordship would believe that his head had been between his daughter's legs. He giggled. William was going to love it. Imagine releasing this to the *Racing News*! Better still the Jockey Club. Hangerford had certainly had quite a ride even if he hadn't finished the race!

# CHAPTER 16

WILLIAM SAT in the Harbour Bar with a large
Scotch and water. After leaving the island he
had arrived at Tortola only to discover that
his flight had been cancelled due to technical problems.
Overnight, a heavy mist had fallen and the next flight
had been postponed until conditions improved. He
wondered how things were going back at the island. He
would have liked to call Justin, but knew that that
would be childish. Although he himself had instigated
his departure, he now had reservations. But he told
himself it made sense and, besides, he knew everything
would be caught on video.

Lost in his thoughts, he was surprised by a nudge on
his shoulder. It was Lady Bellingham. 'Are you stranded
too?' she asked. 'I'm trying to see some friends off.
They've gone to do some last-minute souvenir hunting
so I thought I'd come in for a drink. It's such a bore
this hanging around.'

William was unsure whether he should offer to buy
her a drink. This was, after all, the longest conversation
they had ever had. Boredom must have forced her to
approach him.

'Do you mind?' She indicated the empty chair at his

313

table. 'It's always tricky, a woman alone having a drink in a bar,' she said, sitting.

William ordered a gin and tonic and they fell into an awkward silence. He was trying to think of something to say when Lady Bellingham remarked, 'I hear that your son Charlie has gone into rehab. An old school-friend of Oliver's is in Minnesota too, and he wrote to us.'

'Fingers crossed, he seems to be doing well.'

Another lengthy silence prevailed as she sipped her drink. Then she rattled the ice cubes around her glass nervously. 'Oliver didn't have a chance,' she said, looking down into the glass. 'His body was pumped full of ecstasy, heroin, crack – you name it.' She bit her lower lip. 'I don't know where he got it. I know there's lots of pot around, I take it myself. But we wouldn't let him have the hard stuff, and we kept him under pretty tight surveillance.'

William recalled the party on the night their son had died. He hadn't noticed much 'surveillance'. Lord Bellingham had been stoned out of his head, along with most of the guests.

A tear rolled down her cheek and dropped off her chin. 'I'm sorry, so sorry to mention it. Let's change the subject.' William passed her a handkerchief. 'I thought you'd sold up, or were about to,' she said, wiping her face. 'I've read so much about your place. We're thinking of leaving. You must give me the name of your estate agents. They're doing a grand job of promoting your island.'

'Journalists,' he said, 'always get the wrong end of the stick. I'm not selling, quite the contrary, I love the place.' The silence was descending again, but he found something more to say. 'As a matter of fact I've lent my place to Justin Chalmers and his sister Laura while I do some work in London. I'll just be gone a few days.'

She put her head quizzically to one side. 'Justin Chalmers?' she said, and seemed perplexed.

'Designer,' said William. 'Did the place up for me.'

'Is that the Justin Oliver knew?' she asked.

William nodded. 'Charlie talks about Oliver. He was very upset.'

Lady Bellingham put her hand on William's, blinking back the tears. 'I can't talk about it, I'm afraid. If I do I'll start weeping. It's been quite horrible, the whole business and, er . . .' She swallowed rapidly.

An announcement came over the crackly PA that the weather conditions were clearing and the airport would soon be functioning normally.

'Oh, Lord,' cried Lady Bellingham, rising. 'Must find my chums or they'll be stuck here! Or, worse, I will!' She drained her gin and tonic, then gave a brittle smile. 'Nice talking to you, Sir William. You really must come and join us for dinner some time.'

William was surprised that she had stooped so low as to converse with him, let alone invite him to dine. He, too, downed his drink and walked out on to the quay to get a taxi to drive him the five miles to the airport.

In the lounge, he opened his laptop to discover a welter of e-mails from Michael, requesting he contact London immediately. But he had no time to place a call: the flight was already boarding. The messages worried him. What could be so urgent? Perhaps something had happened to Charlie. He never gave a moment's thought to the idea that it might just be business: his concern was for his son. At last he was taking on the role of father.

As the flight took off from Tortola, the paradise island was silent: most of the resident guests slept late, apart from Max. He wanted to watch the sun rise and had walked to the highest point of the island with a camera.

Max was in the agony of a schoolboy crush on Clarissa, who had played cards with him and James late into the night after they had arrived. The following day she had not come out of her room and when at last he saw her she averted her face and refused to speak to him. Why?

He walked on briskly because the early morning was still dark and the air chilly. He wondered if he was ever going to lose his virginity. With James around, he doubted if he'd get a look in here. He didn't particularly like James: he was so competitive and aggressive. He seemed constantly to have to prove himself, whereas Max was more passive. As inexperienced in worldly and sexual matters as he was, he maintained an adult calm and perspective – which was about to be shattered.

Laura was sitting with her hands clasped around her knees, perched close to the edge of the jagged rock, her hair blowing around her. Max emerged from the woods fifteen yards or so from her and was taken aback when he saw her. Although he was so close, he didn't know whether she had heard him or not. He took a step further forward, but she gave no indication that she knew she was not alone.

'Miss Chalmers,' he stuttered, and her back arched

316

like a cat's. 'It's Max,' he added softly, and wondered if perhaps he should turn back but she beckoned him to join her. Max stepped closer, a little afraid as she was so close to the cliff-edge, but she patted the space beside her for him to sit. He hesitated, edging closer, then got to his knees for safety and crawled up to her.

'You know, if you watch the sun rise close to someone, you are bound together for ever by its rays.' Her voice was a soft whisper. Max could think of no answer. He was close enough now to feel the warmth of her body beside him. They remained silent, waiting, as the amber glow spread before them.

'Here it comes, wait, wait . . . It's coming any second now,' she gasped. He held his breath and she reached out for his hand. 'No one but us will ever have this moment . . . no one but us.'

She tilted her head to catch the rays as they grew stronger, before the golden globe appeared in front of them, bathing them both in its brilliance. But Max had eyes only for the woman beside him. For him, the sun was a pale star beside her, this magical mirage, her blonde hair shimmering like a halo.

Nothing could have prepared him for this moment, nothing in his wildest dreams. She eased her body down to lie on the warming rock, holding out her arms for him to lie beside her. Without a word, he obeyed.

The kiss took his breath away. It was sweet, but it was hungry, and he felt such a surge of emotion that his body shook. She stroked his face, planting delicate kisses on his cheek and neck, her lips tracing his ears, till he felt such ecstasy he let out a moan. Max would never have considered approaching this girl-woman, he was far too shy. But, wrapped in her arms, it was as if he had always known her. He wanted the moment never to end. But it did, as abruptly as it had begun.

'I must go back,' she announced suddenly, and rolled away from him. She was up and running before he could reach out to stop her. All he could do was watch her disappear from his sight. Then he started to cry. He didn't know why: it had just been too much for him.

Max saw her fleetingly again that morning, first at breakfast then down by the jetty. He flushed deeply every time she passed within touching range, afraid she would discover he was following her. His legs shook and his heart beat so rapidly he felt sick. But he thought he had managed to appear in control of himself. After lunch they spoke again. Laura had dropped a hair slide as she passed him on her way to the pool. At first Max had simply wanted to keep it as a reminder of her, but then he plucked up courage to approach her. Just the touch of her fingers against his hand, as she thanked him, rendered him incapable of saying a word. She did not refer to the sunrise and he could not bring himself to mention it. She was, after all, Sir William Benedict's fiancée. He even questioned whether it had happened at all. But he knew it had, and now, speechless before her, it was all that filled his mind.

'You have beautiful clear eyes,' she said softly. He wanted to say something poetic in return, but she walked on.

There were four or five more fleeting meetings that day. At last he stuttered that he had hoped she didn't feel he was stalking her. She leaned closer. 'I'm sorry, what did you say?'

'Nothing,' he replied, as his breath caught in his chest.

To his astonishment and consuming delight, she suggested they walk a while. They went down to the jetty, and twice her shoulder brushed against his. There was one glorious moment when she asked him to hold her hand as she slipped off one of her sandals to shake out the sand. Her closeness made him break out in a sweat and her hand felt cool and soft, like silk.

Over the next few nights, Max could not sleep. All he could think of was Laura, but she did not appear again to greet the sunrise. The dining-room meals became the focus of his day because he knew he would see her there. He tried hard to not make his adoration obvious, but he could hardly contain himself, glancing clumsily in her direction. He started to make elaborate plans for accidentally meeting her and what he would say. But, try as he might, he could never pin down her whereabouts. She never dined at the same time in the evenings, never swam or walked at any specific time. He spent hours hovering round the places he hoped she might be, sometimes sitting in the dining-room for hours. Mostly she didn't appear to notice him.

The meeting that changed everything was when she asked him to help her open a sunshade. They were on the lower beach. He fixed it, then fetched an armful of towels and laid them out along a sun-bed. Laura was wearing a white cotton kaftan, and at certain angles the sunlight shone straight through it to outline her body like a soft shadow. He wanted to kneel at her feet, to kiss each toe, to tell her he was her slave. At one point their eyes met and he was sure she was going to say something to him. With an encouraging smile, she patted the towel beside her. But as she lay back against the cushions, his mother appeared. 'Hello, darling. Get me some towels, would you? And move a bed into the sun for me. Is there a bar down here? I'm so thirsty.'

Max fetched and carried for his mother, who kept up a constant embarrassing chatter about why he wasn't swimming or waterskiing. 'Take your shirt off, darling, you need some sun. You back hasn't broken out in spots again, has it?'

He wanted to die and he shook his head, trying to make the Baroness change the subject, but it got worse as she continued her conversation to Laura with her eyes closed. 'Poor boy, he's got such delicate skin. But, then, they all have acne at that age, don't they? It's ever since he started shaving. At least his face has cleared up. He used to get terrible boils and—'

'Mother!' hissed Max, his face crimson.

Laura got up suddenly, and excused himself, saying she had forgotten her book.

'Are you coming back?' Max asked. He had sounded so desperate and what made it worse was she didn't look at him, just continued walking towards the path.

'Not very friendly, is she?' his mother said, plastering herself in oil.

Before Max could hurry after Laura she insisted he did her back. He hated doing this. She took off her bikini top and lay face-down on the towels for him to spread the oil over her.

'She's really rather rude,' the Baroness continued.

'There's her book under the sun-lounger,' Max said, with delight. His mother looked up as he bent down to retrieve it. It was a volume of children's poems. He wanted to kiss it. 'I'll take it to her.'

'Oh, don't bother, darling, leave it. I'll take it back to the house.'

But Max was already hurrying after Laura. Out of sight of his mother, he opened the book. He could hardly believe his eyes when he saw that a note was tucked into the first page with his name on it. At first he was sure it was a joke, but why would she do that? Then he wanted to weep when he understood that she had suggested they meet by the waterfall. It had to be real.

Max waited for more than an hour past the appointed time. He had almost given up when she came into sight. His heart lurched. The note had said lunch-time, which he had taken as twelve, but she clearly thought lunch was at two. Laura was welcome to take lunch at whatever time she pleased.

Max stepped behind the rushing curtain of water to hide as she approached. She wore a wide straw hat, the same long, white kaftan, and she had threaded flowers through her toes.

'Max,' she said softly, 'I know you're here.' She removed the hat and her hair tumbled down. Slowly, she began to raise her skirt, lifting it to her knees, then her thighs. Hardly able to breathe, Max watched as the white robe inched slowly up her body. Beneath it, she was naked. Like a nymph, she stepped into the cascade of water, holding out her arms to catch the stream, her head tilted back and the water rushing off her. 'Take off your clothes and come and join me. Don't be shy. No one will see us here.'

321

Max hastily tore off his clothes and walked towards her into the clear, thundering water. Slowly her hand reached out for him. She drew him into the recess cut into the rock behind the screen of spray, and cupped his face in her hands to look into his wide, fearful eyes. 'It's all right,' she whispered.

His fear evaporated as their bodies inched closer. 'I love you,' he said, aching to kiss her.

His look of adoration frightened Laura: he reminded her of Justin as a boy. She searched his face, trying to fathom whether he was lying to her, but she saw there only innocence.

To her surprise, when their lips touched she was not thinking of anything or anyone but him. The experience confused her, and she broke away. Then her eyes concentrated on his lips, which she kissed again, as if to make sure the moment between them was real. After kissing him three times she broke away. Max was overcome with emotion and began to cry. She licked his tears as they mingled with the mist from the waterfall, and thought she too might weep. It puzzled her. This was a job, but it felt like something else. She had teased the boy for days, drawing him behind her like a puppy. She had meant to arouse him, play with him then withdraw. But something inexplicable had stopped her. She had never felt this for anyone except Justin. Was that why his kisses felt so nice? They were like Justin's, but they weren't. The feel of them made her want to continue kissing, but she wanted to kiss him as a boy, not as a man.

It was Max who changed the tone. Max became a man then, kissed her strongly and searchingly. Laura allowed herself to be drawn to lie beside him on the cool, mossy earth, his hand clasping hers. She clung to him as if she was afraid to let go.

'I love you,' Max repeated, and she began to sob. She had never known such a powerful, explosive feeling in the pit of her belly. He whispered to her, 'I don't know if I'm dreaming this, if I am mad, or even if it's real. I'm scared to close my eyes and lose you.'

'Ssh!' she said, cradling him in her arms, his head resting against her breasts. She loved his caring gentleness. She liked the way he had put his shirt beneath her head when they lay down, worried that the ground was damp. He didn't paw her or force her hand down to touch him. Their roles had been reversed so unexpectedly and without any calculation on her part. She loved the smell and touch of his lean, young body. He was clean and untouched.

When he asked if she could feel his heart leaping, he endeared himself to her more.

'Do you want to make love to me?' she asked.

Max admitted that he was afraid his inexperience would make her ridicule him.

She held him closer. She felt protective, almost motherly towards him. 'I promise I would never tease you. You will be the best lover I have ever known.' She meant it as a joke, but he gripped her tightly.

She wanted to weep as his kisses on her neck made her thighs ache, and the even sweeter kisses on her lips made her want him to make love to her. But his fingers threaded through hers and rubbed her ring finger. Feeling the solitaire diamond, he released her. 'We mustn't do this, it's wrong, it's . . .'

Laura sighed, and held up her hand. The diamond glittered. 'Don't you ever do anything wrong, Max?' she asked.

'Everyone does, but if you were to make love to me, with me, I couldn't bear to see you with another man.'

She let her hand drop to one side and he caught her fingers, pressing on the diamond with his thumb. 'When are you getting married?'

She closed her eyes.

'Do you love him?'

Again she sighed. 'It's none of your business.'

He sprang to his feet and fetched his jeans, unembarrassed now by his nakedness.

She propped herself on her elbow. 'Where are you going?'

'I can't stay. I can't be with you like this.'

'Why not?'

He zipped his fly, then looked around for his trainers. He sat on the edge of a rock as he slipped on one, then the other. He left the laces untied and looked over; she still lay on his shirt. Suddenly he felt strong, his mind clear.

'We should go,' he said, and moved towards her to pick up his shirt. The whore in Laura had abandoned her, slunk off to hide, unable to deal with the purity of emotion. She couldn't speak. She let him ease away his shirt from behind her. But he didn't put it on: instead, he draped it round her shoulders, as if to hide her breasts. She let him remove the diamond ring from her finger. He placed it carefully on the edge of a rock. 'I want you to marry me.'

She accepted his proposal, but he had no ring. 'Give

me your wedding finger,' he said. She held it out tentatively. He took it and bit it until he drew blood. She touched it with the tip of her finger then licked it.

'That will be our ring,' he breathed. 'Bite me now.'

She bit harder and longer into his finger. It hurt like hell but he wouldn't stop her. Eventually, she drew his head on to her lap. He was unsure what to do, so she told him how to use his tongue. Soon she was begging him to enter her, and as he came into her, she did what she always did: averted her face. Max noticed and withdrew. 'What did I do wrong?' he asked.

'Tell me you love me,' she said.

Max caught her hand and raised it to his lips. 'Right now, if you asked me to, I'd die for you, Laura, and I will kill anyone who takes you away from me. I want you to tell him.'

'Well, I can't straight away. He's had to return to London.'

'When he gets back?'

'Yes . . . yes, I will.'

'Promise me.'

'Yes, if you promise to keep this a secret until I have told him.' She leaned over him. 'This is odd for me . . .' She hesitated, then kissed his lips.

'What is?' he asked.

'I feel such love for you. It is the first time I have felt like this for anyone.'

'You've never made love to another man?' he asked, sitting up.

'I meant I have loved only one man before you, but he doesn't count. Tell me again.'

'I love you,' he said simply.

She laughed, hugging him, not wanting to let him go. 'And I you.'

Justin was furious. For one thing, Laura was not working up to speed: she had disappeared for the whole afternoon. For another he had not been able to capture on film anything that had taken place between her and Max because they had hidden behind the waterfall. Enraged, he confronted her. 'You are so stupid at times. You know where all the microphones are! What the hell did you take him up there for? You must have known I couldn't record you.'

'Maybe I didn't want you to see or hear me with him,' Laura said.

'*What?*'

'Nothing,' she said, looking at her watch. 'I should go. I don't want to keep Angela waiting.'

Justin pretended to pay attention to the dials on the console in front of him. 'How are you going to work on her?' he asked.

'Dahlia is helping,' Laura replied.

'In what way?' he snapped.

Laura ran her fingers through her hair. 'Angela and I share a predilection for lace lingerie, I'm told. Now, thanks to Dahlia "mixing things up in the wash", she has a few pairs of my panties.'

'Well, don't fucking take her up to the waterfall to do it. Did you by the way?' he asked moodily.

'Did I what?' she said, opening the door.

'Screw him?'

'Not yet,' and she closed the door. She felt disturbed about lying to Justin, so to calm her nerves she slipped off the solitaire diamond and felt Max's toothmarks on her finger. It kept him constantly in her mind. A secret.


Angela heard the light tap on her door and removed the ice-pack from her head. 'Who is it?' she asked.

Laura remained silent.

Angela opened the door.

'Apparently, and I don't want to get her into any trouble which is why I came myself,' said Laura, 'Dahlia mixed some of my lingerie with yours.' She held out a small parcel. 'You have mine, I believe.'

'Oh,' Angelia said, and opened the wrapping. She seemed embarrassed as she admitted that the panties and brassière were indeed hers. She went to her wardrobe and opened a drawer to find Laura's. Laura followed her and stood close . . . too close.

Angela moved away. 'You're wearing a lovely perfume,' she said, intent on searching the open drawer.

'Thank you,' Laura said, then leaned close to Angela, who was wearing some kind of gardenia cologne. 'Yours is nice too.'

Angela withdrew Laura's panties from the drawer. 'Oh, they are lovely, and . . .' She took out a brassière and a gossamer-thin silk slip.

'I have them made to my designs,' Laura said, as she laid them on the bed, pressing tissue paper flat to wrap them. 'I love packing,' she said, and went on to explain how a nanny had taught her how to fold garments so they never creased. Eventually Laura looked up from her packing. She indicated the cross stitch Angela had left on the arm of the chair. 'What lovely work,' she said.

'Thank you,' Angela replied, then added hesitantly, 'would you like me to teach you how to do it?'

'Oh, that would be wonderful!'

Angela walked over to an armchair and picked up her bag. She took out some silks then found a small design of a rose. Laura perched on a chair arm. 'Oh, thank you,' she said, as Angela showed her the soft colours, from pink to oyster.

'I think these would be perfect for that rose.' Angela laid out the silks in a row.

'What delicate shades. And the stalk?'

'I'm sorry?'

'The stalk, the leaves and the thorns?' Laura looked into Angela's nervous hazel eyes.

'Oh, yes. Well, I have some greens, but not so many shades to choose from.' Laura leaned in close, her bare arms touching Angela's as the other woman threaded a needle. 'Now, it is imperative you make a good knot. It's so tedious if it works loose.' Angela was rather enjoying the beautiful girl's avid attention. 'Now, I'd begin with the outer, lower petal first. It's very simple and quite therapeutic, but there's an art in getting the stitches even. One tighter than the others leaps out conspicuously.'

Laura was genuinely interested. She had hardly held a needle before, and was so inept that Angela giggled. 'There's no need to be quite so rigid. Hold the needle lightly between your first finger and thumb.'

Laura jabbed in the needle and withdrew it so sharply she dug it into Angela's arm. 'I'm so sorry,' she leaped to her feet with concern as Angela rubbed the place where a pinprick of blood appeared. 'Oh, my goodness me,' Laura said, moving Angela's hand away. 'I'm so sorry.' She kissed the tiny speck of blood, then licked Angela's arm with her tongue.

'It's fine, really, it doesn't hurt,' Angela said, the flush of heat between her legs making her cheeks flame.

But Laura did not pull away. Instead she moved closer. 'I want you so much.'

Angela gasped and, shakily, said that Laura should leave. But Laura did not move away. She slid one arm around Angela, and opened her blouse. Angela felt as if her legs would buckle beneath her.

'I want you to dress in my underwear,' Laura whispered, as she licked Angela's neck, then flicked her tongue into an ear. By now, her hand was working a breast free of its lace, her fingers rubbing the nipple. She knew when she felt the nipple harden that it would be even easier than she had anticipated. 'You have the most incredible breasts.' She nuzzled Angela, then traced Angela's mouth with her fingertips, slipping one into her mouth. Angela began to suck as Laura drew the blouse away from the waistband of her skirt.

'Oh, yes, oh, yes,' Angela murmured, and began to drag her blouse free, to throw it to one side as Laura inched her skirt lower. 'Lock the door,' Angela gasped.

But Laura had drawn her skirt to her ankles and was on her knees, her tongue tracing the band of Angela's lace panties. She brought Angela down on to the floor, and couldn't resist glancing at the tiny red blinking dot in the corner of the room.

She tilted Angela's chin up. 'Surprising what a little prick can lead to!'

They both smiled, and Laura glanced again at the

camera lens, laughing because she knew that every moment had been filmed.

'I chatted to William Benedict this morning,' Annabella Bellingham said to her husband, as they drove back from Heathrow airport. Her husband barely looked up from his paper: it was enough for him that he had had to meet his wife. Conversation was surely beyond the call of duty. 'He seems rather nice, really. Not at all the sleazy character the newspapers had us think. We talked about that fellow Justin, the designer.'

'Wasn't he a friend of Oliver's?'

'That's right. Justin Chalmers.'

'Chalmers,' her husband repeated. Bellingham recalled Justin's face. He didn't know the boy terribly well, but now, somewhere in the fog of his mind, a bell was ringing.

His wife was powdering her nose. 'You remember him, you invited him to the party. Well, he's throwing some sort of bash over at Benedict's island while he's away.' She peered at herself in the tiny mirror. Just mentioning the party where Oliver had died had made her heart sink again and she steeled herself not to cry as she had just finished her make-up.

Annabella snapped shut her compact. 'Justin Chalmers is staying there with his sister, Laura.'

Her husband banged his hand down on the open newspaper. 'Justin and Laura! That's it, Justin and Laura. But Chalmers wasn't their name was it? What were they called?' He clenched his eyes in thought. 'Moorcroft, that's it. Child A and Child B, as they were

330

known in the press. Justin and Laura Moorcroft. I knew I recognized them.'

'What are you talking about?'

Bellingham explained that while he was going through his drawers to find the relevant paperwork required for the shipment of Oliver's body back to England, he had come across some old files and documents belonging to his father.

'I don't understand what this has to do with the Chalmerses.'

'Wait, and I'll tell you. You know Father hoarded everything and that I'd always meant to clear out his desk but never got around to it? Well, I was tossing stuff into the wastepaper basket, when I found this file among a stack of others. It was headed "The Moorcroft Case".'

'The Moorcroft case?'

'Yes, I just said so, didn't I? I flicked through and caught sight of some photographs of a couple of children. I knew they looked familiar, but I couldn't put my finger on who they were.'

Bellingham pressed the intercom to speak to the chauffeur, turning to his wife as he did so. 'Did Benedict say where he was heading?'

'No, but he was on the same flight,' she said, as her husband barked at the driver to pass him his mobile phone.

'Do you know what you dial for Directory Enquiries?' he asked his wife.

'Ask the operator.' Sometimes the way her husband switched subjects infuriated Annabella. It was as if anything she had to say was immaterial. But she was taken aback when she heard him ask for Sir William Benedict's number. She sighed: he wouldn't be listed. She was right, but after numerous calls to friends, Bellingham succeeded. He had to talk to Benedict, urgently.

Angela walked on to the veranda for afternoon tea. The Baron and Baroness were arguing but stopped abruptly as they saw her approach.

'Oh, I'm gasping for a cup,' she said, sitting down primly, cross stitch bag at her side.

'Have you had a pleasant afternoon?' the Baron asked, as his wife poured tea.

Angela gave a girlish giggle. 'Yes, I have, as a matter of fact.' She was hoping Laura would join them, but next to arrive were Daphne and Clarissa Hangerford.

'Was that your husband I saw earlier?' the Baroness asked Daphne. 'On an outgoing boat?'

Daphne nodded. 'It's always the same. He just can't settle. He was worried about a horse or something. I didn't really understand. He just went all silent. To be honest, he's been impossible to deal with the past few days. And this morning, he sprang out of bed, determined to go home. That nice Justin has been so helpful arranging his flight. He asked if we wanted to go as well, but we've only just arrived.' She shrugged. 'So that's that.'

'Sod bloody Daddy,' said Clarissa. Her mother glanced at her. She had been in a terrible mood recently, and no matter how many times she'd asked why, Clarissa had refused to answer her.

Clarissa could not stop thinking about her father and every time she did she wanted to scream. She had washed herself over and over. Now she wanted to hit out and hurt someone, preferably him. Now the bastard had slunk off, afraid to face her. He was a perverted sexual deviant. He had fondled his own daughter's body as if she was a whore, then run away. 'Where's Max?' Clarissa asked, in a strained voice.

'I think he went waterskiing, didn't he?' Angela turned in the direction of the Baroness and smiled at James as he joined them.

'He is,' James said moodily, sitting beside his mother.

'I thought you were supposed to go out fishing with your father?' she tapped James's hand.

'Yes, well, he left without me.'

'Who left whom?' Justin said, strolling in.

'Dad,' James informed him. Justin had noticed, with interest, how keen James had been to talk to him. He seemed just as intrigued by Justin as he had been by Laura, if not more so. Justin decided to play on this.

'We came back hours ago,' he corrected James, and sat down beside him, allowing one muscular thigh to rest suggestively against him. 'Anyone seen Laura?' he asked noncommittally. Angela blushed. 'What about a trip to Tortola this evening?' he suggested. 'Spot of dancing?' James promptly said yes, as did Clarissa. Justin rubbed the back of James's neck. 'Good. Down at the jetty about six. We have to leave early for the tides.' He stood up abruptly and walked out.

When he left, they all fell silent. Only Daphne Hangerford had food on her mind; everyone else was thinking of sex. Daphne was delighted to be able to enjoy the rest of her stay without Cedric's nocturnal importuning. She had not the slightest notion that his last dalliance had involved her only child.

There was an hour to go before the boat left for the disco. Clarissa stood in front of the mirror. Her foul mood was lingering but not all consuming. Sometimes she felt as if two people were chattering away in her brain, one threatening to beat up her father and kick him in the balls, the other crying, reaching out for comfort, because she felt used, dirty and unbalanced. She'd tried on practically everything in her suitcase, but nothing pleased her. She went to the veranda and peered out, trying to see if anyone was on the jetty. She didn't want them to go without her.

'Hi, I was coming round to get you.' It was Justin. He was standing below her veranda.

'I'm on my way,' she said, giving him a coy smile and trying to keep her dress held up; it was unzipped at the back.

'You look as though you could do with a hand,' said Justin, climbing adroitly up the front of the veranda. 'Turn round,' he ordered, frogmarching her back into the room. Clarissa felt the zip being pulled but not up as she had expected. The dress fell round her ankles. 'Mmmm,' said Justin. 'Fancy a quick one?'

'What?' she said, startled.

'Drink,' he said laughing, drawing her closer and massaging her breast. He eased his body on to the bed and slowly unzipped his fly. 'Come here,' he said softly.

She had wanted him from day one. She had almost given up imagining that she stood a chance. There was a moment of fear when she remembered her father's sweating hands on her body, but this felt different, this was what she had been dreaming about. Justin was beautiful, with a perfect body. Clarissa edged closer and opened her mouth.

Justin kept an eye on his watch. To hurry things along he gripped her head and twisted his hands in her hair to force her to increase the rhythm. Clarissa gasped as he pushed himself deeper into her mouth. Mission completed, the little red dot capturing every second, he sprang away from the bed.

'My turn now,' she said, in what she thought was a sexy tone.

'Another time, sweetheart. We don't want to miss the tide.'

She sat on the crumpled bed as Justin left, slamming the door behind him. For a moment she was that little girl who wanted to cry and be comforted. Then she stood up, angry and bitter. Her father had treated her like a whore, and now Justin had too. She began to dress, telling herself she hated men: they were all bastards.


When he arrived in London, William was jet-lagged. He felt bloated and tired. Right away he had been forced to settle the sale of Katherine's house, and had gone straight there from the airport. The urgent e-mails from Michael had concerned the lawsuit against the von Gartens. He was required to make statements. His lawyers had become frustrated by the lack of contact, especially as William had been driving them to get things moving fast.

And there had been a new development: he discovered that lawyers representing Baron von Garten had

had the audacity to ask whether he had any interest still in purchasing the same factory that had been sold to his rival. No doubt this was the reason why the Baron had accepted the invitation to the island! Further enquiries, and illegal investigations into the Baron's financial situation had revealed that his own companies were now in deficit, and he was short of cash. The Baron's main asset was the shares he owned in the company that he had sold to William's competitors, but even they were feeling the pinch because four of their biggest selling items could now be proved to have first been patented by William's company.

The wheels were turning rapidly and in William's favour; he was delighted. He was even more buoyant when his lawyers, having received no contact from Hangerford, filed a backruptcy order. Cedric Hangerford's entire business was being sifted through by the men from the Inland Revenue and also by VAT officers. They were buzzing around his property like flies. While Hangerford was away, he had left his lawyers with power of attorney and his stable manager in charge of business dealings. Had he been there himself, no doubt he would have barred the door.


Now back in London, his business affairs in order, William decided to check up on Charlie at the clinic. He had to hold the line for over fifteen minutes as Charlie was tracked down and then, to his irritation, his son said he couldn't talk for long. He shared a few monosyllabic exchanges with Charlie then hung up. His conversation with Sabrina was equally tedious, but at least he was making sure his children were taken care of. He was just about to replace the receiver, when Sabrina asked if he had heard about Uncle Cedric. He was immediately on his guard: he had made no mention to his daughter that her aunt and uncle were on his island with Clarissa.

'It was in *The Times*. He's been made bankrupt. There was even a photograph. It was all over the racing papers too, even on Channel Four's racing programme. He looked terrible on TV,' Sabrina continued, as William digested the fact that Cedric was in London. He must have left the island shortly after William.

After he had said goodbye to Sabrina he placed a call to the island. He had a long wait before he was put through, and then was frustrated to be told by Dahlia that neither Justin nor Laura was around as they had gone to a night-club. He asked Dahlia to make sure Justin called him as soon as possible.

The phone rang in Michael's office.

'Sir William Benedict's residence . . . One moment, please.' Michael caught William heading for the stairs in the hall. 'Sir, it's Lord Bellingham.'

William frowned. 'Hello . . .' He perched on the edge of the desk, fiddling with the change in his pocket. 'Justin Chalmers, yes, that's correct . . .' He listened then stood up. 'Yes, he redesigned my . . .' His face darkened. 'Laura, that's right.'

'My father, Lord Chief Justice Bellingham, reviewed their case,' said Henry Bellingham. 'He often discussed it, long after they'd been forgotten about.'

He told William as much as he remembered of what he'd read in his father's file. William's hair stood on end. 'I had another look through the file,' continued Bellingham. 'Chalmers was their aunt's name. They must have taken that name after it all blew over. Moor-croft was their original name.' William sucked in his breath. 'Well, thank you for telling me, I appreciate it.' He hung up and drummed his fingers on the desk. 'Get my plane ready, Michael. I have to go to Nice immediately, and I'll need a car standing by. I'll drive myself.'

'But aren't you returning to the island?'

'No, Michael. I said Nice, as in France. Now!'

William found the driveway to Justin's villa even more beautiful than it had been before. There were so many different flowers, and the hidden lights gave a fairy-tale feel to the long lane. Marta was waiting on the steps and gave him a cautious welcome, surprised by his sudden arrival. As she showed him into the bedroom he had occupied before, William was struck by a strange feeling of comfort. The villa somehow felt more like home than any of his London houses or apartments.

He showered and changed before joining Marta in the kitchen, where she was baking bread.

'We need to talk, Marta,' he said gently. She busied herself, avoiding his gaze. 'Marta, we have things to discuss. Justin does not know I'm here.' She opened the oven to remove a loaf. 'I love Justin and Laura, and whatever we say now is not intended to be a betrayal. To be honest, I've grown closer to them than I am to my own children.'

She sat down opposite him, a little uncomfortable. 'I love them too,' she said.

'Tell me about them, from the beginning, or from when you first became a part of their lives,' he said.

338

Marta sensed his concern and intuitively knew that something was wrong. 'May I ask why?'

William hesitated and then explained his situation; his reasons for being there and his growing friendship with Justin. But not until he began to elaborate on the island and the payback game did Marta become attentive.

She chewed her lower lip and sighed. 'The children had an aunt Frances who lived at Mole Cottage in a village near Aylesbury. I had known her since we were schoolchildren. When she discovered that my husband had died and I was in financial difficulties, she asked if I would become her companion. I accepted.' William wondered where this was going to lead, but did not interrupt. 'Frances had lost contact with her brother, Martin, whom she described as a malicious boy. Martin Moorcroft was married to a frivolous Frenchwoman, Madeleine. A great beauty and a socialite. I never met her.' Again Marta fell silent, twisting her hands. 'Martin had two children, Justin and Laura.' She plucked at her skirt. 'He was a man who should never have had children.'

'I don't understand.' William leaned forward.

Marta shifted her weight and her cheeks flushed. Then she spoke quickly. 'He was arrested for molesting a little girl when he was still young himself. He was a paedophile, a masochistic, a horrible man, who married a woman with equally disgusting tendencies. The pair, it seemed, were well matched.'

William looked directly at Marta. 'Were Laura and Justin . . .'

Marta had tears in her eyes. 'From a very early age.

339

They were immersed in a living nightmare. And who could they turn to? How could they know that theirs was not a normal childhood?'

William waited, but this time Marta paused for a considerable time. 'What in God's name happened, Marta?'

She was openly crying now, delving into her apron pocket for her handkerchief. 'A child can only take so much.'

'So what happened?'

'Come with me,' said Marta, and led him through the giant oak door to the wine cellar.


'Are you taking your medication?' asked Justin.

'Of course,' replied Laura. 'There's no need to get snappy. I'm doing everything we arranged. What's the matter with you?'

He caught her in his arms. 'You aren't being silly with Max, are you? I want them to go soon and they'll take him with them.'

'Can't he stay?'

He pushed her away. 'For God's sake, you know why he can't. We've discussed it.' He changed the subject, pointing to film footage of the Baron with the boat-boys. 'When he wasn't screwing them he was pawing Karl in the gymnasium. The Baroness just ignores it.'

'Two such awful parents,' said Laura quietly, 'have made such a sweet child.'

'Oh, God, I don't believe I heard you say that. Sweet child!'

'He's a nice boy, with beautiful manners. He's also

well educated. At least you can have an intelligent conversation with him.'

'Really?' Justin teased. 'Well, perhaps you should make sure you have these intelligent conversations within range of the microphones because so far he's the only one you keep skirting around.'

'I do not.'

'Yes, you do, and I'm sick of it. The rules are clear. You get every single one of them, Laura. That's what you're being paid for. Now, I've got to call William and give him a progress report. What do you want me to tell him? That you think that little prick is a sweet boy?'

'I want to speak to him when he calls,' she said.

'Now you're really annoying me,' snapped Justin. 'So go. Go on, get out.'

Laura wandered to the door then turned back to him. 'Don't get nasty with me, Justin, you know how it upsets me.'

He forced a smile and told her he loved her, but she had gone before he could kiss her and make up. He knew he had been brusque with her, and part of him excused it because he was getting closer to their pay-back. Only one of the guests mattered to Justin, the main man, and he couldn't care less about the others. He didn't want anything to go wrong so he was being over-cautious with Matlock. But although he tried to remain calm, tension was building in him. And he could not admit that he was jealous of that kid Max. It infuriated him.


The wine cellar, unlike the rest of the house, had not been renovated, but remained almost as it had been when Justin and Laura were children. Marta lit some candles.

'They must not be hurt,' said Marta. 'They are still children, especially Laura. She is the most fragile. She cannot be without Justin, she is dependent on him. Without him she would be locked up again.'

'Laura?' asked William, perched on a dusty barrel in the dark. The damp cellar chilled him. 'Has she been locked up in the past, then?'

Marta was rooting about behind a rack of red burgundies. 'Most of her life,' she whispered, and pulled out a dusty cardboard box. Inside was a black leather photograph album filled with newspaper cuttings. She passed it to William and sat silently beside him, letting him read.

The headlines were beyond belief: 'Killer Angels', 'Deadly Babes', 'Devil Children Let Loose'. On and on went the hideous clippings, describing what William now knew to be two tragic children.

'They killed both their parents?' he asked. Marta nodded. 'And the police were called by the nanny?'

'That's right,' said Marta, pointing to a photo of her. 'They stabbed her and pushed her into the pool, but by some superhuman effort she dragged herself out and crawled down to the village where she raised the alarm.'

William wondered why the police hadn't picked up on Justin's background when Maynard died. He had been the main beneficiary of Maynard's will, after all. Then he remembered that children's criminal records are only kept for a few years. As they grew up, the pair must have been given a clean slate and allowed to go free. Furthermore, the children had adopted a new name, Chalmers. Provided they were never caught again, the police would be none the wiser.

'What happened to the nanny in the end?' asked William.

'She died in a car accident, I think. I recall Justin reading something to me a few years back now – well, actually to Laura. I don't remember all the details, just that he was cutting out the article. I think I asked him who she was and . . .' Marta frowned. 'Is this important?'

'Yes, very.'

'Well, that's it, really. He was reading the newspaper and cutting it out. He said she had been their nanny. That's all.' Marta turned a few pages, then paused. She pointed to a clipping. 'This is about her funeral in London.'

'Camilla Maynard.' William's stomach churned. 'Did she have a brother, cousin, any relative called Andrew?'

He had a vision of the dead man floating in the overflowing bathtub, the water pink. He felt the sweat trickle down his back as he recalled Maynard talking about a much older sister who had died in a car accident. It had to be a coincidence, he thought, but he shuddered as he now saw the story's chilling logic.

'Answer me. It's very important, Marta. Have you ever heard Justin mention Andrew Maynard? In connection with this nanny, perhaps?'

'I don't think so.'

'But you must have met him, surely. He stayed here at the villa – a tall, dark-haired man. A young English politician.'

Marta hesitated, and nodded slowly.

'Ah yes, I did meet him, I mean, I served him his meals once or twice. But really, I hardly spoke to him.'

'But he came here frequently. You must know more.'

'Well, Justin explained that he wanted to be alone with him as much as possible, so I sometimes went on vacation when he came. Sometimes I went to see Laura. She was booked into clinics, you know, when she relapsed. She's very fragile . . . physically as well as mentally.'

William asked her to continue her story of their childhood.

'French law decreed that they couldn't be locked up or tried there. They were too young. They were sent instead to a specialist psychiatric unit for disturbed children in England and my friend, Frances, took them into her home, as I told you. All was fine, until a budding young journalist wanted a scoop to kick off his career. He pressed on and on, determined to get his story. It became clear that they could not attend school, could not live in an ordinary home without people throwing bricks through the window. The stress of being hounded made them both become difficult. I don't know exactly what went on. All I do know for sure is that they were taken away, separated.' She showed William a garish paperback book. 'Their case was then taken up by the British courts.'

'Lord Chief Justice Bellingham,' muttered William under his breath. The pieces of the jigsaw were slowly fitting together.

'Justin was sent to borstal, Laura to a psychiatric hospital. The author probably didn't even know what he had done. He wrote about their separation as if he

344

had made some successful coup, but he ruined their lives.'

William glanced down at the cover, emblazoned with a picture of two pretty children wielding an axe that dripped blood. *Angels or Devils?* It was by Humphrey Matlock.

The book smelt of the dank, musty cellar. It contained further pictures: Laura's frightened face as a small child being carried by a police officer, Laura's face at a barred window, Laura in a garden aged twelve. There were more snatched photographs that had obviously been taken from some distance by the spying journalist, each one slightly blurred.

One photograph in particular made William want to weep: Laura in a car with raindrops trickling down the window, waving, a sweet smile on her angelic face. Then came pictures of Justin, who, unlike his sister, showed no sign of terror on his boyish face. He glared out from one photograph after another. There was one of him in a blaze of anger, hurling something towards the camera. There were a few photographs of the children together, hand in hand in sombre school uniforms. In the last section, there were pictures of their parents. William tried hard to imagine exactly what these two inhuman creatures could have been like. Their father's eyes seemed pale and washed-out. His close-cropped hair and tidy beard made him look like D. H. Lawrence. Hard as he tried, William could not detect cruelty in their appearance. The last picture showed their mother holding Laura on her knee, her husband standing behind her chair with his hand resting on his small son's shoulders. They looked like a normal happy family.

William read the book from cover to cover. It was, he hated to admit, well written and engrossing. He was intrigued when he read a quote from a nanny, who had obviously refused to give her name, which described the way the children had made sexual advances towards her and attempted to kill her. She was quoted as saying: 'I knew from the first day I began caring for them that these were not normal children. They were too well behaved. Their manner was formal, and they seemed to be constantly entwined, at times speaking as one. The boy was over-protective of his sister. They even slept together. I saw them feed each other like birds. Yet, on the surface they looked like angels. I soon discovered a terrible, dark side to them. They frightened me. They were truly evil. Maybe they became that way because of whatever they had been subjected to by their parents. But I will never forget the nightmare I became embroiled in, and all I want now is to forget I ever met them. But it is hard to forget the sight of Laura and Justin, with their father's blood dripping from their hands. It has haunted me.'

With that comment hanging in his mind, William closed his eyes. He felt leaden. He, too, had become embroiled in their lives, but he believed them to be far more dangerous as adults. It gradually dawned on him that he had been used. He now knew that the charade into which he had been drawn had been set up for one reason alone. William chastized himself for his blindness. How could he have allowed this to go on? His weakness and vanity gave him the answer. He had so wanted to get back at people and he had believed the lies he had been told because he wanted to. If he had applied just a modicum of his intellect, he would surely have been suspicious. He bowed his head, ashamed. He knew deep down in his heart that he had uncovered the truth. All along he had been suspicious about Maynard's death and particularly the suicide note. Had Justin murdered him and written the note?

He recalled how Justin had gone through his hit-list, leaving only four main targets. No matter which way he looked at the overall picture, it was so sick it beggared belief. He recalled asking Justin whether or not he should invite his victims' children, and he had replied that William's own son and daughter had suffered at the hands of the press, so why not? He felt the ground opening up beneath him; dear God, had Oliver Bellingham been a part of it too? He was Lord Chief Justice Bellingham's grandson after all. Had Justin's revenge been planned to hurt even the younger, innocent generation? His blood ran cold. On the island there were three kids: James Matlock, Clarissa Hangerford and Max von Garten. Was Justin directing his madness against them? Hadn't he said that they deserved to be punished?

William paced up and down erratically, as his mind jumped backwards and forwards. He had *agreed*, he had encouraged Justin! The sins of the fathers ... Dear God! What monster had he released in his name? The fear that Justin would hurt the women and their children escalated in him. But surely even Justin wouldn't do that, would he? But Oliver Bellingham was dead ...

# CHAPTER 17

MAX HAD been waiting almost an hour at Suicide Point and was about to give up when he saw her running, her skirt held high in her hands and her wonderful hair flying loose like a silver wave. His heart leaped with joy as he held out his arms. She threw herself into them and hugged him tightly. 'Oh, I have missed you so much, but I just couldn't get away to see you. We have to be so careful.' They embraced and then she eased him forward.

'Laura, take care, we're very close to the edge,' Max said.

She laughed at him. 'Don't be afraid. Are you scared to look down?'

'Terrified,' he said, holding her hand tightly.

They linked arms and, from a safe distance, looked over the edge to the swirling water thrashing the rocks below.

'Would you jump if I asked you to?' she asked.

'No, because it would mean I had to leave you.'

'Would you jump if I was dead?'

He drew her close. 'Don't say things like that, even as a joke.'

'I'm sorry.' She wrapped her arms around his neck and kissed him.

Justin saw them embracing like lovers and his face tightened with jealousy but he couldn't look away. He called her name. Laura drew away from Max and listened.

'It's Justin,' Max said, pointing, and they looked along the narrow pathway to where he stood.

'We're going to Tortola tonight. Are you coming?'

Max looked at Laura, who hesitated. 'I can't,' she said, then smiled at Max. 'You go. It'll be fun.'

'I want to be with you,' Max said.

'I can't, I have to . . . see someone. It's arranged.'

'Is it Justin?' asked Max. 'You don't want to come because of him?'

Justin was jumping the rocky surface, getting closer. 'Yes, yes. We must keep our love secret. Trust me. I don't want William to hear any rumours about us, not until I've told him face to face.'

Justin was beside him. He hooked his arm around Max. 'You coming?'

'Er, yes, why not?'

'Run along, then. Go get your glad rags on. You've got about twenty minutes to get that fluff off your chin.'

Max looked at Laura, but she averted her eyes and he had no option but to leave them. He hated the way Justin had spoken to him, as if he was a twelve-year-old.

As soon as Max was out of earshot, Laura punched her brother. 'You needn't have done that,' she said.

'I did! Sneaking off to places you know I can't film or record. I'd say you were doing it to make me jealous.'

'Don't be silly.'

'I'm not being silly. We don't have much time and we have an agenda to keep. Next minute William's gonna be back, before we've done the dirty deed. Or deeds.'

'I'm on schedule. Haven't you seen the videos from this afternoon?'

'Not yet.'

'I've done the deed with Angela Matlock so I'm getting the job done. Are you?'

'I'm sorry,' said Justin, pulling Laura towards him. 'It's just this Max thing. I don't want you distracted, and you are.'

'I'm fond of Max and I don't see what's wrong with that. And with him it's fun. It's always horrible with everyone else. I notice you seem to enjoy teasing the Matlocks' son.'

'So you've fallen for him?'

'I have not. He's young, he's naïve, and sometimes it's nice to get screwed without a hidden agenda,' she lied.

Justin lifted her hair away from her face and kissed her neck.

'No, Justin, not here.' She had never rejected him before.

'I want you.'

She felt like weeping: lie was beginning to follow lie. 'I want you too, but please not here. Someone might see.'

Justin nuzzled and kissed her cheek. 'You're right. It's me who's dumb. It's just that seeing you screwing everyone else keeps turning me on.'

'Never bothered you before.' She was calming down

now, more in control. 'You get into such bad tempers, don't you?'

'Maybe because I know we're about to reach the big climax, and I don't want anything to distract us. We're so close, Laura, so close. I just want everyone gone, off the island so we can be together. But we can't until it's done.'

He turned away from her, his eyes brimming with tears, and she could barely hear what he was saying. 'I get scared. I know I couldn't do it on my own, not without you. I've always needed you.'

She linked her arm with his. She could never resist him when he was like this, vulnerable. 'If anyone's around I'm not going inside your room with you.'

'There's no one,' he whispered, but he knew there was. He knew the lovesick boy was watching them.


As they were heading for Justin's bungalow, James looked out of his window. Although he didn't spot Laura and Justin, he saw Max approaching, pushed open the shutters and shouted to him, 'Hey, Max, you coming with us?'

Max whipped around, startled. He wanted to follow Laura and Justin. 'Bit tired. Listen, I've got to go.'

Max tried to walk on, but James was still talking to him. 'You were waterskiing with Justin again today, weren't you?'

'Yes, I was. Listen, James, I really have to go.'

'Where to?'

Max sighed with impatience. 'For Christ's sake, James, I'm gonna see my parents.'

James hesitated, then said, 'Is he coming on to you?'

'What?' Max was confused.

'You heard. Is Justin hitting on you?' James's face was flushed.

'You're talking like an idiot, James. Why? Has he been coming on to you?'

James shouted, 'You calling me a poof?'

'Jesus Christ, James, what's the matter with you?'

James leaped from his veranda and swung a punch at Max, who staggered and fell. Before he could get to his feet, James kicked him in the groin. 'Stay away from him, you hear me? Just stay away from Justin.' He went back into his own room and straight for the cocaine. He didn't bother to chop a line, but stuck his nose over the vial and snorted till his eyes smarted and ran with tears.


Justin's attentiveness to James had gone unnoticed by the others, although he had made sure he constantly brushed against the younger boy as he helped him up into the ski-boat from the water, or to put on his sub-aqua gear. At times, he casually laid an arm across James's shoulders. James was quicker on the uptake than Justin had expected, an easier fish to bait than his father would be. The truth, of course, was that Justin was not at all interested in James.

Justin was sure that James was bisexual and had had more than a few experiences beyond schoolboys' hot kisses. It would have been fun breaking Matlock's son in to some sex games, but he doubted the boy would need much encouragement, which took all the enjoyment out of it for himself. What Justin had not contemplated, though, was that James would become obsessed with him, as Oliver Bellingham had. Perhaps he would die like him too.

Max wiped his bloody nose on his sleeve and took his time getting back on his feet. His balls felt like they were on fire. He rubbed his crotch then headed to his own room, grabbed some ice, wrapped it in a napkin and held it over his face. James was obviously as high as a kite.

'That Justin is a prick,' he muttered, then flopped back on to the bed. He decided he had to talk to Laura. He didn't want to go to the nightclub.

James ran to Justin's bungalow and kicked open the front door, shouting his head off. Hurriedly Laura drew the sheet across her bare breasts, but before Justin could get out of bed, the bedroom door burst open and James barged in. Laura flipped the sheet over her head; she didn't need this, didn't need anyone seeing her being intimate with Justin, let alone naked in bed beside him.

'You lost something?' Justin said casually, leaning back on the pillows and reaching for his cigarettes. 'Don't tell me you've run out of the four grams I gave you last night?'

James shifted his weight from one foot to the other then pointed to the bed. 'I know who's there. I know you've been playing us off against each other and I don't like it. You're a piece of shit.' His face was red with fury.

Justin tossed his lighter on to the bedside table. 'Get out of here, James, before I lose my temper.'

James stuck out his bottom lip like a spoilt child. 'No, I won't.' He dived round the bed and snatched off the sheet. When he saw Laura he stumbled backwards. Confused, he looked from her to Justin, who was smiling, the smoke drifting from his nostrils. 'What's she doing here?' he said. 'She's your sister!'

Justin inhaled deeply and his eyes narrowed. He glanced at Laura, as if to give her a signal. She caught it and, even though she was furious, she controlled herself, stretching her arms above her head, finally dropping the sheet to reveal her breasts.

'Come here,' Justin said to James, the cigarette stuck in the corner of his mouth. James hesitated but then, as if he was hypnotized, walked slowly towards Justin and stood a foot away from the bed.

'Closer,' Justin said, tilting his head so that the cigarette smoke drifted into his eyes.

'No,' James whispered.

Justin reached out and hooked one finger into the leg of James's shorts. 'Naughty boy, come here.' He drew James towards him and began to undo his zip. As he did so he glanced at the bedside clock. 'We don't have long. We're going dancing tonight, aren't we?'

'Yes,' James croaked.

'Mmm, Laura, I think I might need some assistance here.'

James closed his eyes and his legs trembled, but he couldn't move as Laura crawled over the bed towards him. Justin stubbed out his cigarette, eased off the boy's T-shirt and began to pour oil into his hand. Laura drew the frightened boy to lie between them.

*

354

Max looked at his bruised eye in the bathroom mirror. The ice had reduced the swelling so he rinsed his face with cold water and patted it dry. He put on a clean shirt and light trousers, and slipped his feet into rubber flip-flops. Returning to the bathroom he caught his reflection in the mirror. His blond hair was silvery now from the sun, his pale skin tanned a light golden brown. He was struck at first by his resemblance to his mother, and then became rather pleased by the change in his appearance. He could see the effects of his love affair, as strong as the effect of the sun on his slender body. He would have been embarrassed to admit it, but he suddenly realized that he was, as his mother called him, 'a beautiful boy'.

James lay face down on Justin's bed, sobbing into a pillow. He had crossed a line in his life that he had always known was there, but was too afraid to face. He was still weeping as Justin came out of the bathroom, showered and changed. He looked at James, annoyed to see him still lying there. 'You'd better get yourself together. We're leaving in five minutes.'

James rolled over painfully. 'Come on.' Justin hauled him upright. 'Get down to the jetty. I'll see you there.'

James stumbled out of the room. Across his back were deep red welts, and in some places the skin was broken, leaving small beads of blood.

Laura came out of the bathroom, buttoning her blouse. She was angry. 'I said that was risky, but you wouldn't listen to me. What if he starts talking about us?'

'Don't be a fool. You really think that Master Matlock is going to rush to Mummy!'

'Or Daddy,' she said coldly.

'No way is he going to spill the beans on us. I'll make sure of it by the end of tonight.' He left for the boat, and Laura returned to her room. She looked out of her window and could see Clarissa and Justin boarding the speedboat. She wanted to see Max, and be alone with him without Justin monitoring them. She had an agenda, worked out by Justin, but she would follow her own now too. She dialled Max's number.

He sounded so pleased to hear from her that her spirits lifted. They agreed to meet by the waterfall.

'We need to talk,' he said.

'Yes, I think we do,' she said softly, and hung up.

Max flopped back on to the bed. 'She wants me,' he said aloud. 'Laura Chalmers, my beautiful goddess, wants me.' He was unaware that James had overheard him from his adjacent veranda, and had realized he'd been wrong about Max and Justin.

Laura was shaking with nerves, but had almost made up her mind. She was unsure if she had the strength to do it. It would be up to Max to persuade her. Laura was forming a plan to leave the island and Justin. He had said he doubted that he could handle Matlock on his own, and she was sure he couldn't. She was not intending to back out of the murder, though: she just had to make it happen faster than planned. It was imperative to get the Baron and Baroness off the island, leaving Max with her. She knew Justin could easily handle Clarissa and James, and Daphne, that fat, foolish woman, wasn't the problem. Laura's problem was Justin. She had got away with lying to him already. Now she planned on doing much more, because she knew she had to escape him.

'Yes, yes,' she whispered, and told herself that she had made the right decision, unaware that she was pacing up and down the room. If Marta or Justin had seen her doing this, the rapid footsteps, the urgent instructions, repeated to herself more vehemently each time, they would have been worried. Marta always knew this was the first danger sign. The second was when Laura made brushing strokes down her thigh. On these occasions, Marta acted fast, and doubled Laura's medication. But Marta was a long way away. This time Laura was on her own.

# CHAPTER 18

WILLIAM CAUGHT the night flight back to London. He phoned Michael from the villa, asked him to check out Camilla Maynard and arrange a flight to the Caribbean. He intended to leave immediately after his arrival in England.

Michael didn't phone back until William was in the limousine coming into London from Heathrow. He confirmed that Camilla had been Andrew Maynard's sister. Had Justin known from the beginning and used William from the moment he had visited that awful mews cottage in London? He was sure now that Justin had forged the suicide note.

When he got back Michael was waiting for him, although it was after ten. 'Get me Charlie on the line,' William shouted at him, dropping his bag and making for his study.

By the time he was at his desk, the call was put through. William snatched up the receiver. 'Charlie? The letter,' shouted William down the line. 'The one you told me about, from Oliver Bellingham. Have you still got it?'

'Oh, it's somewhere in my stuff,' he drawled. 'But, Dad, let me tell you about—'

'No time,' shouted William. 'Is the letter in the stuff you left here?'

'The big black canvas bag. No! Maybe the duffel bag or in the small gym bag. It's somewhere amongst my gear. What's the problem?'

'Can I read it?' William pressed on.

'Why?'

'It's a matter of life and death,' said William.

'Oh, yeah right, sure, man. I mean it's personal but, like, go ahead.'

William gripped the receiver. 'I love you, son,' he said, 'but I'm in a great hurry. I'll speak to you later, OK?'

William took another deep breath and ran upstairs to the room where Charlie had left his bags. Furiously he rummaged through odd shoes and dirty shorts, until he spotted a gym bag that was full of exercise books, loose pages from *Biker* and music magazines. There were bundles of letters from Katherine to Charlie at school. At last, in a worn and well-thumbed air-mail envelope, he found the letter from Oliver Bellingham. The large sloped handwriting began 'Hello, Wanker!' Next to the greeting, Oliver had drawn a grinning cartoon face. In the first few paragraphs, he described life on Tortola, the surfing and the clubs. He also mentioned that keeping straight was tough on the island, where everything was accessible in vast quantities, especially the ganja. There was another grinning cartoon face. There was some reference to his girlfriend and a lot of dots and dashes after her name, and then an underlined passage about receiving a letter from her so that it appeared 'all was not lost'. This was underlined three times. Oliver mentioned the forthcoming 'wrinklies party'. He was quite looking forward to it because he had met this bloke called Justin in the Harbour Bar. 'He's a really great guy. Very handsome – blond, taller than me and quite a bit older. I've been with him on and off most days and nights.' He wrote that he'd invited Justin to his folks' party – his parents didn't really want him to come, but he didn't care. Justin had promised to bring some gear so it would be a behind-the-bushes job.

A young boy's infatuation with a handsome older man had led to his death. William knew Justin and his sister had been killers as children, but he was also certain they had not stopped killing. He was sure that between them they had murdered both Andrew Maynard and Oliver Bellingham. God knew how many others there had been, perhaps even Maynard's sister. William was determined to find out. The other thought that dawned on him, but oddly did not frighten him, was that perhaps he, too, was earmarked as a victim.

He traced an aunt of Maynard's, his only living relative, as far as William could tell. He did not make excuses as to why he had called out of the blue but came straight to the point. 'This is William Benedict, an old friend of your nephew's.'

'I know who you are. I've read all about you in the press. Why are you calling?'

'I think it is possible Andrew was murdered.'

'Really? Whatever makes you think that? Are you sure you want to open this all up again? I'd hate to have the press coming down here.'

'I'll make sure they don't.'

'I doubt that you of all people would be able to do that. I'm old and I don't want to get involved in any scandal.'

'Please, could you tell me how his sister died.'

'What's she got to do with this?'

'Perhaps nothing, but do you know how she died?'

'A car crash. She was planning to visit me here in Brighton when she died. Her brakes failed on the motorway. I don't know the technical details. It happened years ago, I think it was in March 1992.'

'Did you ever meet someone called Justin Chalmers?'

'I don't think so. Unless . . . Is he the young man who . . .' She trailed off, and William held his breath. 'No, I'm sure I don't know that name. All I do know is that shortly before Camilla's death she met a couple. I thought it was a bit strange because they didn't come to her funeral. They were apparently the last people to see her. If I remember correctly they met her somewhere in London.'

'Did she describe them?'

'No, but I think they were foreign. European, possibly French. I think they had offered her work as nanny to their children. She used to work in France . . .'

'Thank you,' William said, desperate to hang up but forced to hold on out of civility.

William was certain the couple had been Justin and Laura, just as he was sure that they were preparing to kill Humphrey Matlock. He felt powerless to stop them. As for the staff, could he trust them? They had been hired by Justin. He groaned. The last thing he wanted was to involve the police, even though he knew he should. He felt Matlock was probably safe while there were plenty of other people on the island. He knew that neither Justin nor Laura had any personal grievance against the Hangerford family or the Baron – surely they would not harm them? But William was not due to return for three more days. Could he make it in time to stop the madness or had he unwittingly become a party to murder?

The voice of sanity told William to contact the police immediately. But insanity was taking over. Or perhaps it was his own survival instinct. Perhaps he had sensed all along that something was amiss and it was this part of his brain that that had arranged for him to leave them on the island to their own endgame. God Almighty, he mused, I played right into Justin's hands. If he was to contact the police, he would be forced to incriminate himself: he would have to explain how he had come to this conclusion. In any case, how could he possibly explain the situation to anyone? No one would believe him. And he would be humiliated by the press again if they got so much as a whisper of this. He'd probably be arrested as an accomplice, or done up in a strait-jacket.

'Get hold of the goddamn reins, William,' he muttered to himself. 'Stand up and sort this mess out.' It was now imperative he return to the island, but he knew he had to do it without ringing alarm-bells for either Justin or Laura. He closed his eyes, trying to think like Justin. Who could he trust to have a boat standing by to pick him up? He had to arrive without their knowledge.

'Money, you old fool, buys you anyone and anything,' Justin's voice rasped in his ear.

William decided that Dahlia should be the one and only person to know he was returning ahead of schedule and to keep it secret.

*

Max waited almost an hour. When Laura didn't appear, he thought at first he must have misheard the meeting-place. Could it have been Suicide Point? He was sure she had said the waterfall. He returned to his bungalow and called her from there. The phone rang and rang, but there was no reply. He tried Justin's bungalow, but again there was no reply. Max returned to the cliff-tops, making a round trip from one of their secret meeting-places to another. Still no sign of Laura. He returned a second time to his bungalow. He had been waiting for her for almost two hours.

Laura could hear the phone. She was lying on the floor, stiff and cold. Slowly she forced herself to rise and unsteadily made her way into the bathroom to bathe her face. It was another fifteen minutes before she could function fully. Her mind was woolly and she'd bruised her hip when she fell, but she had no recollection of what had taken place. All she knew was that it had happened many times before, when Marta had been at hand to take care of her. Laura examined her body for the telltale marks, but just as she was about to reach for her medication, the phone rang again.

'Laura? It's Max. I've been frantic.'

'William called and I had to be up at the main house. I've got a migraine.'

'I'm back in my bungalow. Do you want to come here or . . .'

Laura was tired. She knew she needed to sleep. But instead she agreed to meet Max, afraid that if she didn't he would turn up on her doorstep.

'Five minutes.'

'No, two,' he demanded, and said he would be outside waiting.

During the long walk to the cliffs Laura felt exhausted. Max rested his arm on her shoulder, and she ached to lie down and sleep, but gradually the cool breeze off the ocean cleared her head.

'Feeling better?' Max asked, concerned.

'Mmm, yes, I'm fine.'

'Good.' He kissed her neck, then held up her hair. 'How did you do this?' He touched the purple marks.

'I fell against the cabinet in the bathroom coming out of the shower. It's nothing.' As if to prove it she began to run as they arrived at the end of the path leading to the open cliff-top. Max watched her spinning and turning, her hair billowing out, her arms raised above her head like a dancer's. She was so fragile, he was afraid the wind would scoop her up and blow her away. She danced to the mossy area where the edge of the cliff dropped to the sheer rocks below, and flopped down. Max joined her. He had picked a posy of blue flowers, and tucked them into her hair by her ear.

'Let me lean against you, as if you were my rock,' she said.

Max swivelled around, and felt her body heat as she leaned her back against his.

'Wouldn't it be nice if life was always this perfect?' she said.

'It would, but it never is. Tell me about Justin,' he said, and felt her spine stiffen.

'You see that little black cloud high in the sky, over there to the right?' She pointed upwards. 'That's Justin. He makes the sun go in sometimes, but then you see it peep out again. Justin has always made me believe that he controls the sun.'

Laura found it easier to tell Max what she had to say without looking at him. Even though she skirted around the horror of her childhood, explaining that the fire that killed her mother was an accident and the attack against her father had been in self-defence, it still sounded like a nightmare. For the first time in her life, Laura was telling someone who was not a psychiatrist about her past. She told him about the long years in homes, about the electrocution therapy, the drugs that left her with no memory for about five years. She admitted that her relationship with Justin must be difficult for an outsider to understand. 'We only had each other, so we must seem unnaturally close.' Laura pressed herself into him. 'He is very dominating and I allow him to be so. If it had not been for him, I might never have been released from the home and allowed to return to France. I owe Justin . . . I owe him everything. And I was content for him to be the most important person in my life until . . .'

'Until?' Max asked softly.

'You,' she said simply.

'Do you love me, Laura?' he asked, holding his breath.

'You are open and trusting and . . .'

'You didn't answer my question.'

He turned towards her and she looked into his face. 'Yes,' she said.

He took her hand and kissed the palm then drew her close to rest against him.

'I know I'm young and inexperienced, just a kid, but

I also know I love you, Laura. I want to make up for all those hideous years and make you happy.'

'You do,' she whispered, loving the feel of his arms around her.

'I want to be with you. Will you leave and come with me?' he asked.

'I don't know. That's impossible, isn't it? Besides, Justin would never let me go.'

'Then don't tell him, just leave. We could leave right now. Will you come with me?'

'Yes,' she said. 'Yes, of course I will.'

'When?'

'As soon as possible, but—' She broke off and took a deep breath as the little black cloud covered the sun, like an omen. 'We're just being foolish. Justin would find me, no matter where you took me. And I don't think your parents would approve. You're much too young.'

Max stood up and drew her to stand in front of him. 'I am not. I have a trust fund, so money is no problem. I knew I loved you from the moment I saw you. My parents will have to know, but so will William.'

'When he calls I'll tell him.'

'No, Laura, you can call him. Besides, I thought you'd spoken to him this afternoon.'

'No, no, I didn't. I had such a migraine,' she lied.

Max put his hands on his hips. 'You told me it came on after you spoke to him. Don't treat me like some idiot. I'm serious. I love you. I want to get out of this place. I want you to get away from your brother.'

'Justin will go to any lengths to stop me leaving with you.'

'Then we'll escape without his knowing. We could

go right now, while he's off the island.' He caught her face between his hands and kissed her.

'Believe me, Justin must not find out.' Her voice caught in her throat.

'You sound as if you're scared of him. Are you using him as an excuse? I don't mind telling him. I'm not afraid of him.'

'Oh, Max, I'm scared he'll make me feel so guilty I won't be able to leave. And I do want to, I really do.'

'Well, I'm not scared. We can go and tell my parents, now, then wait for him and confront him.'

'No, we can't do that. He'll turn you against me and make you hate me. Justin has a powerful hold over me. You have no idea how much it took for me to come to you today. Justin is already jealous of you, he already suspects I care for you, that he is no longer the centre of my universe.'

'How much does he know?' Max asked.

'Enough.' She traced his jaw-line with a finger. 'He only has to look at me to know. I find it hard not to smile when you're close to me. In fact, when you're anywhere near I want to look at you, touch you.'

He clasped her to him again. She was saying words that filled him with passion: words he had only dreamed of hearing. Nothing had ever sounded so sweet.

Suddenly Laura pushed him from her. She felt somehow as if she was flying. 'Wait! I have a plan. The mail-boat docks at our quayside at about six in the evening. We can leave on it.'

'Tonight?' Max tingled, either with fear or excitement.

'No. It comes every other day. It's due tomorrow. Maybe we'll be able to leave then. If not, we have to wait just two more days. We can stay over on Tortola and catch a plane first thing the following morning.' She paced up and down, making brushing motions with her hand, a determined expression on her face. 'We'll stay apart until then, and the night we leave we must be careful not to give a clue to anyone, especially not Justin. You pack your bags, I'll pack mine, and we can leave them hidden close to the jetty. We'll meet up at Suicide Point. Say that you're taking a walk, so that no one suspects. I'll come via the lower path, you take the long route round. No one will be able to see either of us from the house on those routes, and from up there we can see the mail-boat coming in.'

'But if it always comes at six, why don't we just hide down there?'

'It's never on time, and we'll have to wait until Justin has collected the mail. He always takes the crew some beer and chats for a while before he brings the mail and the newspapers up to the house. When he's gone they sit and drink their beer on the boat. That'll give us time to get on board and leave the island without Justin seeing us or anyone suspecting anything.'

Max was so overcome that he didn't notice the deviousness of her plan, or that she had been able to make it so quickly. All he could think about was that she was agreeing to be with him. 'Until then, we keep apart, ignore each other. We must not give ourselves away.' Laura was excited, her face glowing, sure she had not overlooked anything. The fact that he was little more than a child and she an adult woman, fifteen years older than him, was unimportant. They were two people infatuated with each other, holding their world in their arms.

'Whatever you say. I'll be waiting.'

They kissed and parted, then ran back into each other's arms and kissed again, neither wanting to let the other go. Eventually Laura made him turn his back and ran until her lungs felt as if they would burst, her hair flying, her skirt caught in her hands above her thighs.

'We'll get married!' he shouted after her, and his voice caught the wind and echoed. But she didn't hear. He could see her figure darting and jumping, ducking beneath overhanging trees, and then she was gone.

Laura ran full tilt into Humphrey Matlock and lost her balance. He had to catch her or she would have slipped over, dangerously near to the cliff edge.

'Dear God, you're crazy. It's slippery here,' he said, still holding her arm. She gasped her thanks. Her cheeks were flushed, her eyes danced. She rested against him to regain her balance and catch her breath. 'I was looking for James,' he said.

'He's gone to Tortola for the evening.'

'Ah, well,' he said, towering above her. His black hair was tousled from the wind and his face was even more tanned after another day's fishing. 'Are you going back to the house?' he asked, and she nodded, walking backwards a few feet in front of him.

'Did you catch anything?' she asked flippantly.

'You mean apart from you?' He smiled. His teeth were large and slightly stained from the cigars he smoked. She could smell brandy on his breath. 'I didn't have a good day, but tomorrow we're planning to go further afield, start at the crack of dawn. I've not enjoyed myself so much in as long as I can remember.'

Matlock went on chatting to her, indicating with his hands the size of the fish he had lost, describing the dolphins and how close they had swum to the boat. Then he stopped and sniffed. 'God, smell the air, it's so fresh. But that perfume, it's all over the island.'

'It's lilies, Justin has them shipped in.' She spoke softly, glancing coyly at him. He looked down into her upturned, exquisite face. She gazed into his dark eyes as he lifted his hand and hooked one finger into the opening of her dress. He drew her a fraction closer. She felt his rough finger run along the lace of her brassière, then he withdrew his hand, afraid that he had gone too far.

'So you do want me,' she said softly.

Hoarsely he grunted, 'Yes.'

'Maybe one day we'll do something about it.' She turned and ran on, leaving him standing there with a huge hard-on, unfulfilled and feeling idiotic.


'Did you have a good day, darling?' Angela asked, as he turned on the shower.

'No.' He began to strip off his clothes. 'Caught bugger all.'

Angela looked at her watch. It was already almost eight. 'You were out a long time.'

'James didn't show up. I went to have a talk to him, but he's gone off to some disco. About all he's interested in doing.' He stepped out of his tracksuit. 'You do anything?' he asked, not really interested.

'I had a pleasant day.' She smiled. 'Would you like to order dinner before your shower?'

He glowered and said she could order for him, so

she walked out of the bathroom. She hated to see him naked. There was something so monstrous about him: with his deep-tanned face and arms and the hideous vest marks over his torso where his skin was still alabaster white. He was grotesque.

She ordered *filet mignon* for them both, a chilled tomato and lime soup and fruit. Then she called Daphne Hangerford to see if she would join them but received no reply, so she tried the Baroness instead.

'Have you heard?' drawled the Baroness, excitedly. 'Cedric Hangerford has gone bankrupt. The stud farm has gone, plus their two homes. It was all over *The Times*! That's why he ran off from here with his tail between his legs. He must have known!'

'How awful,' said Angela.

'Mmm, isn't it?' The Baroness hung up, wishing she had someone else to gossip with, and Angela realized that she hadn't mentioned dinner arrangements. Oh, well.

She was looking through her wardrobe, undecided as to what to wear, when Dahlia tapped on the door. Angela opened the door in her robe and Dahlia presented her with a small tissue-wrapped parcel tied with a pink ribbon. 'I was asked to make sure you received this before dinner,' she said.

'Thank you,' Angela said softly, and her heart fluttered. She couldn't wait to rip it open, sure of what it would be. And it was. A pair of Laura's panties and a little note asking her to wear them to dinner, as it would make her feel close. As a postscript she added that she longed for their next cross-stitch session.

*

Daphne Hangerford, her hair newly cut and tinted in what would have been a rather flattering style for someone twenty years younger, sat polishing her nails. The manicures had made a world of different to her hands but she had put on a considerable amount of weight over the holiday. Right now she didn't care; her brain wouldn't function and she was confused.

She had placed call after call to her husband, her lawyers, her trainers and the stables but she couldn't get through. She was distraught and even more so when she opened her purse and discovered she had only a small amount of money left. She had a cheque book but she couldn't use that and her credit cards were all heavily in the red. She was sure Clarissa didn't have any money with her. However, she had their return tickets for London and decided she was going to leave as soon as possible. Her panic spiralled out of control when she couldn't get hold of her daughter. When the phone rang she grabbed it but it was only the kitchen staff wanting her order for dinner.

She demanded to speak to someone about leaving immediately, and after a short while Dahlia knocked on the door. 'I have to get off this bloody island. I have to leave,' Daphne screamed.

'Certainly, Lady Hangerford. Would you care for your maid to pack your cases? You will be able to get the launch first thing in the morning – it leaves at seven fifteen. Will your daughter be accompanying you?'

'Clarissa? Yes, of course.'

'I will make arrangements to transport you to the airport, and if you wish I can also arrange for a limousine to collect you at Heathrow.'

Suddenly the panic subsided, and Daphne deflated

like a pricked balloon. 'Thank you, that is most kind. I can't seem to work the phones. I have to call my husband.'

'By all means. Would you care for me to get through for you?'

Daphne clasped her hands in relief.

'It may take a little while – connections have been problematic lately.' She listened, then asked to speak to Lord Hangerford and passed Daphne the receiver.

Daphne's hands were sweating, but she waited until Dahlia had left the room before she spoke into the phone. She could just hear a distant, 'Hello? Hello? Who's speaking, hello?'

'Is that you?' she barked.

'Yes.' His voice was slurred.

She eased herself into a chair, sweat trickling between the rolls of fat on her belly. 'What's going on? I've seen the papers. Is that why you left? And how dare you not tell me, you bastard!'

'Yes, it's true,' he stammered. 'But you know the media – someone must have tipped them off. I couldn't tell you. I just had to get away and give myself time to think.'

'But the money situation?'

He broke down sobbing.

'What about William? Couldn't he help us?' shouted Daphne. She was shaking with nerves. Hangerford began a tirade against William. 'There's more, Piggy!' He used her pet nickname, which she hated: it always spelled trouble when he used it.

'What else could there be?' she said flatly.

'I'm leaving you.'

'What?'

'I said, I'm leaving you.' Then he told her about Judith, the twenty-six-year-old stable girl with whom he had been having an affair. He didn't mention that Judith had a private income, and that although it wouldn't keep him in the style to which he was accustomed, it was better than joining the dole queue and meant he would have a roof over his head.

By the time their conversation had ground to a sickening halt, Daphne Hangerford was in a semi-stupor. She eased her bulk slowly from the wicker chair, opened the fridge and took out a bottle of gin and another of tonic water. She'd never been a great drinker and she was reminded of Katherine Benedict. She remembered the last conversation they had had. Katherine had been sitting surrounded by her dogs. She had been drinking heavily. 'I am sorry to have to ask you this, Daphne, but I need you to repay some of the money I lent Cedric. I'm in a rather difficult position. I've had to use my children's trust funds to tide me over and . . .' This reminded Daphne that Clarissa also had a trust fund. It was still intact and her husband didn't know about it. She giggled. It had been her secret; hers and her beloved father's. He had seen his son-in-law carve his way through his daughter's inheritance, so he made sure his granddaughter's future was secure. There was a few hundred thousand, if not more, that she could get her hands on. Daphne Hangerford raised her glass and vowed that her husband would see her in court if he tried to get his hands on one penny. 'Thank God for you, Daddy!'

*

The Baroness had just showered when Laura tapped at the door of her suite. 'Who is it?' she called.

'Laura.'

The Baroness opened the door and her towel slipped to reveal her breasts. 'Oh, sorry, come in.' She made only a half-hearted attempt to cover herself.

'Are you alone?' Laura asked, closing the door.

'Yes. God knows where my husband is.'

Laura sat down on the enormous sofa loaded with cushions. 'I think you know perfectly well where your husband is.' She smiled sweetly.

'What do you mean by that?'

Laura opened her bag, removed a video cassette and held it between her thumb and forefinger. 'See for yourself.'

The Baroness sat opposite Laura on a low seat, her legs wide apart, knowing she was leaving nothing to the imagination. 'So what is this video, darling? Not of you, is it?'

'It's nothing to do with me, but you'll thank me for passing it on to you. There are two seats reserved on a plane tomorrow morning. The launch will have to leave rather early so that you don't miss the flight. I'll get your maid to help you pack, unless you'd prefer not to use Ruby.'

She slipped the tape into the VCR, then sat back and crossed her legs. 'I wouldn't mention this to the other guests. Just make sure you and your husband leave tomorrow.'

The tape whirred into action. On the screen the Baron, naked, walked into shot, his erection leading the way.

'Or the film will be shown to all the guests in a specially announced screening tomorrow night,' Laura added.

The Baroness was speechless as she watched her husband cavorting with a couple of the boat-boys. 'I'm in love with Max,' said Laura. 'He's asked me to marry him and I have accepted.' She looked at a small flower in the curtains behind the Baroness, her wide eyes clear and focused.

The Baroness was glued to the screen. She had always known of her husband's antics, but seeing him perform had silenced her.

Laura pressed on: 'We want to be left alone, to lead our own lives.'

The Baroness stood up suddenly. 'You lay one finger on my son,' she screamed, 'and I'll scratch your eyes out.'

Laura continued, 'It's not only the Baron on tape. Shall I fast-forward? I notice you have been spending a lot of time with Kurt.' She looked the Baroness in the eye. 'Well, I see I have no need to elaborate. Why not sit and view it for yourself? Think about whether you'd like Humphrey Matlock to get hold of it.' Laura straightened her skirt and stood up. She smiled. 'See you at dinner.'

Left alone in her suite the Baroness played the video through. It was still running when her husband returned. 'Beautiful evening,' he said, as he came in.

'You are in for one big shock,' said the Baroness. 'Sit down and get yourself a stiff drink. And while you sit and watch that video, I'll be packing – without a servant, because it appears you have fucked every single one of them.'

376

The Baron sat in a stupor, staring at himself on the screen. He was mortified. Then his wife was back. 'Oh, by the way,' she said, 'Max is staying on here, with that two-faced whore.'

'Who?' said the Baron, cowering.

'Laura Chalmers has her claws into Max. She said they're going to get married.'

'But he's only eighteen,' he stuttered.

'You think I don't know that?' Tears of fury streamed down her face.

The Baron's shoulders slumped and he started to cry. His wife screamed, 'Get showered and changed. We're dining at nine thirty and we don't let so much as a hint of this show, do you hear me?'

He nodded, and with a sick feeling in the pit of his stomach he turned to watch the video. He felt ashamed. The boys, he realized, were younger than his son. Then the screen went blank. A new scene: the Baroness entered the sauna. Kurt was lying on the top bunk. He eased himself down and began to rub oil over her chest. They were joined by Dahlia. The baron watched in horror. His wife would blame him for driving her into the sex games, but he was too humiliated to argue with her.


Matlock, swathed in a towel robe left undone to reveal his naked body, carried his gin onto the veranda, a cigar clamped between his teeth. 'You ordered dinner?' he looked to his wife, as he slumped on to a cushioned *chaise-longue*.

'Yes.' Angela passed him a bowl of prawn and oyster canapés.

'Odd that Benedict's still not shown. I'd say the Prime Minister's not coming either.'

'I doubt it. He's at some European summit. It's in *The Times*.'

Matlock clicked his fingers. She put down her cross stitch and went to retrieve the newspaper. She hated the way he did that. He was so uncouth at times it made her skin crawl.

Matlock roared with laughter as he read of Lord Hangerford's downfall and held out his glass to be re-filled. 'Probably why Benedict's not shown up. They're related, aren't they?'

Angela poured his drink and returned to her seat. 'By marriage only. Hangerford was his second wife's brother.' She began selecting silks.

'Ah, yes, I forgot you knew so much about them.' He snorted as he turned the pages.

'I find it hard to believe that you would forget that I went out with William Benedict.'

He lowered the newspaper. She didn't meet his eyes, but continued to sort through her silks.

'Slip of the tongue. Of course I haven't. All the same, when you think about it, it's odd that we should be here accepting his hospitality.'

'This was your idea,' she said primly, her lips tight.

'So it was, and I'm glad I did accept. Even if the PM doesn't show, I'm having a good holiday.'

Angela concentrated on threading her needle. Now she understood why Humphrey had come here. It had been too good an opportunity to refuse, no matter what she might feel about facing William. Her husband, she mused, would be able to commit murder and blank it from his self-obsessed mind, just as he had her pitiful threats of divorce. Months ago she had claimed that she could expose Humphrey's indiscretions: they would make headlines. Usually it was an employee who caught his eye, and no one ever lasted longer than a few months, but his callousness hurt her. Finding a credit-card slip from Aspreys for a diamond bracelet that had not been for her had been the last straw. 'I want a divorce,' she had said.

'Don't be stupid.' He had held his hand out for the credit-card slip. She saw him wince as he realized what it was.

'I'm not being stupid. How many women have you played around with? This time I mean it, I MEAN IT.'

Matlock stood up and reached for her, drawing her close. 'Let me make it up to you. What do you want from me? I'll do anything to please you and stop all this nonsense about divorce.'

She had wriggled away from him, still angry, then turned on him again. 'I've been made to look a fool once too often. If you want to make it up to me then ruin William Benedict. It's your choice, because I won't be persuaded to forget about this.'

Matlock had sighed and picked up the paper. The story of Andrew Maynard's suicide had only just been leaked and there would be a lot more to come. Perhaps his wife had hit on something newsworthy in Sir William's indiscretions. And if there weren't any to be exposed, Matlock and his cheque book would invent them. 'Deal,' he said, and lit a cigar. 'I never realized how much he hurt you.'

She did not add that if she had married William, as

she had so desperately wanted, she would not have been tied to a man she detested. 'Just ruin him anyway you can,' she spat out.

He had been as good as his word, had perhaps gone even further than Angela had intended, but she had read of William's disgrace with relish.

'Penny for 'em,' Matlock said now, holding out his empty glass again.

'I was just wondering how late James was going to be.'

Matlock swung his legs off the *chaise-longue*. 'I'm going to have words with that little sod. You spoil him, lazy good-for-nothing.'

'He's with all the youngsters at a disco,' she said, pouring his gin, slicing lemon and scooping up the ice.

'He's missed out on some fantastic hours on that boat.' Matlock had been the first up and the last to return ever since he had arrived, fishing from early morning until dusk. 'You make sure he comes out with me tomorrow,' he said, deep in the article about Hangerford again, hardly able to contain his delight. He checked the journalist's name and wondered who'd leaked the scoop. It was certainly a good one. 'I must call the office tomorrow,' he muttered, tossing the newspaper aside. The photograph of Cedric was on the front page and he chuckled.

Something somewhere was lurking in Matlock's brain, making dull connections, but he didn't have the energy to gather together the train of subconscious thought and link the 'scoop', the 'journalist' and the 'story' that had made his career, so long ago.

*

As the guests on the island prepared for dinner, their offspring, apart from Max, arrived in Tortola. Justin ushered James and Clarissa ahead of him into the dark, dingy back bar of the Coca-Baba club. They were early and the place was only half full, so he suggested they sit at the bar and order some drinks. He felt irritable and tired, and when James leaned close and asked if he needed a hit, he shook his head. He watched James head for the lavatory then ordered a round of rum punches.

Clarissa slid up next to him. 'You were so horrible to me,' she said, pouting.

'Was I?' Justin turned away and lit a cigarette, as she went on to complain about the way he had treated her. It had made her feel terrible.

'You know, sometimes, Clarissa, a man needs to shoot his load. You just struck lucky. Think nothing of it. I don't.'

'You hateful shit,' she said, returning to her stool.

Justin looked around the club, which was slowly filling up with kids on vacation with their parents – the 'Brit Pack', as the locals nicknamed them. James returned from the toilets. He was so high he almost missed his seat and went flying into Justin. When he eventually sat down, he ordered more drinks. 'Pity Max isn't here,' he said.

'Yeah, life and soul of the party is Max,' Justin said flatly. 'Good-looking, and getting more so every day. His body's filling out like his dick.'

James seethed. 'Yeah, well, we all know where he wants to stick it.'

Justin laughed. 'Jealous?'

'I didn't mean you. Max is panting after your sister.'

Justin's jaw tightened.

James leaned closer to him. 'I think she's cute too. I may even try and fuck her again myself. She's easy meat, I'd say.'

Justin hooked his foot under James's stool and tugged hard. The stool slid sideways and James fell awkwardly to the floor, where Justin kicked him hard in the groin. 'Never talk like that about my sister. Now get up, sit up and shut up.'

Clarissa giggled as James heaved himself to his feet and picked up the stool. She was obviously intending to get blotto before the night was over. She was going to show the repellent Justin Chalmers that he couldn't hurt her with his snide remarks.

Laura slipped into William's study to check that the tapes were in order. Satisfied that everything was working and ready to go, she was about to leave when she saw one of the intercom lights flashing. She crossed to it. It was the jetty phone. Then she noticed the light blink on Dahlia's line, which made her worry. She wondered if perhaps the weather had turned bad: sometimes it was too rough to make the trip across. She pressed the speaker button, which enabled her to listen in on any call made anywhere on the island.

'He'll be on the first plane, so be waiting. It is imperative you say nothing, especially to Justin or Laura. Sir's orders.'

Laura gasped. 'Sir' had to be William. Why was he returning before time, and why was his arrival to be kept a secret?

\*

Max was finding it difficult to stop smiling. He was seated at his parent's table and rose to greet them as they arrived. 'Hi, I thought I'd sit with you this evening as everyone else on my usual table's gone clubbing.'

'How nice,' his mother said, as he held out her chair.

'You look stunning,' he said, kissing her cheek.

'Thank you.' She sat with rigid shoulders. 'Your father will join us shortly. As usual he's taking his time dressing.'

'Would you care for a glass of champagne?' Max asked, and his mother nodded. He signalled to the waiter, who crossed to them and poured two glasses. Max looked around the room. 'We're the first down,' he said, trying to make conversation.

'How observant of you!' She lifted her glass, wanting to throw its contents into his silly, boyish face. Max half rose again as the Matlocks came in.

'Are we all dining together?' Matlock said loudly, looking at the table set for eight.

'I believe so,' the Baroness said, forcing a smile, then looked at Angela, who clung to her husband's arm. 'You look quite lovely, Angela, adorable dress. Very flattering colour, lemon.'

'Where's your better half?' asked Matlock.

'He'll be joining us. We've had some troublesome news from Berlin, and I'm afraid we're forced to cut short the holiday. We're leaving early in the morning.'

Max looked astonished. 'You never told me. Does this mean I have to go with you?'

'No, dear. You can stay on. You're enjoying yourself, aren't you?'

'Yes, I am,' he said, with relief.

Daphne Hangerford shuffled in with the Baron. She

was leaning against him and clearly quite drunk. 'Don't get up, please.' She plonked herself into a seat and shook out her napkin. 'This'll be my last night. Clarissa and I have . . .' she hesitated '. . . a few problems.'

The Baroness almost gave herself whiplash she turned so quickly. 'What did you say?'

Daphne broke open her bread roll, scattering crumbs over the table. 'Just personal things. I have to leave.'

'If it's the report in *The Times*, we've all read it.'

Daphne gulped some water, but before she could reply the Baroness leaned closer. 'We're leaving too, we're so bored here. We've got tickets booked, but we're not broadcasting it, and if I were you, I wouldn't say too much. Don't want to appear ungrateful, do we?'

'We're missing one,' Matlock said, nodding to the empty seat at the head of the table. 'Ah, no, she's here.' He looked with admiration towards the door where Laura stood. She was wearing a white sequinned gown that floated around her like stardust, tied in a halter-neck with a white satin ribbon. She crossed to her usual table and signalled to the waiter to bring iced water.

'Won't you join us?' Matlock asked, leaning back in his chair.

Laura turned and smiled. 'Thank you, but I'm rather tired and will retire shortly.'

'Nevertheless we'd like you to at least spend a few moments with us.' Matlock had stood up and was holding out his hand to her. She hesitated before allowing him to guide her to the empty seat next to him.

'Thank you,' she said coyly, smiling at everyone apart from Max, who had flushed. Matlock asked her if she would care for a glass of champagne. Just like his wife, he had eyes only for Laura.

'No champagne, thank you.'

The lights lowered, leaving the room candlelit. The young guitarist entered and began to strum unobtrusively in the corner.

The atmosphere seemed affable, but tense undercurrents were building and Laura was at the eye of the storm. Matlock wanted to fuck her, Max was in love with her, as was Angela, and the von Gartens loathed her. They thought her nothing but a cheap, blackmailing whore. Daphne Hangerford, too drunk to be aware of the immediate situation, was the only person who didn't want either to strangle Laura or make love to her.

Laura behaved as if she was privileged to sit with them, keeping her eyes down and maintaining a sweet, shy smile. Matlock eased his thigh to rest against hers beneath the table.

The big fish was hooked, but his demise was endangering her secret plan with Max. She knew she could not leave the island before the final showdown with Matlock, but time was running out. When Justin discovered everyone was leaving he would be furious, and especially with her for acting without consulting him. She wondered fearfully if she dare carry out the revenge alone. No, she knew she couldn't.

'That was a long sigh,' Matlock whispered. She gave him a tiny, intimate smile and he leaned closer again. 'A penny for 'em.'

'Oh, my thoughts cost more than pennies,' she said softly, her mind jumping. Having orchestrated the imminent departure of the Baron and Baroness, along with Daphne Hangerford and Clarissa, Laura knew that the Matlocks and Max would be the only guests left, and Sir William would turn up at the most inopportune moment.

Laura felt Matlock's leg pressing harder against hers, then his hand fumbling with her skirt. She made the decision. If Justin didn't return on time as they had agreed, she would carry it out alone. She was determined that nothing would stop her running away with Max.

She glanced across the table. They were trying hard not to look at each other, but intuitively Max turned round. His eyes glowed, and she forced herself not to react. Beneath the table, she unzipped Matlock's trousers and began to fondle him, but now she felt disgusted at herself. How could she do this to a man she hated whilst the boy she loved was sitting right opposite her? She concentrated her mind on the plan and drew comfort from the thought that all this was part of a greater scheme.

The plan was for Laura to make Matlock desire her to such an extent that he would agree to meet on the quayside. They would board one of the boats and Justin would be waiting.

# CHAPTER 19

B Y MIDNIGHT, the Coca-Baba club was so crowded that there was hardly any space on the dance floor. Customers perched on the veranda railings and hovered around the rickety steps while the local ragga band pounded away at the microphones, which seemed constantly on distort. The loudspeakers added a high-pitched feedback that almost assisted the vocals and backups. The air was dense with cigarette and ganja smoke, and it was as hot and damp as a sauna. Perfumes mixed with body odour as the dancers writhed to the music. Flickering ultraviolet lights added to the surreal atmosphere: teeth became whiter than white, white clothes glowed with a strange phosphorescence, black skin disappeared leaving only eyeballs and teeth glinting from darkened corners as wraps, joints and folded dollar bills were passed.

Justin sat outside on the roof of a parked car. He had another tepid bottle of beer in his hand and had been eager to leave over an hour ago. Clarissa had danced with anyone who'd have her. She was being passed from partner to partner, necking and clinging to each one as though they were long-lost lovers. Justin watched her, bored. Her eyes occasionally darted him a frenetic glare of hatred. She was proving, if not to him then to herself, that she was sexy and sought-after, which indeed she was. Locally, white meat, especially with money, was referred to as a 'honey pot'. James had become moodier as the evening progressed. He had snorted cocaine, then complained to Justin that it was baby powder or, worse, laced with borax: his nose was dripping and painful.

Justin decided it was time to go home. The tide was in their favour and the water appeared quite calm. Enough, he thought, was enough. His charges were wrecked. He drained his beer, tossed aside the bottle and pushed his way into the heaving mass. Clarissa angrily faced him out: she was not ready to leave. Justin gripped her wrist and dragged her to the steps. 'Get off me,' she screeched. 'I've lost my watch!'

'Shut the fuck up! You want a pack on to us? If you lost your watch, then forget it. Maybe somebody took it in payment for screwing you up the arse in the john.'

She tried to hit him but he ducked. She fell forward and began to vomit.

Justin hauled her away from the onlookers towards the wasteground at the side of the club. There he found James. He was lying face down, his shirt torn, his pants round his ankles.

Justin hauled him to his feet. Get your pants up, man. We're out of here.'

'I was just taking a piss,' James slurred.

Justin signalled for the boys waiting on the speedboat to help him get the pair on to the deck.

'Why did you bring us here?' Clarissa wailed. She continued to snivel about her watch, until she realized her gold necklace was also missing, which brought on a fresh onslaught of tears.

'Think yourself lucky you've not lost a lot more. Stop bleating, and have a good shower when you get in. You're probably lousy with crabs.'

Clarissa gasped and shuddered. 'I didn't let them touch me,' she moaned. But she had, and had lost count of how many.

Justin ignored her. He had noticed James was white-faced, his lips blue. He still seemed unable to focus. 'You okay? James?'

James swung his head round. 'Yeah, man . . . I'm cool.'

The return trip to the island was a long, slow haul. When they arrived at the island, Justin strode off towards his bungalow. He wanted to shower and get the stench of vomit out of his nostrils. As he passed Max's room he crept up to the half-open shutter. The lights were on but, although the sheet had been pulled back, the bed was empty. Justin listened, but heard only the sound of crickets, so he moved on. Where could Max be at this hour?

Laura's suite was in darkness, shutters closed, door locked. He walked on to his own room where the lights were blazing. 'You're late,' said Laura, as he came in, closing the door.

'I couldn't get them to leave the club. I got back as soon as I could.' He began to peel off his clothes. 'Don't come near me, I stink.' He stepped out of his trousers.

'We have to talk,' Laura said.

'Not right now. I need a shower.' He disappeared into the bathroom.

Laura sat drumming her fingers on the bedside table. She had it all worked out. By the time he had left the bathroom Justin was more relaxed. He flopped down on the bed and Laura stroked his damp hair.

'Okay. How did it go with Matlock? You made progress?'

'Yes, he's all over me like a rash. But I don't know whether I can go through with it. The man disgusts me. I don't know that I want to give him the pleasure of fucking me.'

'Well, there's no need, is there? I mean, I think I've done a pretty good job of getting him into the fishing anyway. He'll be dying to get out there tomorrow, and I'll just tell the boat-boys that I'm going to take him out alone.'

For a moment Laura was hurt. She had wanted to be there for the grand finale. Then she realized that perhaps with Justin absent she would have a chance to get her things together for her escape with Max.

Justin saw her look and interpreted it as disappointment. 'Don't worry, my princess. I'll just get him drugged up on the boat then bring him back to the harbour. Keep an eye open for me and we'll finish him down there. I should be back around twelve thirty.'

She took a deep breath. 'Now, just listen and don't interrupt. I've had to push things along a few notches. Tomorrow the Baron and Baroness leave, along with Daphne Hangerford and Clarissa.'

'What?'

'They might have become a problem, and we don't care about them anyway.'

There was something about her tone, her confidence, that alerted him. 'What did you do?'

'Oh!' She shrugged. 'I let them see themselves on the video. They're packed and ready.'

'Is Max going with them?'

'Of course.'

He giggled. 'So that leaves just . . .'

'Matlock, his wife and son,' Laura said softly.

He caught her hand. 'What is it? What's wrong?'

Laura withdrew her hand. 'I think William's coming back.'

'Well, we know he is. It *is* his island.'

She faced him angrily. 'He might be here tomorrow.'

Justin's face drained of colour.


Clarissa walked slowly with the wretched James. He kept stumbling, and had to lean heavily against her. 'What on earth have you shovelled up tonight?' she asked, almost buckling under the weight of his arm around her shoulders.

'Not enough,' he muttered.

'For God's sake, I can't prop you up. We'll have to get one of those golf carts.' She looked around but didn't know where they were kept. She wished she'd asked the boat-boys to help them. 'That bloody Justin just pissed off,' she said, wondering whether or not to leave James where he was and find someone to help.

'He's a shit,' James mumbled, then started to cry, sinking to his knees. 'I'm so messed up,' he sobbed.

Clarissa sighed and caught sight of Max not far ahead of them. 'Max?' she called.

Max had been unable to sleep. He'd read and watched a movie before deciding to walk around the island. 'My God, look at the state of him,' he said.

James was now lying flat on the pathway.

'He's done some drugs, God knows what,' Clarissa said, as they tried to haul him to his feet. 'Help me get him to his room, will you?' Max hooked an arm around him and hauled him upright. The three staggered to James's room. As they reached the door, Clarissa let go of his arm. 'I'm going to bed,' she announced, and walked on.

Max was furious. 'We can't just leave him. He could choke or something.'

'Stick him under the shower, then. I've had enough of him.'

Max stripped off James's clothes and was appalled at the marks all over his body. There were bloody scratches, bites, dark bruises and raw red welts across his back. 'James, who's done this to you?'

James lifted his head, his eyes drooping. He tried to say something but he passed out. Somehow Max dragged him into the shower and turned on the cold tap, soaking himself in the process. Then he returned to the bedroom to brew some coffee and fetch some pyjamas. When he returned to the shower James was still unconscious, but his face was deathly pale and the skin round his mouth was turning blue. Max called Dahlia, who said she would send Kurt.


Laura moved off the bed and began to pace up and down. 'It's got to be him. Why would she say we mustn't be told? And who else could it be anyway? Just to make sure, I asked Dahlia if she had heard from him. She acted a bit cagey and said nothing had been confirmed, that he was possibly coming home but she wasn't sure.'

Justin stood by the shutters. 'She said that? Are you sure?'

'Why would I make it up?' Laura snapped. 'Now you know why I had to move things so fast. I wouldn't have done it if it hadn't been an emergency, not without you.'

'Well, well! Speak of the devil,' he said softly. He walked over to the door and opened it. 'Dahlia! What on earth are you doing up at this hour?'

'It's young James Matlock. He's unconscious. Kurt is with him. He says we must get a doctor.'

'Kurt's a trained nurse,' Justin said.

'A nurse is not a doctor,' said Dahlia, 'and the boy doesn't look good. I've just come from his room.'

'Shit!' Justin dropped his towel and went back into the room to grab a tracksuit. 'Come in for a minute,' he called to Dahlia. As he dressed he asked her if William was arriving ahead of schedule. She was evasive, until he snatched her arm. 'Listen to me, bitch,' he hissed. 'You're here on a massive salary, courtesy of me, so don't fuck me around. Is he coming or is he not?'

She nodded. 'He asked me to tell no one, made me swear not to.'

'Your loyalties are to him now, are they?'

She shifted her weight. 'I didn't mean to do anything wrong, Justin.'

He stared at her. 'I'll let this one go, but don't think I won't remember it. You'd be back in that whore-house, and your kids along with you, if it weren't for me. Now, get out of my sight.'

Dahlia slipped out, terrified.

Justin's face was taut with anger. Then he said, 'I'd better go and see that dumb piece of shit.'

Laura asked if he would like her with him, but he told her to go to bed, she must be exhausted after having to sort so much out by herself earlier. He spoke with the venomous camp lisp she hated.

As the door closed behind him, she sighed with relief. She was sure he had not detected her lie or, more important, suspected anything about Max, and that he had no idea of her intentions. She took a small suitcase, opened it on her bed, and packed the few garments she felt were absolutely necessary. Her heart beat rapidly. She was excited and her hand trembled as she crossed back and forth to her wardrobe, laying out clothes beside the case. Suddenly she felt dizzy and her head throbbed, but she sucked in her breath and didn't stop. Her pace quickened and her hand began to brush at her skirt.

James was now in blue pyjamas. His face above the tight, white sheet was pale and his lips still blue, but his breathing was regular.

Max was in the room with Kurt, who had a medical kit-bag.

'You should leave this to me,' Kurt said. Max chewed his lip. 'Go on, son, you've done more than enough. I'll look after him now.'

Max hurried off and, passing Laura's room, paused: the lights were on. He went up her path and peered into the bedroom between the partly closed shutters. She was undressing, the room lit by candles. Max wanted to call out to her but he couldn't say a word.

He was mesmerized. She was naked now, brushing her hair, her eyes half closed. Suddenly he heard footsteps and ducked down as Justin hurried past. He remained hidden, listening, afraid Justin would discover him.

By the time he straightened up, the candles had been extinguished and Laura's room was in darkness.

If he had been a moment earlier, he would have seen a different Laura, shaking convulsively as she took out her pills. She managed to swallow them, then took deep breaths to calm herself and picked up her hairbrush. With her eyes closed she whispered, 'I'm all right, Laura's all right, Laura's all right.'

James was now lying face down as Kurt dabbed his cuts with antiseptic.

'You shouldn't leave him on his stomach,' Justin said, as he entered.

Kurt shrugged. 'These sores need attention.'

Justin lifted James's eyelid. Only the white of his eye was visible. 'Shit! He's really out of it,' he muttered.

'He needs a doctor, man, the sooner the better.'

Kurt laid compresses over James's back and ran a roll of surgical tape across them to hold them firm, then gently turned him over. Then he said they should take the boy straight to hospital.

'That won't be necessary,' Justin snapped.

'Justin, he's real sick. Look at him! Christ only knows what he's taken.'

'I'll make the decisions. Now get the hell out.'

As the door closed behind Kurt, Justin propped up James on his pillows and snapped open a bottle of poppers. He broke one and held it under his nose.

James heaved, gave a spluttering cough and his eyes fluttered open.

'Breathe in, James, there's a good boy, nice deep breaths. Gonna give you another.'

Max walked in. 'Should you be doing that?'

Justin whipped round. 'It's just to bring him round. We've spoken to a doctor and he's on his way.'

'Should I fetch his parents?' asked Max, concerned.

'No, he's coming to and I don't want them to know the state he got himself into. You just piss off back to your room, there's a good chap. You and your folks are leaving early tomorrow morning.'

Max hesitated. 'Actually, I'm staying on.'

Justin straightened up. 'Really? You're having such a good time, are you?'

'Yes, I am.'

Suddenly James began to cough, chest heaving. Justin sat him up further, shoving pillows behind him. 'Good boy, that's it. Come on. Deep breaths, now.' Justin turned to Max. 'Shut the door as you leave.'

Again Max hesitated, then left. Justin split open yet another amyl nitrate capsule and pressed it beneath James's nose. The boy gasped as his heart-rate soared. His arms flailed and his eyes rolled back. Justin felt his pulse, sat for a while then ran from the room.


James was carried on to the speedboat. Kurt did not say anything as he helped the boys make him comfortable. Justin told Kurt to stay with James while he was in the hospital and to report back.

'You not coming?' Kurt asked.

'No. Tell the boys to return after they've dropped you off.'

'Okay, but don't you think his parents should be told? Maybe they'll want to be with him.'

Justin told them to get moving. It was now almost five, and at any moment the house would begin its morning rituals.

Kurt watched Justin as the powerful boat's engine churned up the water. He'd always known there was some scam going on – that much had been obvious from the amount of money he was being paid and that he'd been hand-picked by Justin. But Kurt was worried that whatever heinous scheme Justin was part of, he was drawing him into it. He decided he'd not risk staying on. Just as soon as he'd sorted James out, he'd go pack his belongings and leave the island. Perhaps Justin intended murdering Sir William.

Her mother had to shake Clarissa awake. She sat bolt upright. 'What? What is it?' When she saw her mother, she flopped back. 'Christ you nearly gave me heart-failure, Mother. What are you doing here?'

'We're leaving.'

Clarissa turned to see the time. 'It's only five fifteen!'

'We're getting the launch to Tortola. There's a flight out at nine and I want to be on it.'

Clarissa sat up. 'Well, I don't, I'm staying.'

'No, you are not. You are coming with me.' Daphne started to sob. 'We're flat broke. The houses are gone, stables, everything. That bastard spent every cent I had. He's borrowed from every one we know and now he's moved in with that bitch from the stables. I wish to

God I'd never set foot in this God-forsaken place. I hate it! It's like a prison.' Daphne stood up. 'Call for someone to help you pack. Don't forget your passport, and if you have any money we'll need it, because I've only got forty pounds to my name.'

'I've no cash at all.' Clarissa sat back on the bed. 'What's the point of going back?'

'We have to. To see what we can salvage. Right now we don't even have a roof over our heads.'

'I see,' Clarissa said softly.

'It would have been nice if you and James had hit it off. The Matlocks have more money than they know what to do with.'

'I wouldn't get involved with that poof,' Clarissa said, searching her make-up bag unsuccessfully for some paracetamol. She had a splitting headache and her body ached all over. She gave her mother a hooded look. Did she really want to go all the way back to London and face her father?

'I'm not leaving,' she said firmly.

'You are,' her mother said, equally firmly. Then she took a deep breath. 'If you want your trust fund intact, you'll not waste a second. I've always known your father's a bastard, but it turns out he's also an accomplished thief. He took every cent Katherine Benedict possessed, including her kids' trust funds.'

'Can he get his hands on my money, Ma?' asked Clarissa.

Daphne looked hard at her daughter and was shocked at what she saw. It was like looking at a stranger: there was no shy, deferential look in her eyes, no innocence left. Here was not a girl who had blossomed into a woman, but a seedy, slovenly girl, brazenly standing with her dressing gown undone, unembarrassed by her nakedness.

'Because if he even tries, I'll have him fucking arrested,' Clarissa continued, as she padded into her bathroom and reached for the paracetamol on the shelf above the basin.

'What has happened to you, Clarissa? I hardly know you any more,' Daphne said.

'Well maybe being almost fucked by my own father had some effect.'

Clarissa took two pills and swallowed them in one gulp.

'You're lying!' her mother said. As much as she loathed her husband, she could not believe what she was hearing.

'I'm not. Ask my father what happened here in the sauna. He groped me. *You* only want me to go back so you can get your hands on my money. Well, it's all mine, Ma, and I need it. You won't get a penny!'

Daphne slapped her daughter's face so hard that Clarissa fell off the chair with a howl. 'If you don't stop acting like some cheap tart and get packed, you might not have any money left.'

Daphne swept out, banging the door behind her. She stopped to catch her breath, and the heady scent of the ubiquitous lilies made her feel sick. How she hated this place!

The Baroness was standing in the hall, her luggage packed and ready to be taken down to the jetty. She looked as immaculate as ever. Her husband, though, seemed nervous and jaded.

Daphne Hangerford was waiting for her cases to be brought down. She didn't want to return to her suite, or to be alone. 'Do you mind if I give you some advice?' she said to the Baroness. 'Don't let your son stay on. Make him leave with you. This is a terrible place.'

The Baroness gave her husband a furtive look then turned away. 'He's old enough to make his own decisions.'

Daphne shrugged her plump shoulders, and saw Clarissa appear, followed by one of the house-boys with her bags. At this moment, a maid approached the Baron with a fax that had just arrived for him. He opened it and froze. Benedict's lawyers were taking him to court. His own team had tried to delay the action, but there was now an even more serious charge of insider dealing. It was suggested he return as soon as possible. He was about to lose everything he owned and the news had been leaked to the European press. Any day now it would hit the British papers.

Angela Matlock came down the stairs to say good-bye, puzzled by what appeared to be a mass exodus. She kissed everyone and asked if Max was staying: she wanted company for James.

'Yes, he is,' the Baroness said.

'I was on my way to James's room,' Angela went on. 'His father is just leaving for another fishing trip and wants James to join him.'

Clarissa grinned. 'I doubt if he'll make it. It was quite a late night.'

Humphrey Matlock was already aboard the fishing-boat and waved to the departing guests from the deck. He had paid little attention to what his wife had said and thought that they, like him, must be embarking on some day-trip. It was a clear, brilliant day, and although it was only seven in the morning, the sun was already beating down. He had hoped James would join him, but there was no sign of his son.

Justin strolled towards him. 'Have you seen James?' Matlock asked.

Justin rolled his eyes. 'He's still in his pit. Rather the worse for wear after the disco, I'm afraid,' he said, jumping aboard. 'Come on, cast off. I'm crewing for you today. The regulars have demanded a day off. I suspect they've got hangovers too.'

Matlock untied a mooring line, disappointed. 'Wretched boy. Spoiled, pampered idiot. I wash my hands of him.'

Justin signalled to the boat-boy to start the engines. 'We're going into deep water this morning and if you get a big catch,' he laughed, splaying his hands out, 'I'll help you reel it in!'

Matlock pointed to the jetty. 'Looks like a mass exodus. Sightseeing, are they?'

'Yes, and hitting the tourist shops.'

'Thank God I'm not roped into that.'

'Yes. We'll have much more fun . . . fishing.'


Angela headed for her son's room. She paused, gazing down at the jetty as everyone climbed aboard the cruiser. Then she went on her way to James. She pushed open the door to his room. It was in immaculate order. The maids had cleaned it and changed the linen.

'James?' she called. This was so unlike her son. His

401

own room at home, even with maids, was in constant turmoil. Angela opened the wardrobe. His clothes were all neatly pressed and on their individual hangers. Even the drawers were tidy. She turned guiltily as Max tapped and peered in from outside. He was a little out of breath as he had run back from the jetty to see his parents off. He had been disappointed to discover he had missed them, and was more than a little confused as to why his mother had not even called into his suite.

'Hi,' he said shyly.

'Hello, Max. I just dropped in to see James.'

'Is he feeling better?'

'Better?' she said, puzzled.

Max came further into the room and he, too, looked around in surprise. 'Well, I saw him last night and—'

'And?' she said quickly. 'Had he been drinking?'

'A bit. He wasn't feeling too good.'

'Then where is he?' she said, now showing her worry.

'I have no idea, but he came home late. They went clubbing.'

Angela gave a soft laugh. 'Of course, he'll be with his father. He was going on a special fishing trip this morning.'

'Oh, that may be it,' Max said, but he doubted it. He excused himself and left, checking the time. It was not too long to wait. He decided he would go for a walk – anything to take his mind off Laura.

Dahlia looked up with surprise as Laura walked into the laundry room. 'Have you heard how he is?' she asked.

'Who?' Laura asked, as she crossed to where her clothes were drying.

'They took James Matlock to hospital,' Dahlia said, watching her intently.

'Justin didn't tell me.'

Dahlia continued folding towels. Laura seemed unconcerned by the news and, to Dahlia's surprise, gathered all her lingerie into a basket.

'Where is my tissue paper, Dahlia?'

'I had it ironed. It's in that drawer.' She pointed.

Laura placed it carefully on top of her basket. 'You're not planning on leaving, are you?' Dahlia asked.

'No, I'm not.' Laura was about to walk out, but then she turned. Her eyes were chilling. 'When do you expect Sir William?'

Dahlia licked her lips. 'Perhaps some time today.'

Laura gave an odd, secretive smile. 'Good.' And she was gone.


Dahlia found Kurt in the gym, working out alone. 'You have any news about James Matlock?'

'They took him into intensive care and said they'd keep Justin informed of his progress. I think he'll be okay . . . Didn't look too good, though.'

'What drugs had he taken?' Dahlia asked, placing pristine white towels in the racks.

'Christ only knows, and in that club they sell shit. They've been handing round Ecstasy tabs like they were M&Ms.'

'His parents haven't been told,' Dahlia said, with a hint of disapproval. Her bleeper went off. 'I've got to go. See you later.'

'You won't, I'm quitting,' said Kurt. 'Be gone by this afternoon.'

'Why?'

'I don't know exactly what's going on here but something is, and it's not smelling good to me. You know Justin's given all the boys two days off, plus the kitchen staff? I reckon whatever's going to happen will happen soon.'

Dahlia hurried out. She began to feel the same trepidation as Kurt, but she had kids – she needed her wage packet. Her bleeper went off and she hurried back to the laundry room.

Dahlia closed the laundry-room door, went to the phone and called William. He was at the airport. If he had been there an hour earlier he would have passed his erstwhile guests, but now the airport was virtually empty. 'I need to be picked up,' he said. 'Is everything all right over there?'

Dahlia took a nervous look around. She knew Justin was out, but was worried that Laura might walk in and catch her. William listened as Dahlia listed those who had left. He asked about Humphrey Matlock. 'Out fishing, sir.'

She hesitated before she told him about James.

William told her he would go straight to the hospital and check on James. 'Where's his mother?' he asked. When William discovered that she had not been told, he bellowed down the phone so loud that Dahlia had to hold the receiver away from her ear. She then told him that half of the staff had been given two days off, including some of the boat-boys and several of the kitchen and domestic staff. 'On whose orders?'

'Justin's,' she said. Then, after another lengthy pause

and feeling even guiltier, she hinted that something odd was going on but she was not quite sure what. 'I may be wrong, but I think Laura is planning to leave.'

'Is Justin going too?' William interrupted. 'Where is he now?'

'Oh, I think he's out with Sir Humphrey on the fishing-boat.' Dahlia listened as William barked instructions down the line, repeated that she must carry out everything he told her to do, without question.

William slapped off his mobile, and remained standing with the phone for a few moments. Then he did what he should have done earlier: he called the coastguard.

# CHAPTER 20

AT AROUND nine, Dahlia found Angela Matlock sitting by the pool in the shade. As usual she was working on her cross stitch. 'Excuse me interrupting you, madam, but I have an urgent message for you. Your son is in hospital on Tortola. He's very sick.'

'What?' Angela stood up and her cross stitch fell to the ground.

'I have arranged for you to be taken there directly,' Dahlia said.

Angela's face drained of colour. 'Has anyone told my husband?'

'He's still out on the fishing-boat, madam. I'm afraid I can't contact him from here. We have tried their radio, but it appears to be switched off.'

Matlock had a cigar clamped between his teeth. It was still early, but he had a glass of iced Pernod which he lifted in a toast to Justin. 'This is one of the best times I've had in years,' he said expansively, then gave a deep rumbling laugh. 'No bloody women on board for starters!' He drank thirstily. 'No son either.' He refilled his glass. 'I don't know what to do about him. He's had every opportunity handed to him on a plate: the best education money can buy, a doting mother, and myself obviously. I'm fond of the lad, but you know ... I hope this will go no further.'

Justin lit a cigarette. 'That's what fishing trips are for. Male bonding they call it, don't they?' He tilted his head to look up to the sky, and squinted against the glare of the sun.

'What do you make of James? You can be honest.'

Justin shrugged his shoulders. 'He's handsome, friendly, good at sport and yet ... He seemed to be searching for the right expression.

'Weak,' Matlock said, and sat down heavily.

They sat side by side, Matlock in contemplation, Justin in reverie.

'Tell me about yourself, Matlock said, helping himself to yet more Pernod. He had been drinking it like lemonade, and up till now it had apparently had little or no effect on him.

Justin stretched out his arms and crossed his legs. 'Well, it's quite a long story. I was born in France . . .'

You hardly have any trace of an accent,' Matlock said, his attention waning as he stared at the ocean. 'Looks like it might get rough.'

'I was educated, if one could call it that, in England.'

'Where?' Matlock still wasn't interested.

Justin paused a fraction. 'A children's detention centre.'

Matlock stopped in the act of raising his glass to his lips. 'A young offenders' institution?'

'Yes. I was sent there at the age of fourteen.'

Matlock was taken aback, but tried not to show it. 'Drugs was it?'

'No.' Justin was enjoying himself, and took his time. He said he had not committed any petty crime and had been only ten years old when he committed it.

'Ten? Good God! What on earth could you have done at that age for them to put you away?'

'Murder. The murder of my parents, to be exact. You may recall the case. My father's name was Martin Moorcroft, my mother Madeleine. I was Child B.'

Matlock had thought he had recognized Justin and Laura when he first saw them together at the island, but had not thought about it again. Until now.

'I do remember something . . .' His mind was spinning but he hid his confusion by drinking, then searching for a cigar.

'My sister, Child A, came to England with me after the murders,' Justin continued. 'We were there as wards of my father's sister, a widow, Frances Chalmers.'

Matlock clipped the end of the cigar. He couldn't look at Justin because the truth was dawning on him. 'We were both accused of the murders,' Justin continued, in a conversational way, as if he was discussing nothing more serious than the weather. 'There was also a third murder, the body found in the swimming-pool, but it had decomposed. It had been one of our first nannies, a horrid woman. Everyone thought she had just upped and packed her bags but she hadn't.' He giggled.

'Then there was Camilla Maynard. She came out to look after us much later. You must remember her. Her brother was Andrew Maynard MP. He committed suicide. Well, his sister Camilla had talked to all the journalists about us. Doesn't ring any bells?' Matlock took out his lighter, and put it to his cigar. He sucked in too strongly and the smoke burnt his lungs. 'My mother died in a fire.' Justin was studying the curling blue cigar smoke.

'Your sister?' Matlock asked, his voice sounding thick.

'Child A was only eight, and they couldn't find a place in prison for her. She was far too young. According to French law, we both were. Instead we were sent to a specialist psychiatric unit in England by the French government.' Justin's eyes bored into Matlock's forehead. 'My sister was always highly strung, very dependent on me. Well, we had never been apart and were very close. After a few sweet years of care in the hands of the psychiatric unit and our dear aunt, the whole thing blew up again. She was taken to a hospital for the criminally insane eventually. I think she was twelve or thirteen when they shipped her off there. She was manic, or so they said. She was moved from one place to another. Not a lot of places could accommodate a little girl like that. She was always on some drug or other and she was hardly recognizable because of it. Her name was Laura.' Justin's eyes were like slits.

'I think I do recall something about the case now,' Matlock said, the sweat dripping from his forehead in beads.

'You should. It made the headlines for months. Do you recall Lord Chief Justice Bellingham? He handled the case in England. His grandson was over here with his parents, Lord and Lady Bellingham, recently. Now, they threw some good parties. At the last one, poor old Oliver OD'd and choked on his own vomit. Sad, really.

He was such a nice kid, about your son's age, and the amount of drugs young James consumes I'm surprised he's not overdosed. Or maybe he has, for all we know.'

'What have my son and this boy Oliver to do with you?'

Justin looked skyward. 'Ah, well, the sins of the fathers and all that. Anyway, before the nightmare began, we were both happily living with our aunt.' Matlock bowed his head. 'You remember the case now I bet,' Justin said softly. 'We made your career, didn't we? You, your alarmist articles and your bestseller. Of course you remember Camilla Maynard. You interviewed her, didn't you? Yes, of course you did! Oh, did I tell you she died in a car accident? Her brakes failed. Bang! Straight across the dual carriageway she went, into oncoming cars. Hers exploded, I think. Awful to watch anyway.'

Justin sighed, leaning back. 'After that novel of yours and all your headlines about us being devil children they didn't dare leave us free. We had to be punished. We had to be publically tried for our crimes. *You* tried us, Matlock. Your filthy articles and your seedy book tried us. You wouldn't leave us alone because we made your stinking fucking headlines. We made your career, didn't we? You are responsible, for Laura's sickness, for the hell she went through in that asylum, for my wasted years at borstal. You are responsible.'

Matlock could not move. He wanted to get up, move away from Justin and his quiet chit-chat voice, but he couldn't. 'Would you like to know about our mother, Madeleine Moorcroft? She was part Argentinian, an olive-skinned woman with large luminous eyes and a hooked nose. She was not plain – ugly, yes, but some people find an ugly woman attractive, don't they? You used some photographs of her in your book, but they never did her justice.'

The movement of the boat was making Matlock feel queasy. 'How long before we drop anchor?' he asked, desperate to change the subject.

Justin stood up, shaded his eyes and looked around. 'Be a while yet. You wanted a big fish! Ever caught a shark?' he asked.

'Not as yet.'

Justin laughed. 'Nor me, but I will today.' His face took on a strange, twisted smile. 'Let me tell you what my mother used to force me to do.' Matlock didn't want to hear, but there was something about the way Justin moved closer, invading his space. He almost brushed against him, but then Justin removed his glass. 'I'll just top you up. It's quite a long story and it's one I want you to hear.'

'I think I've had enough.' Matlock said.

'No, you have not, not by a long shot!' And Justin filled his glass with Pernod and dropped in ice, which rattled against the glass as he handed it back. 'My mother enjoyed pain. She was a masochistic bitch, a woman who became sexually aroused by giving birth. She described the pain as exquisite, said it felt like her insides were being ripped out.'

Matlock felt his skin crawl. 'I don't want to hear this.'

'You have no option. You see, you're now my prisoner.' Justin chuckled. 'You're going to listen to every word I say because I have waited years for this moment.' Matlock rose to his feet but Justin pushed him back roughly. '*Sit*. Sit down and listen.' He was speaking as

411

if to a naughty child. 'I shall begin at the beginning. The first time, she woke me in the middle of the night and carried me into her bedroom, where my father was waiting. I wasn't afraid. They were my mummy and daddy. They loved me. I loved them. They said we would play loving games.'

'Please, I don't want to hear any more,' Matlock slurred.

'I've only just begun,' Justin said.

Matlock held up one hand. 'Listen to me. Perhaps you've harboured some kind of deep-seated hatred against me, understandable from what you've said, but I was just a youngster, and I was paid to allow some other writer to do that book. I had nothing to do with it, believe me. I suppose if I had, you and your sister's faces would have been imprinted on my mind. It's what they call a ghost-writer, do you understand? I didn't write that book.'

Justin watched Matlock as he drank. He knew he had to be lying, not that it mattered. If it hadn't been for him they would never have been hounded. 'Did you coin the phrase "Devil's Children"?'

Matlock drank again. 'I don't recall.'

Justin repeated the phrase, then leaned close and touched the man's knee. 'Maybe it was a fitting description. Maybe it wasn't.'

'Listen, son, if this is about money—' Matlock's head cracked back against the combing as Justin punched him in his face.

'I'm not your son, and this isn't about money. Don't you understand what this is about? This is about me confronting you, my devil. There is no way off this boat, no way you can make it back to the island without me. You are my prisoner, and by the time this is over, you will understand what fear means, understand that you must be punished for what you did to Child A and Child B, like everyone else who hurt them. You are going to die.'

Matlock wasn't sweating any more, he felt icy cold. Justin's face became a blur. 'Dear God, you'll never get away with this.' He tried to stand, but fell back into his seat.

Justin laughed, picked up the empty glass and tossed it overboard. He turned back to stare at the frightened man. This was the culmination of years of secret planning. In some ways it had been Matlock who had helped him to survive all along; without doubt, the idea of destroying him had given Laura the focus she needed to keep her sanity. He had promised they would play this scene together, rehearsed it so often between them. But she had always balked at the killing, and Matlock was the prize that Justin had lived his life hunting.

William had to wait a considerable time before he eventually got through to Dahlia. She confirmed that she had carried out his instructions to the letter, but still had not heard from Matlock or Justin. William placed a second call to the coastguard. They had sent out a launch. William felt relieved enough to leave it in their hands and he hurried to the hospital.

James was on oxygen and a glucose drip, and was linked up to a heart monitor. At this stage they were unable to ascertain if he had suffered any permanent damage. His temperature was stable and a dialysis machine was standing by in case his kidneys failed. His pale face was like a sleeping child's, his arms out straight, like a soldier's, resting on the white sheet. The air-conditioning ensured the room was cool and a ceiling fan turned overhead, making a soft grating sound. Could Justin have had something to do with this? Could he have engineered it? He turned as the door opened, and a nurse ushered Angela in. 'I want to take him home,' she whispered.

'He mustn't be moved,' said the nurse. 'He's still unconscious. We're doing all we can.'

Then Angela saw William. He drew up a chair for her to sit beside the bed. She was twisting a tissue round and round in her hands. 'I asked them to contact my husband,' she said to the nurse. Then she looked pleadingly to William. 'Can you make sure he gets here as soon as possible?'

'Yes, it's being taken care of right now. He'll be here, I'm sure, Angela.'

When the nurse had gone, she said, 'He is so like you, my husband. The only difference is he married me, while you betrayed me.' She threw the torn tissue into the bin. 'You seemed to gain such pleasure from hurting me. You are the most destructive, heartless man.'

'I don't think this is the right place to discuss—'

'No? Funny how there never is a right time, is there?' William shifted his weight from one foot to the other as she stood up and faced him. 'I loved you, you said you loved me. You made me believe you had every intention of marrying me, but within two weeks of making promises, *two weeks*, you took up with that whore! You replaced me in your affections and in my job! I'd had that job for years. You left me when I was ill. You took everything away from me.'

William wished the ground would open up and swallow him. 'It was a long time ago.' He could not believe she was launching such a venomous attack at him while her son lay in a coma beside her. 'You must have hated me,' he said lamely.

'Hated you?' She gave a bitter laugh. 'I tried to kill myself. All I could think about was dying. You almost killed me. I was broke and mentally sick, my mother was suffering from Alzheimer's and I had no one.' She gave a shrill laugh then looked at him. 'But life has a funny way of dealing the cards. My husband's mother was in the hospital too, and that was how we met. Like I said, he reminded me of you – not in looks, just manner. I didn't marry him for that reason. I married him because I thought I loved him. I never did. I tried to make him be like you but he wasn't and then to be used by him with his other women . . . One day I decided that, no matter how long it took, I would have my pound of flesh because I blamed you for my being married to him. I wanted to cause you pain, William, as much as you had caused me.' Her eyes, usually so submissive, blazed. 'Well, I paid you back, William Benedict. You couldn't have had the slightest idea where I was, let alone that I could have been instrumental in . . .'

'It must have been tough harbouring such deep resentment for so many years.'

She was silent for a few moments, then plucked a clean tissue from the box. He could not take his eyes off her hands as they shredded it. 'I never slept a single night without thinking about you. In the end it became second nature, like a ritual.'

'Sleeping cruelty,' he said softly.

'You deserved all you got. Maybe you always were a queer. Maybe that's why you doted on that boy Maynard. You certainly made a big fool of yourself over him.'

William understood it all now. Suddenly he didn't feel any anger towards Angela any more, only sympathy and guilt. Guilt because he had cared for her, and never loved her.

'To begin with my husband always wanted to please me, but gradually I saw through him; I was just a useful appendage. I was afraid he would leave me and take James. It wasn't till I discovered how to control him that I got the upper hand. He was terrified that someone would turn the tables on him. If I divorced him and threatened to feed dirt about him to his competitors he would have been devastated. And believe you me there was plenty of dirt. If you think your little forays with prostitutes made headlines, you should have seen what my beloved husband got up to! He didn't write the articles about you himself, of course, he's above all that now. My husband's only interested in circulation – or money. Rather like you. As I said before, you two are very similar.'

'And you fed him all the inside information about my life to create one scandal after another? My wives, my children?'

'Correct.' She smirked. 'I had always followed your career, William, and your marriages. For God's sake, you even invited me to your first wedding. Can you imagine what that did to me?'

He wanted to explain why he had never loved her or any other woman, but there was no point now.

She looked at the boy in the bed. 'Perhaps now I

will have to pay for it.' She was silent again for a moment. 'Why are we here? I didn't want to come, nor did Humphrey. But he changed his mind. Did you organize this? Did you find out it was me?' she asked softly. She turned to him. 'Did you want me here to hurt me again? Well, if my son is the price, you've won the game. But I don't understand. I believed you never gave me a second thought.'

'I never did,' William said quietly. He hesitated before he continued. 'What do you know about Laura Chalmers?' he asked. 'And her brother, Justin Chalmers?'

'Nothing! Why should I?'

William hooked the back of the spare chair and drew it to the bed to sit next to her. 'Has your husband ever discussed either of them with you?'

'He's never even mentioned them. Neither of us ever met them before we came here. Why do you ask?'

Before she could respond, James began to moan. As they leaned over him, he opened his eyes.

'Oh, thank God, thank God,' Angela wept.

William rang for a nurse, then looked back at the weeping mother caressing her son's face. 'I'm here, darling. Mummy's here, my love. You are going to be all right, I'm here.'

James shut his eyes again. 'I know you are, I've been listening to you two. I just didn't have the strength to tell you to shut the fuck up! I've got to play cricket and I must find my pads,' he said feverishly, trying to sit up.

The heart monitor began bleeping at an alarming rate, and a doctor and nurse hurried in. Angela looked terrified and the doctor asked her to leave, but she hovered at her son's bedside.

417

'Is he going to be all right?' she gasped, and repeated the question over and over as she sat beside William in the corridor outside James's room.

Half an hour later the doctor came out. He said they had given James something to calm him down, and he would sleep for a few hours. Angela went back to his bedside.

'We found not only cocaine in his body but also heroin and Ecstasy,' the doctor said to William. 'I've had three other Ecstasy cases in the last month. One didn't recover, one had irreversible brain damage, the other's back with his family, showing little or no side-effects. Earlier this year we had a young boy dead on arrival.'

'Oliver Bellingham?' William asked.

The doctor gave a brief nod. His other patients had been local kids, and William felt the man's undercurrent of anger.

'Do the police know who's dealing it?' asked William, with a sick feeling in the pit of his stomach.

The doctor was already moving off. 'If your son recovers, I suggest you ask him who he bought the tablets from. Nothing I say makes the slightest difference to the police. Perhaps they'll listen to someone with your wealth!'

William did not correct the doctor with regard to James. Perhaps if he had known he was not related, he would not have been so forthcoming.

'He thought you were his father,' Angela said, bitterly shaking her head. 'How incongruous. If you knew how I longed to be pregnant by you, longed for your child, then prayed that you would marry me. Now here we are praying for my son to live. But he's not yours. I want my husband here, William. Please try to find him – at least do that for me.'

He walked outside, hoping to God the police would get to Matlock in time – not for Angela or for James, but to save Justin from committing another murder. He called the island, only to be told the fishing boat had not yet returned. William wanted to walk away from the wretched Angela, and he worried about Justin, but he went back into the hospital to sit with her. It was the least he could do.


Matlock's big hands were clasped around his knees. They had been anchored for a while, and the boat was rocking gently. 'Please, I'm begging you, turn back,' he said quietly to Justin.

'We can't turn back, Matlock, because I haven't finished,' he replied.

Matlock tried to stand up. To his horror he couldn't. His legs felt like lead, his head throbbed and he started to panic.

'Fix you another?' Justin held up a clean glass.

Matlock looked up, and his vision blurred. 'What the hell have you given me?' His voice was thick.

'What they used to pump into Laura. Largactyl it's called. Just so you know what it feels like. Remember, she was only a little girl.' Justin delved into his pockets and took out one newspaper cutting after another, waving them in front of Matlock's face. 'How much did they pay you for these? Or did they pay you more to write a good headline? How much did you earn for "Devil's Children"?' he screamed.

Sweat dripped down Matlock's back as he fought to

keep his eyes open. His tongue felt as though it was swelling and filling his mouth. His ears were ringing and buzzing, his heart thudding, and he had lost control of his limbs. It was a living nightmare.

'And the book. *Killer Angels!*' Justin prodded Matlock's chest with it. 'I'm going to make you eat every word you say you never wrote. *Liar!*'

He gripped Matlock's jaw, prised open his mouth and stuffed in newspaper cuttings and pages of the book. Matlock was trying to breathe. He felt as if he was dying.

A siren was wailing, growing louder, closer.

Justin looked down at Matlock. The man looked like a rag doll; in his dead eyes he saw the reflection of his own face, a devil's mask of rage.

Justin had his hand on the lever to pull up the anchor when the coastguard's launch came alongside. A man was yelling through a megaphone: 'Prepare to board!'

'No!' Justin screamed, dragging at the lever.

Then he realized he wouldn't be able to stop them. He moved back to Matlock. 'It isn't over. You hear me? It isn't over.'

Matlock tried to stand, but slumped back on the deck. He tried again, clawing at the sides of the boat.

'You got a Humphrey Matlock on board?' the officer shouted.

'Yeah, what's up?' Justin called back.

'We got an emergency. He's wanted back on Tortola. We're coming aboard.'

'He's drunk!'

Matlock clung to the railing and tried to steady himself. He swayed towards the officer's voice, but the boat rocked and he lurched to the side, toppled over and fell into the dangerous water between the boats.

Seconds later, he surfaced, his arms held out for help. But the swell dragged him under. He surfaced again and was thrown back towards the launch. His head cracked open and blood streamed down his face.

Justin uncoiled a rope from one of the capstans and threw it into the water a good six feet from the struggling man. The officers also threw ropes and life-belts, but Matlock was still grappling with the water. Justin pulled off his shirt, shouted directions for the coastguard to move away, then dived into the sea. He swam underwater for a few seconds, resurfaced, then took a deep breath and went under again. He found Matlock easily. The man's eyes were open, his legs hardly moving, arms splayed wide. He was sinking and a small stream of bubbles drifted from his mouth. Justin swam beneath him, took hold of his foot and dragged him down. Then he surfaced, gasping for breath.

'I got him,' he shouted, holding up one hand for the rope. He caught it, took a breath and went down again. He found Matlock and held him down until the last faint stream of bubbles ceased. Then he looped the rope beneath Matlock's arms, swam up and signalled for the men to pull.

Gradually Matlock's body inched out of the water. His head lolled on his chest. The officers hauled him to the deck and tried to resuscitate him. One gave him the kiss of life, but something was blocking Matlock's airway. The coastguard stuck his fingers down the man's throat and pulled out a sodden piece of newspaper. It was an article with the headline 'Devil's Children'.

# CHAPTER 21

WILLIAM HAD sent out one of the orderlies for some coffee and sandwiches, which he now looked at with distaste. Angela, however, sipped her coffee, rocking backwards and forwards on her seat.

'What did you hope to gain by getting us over here?' she asked. William said nothing. 'Oh, come along, there must have been some ulterior motive, knowing you.'

'It was your husband I wanted,' William replied wearily.

'Good God, why?' she asked.

'I wanted to humiliate him, make him a social outcast, like he did to me.'

'Really? And how were you going to do that?'

'Catch him in the act, with his trousers down, photograph him.' He told her about the hidden cameras and the way the island had been set up. 'Laura and Justin agreed to give me explicit footage of your husband, the Baron and Baroness, the Hangerfords, every guest in fact, including their children.' He sighed and stood up. 'I know it all sounds petty, but for a while I was unbalanced. It seemed everyone was against me and I contemplated suicide. Everything in my life had turned sour, and you'll be amused to know that even making money had lost its appeal. I have never known such loneliness.'

Angela put down her cup. All she could think of was her lovemaking with Laura. 'You have all the rooms fitted out with hidden cameras?' she said.

'Yes.' William flushed. 'Only now I see it wasn't really set up for me at all.'

Angela tried to make sense of what he had just said, but all she could think of was the video of her. What would her husband say when he found out? 'Were you going to blackmail us?' she asked.

'It had nothing to do with money. I simply wanted everyone who had made me feel like a worthless piece of shit to know what it felt like. If I chose to, I would be able to make headlines in every paper, especially with your husband being who he is. Can you imagine what his competitors would have done to get their hands on a single photograph? They would have had a field-day with it.' William took a deep breath. 'Now I know that what was really going on was a lot more devious and dangerous than anything I could have dreamed up.'

'What do you mean?' Her chest felt tight.

'It's Laura and Justin Chalmers. This is their revenge.'

Angela was now very scared. 'Why should they want revenge?'

William took out his wallet and passed her some newspaper cuttings. 'Because of these. Read them for yourself. Most importantly, see the name of the young journalist. Your husband built his reputation on the exposure of those two poor kids.'

Angela began reading, then looked at William. 'This

can't be the reason, for God's sake! These are years old. And if Humphrey had anything to do with this, don't you think he would have remembered them?'

'He obviously didn't. As you said, it was a very long time ago, more than twenty years. Why should someone like him remember? They were probably just a step up the ladder. He must have hurt a lot more on his way to the top.'

'Like you,' she snapped, and he turned on her, his face pale with anger.

Before he could reply, a nurse tapped lightly on the door and peered in. 'May I speak with you for a moment, Sir William?' she said, and held the door ajar.

William got up and walked out. In the hospital corridor she told him to call the coastguard station immediately.


Laura was growing impatient. There was still no word from Justin and it was now after two. She had been down to the jetty three times. She knew Matlock would be drugged by now and that Justin should be returning for the final part of the game. She was worried that, if they left it any longer, she and Max would not get away. She had forced herself not to go to him, but had occupied herself with her packing, her obsessive method of laying a sheet of tissue paper between each garment, tucking it into sleeves and around collars. Now her case was ready. They would soon be together.

At four, she saw the fishing boat return and hurried down to the quayside. Justin stepped off the boat alone.

'Where is he?'

Justin hooked his arm around her. 'You want the good news or the bad?'

'What happened, Justin? Don't play games with me. You said twelve thirty. I've been waiting and waiting,' she said.

Justin withdrew his arm. 'What the hell has got into you lately, huh? You're so impatient.'

'I'm sorry, but I've been here all by myself.'

'William's back,' Justin said flatly.

'Where's Matlock?'

'Probably on his way to see William.' Justin laughed, reached into one of the cool boxes near the edge of the quay and opened a can of Coke. 'I just wish I'd had a camera because it was worth seeing. But at the same time there was nothing I could do. William contacted the goddamned coastguards to take Matlock off the boat to go and see his son in the hospital.' Justin gulped the Coke and burped. 'Well, dear Sir Humphrey will be in hospital now, close to his beloved son. You should have seen it – he was all bloated and green in the face—'

'Is he dead?'

'Yes, and I'm sorry. I know what it meant for you to be in at the kill but it just couldn't be helped. I had to do it myself.'

'So, it's over,' she said softly. She hugged her slender body and snorted with laughter.

'Yes, he's gone. They're all gone, all the bad people, darling, all gone.'

Laura gave a soft sob, and spread her arms wide. 'I feel like I could fly now it's all over.'

'I guess it is, bar the diamonds,' he said, moving close to her and rubbing her neck.

Laura looked at her watch. Four fifteen: only two hours to go before she could escape. She had never felt so in control of herself. 'When is William going to show up?'

His hand felt warm and comforting but Laura winced as he gripped her tightly. 'I dunno – but I'm starving.' You want to grab a bite to eat with me?' He nuzzled her and kissed her softly, but laid his hand firmly on her neck.

'No, I'll stay here.'

She inched away from him but Justin drew her closer. This time he kissed her mouth, then broke away and withdrew his hand. 'We'll leave this place soon and go back to the villa. I've missed Marta, missed our home.'

'Me too,' she said. Justin was all hands, touching her, needing her. He wouldn't leave her alone. He cupped her face and kissed her lips again. She felt as if she was suffocating.

'We'll be able to live easy now. I'm sorry about you not being there, but maybe it's for the best – it looked accidental. And with old Willy back, you know what a fuss-pot he is . . . Still, he'll have some exhilarating home movies to watch.'

She held him tightly. 'I love you, Justin, I always will.'

He stepped away from her and looked at her. The way she had said 'I love you' hadn't sounded right. It was as if she had been saying it for the last time. 'And I love you, Laura, and only you, always. We'll always be together, won't we?'

She nodded. 'Nothing will ever come between us. Whatever happens.'

His eyes narrowed. He could feel how tense she was, and his concern deepened. 'Maybe you should lie down. Have you been taking your medicine? I mean, do you think you need it?'

'I'm fine, just . . .' She plucked at her skirt. 'Maybe you're right. I'll go and lie down. Join you later.'

Angela had been given a sedative, but was adamant she would accompany William to identify her husband's body. He suggested that to keep the media at bay they tell no one until the body was ready to be flown back to England. There would be an inquest and the usual documentation to deal with, all of which William promised to handle. At first he was shaken when he heard of Matlock's death, then afraid to ask for details: he was so sure he had been murdered. When the police told him it was an accident, he was relieved. When they said Justin had risked his life trying to save Matlock, he was puzzled, but then even more relieved because he must have been wrong about him . . . and he hoped desperately that he had been.

William's speedboat arrived at Tortola stacked with the Matlocks' cases and a neatly packed envelope containing their passports and money from the private safe in their suite. Angela's jewels were in a small leather case, guarded by one of the boat-boys who handed it separately to William. He arranged for all the luggage to be delivered to the hotel he had booked for Angela. When he slumped into the boat to return to the island, he was in need of a shower, a change of clothes and a good night's sleep. But he doubted if he'd be getting any sleep for a while. He knew he was going to have to face both Justin and Laura.

Justin strolled into Laura's room, where he found her lying on the bed.

' "Why so pale and wan, fond lover?" ' he quoted, throwing himself on the bed beside her. 'It's odd, isn't it? Now that we've done it, somehow it's unsatisfying.'

Laura sighed, and Justin rolled on top of her, tickling her. She tried to move away from him.

'Diamonds, diamonds, diamonds . . .' he said, with a wide grin. He pulled her close and tickled her again. She couldn't stop him; it was the way it had been ever since they were children. He began mimicking Matlock's death scene, plunging off the bed on to the floor, swimming on the carpet. He mimed coming up for air, clinging to the sheet as if it was the edge of the boat, wailing as he fell back.

They laughed until they were exhausted, then lay wrapped in each other's arms. She started to cry and he rocked her back and forth as if she was a baby, making soft sounds to calm her. Then he started to sing. He loved it when she sang with him.

Max had put away the windsurfer, and now strolled to his room to fetch his case. There was an hour to go. He wandered round the house. It was strangely quiet when no one was about.

'Justin?' he called. He stood in the large empty hall, and his eyed drifted to a door he'd frequently seen

Justin disappear through. The office, he supposed. 'Justin?' he called again. No reply.

He entered some sort of control room – it was full of switches and a great panel like you saw in documentaries about rock-stars. Amused, Max sat at the main desk and pressed a button. A monitor overhead flickered and came on. Max discovered he was watching some porn film. But the girl looked familiar. The man had his back to camera and she was sucking him off. God, it couldn't be? It was! Clarissa Hangerford and Justin!

Max didn't like being a voyeur. He stabbed at another button; the VCR stopped, and the monitor flicked to what looked like security mode. The screen showed the front hall. Max pressed the button again. His parent's bedroom! Again. The sauna! This was fun. He wondered whether his own room was included. The dining room, the swimming-pool, the jetty, another bedroom, and another, and another. He flicked again, then flicked back. The last bedroom had people in it: Laura and Justin lying on a big double bed.

'We did it,' said Justin, throwing his head back against the pillow. 'We got every single one of those motherfuckers.' He turned to face his sister. 'Tonight, Laura, we'll dance. I want you to wear that gold dress.'

Laura smiled. She had a faraway look. Max knew it was because she would not be dancing with Justin that night but in his own arms speeding away from this place for ever. 'It was fun killing him, sweet one, I wish you could have seen how cleverly I did it. I pulled him down into the water, and they all thought I was trying to save him. Really I should get an Oscar.'

Laura faced her brother. First he'd mimed it all, now

he seemed to want to go over every detail again. 'Justin,' said Laura, 'you're not kidding me, are you? He is dead, isn't he?'

'Would I lie to you?'

She stroked his head. 'You lie to everyone else. Maybe you would. You know how much it means to me, and now with Angela and James not here, he might just have gone to join them.'

Max leaned in close to the screen. His heart was beating rapidly.

Justin nodded sombrely. 'Would I lie to you? Jesus, how can you even think for a second I would lie about something as important as this? For Christ's sake, he's dead, and the others are ruined.' He wrapped Laura tighter in his arms. 'Oh, sweetness, I've missed lying in bed with you, holding you in my arms. Believe me, I never lie to you, you are the centre of my universe.' He leaned on his elbow, tracing her face with one finger. 'Just as you'd never lie to me. Right?'

She gave a small smile, as he moved his index finger across her perfect lips.

'But I've been jealous of Max. I admit it. For some stupid reason I thought that maybe you really did care for him. I'm glad I was mistaken.' said Justin. 'I understand it now. Max was just part of the scam, wasn't he? He never meant anything else to you?'

Laura shook her head. 'Of course not,' she said, her lips only an inch away from her brother's. 'The only man I have ever loved is you.'

They kissed, at first almost innocently, then the kiss became deeper and more prolonged.

Max gasped. His breath felt as if it had been squeezed

from his lungs and his heart felt as though it was jumping out of his chest. He ran out of the office, out of the house, out into the oncoming dusk. His body felt as if it was on fire. He hurt inside so much that he couldn't get the sight of Justin with Laura out of his mind.

William's stomach churned as the boat crashed over a wave; the sea always got rougher as they headed inshore towards the island. He stretched, then stood up in the boat to admire his paradise as they approached. This evening it looked glorious, with the sun sinking into the horizon and all the outside lights twinkling, making the island appear like a magical mirage. He moved closer to the rails and took deep gulping breaths. It made him feel better: all the anxiety and emotional strain of the day were blown out of him. He was glad to be coming home, and once he'd said that word in his mind, he knew it *was* his home. This was where he wanted to be more than anywhere else.

He had a future he wanted to live his own way, without any interference or guilt. He knew now that it was linked to Justin, because none of what he saw or felt would have existed without him. Now he acknowledged the effect this man, this wild crazy boy, had over him. Never before had he craved to see someone, or felt his belly churn with anticipation at the prospect of being close to somebody. His heart fluttered and he laughed. He would never have believed it was true.

He could hear Justin's laugh, see his face in a multitude of expressions. They overlapped and juggled for space in his mind until he felt weak and had to sit down. Like a lovesick boy, he ached to see Justin, no matter what had happened in the past.

But as the boat drew closer to the jetty his confidence began to waver, leaving him with a terrible dread that Justin might not want to remain his friend. After all, hadn't Justin used him as he had used everyone else? Suddenly he was afraid he would lose Justin. He was unsure whether he could deal with such a loss: Justin was closer to him than anyone else, and no matter what he had done, William would have to confront him with all he had discovered. He fell into contemplation of how he would approach him: he knew he had to be told the truth, no matter what.

When Laura couldn't find Max in his room she was worried. Then she remembered they'd agreed to meet at Suicide Point. She reprimanded herself for being so stupid. She had made the arrangements, after all. She checked her case, stashed behind some ferns, before starting along the winding path up to the point. She'd thought Justin was never going to leave her room. But he'd suddenly heard a boat coming in, and rushed out. It was either William or the mail-boat arriving, he'd called. She waited ten minutes before she dared leave.

Laura ran, panting, to the peak, the highest point on the island. As she turned the last blind corner to climb higher she caught a glimpse of Max in the distance, standing with his back to her, facing the sea. He was barefoot, wearing dark trousers and a white shirt, billowing in the wind. His hands were on his hips and he was standing so still he might have been a statue. Laura began to run, but as she drew closer she froze.

It wasn't Max, it was Justin. She stared at him for a moment, frightened. Where was Max? *What had he done to Max?* She clenched her fists and forced herself to continue towards Justin, who stared out to sea, watching William's speedboat approach the island.

'Where is he?' She was only a few feet behind him.

Justin tensed. He said nothing.

She came closer and her voice was shrill: 'Where is he? What have you done to him? If you've hurt him, I'll . . .' She was close enough now. One hard shove and he would topple over Suicide Point into the crashing sea below.

'He's not coming, Laura,' Justin said.

She raised both hands to push him over but Justin grabbed her wrists. 'He's on the jetty, ready to leave. He's going alone.'

He still held her wrists as her body relaxed and the anger subsided. She shook her head, smiling. 'Oh, no, not this time. I don't believe you. He's waiting for me.'

He grabbed her and held her in his arms so she could hardly breathe. He guided her to the cliff's edge, and forced her to look down towards the jetty. Max was standing with his suitcase beside him. She eased away from him, and stepped closer to the edge. Justin dragged her back.

'What have you told him?' Laura screeched. Justin threw her to the ground and bent down to her. She kicked him between his legs and he howled in agony. 'You bastard, what did you tell him? He loves me.' Laura clawed at the grass. Her eyes were demented and her face twisted with uncontrollable rage. 'You had to spoil it. I knew you would if you found out because you were always jealous, jealous that I had a chance to be free of you. I hate you! I hate you!' she hissed, and with that she came for him, scratching and snarling like a savage.

Then she began to sob. 'I never told him anything. I wouldn't have done that to you.' She could taste the blood in her mouth and gasped, taking deep breaths. She was calming down, bringing her anger under control.

Justin watched her fearfully. The rage quietened, but he could still see it swirling inside her. Her wild eyes belied the smile on her lips.

'You never told him anything, did you, about us?' Laura pleaded.

'I swear on our graves.'

Laura knew he was telling the truth. When they were children they had dug their graves ready for them to lie side by side. They had often laughed about how they would have to dig them deeper and wider if they were to fit into them as adults. His sad, vulnerable face made her open her arms to him and cradle him against her breasts.

Justin was crying. He was so afraid for her when she was like this, when her eyes frightened him. When Laura hid her fury she was very dangerous. He had to stop her seeing Max. He sobbed out, 'I will never leave you, I will always be here for you.'

'Ssh, ssh,' she whispered, kissing his head and rocking him. 'We have to leave each other some day, Justin,' she said. She felt as if her heart would burst open and bleed. Max was not going to get away from her, but she knew that if Justin suspected anything he would never let her go. 'Haven't you ever wanted to be free of me?'

Justin shook his head and slumped to the ground.

She crouched down beside him. 'Oh, yes, you have. Come on, Justin, you can admit it to me. You have wanted to be free of me, haven't you?'

'Sometimes,' he admitted.

'You know, if you could find someone to love and be loved by, I wouldn't stop you or try and spoil it. You do know that, don't you?'

He gave her a sidelong look. This was a route they had never travelled down before. He could not see her eyes or her expression: her hair fell like a curtain across her face. 'Okay, Laura, *would* you feel the same way about me? You know, if I found someone?' His heart pounded. Could he leave her and not feel guilty? Justin took her hand and threaded his fingers through hers. Her hair still hid her face and she made no reply. The pain inside him was like razors slicing into him. A terrible sense of loss consumed him. 'Laura? Is it over now?'

Laura stood up and brushed her skirt down, then took a deep breath. 'I have to go to Max.'

He closed his eyes. 'Let him go, Laura. Let him go.'

She looked down at him. 'No, I won't. It's you I'm letting go, Justin. It's time.'

He had found her hidden suitcase, and knew now she had lied. It hurt him so much.

'We love each other,' she said firmly. 'Not the same way as you and me, that will always be special, our secret. But I have made a decision and you can't stop me. He can take care of me now.'

'No, he can't,' Justin said, his voice breaking.

'Yes, he can. He has a big trust fund and we'll find a little house, perhaps close to the villa in France.'

'I think he went into the control room,' he said softly. But she was talking rapidly to herself, making plans as she brushed down her skirt.

'We could hire you to make our house special.' She cupped his face between her hands. 'This will all be perfect, you'll see. I had better go now, I don't want to miss the boat.'

Justin stared at her as tears rolled down his cheeks. Her eyes were empty. She was already somewhere out of his reach, so he let her go. He watched her walking to her case, brushing aside the ferns, picking it up then turning to wave to him. He couldn't stop her, not this time.

William stepped on to the jetty and was surprised to see Max there, sitting on his case. He rose to greet William. 'Would it be possible to be taken to Tortola, sir?' he asked.

William looked back at the boat-boys. They had made the crossing so many times that day and they looked worn out. 'I'd prefer it if you waited for the mail-boat,' he said. 'It should be along at about six. It'll be a longer trip but my boys are tired out.'

Max checked his wristwatch. It was just past six o'clock.

William raised an eyebrow. 'It'll be here, give or take half an hour. It depends on the tides, and how many deliveries they have to do.' He headed for one of the golf carts then glanced back.

Max was shading his eyes and looking out to sea. He called out, 'I can see it!'

Goodbye, then, have a safe journey home,' William shouted and continued towards the golf cart.

The mail-boat crew agreed to take Max aboard, but said they would need a half-hour break. Max returned to sit on his suitcase. He didn't want to go near the house again. All he wanted was to leave. The more he thought about Laura, the more thankful he was he'd found out. It had been a stupid fantasy. He could not have married Laura. He would never have been able to finish his studies or been able to provide for her. It was just one of those stupid holiday things.

The longer he brooded, the more he reverted to the boy who had stepped off the launch on his arrival. He cried a little, and wiped away the tears with the back of his hand. She was a cheap whore, a slut. Thank God he'd walked into that office. Thank God he'd switched on the tapes.

Laura hurried down to the jetty. When she saw William in the golf cart heading towards the house, she paused, remembering the diamonds. That didn't matter, she'd contact him after she and Max were married: they might need the diamonds to help buy a little house. William wouldn't cheat her. She kept walking, talking rapidly to herself, making her plans.

She didn't realize she was stumbling, almost falling. She felt slightly dizzy. She was so intent on seeing Max that she was unaware of the signals, and blamed the way she was feeling on the weight of her suitcase. She tossed it aside: she didn't want to miss the boat.

Suddenly her legs almost buckled beneath her as the darkness crept upwards. Then came the fear, making its way up her legs to her thighs. Soon it would be dragging at her intestines. Laura gasped for breath as she crawled back to her suitcase. She fumbled with the clasp and got it open to find her medicine box. At any moment now she would be incapable of helping herself. As she opened the box, spilling tablets on the ground, the horror seized her. She tried to stand but her body jerked backwards and she fell heavily on the floor, cracking her head against the paving. Blood seeped into her hair, but she couldn't feel the pain, and she thrashed around, slithering across the stone-flagged path, twisting and turning, spittle at the corners of her mouth.

Not a quarter of a mile away, Max walked along the narrow gang plank to jump down on to the deck of the mail-boat. He watched the boys haul in the planks, the engines started up, and the boat eased away from the jetty. He saw Justin running like a man possessed along a narrow path, saw him bend out of sight. The next moment he was carrying Laura in his arms. Max turned away, not wanting to see them, not wanting to remember what he had seen. He only wanted to forget, but it would take a long time.

Justin pushed open the bungalow door and laid his sister on the bed, praying that it was over, that it would not take hold again. But just as she seemed peaceful, it began again in such force that her body seemed to lift itself up, as if hurled by unseen hands. In a panic he rummaged for her medicine box and realized it was back down the path in her suitcase. He ran out of the bungalow.

Justin's breath heaved in his chest. He'd picked up the pills and the medicine box, shoved them in the case and dragged it back up. Now he opened the box, took out a thick wedge of rubber and stood over her. He calculated how long it had been going on, and tried to hold her down, but her strength was awesome.

'What the hell are you doing?' William shouted from the doorway.

'She's having a fit. It's been going on for a long time. It'll kill her. Help me get this into her mouth – she's biting her tongue. She'll choke herself.'

William could not believe the strength of the fragile woman. At last Justin gripped her head long enough to prise open her mouth, and used a platinum spatula to force her teeth apart. Blood trickled from her mouth where she had bitten through her tongue, but at last he was able to insert the wedge. He stepped away from her, then filled a syringe and injected her with a sedative.

'Get away from her. There's nothing we can do except hope it'll be over soon.'

They stood watching Laura as she continued having spasms and slithered across the floor like an eel. Slowly the fit subsided and she lay twitching and snorting. Her body was black and blue where she had slammed against the furniture and the wound to her head bled freely.

As soon as she was calm enough, Justin lifted her and carried her to the bed.

William fetched wet towels to wipe the blood from

her head, then watched as Justin dressed her in a satin nightie. He tucked the sheet tightly around her and took the wedge out of her mouth. She was still now, in a deep sleep. William was moved by the tenderness Justin showed her.

At last Justin turned to him. 'I'm so glad to see you, Willy.'

'And I'm glad to see you, Justin. I've missed you.'

Only then did he see the scratch marks on Justin's face, the bruises on his neck. 'Dear God, don't tell me she did that to you?' William said, shocked.

Justin shook his head. 'No, I fell. It looks a lot worse than it is.'

William made him sit down, got some disinfectant and bathed the cuts. Some were so deep they bled profusely. Justin remained silent throughout.

Tears slid down Justin's cheeks, which William wiped away. He did not know why it happened, but suddenly he took Justin's face in his hands and kissed him on the cleaned wounds and his neck, but was afraid to move to the lips he wanted more than anything to touch with his.

Justin clung to him as though he never wanted to let go, and the kiss, when it came, was instigated by him. For William it was shocking but also the ultimate pleasure of his life. The embrace took him to a world of love he had believed was beyond his reach. He was filled with desire and hope. This was where he knew Andrew Maynard had been; this was the love he had written about. A shining peace swept through every fibre of his body.

'I'm so glad you're here, Willy,' Justin murmured.

'Me too.' William hesitated before he spoke again.

'I've missed you Justin. I've also been so afraid, but it's all going to be all right now. I'm here for you both. It's all going to be all right, I'm sure.'

'Is it, Willy?' Justin said. 'Promise? I bet you daren't! There's so much you don't know about me and Laura. We're not good people, Willy. I'm not a good person.'

'Justin, trust me, I know everything about you and Laura now, and it doesn't make any difference to me. Marta told me. She loves you and . . . and no one will ever hurt either of you again. I'll see to that.'

He went to the door, overwhelmed by his emotions, but he knew it was not quite over yet: he had to know more. 'I'll arrange for Dahlia to sit with her and we'll get Marta over here.' He faced Justin. 'I have to eat. Would you join me?'

Justin followed him. 'I'm so glad to be with you, Willy. I don't think this time I could have coped. I've been on my own for so long, and I'm tired. Laura needs to be taken care of, she always has. These fits get worse. I've been told that each time it happens, her brain is damaged a little and it terrifies me.'

William put his arm around Justin's shoulders. To his delight, Justin caught his hand and threaded his fingers through it.

'You're not on your own, Justin, not any more. You've got me, and I'll get Laura the best medical attention money can buy. She's my responsibility now.'

'Why?' Justin asked.

'I love you both, that's why.'

Justin appeared to accept his answer and they strolled on into the house.

*

441

William fingered the stem of his glass. He had to choose his words carefully. They had both bathed and changed, and now sat across the table from each other. Yet again, he had a feeling of peace and calm, as if his life at long last had come into focus.

'I have never been what I would call a happy man,' he began. 'There has been little joy in my life. But suddenly I realized . . . you have given me that. It hasn't been plain sailing, but I look forward to seeing you more than anyone. And when I began to think you were . . .' he sipped the champagne '. . . planning murder, it was not that you were about to commit a crime that concerned me, it was the thought that I might not see you again. I realized you had become a very important part of my life. But I need to be told the truth, all of it, so that, if need be, I can protect you both. You must tell me everything. I want the facts, no matter what they are.'

'Maybe you won't like me if you know it all, Willy. You might have taken on more than you bargained for.'

'Try me. I'm offering you this island as your home, a place to stay for ever. What is your alternative? Where else will you go?'

Justin shrugged. 'Oh, back to the villa, get some more design commissions. This place will do me a lot of good as far as that goes.'

'And Laura will go with you?'

'Yep, that's the game plan. I'll earn enough to look after her, and she loves the villa.'

'Isn't that where you both suffered so much? Isn't that the very place she shouldn't return to – or you for that matter? It's there, no matter how you disguise it with waterfalls and flowers, that it all happened to you both.'

'I guess it is, but I've never let us think about it. What it looked like then, and what it now is . . . It's different. It's home.'

'This could also be your home, and you could work from here. You love it here, don't you?'

'Yes, you know I do, but . . .'

'I would like to make it my home, live here with you both.' William sat back, twisting the stem of his glass. When he looked up, Justin was staring at him and his body was rigid. Twice he started to say something and then stopped.

William tried to ease the tension. He poured more champagne. 'I read Andrew Maynard's diaries, and I was envious of his joy at finding love. He wrote of being so happy that it had changed his life. In many ways, you have changed mine, Justin.'

Justin's eyes flicked to the dark ocean. 'Ask me if I killed him, Willy. That's what you really want to know. All this bullshit about being envious, just cut it out.'

'Andrew committed suicide,' William stated.

'Did he?'

William gripped the stem of his glass.

'I wrote the note, Willy, let it sink into the bathwater so the writing would be hard to read. I've always been expert at copying signatures. I also wrote the yellow sticker to make sure you would be called . . .'

'I don't believe you. How could you know that the housekeeper would call me and that I would remove Andrew's diaries?'

Justin leaned back in his chair. 'Because you were in love with him. Maybe you weren't even aware of it. Andrew sussed that you were. Even if it wasn't love, you must have desired him in some way. You certainly saw him often enough.'

William stared at the tablecloth. 'I admired him, I trusted him, I believed that he would have a great future—'

Justin leaned across the table and grabbed his hand. 'You want me to be truthful – why don't you start playing the game straight as well? You didn't lay out all that cash just to be his paymaster. *What did you want out of it?*'

William flushed as he said angrily that he had wanted Maynard's success, nothing more. 'I admired him, yes. Truth was, I bathed in his glory, and I got my knighthood through him, but . . .'

'But?' Justin asked softly, and William couldn't meet his eyes. He told Justin about a little kid who had sat next to him at school, a stammering boy with long eyelashes who had kissed him and had been killed on a level crossing.

'Andrew reminded me of Peter Jenkins, that was his name. Maybe there is something latent in me. I doubt if I could face up to it, but I often wondered why I was so distressed about him. But with Maynard I only wanted him to succeed. I wanted him to be my son. I had little or no relationship with Charlie then.'

'Did you doubt your feelings or did you just not dare show Andrew what you really felt about him?'

William stared hard at him. 'I don't want to answer that, and we're supposed to be talking about you, not me.'

444

'But it all has to be ironed out, don't you think? Lean forward, Willy.'

William did so, and Justin kissed his lips.

'Are you afraid to love me?' Justin asked, and rocked back in his chair. 'You keep on saying how much you love me and Laura, but let's take just me. Are you afraid to lie naked next to me, Willy, afraid to let me make love to you?'

'Yes, I am, and that's not why we're here. I have offered—'

'To take care of me and Laura. But you want me to tell you all my secrets yet refuse to tell me yours, or admit them. I'm not your son. I'm not Charlie. I'm Justin. To what depth does your love want to go?'

'I won't answer that. I'm just confused, and I need to know – did you kill Andrew?'

Justin kicked his chair back and walked to the window. 'Yes. He had to die because he was becoming dangerous. He found out about my background. He was always delving into drawers and trying to find out more and more about me and Laura. Then he found out about his fucking sister and—'

'She died in a car accident,' William said, hardly audible.

'I know. I fixed her brakes. I even followed her along the motorway and saw her car veer across the lanes. Camilla Maynard gave exclusive interviews to Humphrey Matlock. She was part of it. By the way, I held Matlock under the water until he drowned. What do you say about that? I mean, surely you don't need to ask me why? You said you knew why. You said you knew everything. Well, now you do, and what do you think of me?'

445

William pushed back his chair and crossed to Justin. He held out his arms and Justin's bravado evaporated. Like a small boy, he went to William and clung to him, sobs shaking his body. William held him tightly, soothing him, letting him weep until he was silent.

The thoughts that zigzagged through William's mind made it difficult for him to remain calm. What Justin had said was shocking, yet he had suspected it all along, suspected and been afraid of it since he had talked to Marta at the villa. But it did not feel as if he was holding a killer in his arms, only a wounded boy whose suffering had obsessed him.

'You're the only friend I have ever had in my life,' Justin whispered. He rested his head against William's shoulder. 'Sometimes I feel like I am insane. But the need to hurt those who tortured me and Laura would never go away. I had to do it, William, otherwise I would have gone crazy, like Laura.'

William led him back to the table and sat him down. He patted his shoulder, then used a napkin to wipe his tears. 'How much a part of it is Laura?'

'Oh, nothing but the planning. We planned everything together. We're not just brother and sister. We're lovers. We could only ever trust each other, you see? Can you understand what we became to each other? We were each other's parents. We were all we dared to love because everyone else seemed intent on destroying us, and the more pain we experienced, the more we were drawn together. Only by being so close could we protect each other.'

William returned to his seat. His mind was in turmoil as he tried to assimilate the terrible things Justin had just told him. But he knew he must now allow Justin to see how affected he was by the truth.

Justin drained his champagne. 'You're confusing me,' he said softly. In the candlelight his face was astonishingly beautiful, his high cheekbones shadowed, his jaw-line chiselled and his eyes glittering like azure stones.

William turned away on the pretext of pouring more champagne. 'I'm sorry, I didn't intend to . . . er, confuse you. I'm trying to be as honest as I can. You've helped change my life. Now I want to help you straighten out yours. After what you've told me . . .'

'What if it's too late?' Justin said.

'It's never too late. Look at what you did for me. And I'm not just referring to making me lose my gut. It's what you did for me up here,' William said, tapping his head.

'But what if my confessions repel you, frighten you? You may betray me out of fear.'

William kept his gaze steady. 'I will never betray you, Justin, and I mean it. This island will be a safe place. Do you understand what I'm saying? No one can get to you, or harm you or Laura. I will protect you both.'

'Does that mean you can forgive me and forget what I have done?'

William watched as a multitude of emotions played across Justin's handsome face. 'No one is aware of what you have done. Unless they are told or the police reinvestigate Maynard's suicide, they probably never will be.'

'Unless you tell them. You see what I've just done? I've put my life in your hands.'

447

'I have promised that I will protect you.'

'Why? What makes you want to do that? Or, for that matter, what will stop me killing you? Now that I know you know, and you are the only one apart fom Laura who does, what do you think will stop me killing you?'

William met Justin's eyes, and this time he didn't look away. 'Because I love you, and you have made a difference to my life. I am prepared to—'

'Be my lover?'

'*No!* Stop that! I am offering to be . . . like a father to you.'

'My father is dead,' Justin said. Suddenly he stood up and his chair fell behind him. 'Just give me Laura's diamonds, the ones you promised, and we'll both leave. I don't want to hear any more crap from you. You've had too much to drink.'

William stood up too. 'The diamonds are under your sister's pillow.' He noticed this freaked Justin. He continued, 'I've also destroyed the tapes. You will never be able to use them against anyone.'

'Oh, I see. So you want to destroy me next,' Justin snarled.

'No, I don't. You've not been listening to what I've been saying. I'm offering—'

'What the fuck do you want from me? What do you expect me to say to you? Do you want to keep me here like some fucking plaything? What's happened, Willy? You still afraid to come out of your closet? Why don't you admit it now? Go on, look at me. Tell me you want me to fuck you. Do you think that's what I want? You? With your wispy hair and flaccid belly? I don't want you near me, you repel me, and this bullshit about protecting me is all for one reason. You want my body just like that prick Maynard did.'

William hit him hard across the face. Justin stumbled to one side then laughed and started to give William a slow handclap. Then he glared and became the waspish, lisping man Laura and William hated. 'Well, well, how the worm turns!'

'What did I say that was so bad, Justin?' William was not going to be drawn into a shouting match.

Justin pushed his face forward so that he was almost nose to nose with William. 'You wiped my precious tapes. I needed them. You're a liar and a two-faced bastard. And you, Willy-boy, are not my father. If you were you'd have a knife stuck in your chest. As it is, if you keep me prisoner on this island you'll never be safe. I'll hurl your body off Suicide Point. Just another accident.'

'You wouldn't do that to me.'

'You want to bet?'

Justin turned and walked out, knocking aside the waiter as he carried in their tray. The dishes crashed to the floor but Justin did not turn back. William sat up and shook out his napkin, anything to stop his running after Justin. He had just seen the madness in him, the killer, and it scared him. Whatever he had dreamed up about being a fatherly figure to that wild creature was insanity, and he knew it. But he did not want to back away. He had come to see Justin and to explain himself. But explain what? The reality was that he was in love with Justin. He wanted that love reciprocated, and for a moment when they had embraced, he had felt sure that it was. But instead of telling Justin this he had offered to be a substitute father, and Justin had snarled in his face. And he *did* want to lie naked beside him, to make love to him. He wouldn't let Justin's rejection alter the fact that he was still the most important person in his life, and he would stand by what he had offered: his protection.

William forced himself to eat his dinner. Each mouthful was hard to swallow, but he was not going to chase after Justin. He needed to cool off. They had to talk again.

Dahlia put her finger to her lips and pointed to the bed. Laura was propped up with pillows. Her hair had been combed and tied with a ribbon, and there was a plaster across the cut on her head. However, her eyes were clear and bright and her cheeks slightly flushed. She looked like a little girl. A square of black velvet lay across the white sheet. It was covered with sparkling diamonds.

'She's had a sedative,' Dahlia whispered, gesturing for William to move to her side. 'She doesn't seem to know where she is.' Dahlia showed William the tablets, vials and hypodermic needles in Laura's medicine box. 'Justin was here. He told me she sometimes reverts back to childhood. It takes time for her to readjust, he said. He also said—' She faltered.

'Said what?'

'That in the past she had electro-convulsive therapy if she remained in her own world. But it was a last resort.'

William nodded then asked her to make him some

coffee. As she left, he took her seat by the bed. 'How are you feeling, Laura?' he said softly.

She turned and gave him a sweet smile. He was uncertain whether she knew who he was: there was a deadness in her eyes. She blinked slowly at him, then turned her attention back to the sparkling stones.

'They are diamonds,' she said slowly, as she began moving them from one side of the black velvet to the other. 'One for Lord Cedric, one for his wife, one for Clarissa, one for James, one for the Baron, one for the Baroness, this big one for Matlock, and this one for Angela.' She counted them again, moving them back to the other side of the velvet, her brow furrowed.

Dahlia returned with a tray. 'She's been doing that for quite a while. She remembers who was here, so she can't be that bad,' she said.

They both turned as Laura spoke. 'One missing! There's no diamond for Max. Max should be the biggest.' She turned to William. 'Are you jealous, like my brother, because I love Max? I'm going away with him.' She busied herself again, smoothing the black velvet.

William leaned forward. 'I must have miscounted, Laura, I'm sorry. You'll have another tomorrow, the biggest one of all. And then Marta's coming to look after you,' he said.

'Thank you,' she said.

'Do you like being here?' he asked. She made no reply. 'If you want to stay on the island for ever, I will always take care of you, Laura.'

'Thank you,' she said.

He turned to Dahlia. 'Is that true, about Max?'

'They were planning to elope, but I think the boy changed his mind.'

'Thank you,' said Laura, to nobody.

Dahlia stood behind William and put her hand on his shoulder. 'I have never heard anyone say those words so sweetly, or so sadly. When Justin said he was leaving, that was all she said to him. She looked up, smiled just as she did now and said, "Thank you."'

William gasped. 'Justin said he was leaving? But he can't have! The mail-boat went ages ago.'

Dahlia nodded. 'I know, but it stops off at all the islands. Fifteen minutes ago he said he was taking the speedboat with one of the boys to catch it up.'

William left the room and ran panic-stricken to the jetty. The speedboat was just returning. There was no sign of Justin. His heart sank. He called to one of the boys swabbing down the decks on the cruiser. 'Have you seen Justin?'

'He left, sir. I took him to the mail-boat. He went aboard at Mustique. He and the young man, Max, left for Tortola together.'

William felt as if his panic would spiral out of control. He shouted orders for the crew to come immediately to the dock and get the speedboat ready.

'But, sir,' said the boy, 'look at the sky! There's going to be a storm.'

'Just do it!' he shouted.

He had to sit down, his legs were shaking so much. Why had he said it all? He had forced Justin to run away. Then he thought of what Justin might do to Max. He knew he had to get to the mail-boat – had to reach Justin before he killed Max.

# CHAPTER 22

THE STORM that had been threatening made a spectacular entrance with a terrifying crack of electricity. Lightning lit up the sky and the ocean, before everything was plunged into darkness again. A second later, a shorter bolt flashed, heralding the thunderclap that followed, and showing Justin in silhouette on the deck, as he waved farewell to the speedboat crew. Max was already worried about the storm and was sure Justin had come after him. He moved closer to one of the men on board, expecting some kind of argument to break out. But Justin never even looked at him.

The mail-boat rolled on the choppy waves, but the crew seemed unconcerned. Max constantly looked sky-ward in trepidation. He wasn't sure which was worse: Justin being on board frightened the life out of him, but the crew regaling him with stories of real 'horror storms' they had survived made him tremble. They had been at sea more than three-quarters of an hour after delivering the mail to the islands, and it was coming up to eight o'clock. The sky was already pitch black when the rain started. Thankfully it was not heavy. One old man smiled at Max, said the worst was over, but it didn't make him feel any better.

Justin sat hunched at the stern. He had ignored Max from the moment he had come aboard. He knew the boy was constantly looking at him, knew he was afraid of him, but he wasn't interested, not yet. He had no desire even to speak to him. His face was set in an expressionless stare looking out to sea. He had taken money and his passport, but wasn't sure what he intended to do after he had completed his new mission. He was a little ashamed of having taken off in the way he had, but William had unwittingly touched a raw nerve that had made him act on impulse . . . he had felt the terror rise, the memories of his anguish. Only Laura had dried his tears. Then came the shame he felt when they had taken tiny Laura into their room, not him. He had covered his ears when he heard her calling for him. Later that first night, he had crawled in beside her, bathed her tiny bruised body. Then they had clung to each other, night after night, waiting with fear for their bedroom door to creak open.

'Come with Mummy, Laura.'

'Come to Daddy, Justin.'

They had been subjected to such perversion, such pain, and threatened with more if they whispered to a soul what had happened to them. The devil would eat them alive if they ever told anyone about their mummy and daddy's games. They were special secrets, and they would die if they ever told them. They would be buried alive – and to make sure they understood, they had been forced to watch the burial of their pets, forced to watch the earth cover a tiny canary's feathered chest, a pet spaniel tied by his paws. They had waited to dig him up and seen the maggots and bugs filling his mouth, his ears and his eyes. They reburied him, more afraid than ever. So they kept the hideous secret until Laura lit the candle and held the flame to her mother's sheets. Then they had another secret to hide, and another, and another . . .

Justin had had no option but to get away. He had been afraid of what he might do to William. Seeing Laura regress yet again had not helped: it had made him feel wretched, even though he had seen it many times. He knew she had come out of them before. Sometimes it had taken days, months, but Justin was certain that, whatever happened to him, William would care for Laura. He had never entrusted her to anyone but himself and Marta, but knowing their old nurse would soon be arriving had made his leaving easier to bear. He blamed Max for Laura's collapse, and now he would make him pay. He would be the last, he swore to himself. After Max there would be no more.

Like a dark shadow, the island disappeared from view. How he had loved it, built it with such dedication and care. Never before had he been so content or happy in a place. He knew every flowering bush, every tree and every cove. He would have liked to spend the rest of his life there because it was his paradise. In his heart, it had become his the moment he had stepped ashore for the first time. That was where he could find peace, forget the horrors that tormented him. Now he was leaving it and he didn't know or care where he was going to. He would not let his mind drift back to William, who loved the island as much as Justin. If only William had been honest, if only he could just have offered to love and nothing more, but he hadn't. Instead he had used the hated word 'father', which had cut through Justin's heart and turned him back to the madness that lurked just beneath his beautiful exterior.

William had touched a raw nerve in the hope of gaining some understanding. How could he know he had pressed the button that made Justin want to kill? He turned to face Max, and their eyes locked.

'They say the storm's passing over,' Max said, as justification for speaking to Justin. Their proximity had given him the confidence that no harm would come to him, but he saw Justin flinch. 'How much longer do you think it's going to last?' he asked.

'As long as it takes, Max.' Justin's voice was low, and his eyes bored into the boy's fearful face. He wondered if it would appear too much of a coincidence if Max were to drown like Matlock. But the crew were everywhere. He would have to think of some other way, but he felt so tired.

He watched Max slither back to the shelter of the little cabin. Maybe the storm would toss the boy overboard without any assistance from him: it was not blowing over by any means. The rain had only just started to fall and would come down much heavier. The distant booms of thunder would soon return seaward.

Max hovered close to the cabin door, and was told to go below deck. But he preferred to cling to the guard rail. 'It seems to be getting rougher,' he said, and was frightened by the seamen's looks as they dragged on their rain capes and hooked safety harnesses to their belts.

'You go below when we tell you, son,' one man shouted.

'Isn't the storm over?' Max shouted.

'No,' came the reply.


Justin focused on the mounting angry waves. He wondered how long it would take to drown and be really free. How would it feel?


William wore a cape and sou'wester. The rain dripped off him as the speedboat cut through the swell. They had made radio contact and discovered the route the mail-boat would now be taking. William planned to overtake it. He hoped he had not misjudged the journey. He had no intention of trying to get aboard mid-way, sure that Max would be safe until they had landed. He just hoped to God he would get there in time.

The storm was at its zenith when William landed on Tortola. He stood at the quayside waiting for the first sighting of the mail-boat. He knew he had overtaken it, but worried now that perhaps it had anchored in one of the inlets until the storm blew over. It was almost ten o'clock. He bought a bottle of brandy from the Harbour Bar. He felt stiff and cold. It had been the longest day and night of his life. Nothing he had ever been through had made him so emotionally drained yet so positive. He was there for Justin and he hoped to God that Max had come to no harm.

*

457

Max clung to the sides of the cabin as the boat thudded and rolled, the waves crashing over the deck. He was now wearing a cape and a safety harness hooked to the guard rail. He had gone below for a moment, but had started to vomit so had returned to the deck. Tears of fright mingled with the relentless rain; he could see nothing but blackness. The crew had started pumping out the bilges – they had taken in a lot of water. Using a rope and hook to edge along the railings of the deck, one of the crew made his way to the stern. He was shouting for Justin. There was no reply. He called again, screaming against the wind.

Then, to his horror, Max saw him, balanced like a trapeze artist outside the rails, arms raised, face tilted back.

'Justin! Justin!' Max's voice, too, was lost in the howling gale.

Justin remained upright for a few seconds. Then the boat banged against a twenty-foot wave and Justin sailed into the air, as if he was flying. His body lifted above the boat then dropped into the churning sea.

'Man overboard!' the cry went up.

'Justin! *Justin!*' screeched Max.

The crew risked their lives in leaning over the edge of the boat to find him in the swirling water, and the skipper turned on a searchlight, but there was nothing. Only the deafening howl of the wind, and the thundering waves. They searched for over an hour, before the skipper accepted that he was dead.

At midnight William saw the old mail-boat cruising into the harbour. The coastguards had been informed of a man overboard, but had been unable to launch a rescue craft. When the old boat dropped anchor, there was no mistaking the despair of the crew over the recent loss. William searched for Max. He was sobbing, but safe, being helped down the gangplank on to the jetty. His relief was short-lived however— 'Where's Justin?' he called, running towards Max.

Max's teeth were chattering, his whole body shaking, as he stammered. 'Overboard!'

William sagged. He didn't want to hear this. It couldn't be true.

The sun rose, an amber globe that turned into a deep crimson ball and seemed to come up from the sea-bed to send shimmering rays across the now quiet waters. William was on his way back to the island. All the way he scanned the ocean with his binoculars. As they passed the two jagged rocks, he looked up at Suicide Point, hoping to see Justin, but no one was there.

The coastguards had been searching, and reported that no body had been found. With the storm at its height when he went overboard, he might have been swept for miles down the coast. They continued their search, in small coves and inlets, but they knew there was no hope of finding him alive after twenty-four hours.

William left the boat and went up to the house for breakfast. He had not eaten for hours, and he wolfed down the food, though he tasted nothing. As the perfect day took hold news spread round the island. William saw huddles of gardeners whispering. One man, older than the others, was squatting on his heels, sobbing loudly. The boat-boys sat side by side, their legs dangling over the jetty, arms around each other. They had loved him too. Everyone here had loved Justin. He was there in every blade of grass, in every secret path, even in the air, perfumed by the blooms he had chosen.

As William was about to enter Laura's room, Dahlia appeared and drew him aside, inching the door shut behind her. They walked a short distance before she spoke. 'I can't believe it,' she said.

'Have you told Laura?' William asked.

She shook her head. 'On the night of the storm, she woke up. It was about ten o'clock. She seemed frantic. Then . . .' Dahlia started to sob. Eventually she blew her nose and her face puckered. 'She turned to me and said, "Justin has gone now. He's never coming back." I tried to calm her and said everything was all right, but she said, "No, Dahlia, Justin isn't ever coming back." How did she know?' William could say nothing to comfort her. As she gradually became calmer, she wiped her eyes. 'I said I would sit with her, and she thanked me. She didn't cry, Sir William, it was the most heart-breaking thing I have ever experienced. She said she didn't need me as he was with her, Justin was taking care of her.'

William entered the room and looked down at Laura. He was as memerized by her as he had been from the first moment he saw her portrait in his bedroom. Her silken hair was loose around her shoulders, her eyes were clear, the helpless look had gone. Her face, devoid of make-up, had a luminous quality.

'Hello, Laura.' His voice was a hoarse croak.

'Hello, Willy,' she said, patting the bed for him to sit beside her and reaching for his hand.

He was unsure of what to say. 'How did you know?' he asked.

'That he'd gone? Well, how could I not?' Her voice didn't waver. 'We have always read each other's minds. Since we were children.'

'I loved him,' William said, head bent.

'I know you did. He couldn't believe you meant it. You see, Justin always believed he could control everyone. But when you grew to love him, he didn't know how to handle it and then . . . you said something to him. You killed him,' she said.

William gasped. 'No – no! I never wanted him to leave.'

'Ssh.' She put a finger to his lips. 'You couldn't have understood. You told him you wanted to be like a father to him. Isn't that what you said?'

'But – but I . . .'

She lay back on her pillows. 'Our Father who art in Heaven . . . If he had stayed, Justin would have had to kill you, Willy, because a father figure represented evil to him. A father would control him, punish him, as our father did. You see, whenever we needed the strength to . . .' she couldn't bring herself to say 'murder' '. . . we would just remember our father and what he did to us. Then we could do whatever we wanted. It made it all right.'

William bowed his head. His eyes brimmed with tears.

'But he would never have *wanted* to hurt you, Willy, not you. He knew you would take care of me so it meant he was free. I have been a burden to him, I know that.'

William could say nothing.

'He didn't hurt Max, though, did he?' She smiled.

'No. Max is back in London now.'

Her face twisted and then she unfurled her fingers. 'Good. No harm done. And with no one finding Justin, he can't be buried, can he?' she asked, puzzled.

'I can arrange a memorial service.' William gulped.

'No, this island is memory enough. And he's here, William, he won't ever leave. I don't want any service, he only loved me, you and this island.'

Laura drew him into her arms as if he was a child.

'Marta will be here today,' he said.

'Marta will like it here. She will take good care of us.'

William's heart leaped as she said 'us'. 'Will you stay on?'

'I would like to stay here always,' she said, without any hesitation.

'I will never let you down, Laura. Please believe that, without him, you are now the most important person in my life.'

'Thank you,' she said.


Marta arrived late in the afternoon. William was waiting for her and held her tightly as she cried. He gestured for the boys to carry her luggage to the waiting golf cart, and hooked his arm through hers. Later she sat with William on the veranda, sipping a glass of chilled champagne. 'You can feel him here,' she said, 'in the plants, on the breeze.'

William nodded: he believed it. In some ways it had eased his grief. Marta's eyes filled with tears, and when she patted her pocket for a handkerchief, William handed her his.

'Thank you,' she said, and dabbed her eyes. She asked if he had noticed how often Laura said that phrase.

'I have. It's very endearing.'

Marta folded and refolded the handkerchief on her lap. 'It isn't. It's heartbreaking. If you were to rape her or to brand her with a red-hot iron, she would thank you.' Marta sighed. 'They were both forced to say it after whatever they had been subjected to. Justin used to say it as much as Laura. Once he stole some money from my purse, just some loose change, but I was angry. I smacked his hand and he looked at me and said, "Thank you." When he brought Laura home from the asylum, I used to watch him looking at her as she repeated over and over: "Thank you, thank you for the pain."'

'I am in such pain now, Marta,' he said bleakly.

'You are not to blame,' she said kindly.

'I am, Marta. I said I wanted to be a father to him. I know now it was the worst thing I could have said to him and, anyway, it was a lie. I was incapable of admitting to him, and to myself, that I wanted him to be . . .' he swallowed, unable to admit even now that he had wanted Justin in every way a man can love another man. He was still ashamed to acknowledge his feelings.

'You don't need to say any more, I understand. Remember I used to see you together, see the way he looked at you, and you at him?'

He leaned over and kissed her cheek. 'Marta, I will

protect Laura with my life. No one is ever going to hurt her again.'

Marta was frightened: he had to have an ulterior motive. William saw her anxiety and understood.

'I want only to care for her,' said William. 'Justin changed my life. I intend to come back here to live, because he is here. Here I'll be close to him.'

William's life took on a different perspective in the period after Justin's death. The coverage of Matlock's funeral was on the front page of every newspaper, and in all the television news broadcasts. Angela gave the performance of her life as the grieving widow, dressed by Valentino. At long last she was the focus of everyone's attention. James remained in a child-like state, dependent upon his mother, most of the time unaware of where he was, or that his father was dead. Max returned to the dominant arms of his mother as she searched for a suitable, rich wife for him. They rarely, if ever, saw the Baron whose downfall had been written up in the press world-wide. They now lived totally separate lives.

The Hangerfords divorced and Daphne was obliged to live in more meagre circumstances. The lack of money, however, meant that she lost more weight than she had ever done before and she felt considerably happier with herself. Clarissa discovered that her father had also plundered her trust fund and she conceded to finding work as a nanny.

William returned to London when Sabrina went into labour, producing robust twin grandsons. Considering her new 'free' lifestyle, she was appallingly conventional:

she had a Harley Street consultant and a private room at the Portland Clinic. Jacob remained steadfastly at her side, only rushing in and out to tell the pacing William that everything was going to be fine. When William held the babies he felt a tremendous rush of emotion. 'They'll love to play on my island,' he said to Jacob.

Charlie seemed to have got his life on some kind of path. He had formed a 'steady attachment' to a wisp of a girl, who made wheat-free pies and bread, and wanted to open a 'health-food café'. William discussed with him where it might lead, but could feel no deep, emotional bond with his son. He knew he should be ashamed of this, but his children had been brought up by Katherine and he had spent so little time with them. He set aside large trust funds for Sabrina, Charlie and his grand-children, even though he initially balked at the idea of making their future lives financially secure. Although William now accepted he would never be close to either his son or his daughter, he cared for them deeply. They were getting on with their lives, and he felt no guilt at cutting loose from them. He would always be there for Charlie and Sabrina, if they needed him, but he doubted it would be for more than money. He also drew up a new will, leaving vast sums to charitable foundations, particularly organizations against child abuse.

To his employees he became a calmer figure. One by one his companies were restructured to enable him to have as little to do with them as possible. Rumours spread that he had some incurable illness, and was preparing for death. Nothing could have been further from the truth, of course: he was preparing to live his life and to enjoy it to the utmost. But William had ceased to worry about what other people said. He knew that what you feel inside is more important than anything anyone else thinks.

While in England, William put in order his financial affairs, to leave him free to relocate to the island. He wrote to Laura every week without fail, and telephoned every two or three days. He hired an art teacher for her as she had begun painting, and he was delighted when she said she had been learning to sail. He became paternal, even over-protective, towards her, warning her not to go too far out when she swam, to use sun cream and always to wear a lifejacket. He loved to hear her giggle and call him an old fusspot. Laura became the child he had never been allowed to enjoy.

Marta gave him bulletins on Laura's progress, and she, too, sounded pleased to hear from him, saying how much they missed him. She listed the new plants she had put into the flower-beds and worried about over-spending: she was now keeping the household accounts. William enjoyed these lengthy discussions with Marta, who always asked his advice, even on the smallest matter. He liked her consideration, but above all he loved her honesty. Only half the staff had been retained on the island, and Dahlia had brought her son over to live with her. She and Marta had become friends and ran William's island home with an attention to detail that ensured it was always immaculate and ready for his arrival.

Over the course of a year, William saw his work come to fruition. He had handed over to others the day-to-day running of his business affairs. He had sold off many of his homes, and shares in his major US and Japanese companies. The last to go was his London house.

*

466

William was overjoyed to return to his paradise island and Laura. As the launch neared the jagged rocks, he saw her, way up on the cliff edge, waiting for him. His heart pounded: she was waving a big yellow towel to make sure he saw her. He watched her run down the path to be on the jetty as the boat came into the harbour. Laura was fit and filled with energy – she was a different woman. She ran towards him, arms wide. William picked her up and twirled her around. She clung to him, kissing his cheeks.

'Welcome home.' She held his hand, dancing alongside him as they headed for the golf cart, hopped aboard and drove him herself. She was full of a new confidence, pointing out all the plants and shrubs Marta had told him about.

As they reached the house, Marta came running down the wide stone steps. She hugged him, then both women insisted he inspect everything they had been doing to make the house into his home. After that he had to view Laura's paintings. Many were of himself, copied from photographs. His heart lifted so high it was flying.

Then Laura tugged at his hand, wanting him to go into his suite. 'But keep your eyes shut,' she said. He stumbled and she steadied him.

'Stop now,' she said, 'but keep your eyes closed.' She and Marta moved away from him. 'You can open your eyes now, Willy,' she said breathlessly.

Straight in front of him, in place of the painting of herself, Laura had hung a new picture. She had commissioned a well-known artist, recommended to her by her painting teacher, to execute a full-length portrait of Justin, barefoot, wearing torn jeans and white T-shirt.

His blond hair was bleached by the sun, and his skin deeply tanned. The artist had caught the way he tilted his head before his face creased into his wonderful smile.

'It's for you from me,' said Laura, searching his face for a reaction. She whispered in his ear that she had used her diamonds to pay for it.


William stood in front of the painting, his heart pounding. Laura had seen his dream. It was a dream he had often had since Justin had died, that one day Justin would return, that one day when William was heading back to the island he would see him waving from the high point and would watch him run to greet him as Laura had that day. Now William could walk into his bedroom knowing that Justin would always be there. It was painful, but the pain would be his reminder not only of what he had lost but of what he had gained. Slowly William smiled and his eyes filled with tears. All he could say in a soft, painful whisper was, 'Thank you.'